EX LIBRIS

Romance
Treasury

THE ROMANCE TREASURY ASSOCIATION

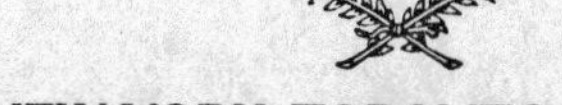

NEW YORK · TORONTO · LONDON

These stories were originally published as follows:

THE SYCAMORE SONG
Copyright © 1975 by Elizabeth Hunter
First published by Mills & Boon Limited in 1975

AUTUMN CONCERTO
Copyright © 1974 by Rebecca Stratton
First published by Mills & Boon Limited in 1974

BEWARE THE HUNTSMAN
Copyright © 1975 by Sophie Weston
First published by Mills & Boon Limited in 1975

ROMANCE TREASURY is published by
The Romance Treasury Association, Stratford, Ontario, Canada.

Dust Jacket Art by Len Goldberg
Story Illustrations by Len Goldberg
Book Design by Charles Kadin
Printed and bound by R. R. Donnelley & Sons Co.

ISBN 0-373-04062-8

Printed in U.S.A. A062

CONTENTS

THE SYCAMORE SONG

The Sycamore Song

Elizabeth Hunter

It was a mystery to Victoria why her father had left her the financial responsibility for his archaeological dig in Egypt. She had not known her father well, but she was determined not to let him down.

Then she discovered that, as a woman in that male-dominated land, her hands were tied. At their first meeting Tariq Fletcher had told her, "I have an interest in that expedition and I mean to run it for you."

Could she trust him? It seemed that her father had not; but the handsome stranger had struck a deep unexpected chord within her and she decided to listen to her heart. She just hoped it wouldn't suffer permanent damage!

CHAPTER ONE

THE GUIDEBOOK had said the tree was a sycamore. Victoria had no way of knowing. She leaned against the wall of the enclosure and tried to catch her breath. She had been stupid to come alone, but she had thought the tree would be in a recognizable tourist area where people would be accustomed to strangers—even foreign women—walking through their streets and staring at the sights. Instead, it had been raining the night before, making the streets muddy and full of puddles, and the children had practically mobbed her, shouting things at her that she didn't understand, until she had lost her head and had taken to her heels, making a mad dash for the sanctuary of the Virgin's Tree and the comforting smile of the watchman who had accepted her overly large tip and had pushed her through the iron gate, shrieking at the children as he did so.

Victoria thought the tree was dead. There were some leaves that she had thought at first belonged to it, but closer inspection showed that they belonged to a creeper that was growing up the far wall. It didn't matter much. The tree had a magnificent, curling shape, spreading itself right across the enclosed space. It was supported in one place by a stout X-shaped cross that emphasized the silvery, weathered look of the tree itself. It was undoubtedly old. Perhaps it really had given shelter to the Virgin Mary and the Infant Child when they had taken refuge in Egypt. It was easy to be cynical about such stories, but this legend was venerable indeed. Even the local district was called Matareya, meaning fresh water, after the spring of water that the Virgin had used. Of all the local sources of water, it alone was free of the brackish taste of standing water.

The iron gate creaked open to admit another visitor, a man this time, taller than the average Egyptian, with strange, light eyes that Victoria noticed at once and found fascinating against the clean, tanned texture of his skin. She regained her composure with difficulty, aware that she was staring, and tried to pretend that she had not noticed him at all, putting out an inquiring finger to touch the rusty notice that bore the legend in English and Arabic that this was the Virgin's Tree.

"It is said that it is three and a half thousand years old," the man said, his English so perfect that Victoria couldn't resist the impulse to turn and stare at him.

"I know. I read up on it before I came," she snubbed him.

The man's eyes swept over her, making her vividly aware of her torn stockings and the dust on her coat that had resulted from the buffeting the children had given her.

"It was unwise of you to come sightseeing by yourself in such an area, Miss Lyle."

Victoria started. "How do you know my name?" she demanded.

"I knew your father." The words were dry and held a message that she didn't understand. She suffered his searching gaze with barely suppressed irritation, lifting her head to a proud angle and giving him back look for look. He was worth looking at, she thought. He had wiry, light brown hair and those strange, enigmatic eyes that gave away nothing of what he was thinking. Even his polished black shoes had somehow escaped the mud that had gathered in the gutters of the streets outside. She didn't present nearly such an attractive picture, she thought ruefully. Her black hair hung loosely over her shoulders because she had lost the ribbon with which she normally tied it at the nape of her neck; her skin, always whiter than she liked, was paler than ever from the English winter, and while she knew herself to be slim and attractive, she couldn't help recalling her father saying that most men of the Middle East preferred their women to be rather more curvaceous and more obviously feminine to look at.

"Did you know my father well?" she asked him at last, losing the battle of the long silence between them.

"Well enough."

Victoria wondered what that meant. She had long ago admitted to herself that her father had remained a stranger to her right up to his death. They had, after all, only met on a few occasions when both of them had been inhibited by their lack of knowledge of each other. Her parents had separated when Victoria had still been a baby and she had lived perfectly happily with her mother on the outskirts of London all through her childhood and school days. Her father, on the other hand, had spent the greater part of his life abroad, unraveling the mysteries of the ancient civilizations of Egypt, Mesopotamia and Persia. His last expedition had been to Egypt and it had been there he had died. Victoria had only known of his death when she had been called to the offices of his London lawyers and had discovered that he had left his considerable fortune to her, provided only that she continue to finance his present expedition.

Mrs. Lyle had been pleased that Victoria had been remembered by her father, but she had been quite adamant that nothing was going to make her leave the comfortable shores of England again, not even her daughter's agonized plea that she couldn't possibly face Egypt all by herself.

"I would not go with your father after that first disastrous expedition to Babylon, and I will not go with you," her mother had said grimly. "Besides, why go at all? All you have to do is provide the money."

"But there's no fun in that!" Victoria had retorted. Frightened though she might be by the prospect of stepping into her father's shoes, she nevertheless had every intention of going to Egypt and seeing personally how every penny of her money was spent. Why else had her father left it to her?

Perhaps, Victoria thought, this man had known her father much better than she had.

"How did you know who I am?" she demanded. "And how did you know I was here?"

"I followed you from your hotel. I knew you were staying at the Mena Garden Hotel at Giza and I bribed the guide at the gate to tell me when you took a taxi anywhere."

"But why?" A dawning indignation lit her blue black eyes. "If you were following me," she added with a good deal of feeling, "you might have rescued me from those—those brats out there!"

He laughed. "It was your own fault for coming to such a place alone. It was the easiest way of teaching you that you're going to need help in running your father's expedition. I wanted to get in first before someone else from the dig gets to work on you. There's been a whole lot of trouble on the site—"

She raised her eyebrows. "I don't think this is the

time for discussing my father's business," she said coolly. "I prefer to see how things are for myself."

"I'll stay around anyway," he said. "Has anyone from the expedition been to see you yet?"

She shook her head. "Not yet." She looked at him with increasing curiosity. "How do you know so much about it?"

"I've made it my business to do so. I have an interest in the expedition and I mean to run it for you—" he smiled slowly "—when you've found out that you can't manage without me, as your father was beginning to discover. Our quarrel was a personal one and should never have been allowed to interfere with our work. I want to make amends for my part in that."

She wondered how much she could believe him, and decided to reserve judgment until she had seen the site and the people working there, for herself.

"I wanted to see the Pyramids," she said, "but the camel drivers were so pressing that I went back to the hotel. Are there any organized tours that I could join?"

His smile reached his eyes with a mockery that made her regret being so open with him. She hadn't meant her words as an invitation, but he might well have taken them as such.

"I'll be pleased to escort you wherever you wish to go, *Fadehat el D'emal*, if you've finished looking at this tree?"

His brief break into Arabic reminded her that she still had no idea who he was, nor did she know anything about him.

"I don't know that I wish to be escorted anywhere by you," she said frankly.

By way of answer he signaled to the watchman to open the iron gate, giving Victoria a glimpse of the crowd waiting for the excitement of watching her struggle down the street through the children once again. "Well," the man prompted her, "why don't you go?"

Victoria bent her head. "If you'll take me back to the hotel I'd be very grateful," she acknowledged meekly.

"To your hotel," he agreed. "Or I could take you to my foster mother who would be glad to look after you for a few days?"

"But I don't know anything about you," she protested. "I don't even know your name."

"I'm sometimes called Tariq," he told her.

"Then you are Egyptian?" she exclaimed.

"Does it matter?" he retorted.

"I suppose not," she said. But it did. She wanted to know about him and she was afraid she would be disillusioned when she did. There was something about him that sounded a deep, unexpected chord within herself. She lifted her eyes to his. "All right, Tariq, why did you follow me here?"

"Because you're your father's daughter," he responded immediately. "Did you think I might have another interest in you?"

"I thought it possible," she admitted. "Especially as you won't tell me your full name, nor who you are."

"What does that prove? I could tell you a lie, a believable lie, and you still wouldn't know anything about me."

She considered that for a moment. "You could tell me the truth," she suggested.

"I'll tell you this much," he said, "I used to work with your father, but we parted company a few months before he died. There has been trouble at the site ever since I left and the government is now employing me to look after their interests at Sakkara, and that involves keeping an eye on you."

"I see. That's how you knew I had arrived in Egypt, I suppose, and that I plan to continue my father's work where he left off?"

"They told me you know nothing of your father's work," he retorted. "You would have done better to stay in England like your mother, and leave it to the Egyptian authorities to organize the work for you."

Victoria sighed. "I know," she admitted. "But I wanted to come so badly. I don't have to know much to hand out the money, do I?"

"More than you think. Are you going to trust yourself to me, Victoria Lyle?"

She chewed on her cheek, enjoying the sensation of power it gave her to tease him a little. "I'm not sure," she murmured, modestly lowering her eyes.

"Like any woman?" He put a hand on her arm and drew her through the gate after him with a shouted imprecation at the crowd. He opened the door of a nearby car for her and pushed her into the passenger seat with such force that she subsided onto the leather-covered springs with an outraged gasp. The pressure of his fingers tightened on her arm. "You will need to trust someone," he warned her. "You would do well to do things my way."

Victoria rubbed her arm, annoyed that her heartbeat should have quickened at his touch. Attractive he was, but he was not that attractive! "I dislike being manhandled," she complained.

His eyebrows shot up as her eyes met his. She had never seen anything like the pale greenish yellow of his irises. They reminded her of the eyes of a cat and she was not at all sure that she liked them on a human being. "Manhandled?"

"*Pushed!*"

His eyes narrowed. "My dear girl, I barely touched you."

"You did? You practically threw me into the car—and I don't like it!"

"Very well, I apologize," he said smoothly. "Though I think it is you who are trying to annoy me. Why, Victoria?"

Why indeed? She could hardly tell him that his presence disturbed her, making her uncertain and not at all like her usual self. Normally even-tempered, she didn't know why she should feel herself prickling at every remark he made.

"I accept your apology," she said.

He got into the car beside her, watching her through half-closed eyes. "You are more like your father than I thought," he said. "Prettier, but impulsive to a fault. Have you thought you might be in danger while you are here?"

She shook her head. "I came because my father wanted it that way. I had a letter from him—but that is *my* secret."

He touched the line of her jaw with gentle fingers, turning her head to face him. Surprisingly, she didn't find the gesture at all disagreeable. On the contrary, his fingers felt cool and firm and as familiar as her own against her cheek.

"You can trust me, Victoria," he said again. "Take your time before you make any decisions about anything to do with the site. Will you promise me that? It would be a shame if anything were to happen to your father's daughter. You ought to be enjoying your first visit here. Go very slowly, and if you have any doubts—any doubts at all—come to me with them. Okay?"

Her instinct was to trust him completely, but she didn't trust her own judgment as far as he was concerned. She felt as though she was on the brink of something wonderful, but it could just as easily be something disastrous. The truth was that no one had ever affected her in quite this way before, and she wasn't sure she liked the sensation.

"My father wouldn't have written to me if he hadn't thought I could cope by myself. I'm not a fool, Mr. Tariq!"

"No, Miss Lyle, I'm sure you're not. But there are many things that are difficult, if not impossible, for a woman to do by herself in this country, and you're going to need help whether you like it or not."

"Your help?'

He nodded. "My help. What did your father have to say in his letter to you?"

Victoria stirred uneasily. "I told you, it's a secret." She picked at a loose thread in her skirt, hoping she hadn't snagged it beyond repair. "I don't know anything about you," she added. "Why should I trust you?"

"What do you know about your father?"

She was effectively silenced. What did she know about her father? About as much as she knew about archaeology and digging up ancient civilizations. A great big fat zero. And if this Tariq worked for the government as he said, perhaps he was worthy of her trust.

"Are you an archaeologist yourself?" she asked him cautiously.

"That's right."

"Have you worked at Sakkara?" She waited for his barely perceptible nod. "Some pretty valuable things have been dug up there, haven't they?"

"A few."

"My father was worried because some of the

things have disappeared. He told me to watch out for a man called Torquil Fletcher. And he said not to allow anything to leave the site without my personal supervision."

Tariq's hands closed around the steering wheel until his knuckles showed white. "Did he say why he suspected this Torquil Fletcher?" he asked. He turned the ignition key and set the car in motion down the street, but she could feel his tenseness as he waited for her answer.

She remembered her first excitement when she had read the letter the lawyers had given her. "He's a gold thief!" she announced dramatically. "He's no better than the tomb robbers of old, only they, poor things, suffered from the curse of the Pharaohs and always came to a nasty end. Nothing seems to happen to this man!"

Tariq laughed. "Is that what your father told you?"

"Not exactly, but he implied as much. It was rather awful how much he seemed to hate him. To tell you the truth I wondered if there wasn't something personal between them. My mother always says my father could be terribly spiteful, but it's difficult to know—" She broke off. "They didn't like each other very much," she added abruptly.

"Torquil Fletcher is no thief, Miss Lyle. I know him well and I can assure you of that. If things have been disappearing, you'll have to look elsewhere for your villain. Are you sure your father really suspected Fletcher?"

She nodded violently. "He said there was no one else it could be. He had worked with everyone else on the team before. Mr. Fletcher wasn't working for him exactly—I don't know what his position was."

"He represented the Egyptian government."

"He did? How strange. That's what you do, isn't it?"

"Sometimes. There's been a great deal of talk about this latest dig of your father's." He looked at her and smiled and she began to think that his strange eyes were rather attractive after all. "But you don't have to worry about it anymore—you have me to do that for you! All you have to do is enjoy yourself and see the marvels of Egypt as your father wished."

She took a quick breath of relief. She had been worrying about her role at Sakkara and she was more than glad to unload her difficulties onto the shoulders of the man beside her.

"I have so much to learn," she said. "It seems rather selfish to leave it all to you, though. What will you do?"

He shrugged his shoulders. "I shall go with you to Sakkara." A harsh note entered his voice and she thought he would not be a man to cross lightly. "I shall stick to you like a leech, Victoria Lyle, to make sure you're not used in any racket with or without your consent, and I'll tighten up the security until not even a mouse can get in or out without my knowing about it."

"But I wouldn't have anything to do with any racket!" she objected.

"That, my dear, has yet to be proved to the Egyptian government."

He drove well through the dizzying traffic that raced along the streets, honking at every opportunity as though silence was more than the Cairenes could bear. Victoria had always understood that Cairo was an elegant city, but she thought it had a dusty, unkempt appearance. Perhaps it was tired from the constant battle with the surrounding desert that colored the buildings and reclaimed the spaces between one district and another. Still, the Nile, surprisingly really the color of *eau-de-nil* in certain lights, was a noble ally in keeping the desert at bay, besides being the source of the city's prosperity. Its green banks refreshed the eye and formed the central feature of the city, dividing one island from another, entwining the land, as it had entwined and awed men's hearts for countless centuries in the past.

"Are you particularly devout, Victoria, that you came first to visit the Virgin's Tree when there is so much else to see?" Tariq's voice mocked her.

"I thought it would be safe to come by myself," she answered. "I suppose I should thank you for rescuing me from the children there." The uncertainty in her voice betrayed her doubts as to the wisdom she had displayed in taking him into her confidence. Supposing he was not who he said he was? Supposing he wasn't taking her back to the hotel at all?

"I'm only doing my job," he said.

Is that how he saw her? As a job and not as a person at all? The idea didn't please her. It didn't *matter*, of course; it didn't mean a thing. Everyone preferred to be seen as an individual and she was no different from anyone else in that. He was just a man doing his job, and that was how she would see him, too, from now on.

"Did the taxi bring you around by the obelisk?" he asked her, a faint glimmer of amusement in his eyes.

"No. What obelisk?"

"Heliopolis, which is the suburb where we are, was called that by the Greeks. It is the old city of On, where stood the oldest university in the world, the center of astronomy and mathematics, built for the sake of the sun god Ra. There's an obelisk that marks the spot where the university stood. It was one of the great centers of the ancient Egyptian religion. As a matter of fact, Cleopatra's Needle in London was erected in On—Beth-shemesh in the Old Testament—or the house of the sun god, thirty-two centuries ago. What it had to do with Cleopatra isn't known, but she may have been the one to order its removal to Alexandria where it stood for the eighteen hundred years before it went to England. Obelisks and standing stones were all sacred to Ra."

"Was Ra the greatest of the gods?"

"In Heliopolis he was. He was known there as the creator god. There was another school of thought at Memphis, the first capital of united Egypt. There Ptah was the creater god and the most important."

"Memphis," Victoria repeated, an edge of excitement in her voice. "Isn't that near Sakkara where my father's dig is?"

Tariq nodded. "Sakkara is the necropolis of Memphis. The remains of the city, such as they are, are on the east side of the river. Sakkara is on the west side where the dead were sent to reside with the setting sun. The departed were sometimes referred to as westerners—a salutary thought, don't you think?"

Victoria laughed in spite of herself. "I can't wait to get to Sakkara and see it all for myself!"

He smiled at her. "Life isn't very different here today," he said. "Or death, either. Cairo has its own necropolis to this very day. We go past it on the way back to the hotel. It's different only that it is on the east side of the city, but it is wholly dedicated to the dead. You see the bare hills of Mokattam over there?"

"It looks more like a quarry to me," she responded.

"It was," he said dryly. "It was the quarry that provided the stone for the Pyramids at Giza."

She was astonished. It looked as though the stone had been wrenched out of the steep sides of the hills only yesterday, or at most the day before.

"Well," Tariq went on, "between those apartment blocks over there and the hills lies the city of the dead. It's not an ordinary graveyard, but it has streets with numbered houses just like anywhere else, only very few of the living live there. Most families have a kind of chalet there, though, quite like an ordinary house, with cooking facilities and so on, and two adjoining rooms with an oblong stone opening in the floor. Under one floor lie the male members of the family and under the other the females. Often, whether the family is Muslim, Copt—that is Christian—or Jewish, they will celebrate a feast of forty days after a death in their house. This represents the time it took to mummify a body before it was entombed in Pharaoh's Egypt. The Egyptian has always been on very intimate terms with death."

The necropolis was lower than the road, and the desert was doing a good job of returning the narrow streets to the dun-colored dust that pervaded everywhere. Watchmen roamed the roads, giving a semblance of life to the place, and there were even small shops selling tea and other necessities to the mourning families.

"Surely people don't still rob the dead?" Victoria surmised, wondering why the watchmen should be considered necessary.

"Why not?" he answered her. "Robbers don't distinguish between the living and the dead in their search for victims. Most people here tear the shrouds of the dead to prevent them from being looted. They don't bury their dead in coffins, they only carry them from one place to another in wooden boxes, so the dead are rather vulnerable to the attentions of the grave robbers, just as they were in olden times."

"How ghoulish!" Victoria commented.

"Indeed," he confirmed. "The superstitious will have it that hundreds of ghouls walk the streets down there every night, and they don't go near when the sun's eye isn't there to protect them. But in the daytime, at all the great feasts of the year, the place is alive with the living visiting those members of their families who no longer smell the air or wear new clothes."

Victoria made a face at him. She was beginning to feel more at ease with him than she had before. Even when he slowed the car to a crawl she wasn't worried.

"I thought you might like to look at Saladin's citadel," he said.

"Saladin? Richard the Lion Hearted's Saladin from the Crusades? What was he doing here? I thought he lived in the Holy Land. And wasn't he a Kurd anyway?"

He seemed impressed by her last question. She saw his start of surprise and felt a satisfaction that she had at last jolted him into looking at her as a person with her own thoughts and feelings.

"Yes, he was a Kurd," he agreed, "and he wasn't here for very long, but he built the citadel. It's a magnificent pile, isn't it? You must go and look at the mosque there sometime."

Victoria allowed her eyes to dwell on the lion-colored, massive ramparts that led upward to the dome of the mosque and the minarets pointing up into the blue sky. "You're very proud of Cairo, aren't you?" she said. "You must know it well."

"I was born here," he explained. "My mother died here when I was two weeks old, leaving my father to cope with me and his army career as best he could. My foster family is Egyptian. Does that satisfy your curiosity?"

She ignored the impatience of that final question. "They're a handsome people," she said. "I think I'm going to enjoy my time here very much."

"Tell me that in a month's time," he retorted. "You've yet to meet the people who were working with your father. They won't accept you easily, a complete amateur holding the purse strings. You know that, don't you?"

Her mouth twitched into an impertinent smile. "Why should I worry? Or have you changed your mind about protecting me from them?"

"It's not a joke!" he said sharply. "You may well come to hate me for what I have to do in the future." His eyes rested for an instant on her face. "And that would be a pity," he added. "You're far too pretty for any man to want to quarrel with you for long."

"You may be surprised at how quickly I pick things up. I'm not just a pretty face, you know! Besides, you have an advantage over me. You do know my name!"

"You wouldn't appreciate my name at the moment," he told her. "It will have to be enough for you that you met me in the shade of a sycamore tree. The sycamore is a traditional symbol of romance in Egypt, even three thousand years ago. 'A sycamore sang to a lady fair—' "

Why, he was flirting with her! Victoria pursed up her lips and glared at him. He quoted softly:

"Papyri green are my leaves arrayed,
And branch and stem like to opal gleam;

Now come and rest in my cooling shade
The dream of your heart to dream."

"Very pretty," Victoria said. She thought it beautiful and she was beginning to wish that she had met Tariq under other circumstances, when it wouldn't have mattered if she had flirted, too, just enough to find out if he really liked her. But she had to remember that he was a man on the job and he had to put up with her whatever he thought of her, just as she had to put up with him.

"I didn't come to Egypt for romance, or to dream dreams," she said. "It's a long time since the Virgin's Tree had any cooling shade. Perhaps that makes a difference."

The glint in his eye was unreadable. "Perhaps one day we'll find out," was all he said.

CHAPTER TWO

VICTORIA'S ROOM at the hotel was on the ground floor. From it she could see the colorful scene of the tables set on the grass for people to have their lunch in the open air and, behind them, the towering triangular shape of the Great Pyramid, the largest in Egypt, the tomb of Khufu, more familiarly known by his Greek name of Cheops. The maid had drawn the curtains, shutting out the view, but Victoria pushed them back with an impatient hand before sitting on the edge of the bed and making an effort to decide if she had been right to accept Tariq as the man from the government, the man who had the right to oversee her every movement on her father's dig at Sakkara.

It would have been easier if he had been less attractive. She stared out of the window, remembering in detail his strange yellow green eyes. No Englishman had ever had eyes like that! She would have liked to be able to attribute them to the great Mameluke dynasty that had ruled Egypt for so long, or even to the Berber tribesmen who still roamed the edges of the Sahara—didn't they sometimes have green eyes? Yes, she was sure they did, but never yellow eyes. Nobody, but nobody, had yellow eyes!

Victoria's experience of men was small. She had been brought up in an all-female household and had gone to a single-sex school. Afterward, when she had held down her first job, she had had several brushes with romance, but none of them had been serious. They had amounted to no more than a pleasant exploration of the possibilities that lay between any two people of the opposite sex—enjoyable, sweet, and holding out a promise of what might be—sometime in the future with somebody else. None of the men she knew had been anything like Tariq.

He had said that she could trust him, but he had not trusted her, not even with his real name. Perhaps that was understandable as he only knew her as her father's daughter, and if things had been smuggled from the site, she could be in the know, in which case he would be her enemy. Only she was aware of how little she knew of her father's affairs. If she had known more she might not have cast herself into the breach so willingly—but perhaps she would have done, for she had longed all through her childhood to leave the comfortable existence her mother had carved out for her and to share her father's hazardous, but infinitely more exciting life in the forgotten places of the world. Yet her first doubts that she would be able to cope with handling the finances of the expedition had been strongly reinforced by Tariq's few remarks on the subject. She would be very glad to have him behind her, though she would have preferred it if he had been more like other men and had not had a pair of fine yellow eyes and a pair of hands that talked with a facility that had never been learned in England.

She took a deep breath and started to change into a dress with a wider skirt that would be more practical for visiting outsize monuments like the Giza Pyramids. It was not, she assured herself, because the color of the dress also set off the shimmering black of her hair and stressed the extreme whiteness of her skin. What did that matter, she asked herself, with only Tariq to look at her, and her without the least ambition to attract him and add to her difficulties in the near future? That, at least, was almost true, for she wanted badly to know more about him, but he rubbed her the wrong way, too, treating her as a dreamy fool who couldn't be trusted to deal with the realities of life.

She wandered out onto the balcony, hoping to see Tariq before he saw her. One could tell quite a lot by observing people when they were unaware that they were being watched, or so one of her girl friends had frequently told her. But she couldn't see Tariq anywhere, and she felt a moment of panic when she thought he might have gone away and left her on her own.

"Are you ready for lunch, Miss Lyle?"

She clutched the edge of the balcony, berating herself as a first-class fool for getting upset about nothing. "I wasn't sure you were staying for lunch," she said. "Why don't you find a table?" she added with creditable hauteur as he said nothing at all. "I'll be out in about ten minutes."

"Ten minutes? Oh, come on, Miss Lyle, it won't take you ten minutes to lock your door and come out here." He looked up at her and smiled. "It would take you even less if you climbed over the balcony."

It wasn't high, but it was high enough to discourage her. For most people it would have been quite easy to climb over the rail, avoiding the flowers that were growing in the top of the marble wall, and jump down onto the ground below, but Victoria had suffered all her life from a fear of heights and even such a small hazard as this one was more than she felt she could attempt.

"I prefer to be more conventional and use the door," she told him.

His expression openly mocked her. "Are you a conventional person, Victoria Lyle?" he asked her.

"I've never had the opportunity to be anything else," she admitted. "How about you?"

He shrugged. "It's difficult to say. What is conventional in Egypt might be considered very unconventional in the kind of place you were brought up. Your independence of any man's influence is in itself unconventional here, for instance."

"Would you rather I had a brother for you to deal with?" she asked, more curious about him than ever.

His lips twitched. "It might be simpler." He glanced down at his watch. "I am very hungry, even if you are not, so shall we continue this interesting conversation over lunch?"

Her eyes fell before the impatience in his and she made a hurried exit from the balcony into her room. Now that she came to think of it she realized she was hungry, too. It would be fun to share a meal with Tariq, and she was suddenly in a great hurry to join him outside, grabbing her handbag and running down the corridor toward the entrance in order not to miss a single minute of his company.

Tariq was waiting for her. "A brother would be a less attractive proposition," he murmured. "You are looking very beautiful in that dress!" He put a hand under her elbow and led her through the maze of tables on the lawn toward one that had its own sunshade and that was already set for lunch.

"Is it part of your work to pay me compliments?" she asked.

"No, that is my pleasure."

"Then you might have lunch with me, even if I weren't my father's daughter?"

"It's possible," he agreed.

"I suppose you'd prefer women to stay out of the public eye, to be quiet and do as they're told. That's very Egyptian!"

He ignored the edge to her voice, smiling fully at her. "Is that how you intend to behave at Sakkara? It would certainly make things easier if you followed my advice without too much argument."

She colored a little. "Oh, I'm not Egyptian at all!" she exclaimed.

"No, but one can learn something from everyone." He held her chair for her, easing her into her seat and arranging the sunshade to protect her face from the sun. "I have ordered shish kebab for you, and some Egyptian wine that I think you will like, and coffee to finish with. Will that suit you?"

She didn't know what a shish kebab was, and she was quite unaccustomed to having wine with her meals as a matter of course, so she gave him a quick nod. She also tried not to compare how long she had had to wait for service when she had been by herself the night before, with the magical way the food appeared now at a mere flick of Tariq's expressive fingers.

When the waiter had moved away, Tariq gestured toward her plate, smiling at her. "*Itfaddalou*! Enjoy yourself!" he invited her.

The shish kebab was very good. There were little bits of barbecued lamb cooked over charcoal in the open air, and some barbecued groundmeat, more properly called *kufta*, served with chipped potatoes instead of rice, and with a yogurt sauce that broke up the fat of the tender portions of meat. Victoria ate her lunch with appetite. She was surprised that a Muslim country should produce wines when alcoholic drinks were forbidden to them, but it had a pleasant if slightly sweet taste on her tongue, and as Tariq drank it, too, she thought he might be an Englishman and a Christian after all.

The waiter took away their plates and Victoria sat back in her chair to await her coffee, trying not to speculate too openly about the man opposite her, but to enjoy the luxury of the bright sunshine that, even in January, felt warm against her bare arms. It was only the sun that was hot, however. When a cloud crossed its path, one immediately felt cold and shivery, and the people in the restaurant began clicking their tongues in displeasure and reaching for their sweaters, only to take them off again the next moment when the sun reappeared.

It was in one of these cloudy intervals that Victoria discovered that if she were to watch the family at the next table, she could also keep an eye on Tariq opposite her without appearing to stare at him. She found she liked looking at him. If she had had the gift, she would have liked to carve his face in stone, for it was an interesting face by any standards, and it would have appealed to anyone's artistic senses. So she allowed herself to indulge the pleasure she obtained from his strong eyebrows, his too big nose that destroyed any pretensions he might have had to classical beauty, and the mobile, rather cruel mouth that lent a touch of stern disinterest to his whole face.

When he stood up, she started, aware that the silence had been too long and that he might have asked her something but she hadn't heard a word. However, it was not her he was looking at, but someone else who was approaching from behind her. Victoria turned, also, and saw that the newcomer was a youngish woman, small in stature, attractive rather than pretty, with a pair of large, dark eyes that she used to very good effect in greeting Tariq.

"So, Tariq, you are pleased to see me, *non*?" Her French accent gave a charming lilt to a voice that was otherwise rather harsh and quite unlike the soft, feminine curves of her body. "Didn't you expect me?"

"Sooner or later," he answered. "I thought you might have been too busy at Sakkara to have the time to come to Cairo."

"When I knew Miss Lyle was here?" The French girl threw back her head and laughed softly. "Naturally I came at once, as soon as I knew that her father left her in charge of our finances. I wanted to get my word in, too!"

Tariq raised an eyebrow in Victoria's direction. "Miss Lyle won't be challenging your position on the site. She doesn't know a thing about Egyptology and doesn't pretend to."

"I see." The French girl expelled her breath thoughtfully, turning her attention to Victoria. "I presume this one is Miss Lyle? She is not much like her father to look at." She twisted her lips into a wry smile. "Me, I loved your father! He was a great man."

Victoria looked grave. "I didn't know him very well," she admitted.

"What chance did you have?" The Frenchwoman shrugged. "His marriage was unsuitable and he stayed away from England because of it. There were more—compensations abroad, you understand? I am Juliette Mercer, your late father's assistant. Welcome to Egypt!"

"Thank you," said Victoria.

"I hoped to see you by yourself," Juliette went on breathlessly. "I wanted to be sure that you understood the situation at Sakkara before you arrived there. It is—complicated, you understand?"

Victoria leaned back in her chair. "I'm afraid we've finished lunch, Miss Mercer," she said, "but you'd be very welcome to have coffee with us."

"Mrs. Mercer," Juliette corrected her quickly. "Does Tariq stay for coffee?"

"I do," Tariq answered her, without even looking at Victoria.

"But—" Juliette began to protest.

Victoria blushed faintly, knowing that she was about to tell what amounted to little less than an outright lie. "Tariq is lunching with me at my direct invitation," she said gently.

Tariq's eyes turned on her. They were less like a cat's and more like those of a bird of prey, she thought uneasily. "Is that how it was?" he mocked her.

Victoria did her best to ignore him. "What did you want to tell me, Mrs. Mercer?" she prompted the French girl.

"Juliette. You had better call me Juliette. I was such good friends with your father that I am sure we will be good friends also. But it is awkward to talk frankly with you, *chérie*, while we have Tariq with us. He was not friends with your father. Did he tell you that?"

"He said there had been some misunderstanding between them," Victoria admitted.

Juliette rolled her eyes heavenward. "Is that what he called it? Tariq, *mon cher*, that was not well done of you. Victoria is a woman of the world, no? She would have understood." She made a dismissive gesture, turning her wide eyes fully on Victoria. "Your father didn't trust Tariq, not at all!" she went on with considerable drama. "First there was the stealing—has he told you about that? And then there was the renown. Your father was a good archaeologist in his own field, and famous, whereas who had ever heard of—"

"That was not what we quarreled about, Juliette."

"No, no, we are knowing that. But he did think you had something to do with the stealing that was going on—"

"Although it went on after I left?"

"He was ill then, *chéri*. It was not mentioned to him that still more articles were disappearing. It was not considered good for him to know." Her eyes narrowed momentarily. "Are you coming back to Sakkara?"

"Yes, he is," Victoria broke in. "He's going to help me run things—as the government's representative, of course."

Juliette looked concerned. "If you wish him to know all about your affairs that is your business," she acknowledged, "but it is not a good thing for the Egyptian government to know too much of what the expedition is costing you. There will be enough fuss about making the permit over to you as it is. That is one of the things I wished to speak to you about. It may be better to take out the permit in my name—what do you think?"

Victoria looked despairingly at Tariq, but he was no help at all. He only looked back at her, his tawny eyes mildly interested.

"I shall take advice," Victoria said finally.

"Good," Juliette commended her. "And I shall stay for coffee after all. I like it black and very hot, if you please. What do you do with yourself after lunch?"

"I want to see the Pyramids," Victoria volunteered, glancing over at the huge geometrically shaped monuments that towered over the hotel.

"It is good to see them while you are here. You will learn much," Juliette agreed. "But they are not the same period as the tomb of Kha-sekhem. He was Second Dynasty, in the Archaic Period. The Pyramids belong to the Old Kingdom."

Victoria struggled to put an intelligent expression on her face. The name Kha-sekhem rang a faint bell in her memory. Had he been the occupant of the tomb her father had been excavating?

"Kha-sekhem's tomb was unknown until George found it last summer," Juliette went on. "We knew about Kha-sekhem himself, of course, because his statues and steles had been found in Hierakonpolis."

"I see," said Victoria. "Was he somebody important?"

Tariq made an expressive gesture with his hands, but it was Juliette's yelp of dismay that claimed Victoria's attention. "Is it possible that you know nothing of your father's work? Nothing at all?"

"I've never pretended that I did," Victoria answered, nettled. "Why should I?"

Juliette stared at her, unable to believe her ears. "*C'est incroyable*! That it should be this one, who knows nothing, who should now control the finances of the whole expedition! It is clear that George Lyle was mad to think of such a thing! To hand us all over to an *imbécile*, just because she happens to be his daughter!"

"You are not being very polite," Tariq told her dryly. "Besides, Victoria knows some things. She knew Saladin was a Kurd."

"Oh, Saladin!" Juliette said with contempt.

"Some people find the Crusades more interesting

than Ancient Egyptian Pharaohs." Tariq's tone was dry.

"Oh, but I don't know anything about the Crusades, either," Victoria denied, honestly. "I just happened to have read that Saladin was a Kurd in a book about Richard Coeur de Lion, who was a complete bore if ever there was one. He made a wretched husband, and poor old John had to clear up the mess for him at home and has taken all the blame ever since."

To her annoyance, Tariq burst into laughter. "So much for the propaganda of Robin Hood, the Magna Carta, and the legend of the wicked king!" Then he stopped laughing. "Isn't it more usual to feel sorry for Richard for being such a bad husband to only one woman? Why not object to Saladin for being husband to so many?"

Victoria cast him an expressive look. "At least he was a man! I daresay all his wives were a great deal happier than poor Berengaria!"

His eyes showed amusement and she was strongly reminded of the sunlight dancing on the Nile as she had seen it that morning. "Thus the eternal female mind! Poor Richard indeed!"

Juliette frowned. "Me, I have a great admiration for Richard," she claimed. "He was renowned for his great chivalry and his romantic nature. But *naturally*, because he was really a Frenchman!" She waited while the waiter brought and served the coffee, then she said, "I am tired of Saladin! I have more important things to talk about. Victoria—I may call you Victoria, I hope? It is important that you should have some idea about what has been going on at Sakkara. Hardly any work has been done since your father's death. There has been no money with which to pay the workers, and apart from Jim

Kerr and me, the whole team has departed. We cannot possibly finish the excavation as we are, but that is your problem. I would have left myself if I had not felt I owed it to George's memory to try to help his daughter. But now I must know if we are to go on or not." She sipped her coffee with a grimace. "I imagine not. Jim and I are not miracle workers that we can do it all ourselves!"

"I shall be there," Tariq drawled out.

Victoria felt a warm sensation of relief creep through her. If he was there then everything was bound to be all right. "And we will find more workers, surely?" she added.

"Never!" Juliette exclaimed. "You will never allow Tariq actually to work inside the tomb? Your father would never have permitted it!"

Victoria cast Tariq a quick look of dismay. "I have to make my own decisions," she pointed out. "I may be his daughter, but I am not my father, and his quarrels are not mine. Besides, Tariq works for the government and he has their authorization to be on the site."

Juliette made an irritated noise with her lips. "Is that true? How did you persuade them you were to be trusted?" She turned to Victoria, sighing lustily. "I wish I had come to you earlier. I could have warned you not to have anything to do with him for your father's sake. If he comes back to Sakkara you will certainly regret it. It was terrible what happened between him and your father. George wouldn't speak of it afterward, but we all knew he had quarreled with Tariq over the missing objects. He ordered him away from Sakkara, never to return! Me, I thought he should have sent for the police.

"I thought so, too," Tariq said unexpectedly. "It would have been better all around if he had." He stretched and yawned. "Have you finished your coffee, Juliette? If Victoria and I are to explore the Pyramids this afternoon, it's time we were starting up the hill." He grinned across the table at Victoria. "If you're feeling very lazy, I may allow you to ride up on a camel!"

"Oh, I couldn't!" She was ashamed of the vehemence and sheer fright in her voice. "They're rather tall animals," she amended more moderately. "I'd really much rather walk. I suffer from acrophobia—vertigo—if I get more than two feet above the ground. I'd really much rather walk."

He put his hand over hers. "You would be quite safe with me," he assured her.

"I'm sorry," she murmured. "That isn't the point. It isn't reasonable to be afraid of anything so silly, but I go into a panic even at the thought of it. I know it's quite safe, but it doesn't make any difference at all." And now he would think her a proper fool, she thought wryly.

"You should always make yourself do things you are afraid of," Juliette advised her with all the overbearing patronage of someone who hasn't a nerve in her body and can't imagine why anyone else would be afflicted by something that had never disturbed her.

"I have tried," Victoria said. "I used to force myself to climb trees, but I fell out of one and when I came out of hospital I decided I would learn to live with the fact that I do better with my feet firmly planted on Mother Earth." A faint smile lifted the corners of her mouth. "I've kept them there ever since."

To her surprise, Tariq was smiling too. "And your head in the clouds? Never mind, we'll both walk."

Juliette stood up abruptly. "And I shall leave you.

I'll see you tomorrow in Sakkara, Victoria. You are a silly girl to bring this man with you, but if you will not be advised by me—"

"You are scarcely an unprejudiced witness," Tariq put in. "Let Victoria make up her own mind about me."

The French girl flushed an unpleasing red. "I would have thought you were too much of a gentleman to remind me of something I would sooner forget all about. I'd have you remember that I chose George—"

Tariq surveyed her calmly. "There was no choice, Juliette, nor have I ever pretended to be a gentleman."

Juliette jerked her head in Victoria's direction. "Have you told *her*?"

"Not yet. George was her father, after all. Go back to Sakkara, Juliette, and mind your own business. If you want something to do, you and Jim Kerr can think about how to rescue the expedition from total disaster."

Juliette gave him a bitter look. "Jim is a fool! He hasn't a clue what to do next. He and Victoria will make a fine pair!"

Tariq frowned, superbly arrogant. "Victoria will do very well," he bit out. "Tell Jim to keep out of her way. She will be better off without his advice. His job, like yours, is to finish the excavation as quickly and as well as possible. You'd both do well to remember that!"

Juliette said nothing more. She turned on her heel and marched away from them across the grass, her arms swinging wildly at her sides. She had a typically French figure, small and neat, with rather short legs that made her indignant steps funny rather than dignified, as she had intended.

"What was all that about?" Victoria asked as Tariq sat down again.

His eyes flickered over her, sparing her nothing in the intent way he summed her up, assessing her with an intimacy that she resented, but met head on with a cool stare of her own.

"There is often a conflict of personalities on a dig," he said. "When it gets mixed up with sex, as well, it can be pretty explosive. With Juliette, you never know which role she is playing at any particular moment—the woman or the archaeologist—and in a closed, intimate society where women are apt to be trouble anyway, her particular brand of charm can stir things up in a way that has to be seen to be believed."

Victoria looked away. Had he been attracted to the French girl too? It was pretty obvious that her father had more than liked her. But she didn't like to think of Tariq flirting with Juliette, and felt a sharp pang of jealousy that he might have done so in the past.

"Men always blame women," she murmured. "Surely they bear some of the responsibility? They should be used to women working alongside them in almost every field nowadays."

He seemed amused at her again, and she found that she resented that, too. "True, but we are not emotionally involved with most of them and don't wish to be. It isn't as a work colleague, for instance, that I prefer to think of you."

"You shouldn't make personal remarks," she told him sharply. "I think Juliette was right about you. You're no gentleman!"

"She wouldn't like it if I were," he drawled. "She likes me well enough as I am."

"But she's married," she protested, and wished

that she had had the sense to hold her tongue. If Tariq wanted a woman, he wouldn't allow a mere detail like that to stand in his way. "Where is her husband?" she demanded.

He looked amused. "Her husband received his *congé* a long time ago. She thought about marrying your father for a while, but he was too sprightly a bird to get caught in her trap—"

"He couldn't," Victoria said. "He was still married to my mother."

Tariq raised his eyebrows. "Didn't she want to marry again?"

Victoria shook her head. "I don't think so. She didn't like being married at all, certainly not to someone like my father. My mother can't bear to live anywhere but in England. She likes to have the familiar world she knows around her—the shops she has always been to, the friends she made at school and has seen twice weekly ever since. And my father, of course, was quite the opposite."

"And which parent do you take after?"

She had never given it any thought until that day, but the Virgin's Sycamore Tree had given her the answer before she had even asked the question. She had all her father's passion for the unknown, the incomprehensible, even the exotic. If it weren't so, she wouldn't have looked twice at Tariq himself, for he was all of those things.

"I haven't been away from England long enough to tell," she answered.

"Well, the Pyramids should help you to make up your mind," he observed. "I'll ask you again tonight by moonlight. I expect like most women you find it easier to talk about yourself in the dark!"

She didn't like the sting in the tail of that remark, but she allowed herself to be helped to her feet and even managed a small smile. "I don't go out with strange men after dark," she said.

"Not even with the Sphinx as chaperon?"

She was tempted. Had he known many women, she wondered. And had they all poured out their innermost thoughts to him at his bidding? The thought made her steel herself to refuse to do any such thing.

"Not even then," she said.

"You're very hard to please," he said. "But I haven't given up all hope of persuading you." He put up a hand and touched her cheek, and some of the sternness left his face. "I'm not a stranger, Victoria Lyle, or I shan't be for long. I can't be and do my job properly. I'm going to stick as close to you as a barnacle on the side of a ship." He tapped her chin with a light blow that warned her that he meant what he said. "Perhaps you should have been your brother after all."

Victoria swallowed, unable to think of any adequate reply. Her heart took up an erratic beat within her and she stooped quickly to pick up her handbag.

"A government barnacle," she reminded herself as much as she was reminding him. "My being a girl or a man doesn't come into it."

"You think not? You may be right. But whichever you are, come along and we'll start your first lesson in your father's trade."

CHAPTER THREE

"CHEER UP, SWEETHEART!"

It was an impertinence for him to call her sweetheart. She was of two minds whether she would rebuke him for taking such a liberty. It was worse, she knew, because if she decided against it, it would only be because she thought he would find some stinging retort that would discomfort her still further. She began to hope that she wouldn't have to see much of him at Sakkara, not until she had a better idea of how to handle him.

"Tariq, Juliette is quite right. I don't even know how to begin to cope with the excavation. I can't imagine why my father thought I could."

"You have me," he reminded her.

Yes, and a lot of good that was going to do her when she didn't even know if she could trust him or not. "Have I?" she said aloud. "I can't know that. How can I? And what am I to do if Torquil Fletcher turns up? Will you cope with him, too?"

"I think I can safely promise that. You don't have to worry about Fletcher, Victoria. It's true he quarreled with your father, but it was a personal matter, and it had nothing to do with their work."

Victoria sighed. "A woman?" she said.

"A woman," he agreed.

She sighed again. "I suppose it was silly of me not to have realized. I never thought of my father—"

"Why should you, if you barely knew him? How old are you, Victoria?"

"Twenty-three." Twenty-three was old enough not to be surprised and shocked by such matters, she thought gloomily. "How old are you?" she added, not to be outdone.

"Thirty-four. But it isn't only the years that count. I'm an old man compared to an innocent like you. I've lived my life to the full, while you, at a guess, have scarcely lived at all, keeping your mother company and she keeping the local swains at bay from her little ewe lamb!"

"It wasn't quite like that," she said. "If you knew me better, you might be surprised!"

"Would I?" He sounded amused.

No, he wouldn't be! "My mother would have been lonely if I had left her on her own," she defended herself. "I'm all she's got. She isn't possessive exactly, but she does want me to marry a nice local boy and live around the corner so that we can call in on each other every day. You know the sort of thing."

"I'm surprised you could tear yourself away to come to Egypt," he commented gravely.

"But it was the most marvelous opportunity!" She made an expressive gesture. "I want to see something else before I settle down, but I don't love her any the less."

"And you think you'll go back there more or less unchanged when you've finished here?"

"I don't know," she admitted. "Things look different out here."

He looked her over, noting the eager interest she had in everything she saw.

"Very different," he agreed.

She wondered what he meant by that, but at that moment they reached the main gate of the hotel, and her attention was claimed by the hustle and bus-tle outside at the foot of the hill that led up to the Giza complex of Pyramids. It was very steep and the urgency of the vendors made any progress upward quite difficult.

"Welcome to Egypt, *madame*! Welcome, welcome! Will you ride my camel? Just to have the photograph of you? Very comfortable camel! Please, *madame*, you come this way! Nice view of Sphinx! No camel, then I find a donkey for you, yes? But, *madame*, I have a lovely chariot—"

Tariq looked as though he actually enjoyed the exchanges that beset them on every side. Occasionally he would say something to them in Arabic, and they would laugh, bow gracefully and go away, to Victoria's great relief.

"Why are they so persistent?" she asked him.

He put his arm right around her, guiding her carefully around a group of animals and oblivious tourists. "They have no other way of making a living. There's compulsory schooling in Egypt now, but most of these men are too old to have benefited from the new ideas, and they scratch a living as best they can. If you can't read or write, there isn't much you can do in the modern world."

She pulled away from him because the close contact with him disturbed her, but his hand shot out, anchoring her firmly back against his side. "You'll get run down if you dart about like that," he reproved her, and as if to prove his words, an enormous American car shot past them, just shaving the robe of one of the camel drivers.

At the top of the hill, Tariq bought their tickets at a little booth and stuffed them into his pocket, leading her away from the largest pyramid of them all, the Pyramid of Cheops, an edifice of such magnificent proportions that it towered above them, looking to all appearances, even in these days of high-rise buildings and engineering miracles, as though it did indeed reach right up into the sky. Close up, it was possible to see the huge slabs of granite that had gone into its making, and that once had been clad in an outer coating of Tura limestone that had long since been carted away for other buildings. The height of the pyramid had been reduced for the same reason and it was possible to climb up the sides to the top, to look right across modern Cairo, and to Memphis, the first capital of the Two Kingdoms, and to Sakkara, the necropolis of that capital.

"I never imagined it would be so big!" Victoria confided. "It's huge!"

Tariq smiled. "You're not the first person to think that. All sorts of calculations have been made to give some idea of its size. It's been said that you could fit the Houses of Parliament and St. Paul's Cathedral in its base and still have some room left over. Or, alternatively, Florence and Milan Cathedrals, and St. Peter's in Rome, and still be able to throw in Westminster Abbey and St. Paul's for good measure."

"That's big," she agreed.

"Something of a triumph for those days," he said dryly. "Imagine what they must have been like when they were gilded to catch the rays of the morning sun! The ancient Egyptians may have been obsessed by death, but it was a magnificent obsession. There was nothing paltry about the grandeur with which they endowed the Kingdom of Osiris."

"The god Osiris was killed himself, wasn't he?"

"He was. He was killed by his brother Set. His sister-wife Isis, combed the world looking for him, and when she found his body she mummified it to keep it forever. But Set's hatred was such that he couldn't bear to leave well enough alone and he chopped up the body, scattering it over the countryside. Poor Isis set out on a further search and collected up all the various parts of her husband's body. Life was breathed back into it and Osiris became the King of the Dead."

Victoria commented, "Isis was some lady, wasn't she? I know she was considered to be very beautiful."

"So lovely that many of her statues in Rome came to be called representations of Our Lady so that they wouldn't be broken up, which was the fate of most pagan religious objects. Probably the picture we have of Mary, even today, owes a lot to the ancient Egyptian's vision of his goddess Isis."

Victoria caught his arm, reluctant to leave the Great Pyramid without having seen inside. "Please let's go in there," she begged him.

"We'll come back," he promised. "I want you to see Chephren's pyramid first. It was built later and it hasn't quite the same marvelous quality as Cheop's, but it makes a very good introduction to how they were planned and built. I'm afraid you're going to find it an exhausting afternoon. You must tell me if you get too tired."

His concern for her was rather nice, she thought. She wondered if he thought her particularly fragile, but dismissed the idea as absurd. He probably always treated all females, young and old, in the same old-fashioned way, expecting them to respond in kind by allowing him to have the last say in everything. She thought there had probably been a good many who had chosen to bask in the warmth of his approval rather than strike out for themselves against his wishes for them. Had Juliette?

She turned away from the thought. It was none of

her business, she told herself, and she had no right to be hurt by anything to do with him. He was nothing to her, just as she was nothing to him.

Somewhat reassured, she gazed up at Chephren's pyramid, noting that part of the limestone casing had been left on this second monument to show what the whole had once been like. From ground level it seemed to reach almost as high as that of Cheops's, and because the sides were less ragged, there were no climbers scaling its heights, looking as small as ants as they worked their way up and down the huge blocks of stone.

The entrance to the pyramid seemed dark after the sunlight outside. A tunnel stretched downward, lit by a few naked bulbs. On the floor had been placed some planks of wood onto which small strips had been nailed to give some grip. The guide hurried forward to greet them, arranging their progress to his own satisfaction by taking a firm grasp of Victoria's hand and hurrying her onward, farther and farther down into the bowels of the earth. The roof was not high enough for her to stand upright, so she had to bend almost double to avoid hitting her head, which added considerably to the discomfort of the breathless rush down the makeshift catwalk. She arrived at the bottom sadly out of breath, and pretended to look determinedly around until she had recovered.

"This was the first burial chamber, but it was later abandoned for the one that's almost in the center of the pyramid," Tariq told her. He, of course, had had no difficulty in keeping up with the impetuous guide, she noticed with disgust. He caught a glimpse of the expression on her face and chuckled. "Don't think about the weight above your head," he advised her maliciously. "We can't have you suffering from claustrophobia as well as acrophobia."

"But we must be well below ground level," she answered, unamused.

"Yes. We climb up again now to just below ground level where the actual tomb was situated. Do you want to go on?"

It was easier going up than going down, she discovered. At one point they passed some frightening, unguarded steps, but the guide pressed onward, and her relief that she was not going to have to climb up them was such that she found she could hurry on almost as fast as he, as if she had done this sort of thing all her life.

The reward when they reached the burial chamber was great. The tunnel opened into a large-sized room, nearly fifty feet in length, she judged, by perhaps twenty feet wide, with a high, gabled roof, the stone of which had been laid at the same angle as the outer sides of the pyramid. Except for the roof, it had been hewn wholly out of stone, and she wondered what their tools had been to embark on such a task.

"Is the tomb my father discovered anything like this?" she demanded with suppressed excitement.

"Well, it's smaller," Tariq answered her, "but it has its own grandeur. You'll see it for yourself tomorrow. It's earlier than any pyramid. It's thought that the pyramids grew out of the *mastabas* of the Pharaohs and noblemen who preceded them."

"A *mastaba* being what?" she asked.

"A flat-topped tomb, like the one that's being excavated at Sakkara. *Mastaba* means a kind of seat in Arabic, rather like a bench, which the shape of the tomb is supposed to resemble. During the first two dynasties, in what is known as the Archaic Period, Pharaohs as well as noblemen were always buried in *mastabas*. Noblemen were never allowed to be buried in anything else."

The way back seemed shorter. The guide still hurried ahead, firmly grasping Victoria's hand and pulling her along behind him. She tried at one point to make Tariq go ahead of her, but this met with a flat refusal on the part of the guide to let go of her.

"He likes holding your hand," Tariq told her with a laugh. "He thinks you very *gamîl*."

"Thank you very much! I don't like camels!"

"Not a camel. *Gamîl*. It means beautiful."

Diverted, Victoria looked over her shoulder at him. "You can't possibly know he's thinking that. He probably only wants to make sure that we hurry up."

"All Arabs have an eye for a pretty girl," he answered her. "And not only Arabs!"

She laughed with him. She was glad that he thought her pretty at least, for he certainly thought her a fool. Indeed, she was so entertained by the compliment he had paid her that she scarcely noticed they had come back to the unguarded steps she had seen on the way in. They drew level with them and the guide put a slippered foot on the lowest stair, urging her to follow him.

But she could not. The mere thought of climbing those steps froze her into immobility. They reached up above her, white and ghostly in the dim light, with the well of the passageway disappearing into the darkness below her. Terrified, she jerked her hand out of his and turned blindly back the way they had come.

"I'm not going up there!" she cried out.

Tariq put an arm about her body. "It isn't very high. Take it one step at a time."

"I can't!"

"My word, you do get yourself in a state over heights," he said. He put a hand under each elbow. "Up you go!"

She tried to turn around, to bury her face in his chest, beside herself in her anxiety to get away from the wooden steps, but his hold on her arms increased and he would not let her go.

"I'm not going up there!" she wailed.

"Of course you are!" he said in her ear. He answered something the guide had said to him in Arabic, and the Egyptian climbed the stairs, looking back at them with a gappy, toothless grin that Victoria was sure would haunt her as long as she lived. She shut her eyes with a gasp of sheer panic and the pressure on her elbows increased.

"Go on, *yâ habibi*, I'm right behind you. I shan't let you go!"

"Are you sure? I'm sorry—"

"Don't be! It's a very good excuse to hold you in my arms without your thinking the worst of me." She could feel rather than hear the rumble of laughter in his chest, and she hated him. "I have an eye for a pretty girl, too," he claimed. "Especially one who has hair as black as night, eyes as dark as the evening sky, and a skin as fair as the light of the moon." He laughed out loud. "You can open your eyes now, Victoria Lyle. You've made it!"

She opened her eyes, the better to berate him for talking such foolish nonsense to her at such a moment, and was surprised to discover that she was indeed at the top of the staircase. She rubbed her elbows where his hands had held her, confused by the memory of what he had said. "You hurt me!" she complained.

"Little liar! At least I got you up here. Why don't you thank me for that? You felt safe enough as soon as you knew I wouldn't let you fall, didn't you? You must trust me more than you think."

"You don't understand," she retorted. "One

doesn't reason logically at a time like that. Besides, I didn't have any choice. You forced me up here!"

"Oh, no, I did not," he said. "You walked up here by yourself because you knew you were safe with me behind you." As she opened her mouth to contradict him, he touched her lips with his forefinger, effectively silencing her. "Don't you dare deny it, or next time I'll leave you to the mercy of the guide!"

That stopped her for a moment. "You wouldn't!" she breathed.

"No, of course I won't. But I do wonder if you should attempt Cheops. It's a pretty stiff climb."

"I'll be all right if you're there. It can't be much worse than that!"

"The Grand Gallery goes right up into the center of the pyramid, but you should be all right if you don't look back—"

"And if you're right behind me!" He gave her a push along the short catwalk that led to some stone steps at the other end of which she thought she could see daylight. She plunged upward, scraping her shin against an uneven stone in her hurry. She hardly felt the pain at all. "I'm sorry to have made such a fool of myself," she apologized as they came out at the original entrance to the pyramid and started down the uneven steps to the ground below. "But you didn't have to say pretty things to me to give me something to think about. I know I'm just a job to you." She blinked in the sunlight. "You've probably said them all a hundred times before!"

His eyes shone gold and spelled out the message that she was treading on dangerous ground.

"You don't have to worry," she assured him hastily, "I didn't believe a word of it!"

He took a well-handled note out of his pocket and

gave it to the guide, slapping the man companionably on the shoulder. After they had all shaken hands, he turned back to Victoria, his eyes very bright.

"I've never seen anyone with yellow eyes before!" she exclaimed. "I'm sure you didn't get them from your English father."

"From my mother," he admitted. "She was a little French hen of a woman. I've always regretted that I never knew her, for French women often have a *je ne sais quoi* that other women lack."

"Like Juliette?" Victoria suggested, chancing the remark.

"Uh-huh. Sophisticated, chic—"

And no better than she should be, Victoria finished for him in her own mind. And Juliette was not, but perhaps he thought that that, too, added spice to a woman.

"Don't you think we ought to get on?" she said with admirable aplomb. "The afternoon is half-gone already." She ignored the twinkle in his eyes and pointed vaguely in the direction of the Great Pyramid. "I want to see everything while I'm here!"

He shrugged his shoulders and walked beside her across the rough ground, holding her back for an instant as they again crossed the busy road that ran between the two pyramids. They rounded the corner of the enormous edifice and made their way to the present entrance that had been cut out by robbers not very many years after the great Pharaoh had been laid to rest in what had been thought to be perfect safety.

Forever afterward Victoria was to remember her first visit to Cheops's Pyramid as the great turning point of her life. It came upon her unawares, before she had begun to realize what was happening to her.

One moment she was as she had always been, and the next she was aware of a new self that had been brought into being, against her wishes, by the man beside her. A man she wasn't sure she liked, let alone loved, but who had already become more important to her than any other person she had ever met. And she didn't even know his name.

So bemused was she by this discovery that she could have climbed the whole way up to heaven and scarcely noticed. As it was, she had done the greater part of the seventy meters up to the King's Chamber before she realized what a long way down it was behind her. The same kind of strips of wood had been nailed across the planks that covered the ancient stone steps that the Egyptians had used to haul up the coffin of the dead king, but here they had been reinforced with metal, perhaps because of the steepness of the angle. The first flight took them halfway, to a low corridor leading to the abandoned Queen's Chamber, which had never been completed.

It was a fairly small tomb compared to the others, hewn out of a single slab of granite. At one end was a recess that might have held a statue of Cheops himself, so that if anything happened to his body, his second self, his *ka*, would have some place to return to that he would recognize as his own likeness. From there on upward there was a choice of two stairways, one on either side of the smooth, central ramp, up which the sarcophagus had been hauled.

It was there that Victoria was foolish enough to look back at the way they had come. She held onto the thin metal banisters until her knuckles shone white and trembled.

"Look up!" Tariq's voice said immediately behind her. He came so close to her that she could feel the hard muscles of his thighs against hers and he put one arm around her, holding her firmly against him, his hand against her heart.

Now she had something new to worry her. Forgotten were her fears of the height they had attained. Forgotten, too, was her immediate interest in the architectural splendor of the Grand Gallery. She was conscious only of the feel of his body against hers and an urgent longing to be closer still. Her palms slipped on the metal banister and the lights blurred before her eyes.

"Easy now," Tariq bade her. "You're nearly there."

She reached the top and stood as far away from him as she could, gasping for breath. Her legs had turned to rubber and she was afraid to look at him for fear that he would read what she knew must be reflected in her navy blue eyes. Instead she stared down at the bottom of the shaft up which they had climbed, and for once she knew no fear at all of the depth of the fall below her.

"Well, well," said Tariq, "you're getting very brave!"

She trembled then and clutched the rail in front of her. "I made it!" she said faintly. "I actually made it!"

"You have to go down yet," he reminded her.

"A mere bagatelle!" she declared, but a wave of panic swept through her at the thought. "And not quite yet," she added with great caution. She bent her head too quickly to go through the low, narrow passage that led to the King's Chamber, and hit it hard on the entrance. Tariq swept her around to face him, rubbing her scalp with gentle fingers.

"Better?" he asked her.

She wondered what he would say if she were to tell him exactly what she was feeling—that he himself had become the center of her thoughts. She tore herself out of his embrace and flung herself into a headlong charge down the passage, emerging into the King's Chamber with such force that another tourist, waiting to come out, put out an anxious hand to steady himself.

Tariq followed at a more leisurely pace. He walked over to the stone sarcophagus and leaned against it, crossing his arms in front of his chest, and watching her as she wandered nervously around the chamber, looking at the markings on the walls—modern, she feared—and the vent that brought in fresh air from the outside, though its original purpose had probably been to allow the Pharaoh's *ka* to come and go at will.

"Tariq," she said at last, "about going to Sakkara tomorrow. Will they expect me to bring the money with me?"

He shook his head. "There's the license to sort out first. If you have some money with you, I expect Juliette and Jim Kerr will be glad to be paid up to date, but I shouldn't worry about it too much."

She felt suddenly helpless. "Juliette is right. My father must have been mad to let me loose on such a project. I don't know the first thing about it and I'll only be in the way."

"Are you thinking of running back to England?"

She was. She couldn't deny it. England spelled safety and a cozy security where she would never have to think about him again. "I might," she said.

"That would be a pity. I think you must stay, Victoria, until we get to the bottom of these thefts and clear your father's name—"

"But nobody has accused him!"

"As far as the Egyptian government is concerned he was as much a suspect as anyone else. You may have come out here to finish the job for him."

"Is that what you think?" she asked.

"I'm not paid to think. I'm paid to find out the facts, whatever they are. My guess is that you know nothing about it, but it's more than likely you'll lead me to whoever does."

"You mean you're going to use me as bait?" She hoped she didn't sound as frightened as she felt.

"You'll be all right," he said roughly. "You may even enjoy most of it. It seems a long time since I slept in a tent in the desert. What more can you want?"

"I want to go back to the hotel," she said. "It must be nearly dark outside."

He stood up, capturing her hand in his. "If it is, you'll be able to see the Sphinx by moonlight as I promised."

"I don't know that I want to," she denied.

He let go of her hand and followed her closely through the passage back to the Grand Gallery. "I want to show it to you," he said. He caught her hand again, bringing her to a standstill so that he could pass her in order to go down the ramp first. "Turn around and come down backward," he commanded her. "Slowly!"

Victoria looked resolutely ahead of her and tried not to think of the great, gaping shaft below her. One step at a time and she would manage it. One step at a time, making sure he had no opportunity of touching her. Perhaps Sakkara would be fun. England might be safe, but it would also be lonely.

She felt a strong sense of satisfaction when she found herself on level ground again. A smile spread over her face. "I did it! You didn't think I would, but I did it all by myself!"

"*Il hamdu li'llah*! Thank God," he said devoutly.

"*He* may have had something to do with it," she

acknowledged, "but you didn't have to do a thing. You needn't have been there at all!"

"That's something you'll have to answer for yourself," he said dryly.

"Perhaps. But at least I did it. I've never done anything like that before."

She stepped out of the pyramid before him, shivering a little in the coolness of the evening. "Oh, look!" she exclaimed. "It isn't quite dark! Isn't it a beautiful sunset?"

"Beautiful," Tariq agreed without evident interest.

"You could at least pretend to look at it," she said.

"I can see it reflected in your eyes," he said easily. "If you came closer, *yâ habibi*, I'd see it better still."

She had no intention of obliging him. For one thing, many of the camel drivers had not yet gone home, and for another, she didn't trust herself anywhere within his vicinity. His hands pulled her roughly against him and his lips claimed hers, warm and searching, until she flung her arms around his neck and began to kiss him back. She thought she had known it all, but she had never known anything before that moment. He made a movement to release her, but ended by pulling her closer still, putting his mouth against hers again, and she forgot everything else in her urgent need to respond to him.

CHAPTER FOUR

"TARIQ, NO!"

He lifted his head. "I'm afraid you've missed your sunset."

"Have I?" She turned her head to look at the western sky still ruddy from the sun, which had just sunk below the horizon. "Even my mother admits there's nothing more beautiful than a sunset in the desert," she said. She didn't have to make conversation, but how else could she make the transition back to reality?

"There will be others," he said.

She nodded her head. "You don't have to worry," she told him. "This has hardly been the biggest moment of my life."

He shrugged his shoulders without apparent regret.

"You don't have to feel sorry," she said coldly. It would be the last straw if he should retract in any way from that moment that had stirred her to the depths of her being. Of course he hadn't meant it! He would have kissed anyone who had been on hand. But, just for a few moments, she wanted to pretend that it had meant as much to him as it had to her. "Or do you want to apologize, too?"

"I'm not apologizing for kissing you, Victoria Lyle. I'm only sorry about the timing." But he did not seem at all sorry.

"Then you don't have to worry, do you? It was nice, but it meant nothing to either of us, *habibi*. I shan't make any demands on you—none at all! I don't even like you very much!"

"Then you shouldn't call me your darling," he observed. "If you want to use it for a man, it should be *habipi—habibi* is strictly feminine!"

"I'll never use it!" she retorted. "I don't intend to learn any of your bad habits. I wish you'd go away and leave me alone!"

"Do you?"

"I don't care in the slightest what you do!"

It was too dark to read his expression, but she felt his tap on her cheek and knew that he would have liked to make it much harder. "Do you still want to go and look at the Sphinx, or do you want to go back to the hotel?" he asked her.

"I want to see the Sphinx." Her tone was even.

She could see his teeth shining white in the twilight, as he replied, "You're not half as sophisticated as you pretend, my dear. It's a pity, because I'm not used to having to resist temptation, and I intend to see this Sakkara business through from start to finish!"

"I'm not stopping you."

"You could, if you tried hard enough. That's what's worrying me. You should have been your brother after all!"

Her temper stirred within her. "I didn't ask you to flirt with me," she said. "You can't accuse me of inviting—"

"The very look of you is an invitation!" he mocked her. "When this is over—" He broke off. "Never mind," he went on. "At least you'll be able to see the rise of the moon, even if you did miss the sunset."

"Yes," she said. "Tariq, you don't have to come with me to the Sphinx if you'd rather not. I shall be quite all right by myself."

"While I have nightmares thinking about the scrapes you might be getting yourself into? No, thank you! We'll go and see the Sphinx together. All right?"

"All right," she agreed against her will, acutely aware of him.

She walked beside him, stiff-legged in her anxiety not to betray her feelings, past a barrier erected to stop cars from using the road that led down past the Pyramid of Cheops to where the Sphinx guarded the whole burial complex of the three large and six small Pyramids of Giza. One of the watchmen came hopefully toward them, looking for an easy tip for escorting them down the road toward the Sphinx. When Tariq waved him away, he angrily retorted that the road was closed, but a few words of Arabic sent him back into the shadows from whence he had come, muttering beneath his breath.

"Why doesn't he want us to go this way?" Victoria asked.

"They're about to hold a rehearsal of the *son et lumière* and so they've closed the road. There's no reason why we shouldn't go on, though; they only want to stop the cars because of their headlights."

At that moment all three of the major pyramids were bathed in light, a light that changed from green to red to blue, and back to green again. It seemed as though a whole concert of music was coming from the center of the Great Pyramid, and it was hard to believe that the sound was a reflection from the microphones that carried the sound to the seats in the arena below them.

Then, before them, Victoria could make out the lionate shape of the Sphinx's head. They were standing above the left shoulder and she could see the clean line of the cheek and jaw as the spotlight came into play, highlighting the age-old face that had awed the world for more centuries than any other monument made by man.

"Oh, it's beautiful!" she said.

She knew that Tariq was smiling at her enthusiasm and she didn't care at all. Let him laugh at her if he wanted to.

"When the lights go out, you'll be able to see the rising of the full moon," he told her. "Do you want to go farther down?"

She did. "Can one go right down to the bottom and climb up there below the face? I'm sure I've seen people there on postcards."

"When the lights stop. But you can see the face much better from a distance. The ravages of time are more obvious when one stands on the paws of the beast."

"I don't care! I want to sit at his feet and feel romantic!"

"And this is the girl who doesn't invite people to flirt with her!"

She gave him a mischievous look. "You can stay here if you like," she suggested.

"I could," he agreed, "but I don't think you'd make it without me. You'll need me to get past the guard."

"Oh." She hesitated. "I would like to see it properly, but if you don't want to, I shan't mind very much."

The moon, round and very white, burst up over the horizon, looking four times as large as it would when it climbed higher into the star-spangled blackness of the night sky.

"You've talked me into it," he drawled. He crossed the road and stood by the parapet, watching the lights playing on the face of the Sphinx. "I don't want to hurt you, Victoria," he said at last. "I have to do my job."

"Does that prevent you from being my friend?"

"It depends what you mean by friend. Your father wouldn't have approved of any kind of friendship between us. He thought I had far too much success with the ladies without getting involved with his own daughter."

"But you're not involved," she pointed out. "I'd like you to be my friend, though. I think I'm going to need someone on my side at Sakkara, if Juliette's reaction is anything to go by. Is that asking too much?"

"It may be. It isn't your *friend* I'm tempted to be, but if that's the way you want it, I'll do my best to oblige—from tomorrow on!"

She was silent for such a long time that he turned and came back to her. "What about tonight?" she said.

"Tonight you'd better stay out of my way," he said.

She stared at him, trying to make out his expression. "It's only the moonlight," she said in her brightest manner. "The sun will be shining tomorrow."

He put his hand on her shoulder. "I hope it shines for you," he said. "I hope it shines for us both. But what if your father was involved in this business himself? Have you thought about that? You could end up hating me thoroughly."

The lights of the *son et lumière* rehearsal flickered and died. Victoria blinked in the sudden blackness and suddenly began to run down the hill toward the Sphinx before Tariq could read the emotions written on her face. He caught up with her at the foot of the hill, his longer legs gaining on her with an ease that defeated her.

"You could have broken your neck dashing off like that," he said. "But I suppose you didn't think of that?"

"No, I'm reasonably surefooted," she told him. "I very seldom take a tumble."

"Maybe, but when you don't know the path, that might not have helped you much!"

She forced herself to laugh at his concern because she didn't want him to know that she had been running away from him as much as anything. She had to make up her mind about him, and she couldn't do that when he was close to her. She had to make up her mind whether she really trusted him or not. That her father had not done so didn't weigh much with her either way. It didn't sound as though he entirely trusted her father, either. Her instinct bade her allow him a free hand where she was concerned—with her money, with everything—but her instinct remained an unreliable guide, for she had never been tested in this way before. Of course, he had taken the sting out of her fear of heights by forcing her to admit that she had known he wouldn't allow harm to come to her. But could she be as certain that he would protect her from her own ignorance at Sakkara?

"If I'd fallen, would you have picked me up?" she asked.

His grasp on her shoulder tightened. "Are you deliberately trying to be provocative?" he demanded.

"*No*! I was trying to make up my mind about you."

"And what did you decide?"

"I didn't come to any decision," she said. "I can't make you out at all!"

"I'd say you already have, in your heart, where it

counts." His tone was confident. "You don't like me much, but you've made up your mind about me."

"Oh? And what conclusion have I come to?"

"That I'm the best bet you've got!"

"Do you really think so?" She pretended a nonchalance she did not feel. "I think I'll keep my options open."

They had reached the foot of the Sphinx and an armed guard stepped forward, startling her. Tariq spoke to him and he pulled back part of the barbed wire fence and let them through. It was easy enough to climb up to the feet of the huge man-headed lion, and even up onto the beast's chest, from where one could look directly up at his chin.

Tariq held out his hands to Victoria. "Are you coming down to my level?" he said. He lifted her down from her perch, right into his arms, and she made no protest at all. He kissed her on the lips. "This was a mistake, Victoria." He ran his mouth over her face and then took her lips again, suppressing her faint gesture of protest with an impatient movement of his hands. She abandoned the unequal struggle and let him do as he liked, intoxicated by the feel of his lips on hers.

Slowly he lowered her onto her feet, his hands hard against her hips, pulling her closer still against him. "A big mistake! But you look so lovely in the moonlight and I can't resist you!"

She clung to him. "I'm sorry," she said.

He made an exasperated noise in the back of his throat. "Because I want to make love to you?" He put his hand over her mouth, effectively cutting off her answer. "I should have known better than to have brought you here. I'm going to kiss you once more, Victoria Lyle, and then I'm going to take you to dinner with my foster family—"

"I'm going back to the hotel!"

"Very wise. You should have gone when you last said that, my love. It's too late now. The damage is already done!"

"No, no, it isn't! Let me go, Tariq—"

"There's stardust in your eyes, did you know that?" He brushed her lashes with his fingers.

She made an earnest effort to pull herself together. "Stardust indeed! You must think me a fool if you think I'm going to swallow that!"

He put a hand under her chin and forced her face up to look at him. She struggled feebly, twisting away from his strong fingers. She felt torn in two. One half of her longed to go on where they had left off, but the other, more sober self couldn't help remembering that he had probably kissed a dozen or more girls in the moonlight, whereas she, despite her earlier claims, was a novice in the art of dalliance. She feared she would lose her head, and perhaps even her heart, if she stayed a moment longer.

"Is your foster mother expecting you?" she asked in desperation.

"She lives from moment to moment. There's always a place for me at her table, and also for anyone else I care to take along. You'll be welcome there, even as your father's daughter and despite the fact that George and I quarreled. Omm Beshir is a little woman, but she has a very big heart." His hand stroked her back. "But first I'm going to kiss you just once more. Stand still, little one, and look up, or you'll never know how it feels to have the man, and the moment, the Sphinx and the moonlight—"

"*No*!" she gasped. She had to remember that he wasn't serious, that it meant nothing to him that she was perilously close to falling in love with him. It was too late. Her blood thundered in her ears and her bones melted within her as his hands caressed her, drawing her ever closer until her whole world consisted of the smell and feel of him and the demanding mastery of his mouth on hers. He was not very gentle, making no allowances for her lack of experience, and when she tried to take a step away from him to catch her breath, he pushed her hard against the chest of the Sphinx until the rough stone bit into her back and she was completely helpless in his arms.

Then quite suddenly she was free and he had turned his back on her. "You're too much!" he said huskily. "And don't dare tell me again you've been kissed before, Victoria Lyle, because you've never felt *that* before!"

"I wasn't going to," she said faintly. "But that doesn't mean that I approve—"

"Oh Lord," he exploded, "you were well named, Victoria!"

"She was the one who wasn't amused," she retorted. "I said I didn't approve of casual affairs. I don't—I mean, I never have before and I don't intend to start now!"

He was silent for a long moment. "My word, you don't pull your punches, do you?" he said at last. "I don't regard you as a flirt, my dear, if that's what you're afraid of. I only had to look at you to know that." He turned his head. "Well, are you going to believe me?"

"Yes, but I want to go back now."

He smiled wryly. "When you look so delightfully demure you tempt me to break my resolution not to mix business with pleasure, and I refuse to be tempted by you once more tonight. So come along, my lovely, and I'll take you to Cairo before I change my mind!"

He took her by the hand and pulled her after him,

helping her down from the feet of the Sphinx to where the armed guard waited below. Her hand trembled in his and he looked back up at her and saw the fine pieces of stone that had caught on her dress when he had pushed her back against the Sphinx. With an unreadable expression, he waited for her to catch up with him and brushed her off with a gentle touch.

"You'll like my foster mother," he told her. "She'll be on your side, *habibi*, even against me!"

VICTORIA SAW a new side of Tariq that evening. She was entranced by the strange household to which he took her and especially by the dumpy little creature he introduced to her as his foster mother. She was seated on the floor, her legs drawn up under her, her prayer beads dangling from one dainty hand as she spoke to one or other of the assembled gathering. Victoria thought that some of the people there must surely be guests rather than relatives, for surely not even an Arab family could be so large, or so varied in age and coloring.

Tariq kissed the old lady's cheek, addressing her in Arabic. Her green eyes, which she attributed to the royal blood that had entered her family sometime in the distant past, twinkled up at her foster son as he drew Victoria forward to meet her. She reached up and saluted the girl's hand with her lips, presenting her own beautiful molded little hand for a similar salute from Victoria.

"Welcome to *Masr*!" the old lady bade her, using the colloquial name for both Cairo and Egypt. The green eyes were bright with speculation. "Victoria Lyle," she said in her heavily accented English, "I heard much about your father from Tariq, but nothing before today about you. Victoria, like a queen, like Kilopatra, no? You would be better called for her, for she was more beautiful than the English queen, I am thinking. Tariq was very clever to find you!"

Victoria sat down beside her on the floor, wishing that her limbs had been better trained for such a position. She was amused by the Egyptian pronunciation of Cleopatra, and by the sly compliment to her own looks. She liked Tariq's foster mother very much indeed and it was a decided point in his favor that the little Arab woman obviously adored him as much as if he had been her own child.

"Does Tariq come here often?" she asked, hoping that he did and that he would bring her with him when he came again.

"He is a son to me, *mashallah*!"

Victoria was to discover that *mashallah* was a favorite imprecation of her hostess to divert the Evil Eye from whichever loved one she happened to be speaking about.

"You mean he spent his whole childhood with you?"

"Only the long holidays after he went back to England to the school his father chose for him. It was a sad day whenever he had to go back again. How we all wept! He, too, even when he was quite a big boy. But now he is here most of the time and we are happy that it is so."

"But you must have a great many children of your own," Victoria commented, observing that yet more people were crowding into the already packed room.

The old lady chuckled. "So many, but there is always room for more! Tariq was my first baby. It is sad that he is not my own child, but he is better than a son to me. He takes me out shopping whenever he is in Cairo and he spoils me in my old age." Her eyes rested affectionately on her foster son. "He has much kindness in him, especially for us women, and we—we all love him in return!" She gave a little crow of laughter. "But you are the first girl he has brought here to see me. Did you know that?"

Victoria blushed. "We only met this morning."

"*Alallah*! Leave it to God! We are all in his hands and are nothing without Him. It is time Tariq found a nice girl for himself. There have been others, but they have had no understanding of him, wanting only what they could get out of him. Are you different from these others, Victoria?"

"I don't know," Victoria admitted. "Tariq and I are friends—nothing more." She met the bright green eyes bravely and the older woman nodded her head, satisfied.

"Your father did a bad thing to Tariq," she said slowly. "You will need to do better by him than he did, but if you are good to him, he will be good to you. I think he will find it easy to be good to someone as pretty as you, no?"

Embarrassed, Victoria never knew what she would have answered, for at that moment Tariq came and sat on the floor beside them, picking up his foster mother's prayer beads in the most natural way, slipping them through his fingers with such grace that Victoria found herself quite fascinated by the sight. She had never seen anyone who had such expressive hands, she thought.

"What has Omm Beshir been telling you?" Tariq smiled at her. "Has she been telling you all my secrets?"

His foster mother put a tiny hand on his arm. "This one pleases me well," she congratulated him smugly. "Does she go with you to Sakkara tomorrow?"

His eyes rested on Victoria's face, alight with warm, affectionate laughter. "I go with her," he corrected. "Her father has left her in charge of the expedition's finances. But you needn't worry. I shan't let her out of my sight until that old business is finished."

Omm Beshir bridled. "And will that other one be there also?"

"She won't worry Victoria. Juliette and I have always understood one another, and anyway, it was George she preferred in the end."

Omm Beshir sighed, spreading her hands in dismay. "I don't pretend to understand your Western ways! If she were one of us, we would know how to treat such a one, but I'm told she's in no way remarkable in your country. I'm not surprised her husband will have nothing more to do with her!"

Tariq grinned. "You do her an injustice. It was she who divorced her husband. It was only afterward that she began to look around at other men."

Omm Beshir sniffed disapprovingly. "How many husbands does she mean to have?"

He shrugged. "She claims she doesn't want to chain herself down to any one man again. She likes being free and being answerable only to herself. She wants to make her own way in the world by her own efforts."

Omm Beshir was shocked and contemptuous of such an idea. "What kind of freedom is that?" she demanded. "What is so good about having to do a man's job? What comfort does she find in her ambition to be like a man? Am I less free than she because my husband lives his own life and I live mine, serving him and my children, and living as a woman was meant to live?"

Tariq looked amused. "No one would dare deny

that you are happy living the way you do, but other women want other things nowadays. Juliette wants to rejoice in her own achievements, not in her husband's." He turned to Victoria. "What about you?" he asked her.

She hadn't expected the question and she didn't know how to answer. She was all too conscious of his observant, golden eyes on her face and was afraid that he could read her indecision all too clearly and would despise her for it.

"I'm happy to be a woman," she said at last.

Omm Beshir gave her a good-natured poke in the ribs. "It is easy to see that you are happy to be a woman today, *yâ bént*, but what of tomorrow when they will all be looking to you to make the decisions?"

"But they won't!" she denied too quickly. "They must know that I don't know the first thing about such things. Anyway, Tariq will be there," she added, completely demoralized.

"And will you do what he tells you?" Omm Beshir teased her.

They were both laughing at her, she saw, and after a moment she joined in, knowing that it was kindly laughter.

"I may do," she said, her nose in the air. "It depends what he tells me to do—and what the others want me to do, too!"

Omm Beshir shook her head at Victoria and laughed again, breaking into Arabic, which she found easier and more comfortable when talking to her family. Victoria changed her position to ease her aching thighs and began to look around the crowded room at her leisure. Tariq and his foster mother soon forgot her presence as they talked to one another, and she listened to them idly, liking the sound of the liquid language they were speaking, half wondering if she would ever master the glottal stops in the back of the throat that seemed to be so important to the Arab speech, and half wondering if the room she was in was typical of the average Egyptian house.

The house was very simply built, with few defenses against wet weather such as they had had the day before. The bright green color wash on the walls showed large dark patches where the water had come in, and there was a faint, musty smell that pervaded everything and must also have been caused by the rain. Or, less likely but possible, it might have come from the strange furnishings that were packed around the walls of the room with an indifference to comfort that was strange in a people noted for their sensual tastes. There were couches galore, mostly too high for one's feet to reach the floor when sitting, and a few iron hard cushions covered in highly colored materials. The chairs had spindly wire legs and stood in drunken disarray in whatever corner they had been shoved to get them out of the way. Some of the younger members of the family sat awkwardly on the edges of the couches as if it were a duty for them to do so, but their elders, more intent on their own comfort, either pulled their legs up under them where they were sitting, or followed Omm Beshir's example and seated themselves on the floor.

Victoria came out of her daydream as someone touched her hand, and she looked up to see a small boy holding a tray of glasses beside her.

"*Itfaddal!*" he said shyly.

Victoria looked at the thick, exotic-looking mixture in the glasses with distaste. A sweet, sickly smell assailed her nostrils and she shook her head vigorously. "No, thank you," she said.

Tariq reached across her and pressed one of the glasses into her hand. "It's considered very rude to refuse anything one is offered," he said in her ear. "It offends against their hospitality. You must drink it, if only because they have gone to a lot of trouble to prepare it for you."

"What is it?" she whispered back, accepting the glass. "It will be your fault if I throw up," she added mendaciously.

"Don't you dare! It's a drink made from prickly pear—an acquired taste, you might say, and one which I haven't acquired. The best method is to hold your nose and swallow! Like this!" He took his own glass from the tray and poured the contents straight down his throat.

But Victoria found herself unable to emulate this feat and she was still playing with her glass when Omm Beshir called them all to the table to eat.

It was a strange meal that followed. There was cooked millet, which Tariq told her was called couscous; cabbage leaves stuffed with spiced rice; a roasted duck, which was given pride of place in the center of the table; and a great many side dishes of vegetables and hot, peppery sauces. Victoria was relieved to discover that she liked most of the different foods that were put in front of her, and actively enjoyed trying out all the various concoctions, to the delight of her hostess who kept pressing her to eat more and more, until she began to feel rather like a stuffed delicacy herself. It was halfway through the meal when she realized that she was the only woman eating; everyone else at the table was a man.

"Isn't your foster mother hungry?" she asked Tariq, taking advantage of a sudden burst of laughter.

"It would embarrass her to eat with men she

didn't know well," he answered. "All her neighbors have come to look at you because they heard I had brought you to see Omm Beshir, and some of them she hardly knows at all. When I was a child," he remembered with glee, "she used to rush behind a curtain if her husband brought home a strange man, but she has been living in Cairo for a long time now and has become very sophisticated and modern."

Victoria laughed. "I think she's a darling!" she said warmly.

His golden eyes mocked her. "That's more or less what she said about you," he told her. "You may be complimented, for although she seldom goes out, and even more seldom meets people outside her family, Omm Beshir is a very shrewd cookie indeed!"

And rather to her surprise, Victoria found that she was complimented, that she had wanted Tariq's foster mother to like her, more than she had wanted anything for a long, long time.

CHAPTER FIVE

THE ROAD TO Sakkara led along one of the irrigation channels that had watered the fertile land beside the Nile for more generations than even the lengthy history of Egypt had recorded. Much the same methods were used to raise the water then as now: a blindfolded ox walking endlessly around and around pumping the water up into even smaller irrigation channels, or a series of buckets on a belt operated by hand, or even by the simpler method of a bucketful at a time. In the ancient days if a man were to take more than his fair share of water he would be punished not only in this world but in the next. The crime is scarcely less heinous today, and every drop is measured with the same care as it was long ago.

It was not far to Memphis. Victoria had gone in to breakfast with a businesslike glint in her navy blue eyes, determined to show Tariq that yesterday had been yesterday, but now she had to concentrate on her father's excavation and wouldn't have time for any other diversions. When she had sat down opposite him at the table, her resolution had been dented somewhat by the swift appreciation she read in his falcon's eyes.

"Tell me something about the tomb my father found?" she had invited him.

"I'll tell you at Memphis," he said. "You'd better see the remains there on the way to Sakkara."

And now here they were almost at Sakkara, and

he hadn't told her anything at all. She wondered if that had been her fault. She had sat beside him as stiff as a poker, answering everything he had said in monosyllables, but she hadn't wanted to confide in him that she was afraid of the reception she was going to receive at the excavation, that she was so nervous that her tongue felt like a lump of dry wood in her mouth.

"You'll be all right," he said out of the blue. "I won't let them eat you, not on your very first day."

She started, summoning up a smile. "I know I'll be all right. If my father thought I could cope, I must be able to, mustn't I? Besides, I know I can manage as long as Torquil Fletcher doesn't turn up. I've been telling myself that all morning." She stared out of the window. "I know he's a friend of yours, but you have to admit that he did make trouble. Everybody says so!"

"I haven't said so," he pointed out. "I agree that the team began to fall apart just about the time he quarreled with your father, but that was a coincidence. It came at the same time as your father began to suspect that some of the most valuable objects he was finding had disappeared. He wanted to blame Fletcher, but he knew that Fletcher hadn't done anything of the sort. The trouble was, he was so angry that he didn't care what bricks he threw at him."

"Did they quarrel over Juliette?" Victoria asked him.

"In a way," he admitted.

"Was my father—fond of her?"

"He liked having her around. You mustn't blame him if he found her attractive. She fell into his hands like a ripe plum and he was absolutely delighted with everything she said and did."

"Until Torquil Fletcher upset everything?"

"He didn't realize how serious George was about her. If he had, he would have left her alone. As it was, he went all out to have some fun himself, and Juliette wasn't exactly averse to his advances." His lips twisted into a wry smile. "I think she rather liked having two strings to her bow. Only George found out, as it was inevitable that he should, and there was a battle you could have heard down in Cape Town. It was a bad scene."

"It was cruel, too," Victoria considered. "My father wasn't a young man and he had been rejected by my mother, too, in a way. I mean, she wouldn't go anywhere with him. She didn't like him, let alone love him, and he must have known that. It was obvious even to me as a child. I don't think I'd like your Torquil Fletcher very much."

"I don't imagine he took your father's past life into consideration," Tariq said dryly. "Juliette was there and available. That was all there was to it as far as he was concerned."

"Probably not," she agreed with disapproval. "My father had other reasons for disliking him, though. He said so."

"Not really," Tariq denied. "George wasn't normally a small-minded man and he would have got over the rest quite easily if Juliette hadn't been sticking in his gullet. Fletcher questioned her judgment, too, in an article he wrote and she isn't going to forgive him for that in a hurry!"

Victoria didn't mind the thought of the French girl's discomfiture nearly as much as she did her father's. "What happened?" she asked, intrigued.

"Your father and Juliette had decided that their tomb was the tomb of the Pharaoh Kha-Sekhem, because they had found a statue of him in the outer doorway. Fletcher disagreed. Quite a few statues and stelae of Kha-Sekhem have been found in the past, always in the south, and always wearing the white crown of Upper Egypt *without* the red crown of the northern delta kingdom. When he wrote an article saying so, Juliette went up in smoke, and your father ordered him off the site."

"Was he right?" Victoria asked.

"I think so."

"Then how do you explain Kha-Sekhem's statue being in the tomb?"

"I don't. We shan't know for certain until they get farther into the tomb and sort out all the finds. At the moment they're still arguing about the probable dating of most of the objects, when they're doing anything at all. It's been a pretty slack operation from the start. Don't expect them to like it when you begin to apply the big stick, Victoria. Neither Juliette nor Jim Kerr is going to enjoy being handled by a complete amateur."

"But you'll be there," she pointed out, trying to sound less anxious than she felt.

"They won't relish that either!" He felt her stiffen and put a reassuring hand on hers in a brief contact that made her heart swoop within her. "They can't get rid of me without your say-so," he said. "And you'll have to talk to the Egyptian authorities to persuade them to withdraw me before I'll go. So it looks as though you're stuck with me for the time being, come what may!"

It was a comforting thought, but not one she could afford to indulge if she wanted to impress on him that their relationship was going to be a working one and nothing more.

"Are we going to Memphis now?" she asked brightly.

"If you like." He looked across at her, his eyes

full of mockery. "There's little enough there for you to dream about."

"I told you it would be different in the full light of day," she retorted. "We both knew it didn't mean anything!"

"Does that mean we have to behave like strangers?"

"We are strangers," she claimed. "We only met yesterday—"

"So we did. But you recognized me at once in the shade of the sycamore tree, just as I knew you."

"There wasn't any shade," Victoria objected. "I don't believe there's been so much as a single leaf on that tree for a hundred years!" She waited for him to say something and when he didn't, she felt thoroughly cross and ill-used. "What is there at Memphis?" she demanded.

He parked the car under some palm trees and leaned back, watching her lazily through half-closed eyes. "Put your prickles away, Victoria," he said. "I don't like being scratched, and I don't intend to be by you."

She blinked, her lashes showing very black against her milk-white skin. "I don't know what you're talking about," she declared.

"Think about it," he recommended. "We'll be seeing a great deal of each other in the next week or so, and if you're going to be on edge all the time you'll wear yourself out."

"It isn't only me!" she flashed at him.

He reached out a hand and brushed a lock of blue black hair out of her eyes. "But I've been here before, and I think I'm better able to cope. Make it easy on yourself and leave things to me. All right?"

She nodded, unable to say a single word. It was something of a relief to have it out in the open, she admitted to herself. For the first time that morning she relaxed her taut muscles and smiled at him. He held out his hand to her and she put her own into it to seal the agreement.

"There's a sphinx here, too," he told her. "Come and see if you think it resembles its big brother at Giza."

She got out of the car and looked around her. "You haven't told me why Memphis was important," she reminded him.

"It was the first capital city of the united Two Kingdoms," he said, and he began to tell her about the fabled Menes, or Mena, the first Pharaoh of the First Dynasty, who had united Upper and Lower Egypt into one administrative unit, making it into perhaps the first real state, or country, that the world had ever known, around the year 3500 B.C.

If the Sphinx was small and dainty and in no way comparable to its mighty cousin at Giza, the unfinished statue of Rameses II lying on its back in a specially constructed museum was positively huge. Victoria thought he had rather a nice face. The royal wig and the false beard, which all the Pharaohs had worn, set it off well, giving the nose and mouth a clean-cut look that was almost modern in its execution and design.

"Was he the one who chased after Moses?" she asked Tariq.

"It was more likely his successor who did that. Rameses had other claims to fame. He was a very great man." He put his hand in his pocket and drew out a handful of blue scarabs, holding them out to her. "I meant to give you these before," he said. "A charm to watch over you when I'm not close by. They represent the dung beetle that was sacred to the sun god Ra—"

"The one you were talking about yesterday at Heliopolis?"

"Where we met," he agreed with a faint smile. "You can see these dung beetles sometimes in the desert—shiny, black little things that roll a great ball of dung in front of them that contains their eggs. It seemed to the ancient Egyptians that they produced new life out of nothing when the young beetles broke out of their eggs, and they imagined a huge, similar beetle rolling up the sun into the sky every morning, bringing new life to the world."

Victoria examined the small scarabs with care. "But these aren't old, are they?" she exclaimed.

"No, they're mostly made as souvenirs for the tourists. But this one is old." He picked out a pale gray one from among its brighter brothers. "This one I found myself. It has beautiful markings underneath." He put it back into her hand, closing her fingers over it. "It was the first I ever found," he told her. "Keep it safe for me as a symbol of the trust you have in me. You do trust me, don't you?"

"You know I do! But don't you want to keep it? Why isn't it in a museum?"

"They have too many of them already, and so I was allowed to keep it. If you're afraid of losing it, you could wear it around your neck on a string."

"I will," she promised, pleased. She held it tightly in her hand and smiled back at him. Perhaps the beetle would roll up the sun for her one day, and in the meantime, Tariq must like her a little or he wouldn't have given it to her. "Does the charm work in the dark?"

"I've never tried it out," he answered her. "You'll have to let me know if it does."

"I might not know," she said uncertainly.

"You'll know!" he assured her. "You'll know if you feel as safe by night as you do by day!"

Victoria smiled. "I'm not afraid of you at any time," she told him.

"But it won't be only me you'll have to contend with." His face hardened, a muscle tightening into a hard knot by his jaw. "I wish it were, my dear. I'd feel a whole lot happier about you if I thought that!"

THE DEMARCATION LINE between the green of the Nile valley and the sand of the desert was as clear as the line that runs between a highway and the grassy shoulder beside it. On the one side lay black, productive soil; on the other, the crumbly stone of the eternal desert, stretching most of the way across North Africa. It must have been as obvious in the old days, when they had carried the dead to the western side of the river to join the other subjects of Osiris and take up their final residence in his kingdom. But they did not seem to have approached death in a morbid spirit. On the contrary, the tombs of the various notables had been hardly different at all from the houses in which they had lived when they were alive. Some of them had had gardens attached, and one had even had a bathroom put in for the convenience of the great man who had been laid to rest there.

In the distance Victoria could see the famous Step Pyramid of Zoser, the first edifice in Egypt to be built entirely of stone. Nearer at hand were several other pyramids, so badly ravished by latter-day builders who had taken their stones to save quarrying their own, that they looked like nothing more than piles of loose rock that mattered to no one.

The road petered out into a track across the sand and they went quite close to one of these pyramids where, to Victoria's delight, a fox had made his home among the tumbled stones and was peering out at them, not even bothering to move away. A group of camels, chariots, and donkeys waited patiently a little farther along the track for the next group of tourists who would come to see the Serapeum, the underground corridor of tombs of the bulls that in their lifetime had been sacred to Ptah, the creator god of Memphis.

Tariq chose another track leading away from the Serapeum at the junction by the donkey boys' hut. Looking back to catch a last glimpse of the colorful group of men and animals, Victoria saw, far down below the level of the other road, a semicircular area that contained a number of battered busts of Greek poets and philosophers looking so out of place in that setting that a giggle escaped her.

"Why here?" she asked.

"The Greeks were lavish in the homage they paid to a civilization that they recognized as being far more ancient than their own. They recognized the debt they owed to Africa and Asia Minor, a debt that in modern times we more often prefer to ignore."

And then, suddenly, they were there. A small mound of sand was all that was visible of the actual dig. To Victoria's eyes it looked rather dull, but she got out of the car and peered down into the opening that had been dug into the side of the old tomb. She stood up straight, disappointed, and her heart knocked uncomfortably against her ribs when she realized that Tariq hadn't waited for her, but had driven on nearer to a group of white canvas tents that had been erected not far from the site.

A man on a donkey, unshaven and with his shaggy hair full of sand, rode over to her and sat there for a long while looking at her.

"You must be Victoria Lyle," he said. "I'm Jim

Kerr. Did someone bring you here, or did you materialize out of the desert?

"I came with Tariq," Victoria told him.

"So he's back again, is he? That won't sweeten Juliette's temper any, or is everything forgiven and forgotten between them?"

Victoria raised her eyebrows in a haughty expression she had borrowed from Tariq. "How should I know?" she countered. She turned back to the entrance of the *mastaba*. "May one go down there?" she asked.

"Who is there to say no to you? I'll get a light and come down with you, if you like. But you don't have to prove anything to me, you know. It's no skin off my back if you take your responsibilities here seriously or not. Only Juliette cares about that, and her first impression was so unfavorable, you'll have a tough job making her believe that you know anything about Egyptology."

"I don't. I can't pretend I do—not even to please Juliette!"

"Oh well, as long as the money keeps flowing she'll forgive you that. She's a great deal less likely to forgive George Lyle's daughter for turning out to be a raving beauty. If you take my advice, you'll stay away from Torquil Fletcher when she's around. With your father dead, there's nothing to prevent them getting together now."

"Except he isn't here—"

"He is, if Tariq brought you here. Didn't he introduce himself? Tariq *is* Torquil Fletcher!"

For a moment Victoria thought she was going to faint. She sat down hurriedly on a pile of stone and sand before her legs gave way under her. "He wouldn't tell me his name—only Tariq!"

"Most people call him that," Jim Kerr admitted.

"That weird foster mother of his called him Tariq as a baby when she couldn't get her tongue around Torquil."

"She isn't weird," Victoria defended her. "I like her!"

"My, my," said Jim. "He has been busy, hasn't he, if he took you there?" He scratched some of the sand out of his beard. "Wove you a fine tale about himself, did he? Never mind, you're not the first female to be hooked on that line of his. He's quite the lady's man—as your father would have told you. He knew. Oh, brother, he knew all about it!"

To Victoria, that was no comfort at all. She felt betrayed, and not even the feel of the scarab in her pocket did anything to console her. She had *trusted* Tariq, and not only with her father's affairs, and it was obvious that he didn't care at all, or he would have at least prepared her by telling her his real name.

"I don't think I want to go inside the tomb now after all," she said. "I'd rather go to wherever it is I shall be staying."

"Right," Jim approved. "I'll take you." He dismounted from his donkey, clapping his hands behind its back to make it go back to the others. "There hasn't been much happening recently," he explained. "There wasn't enough in the kitty to keep things going as we'd hoped. Juliette and I stayed on to be here when you arrived, but we couldn't persuade any of the men to hang on, especially not with the government breathing down our necks."

"Tariq is working for the government—"

Jim shook his head. "Another tale, my dear. You'd do better to get your father's license transferred to Juliette or me, unless you mean to take it out in your own name?"

"I'll have to think about it," Victoria said. It didn't take much thinking, though, to know it wasn't likely that anyone in his right mind would grant her a license to take control of an excavation she knew nothing about, and wasn't qualified to direct in the first place. She would have to trust Tariq after all, she thought, or go back to England and admit total defeat. He hadn't made it easy for her to back him up if he wanted to take charge himself.

They had almost reached the group of tents when Jim said suddenly, "You only got the money as long as you came to Egypt, didn't you? What would have happened to it otherwise?"

"If I hadn't come it would have gone to his assistant—I suppose that must be Juliette? But he didn't want her bothered with both the finances and the everyday details of the dig. He didn't leave me anything personally, or her either, if that's what you want to know."

Jim grinned at her. He looked more like a hippie than a serious man of science, with his wild hair and beard, and not a very clean one at that. He should have been likable though, yet Victoria found she didn't care for him at all and she wondered why not. She liked most people unless they were obviously horrid, and Jim Kerr was certainly not that.

"I was curious, I guess," he said. "It's a bad habit diggers in the dust are apt to get into. It doesn't mean I'm any less glad you've come!" He waved across the sand to Juliette who had just emerged from one of the tents. "Hey there, where are we putting our new boss? Shall I show her to her father's old tent?"

Juliette gave Victoria an indifferent look. "It's the largest," she said languidly. "Are you afraid of being by yourself, Miss Lyle? Your father's tent is rather far from the others as George didn't care to be observed by anyone. You won't get lonely, will you?"

"I'm sure it will do very well," Victoria murmured, accepting the challenge implicit in her words. She turned and looked full at Tariq, who had come out of the tent behind Juliette. "As long as it's as far away as possible from Mr. Fletcher's," she added meaningfully.

He didn't look in the least bit guilty. Indeed, she might have fallen into the trap of thinking he hadn't heard her if it hadn't been for the quickly suppressed twitch of the corners of his mouth. "I thought we were on first name terms," he said.

She looked at him with a flash of anger. "Which one would you like me to use? It may take me time to get used to Torquil."

"Tariq will do," he returned. "I'll show you to your father's tent," he added abruptly. He put his hand on her elbow, anticipating her refusal and, when she tried to win free, increased the pressure of his fingers until she gave way and consented to go with him. "I want to talk to you," he said in her ear.

"Well, I don't want to talk to you!" She waited until she was sure they were out of earshot before continuing. "How dare you even *speak* to me? You could have told me you were Torquil Fletcher, instead of leaving me to find out from someone like Jim Kerr!"

"So you don't like him," he murmured. "I wonder why not?"

"That's none of your business," she snapped.

"I thought you'd have more faith in me," he said.

She felt unaccountably guilty. "I haven't made up my mind about you. Tariq, what am I to do?"

"Nothing's changed, *yâ habibi*. Either you trust me or you don't."

"I have to trust you," she sighed. "There isn't anyone else." She forgot to look where she was going and fell heavily over one of the guy-ropes of the tent, letting loose a cry that would have done credit to a banshee. She got to her feet and examined the grazed palms of her hands, wincing as she pulled a sliver of stone out of her wrist.

"Let me look," Tariq said wearily.

"*No*!"

"Don't be a fool!" He grasped her arm and swore under his breath when he saw what she had done to herself. "You'd better have some disinfectant on that. Come into the tent and I'll do it for you."

"I can quite easily do it myself," she said with a pugnacious lift to her chin.

He didn't bother to answer that. Taking a firmer grip on her arm, he hurried her before him into the tent, ignoring her astonished cries of pleasure as she saw the beauty of the interior. He splashed some water out of a jug into a bowl and added a measure of disinfectant with a liberal hand. Then, standing behind her, he pushed both her hands palm downward into the mixture, wincing himself at her indignant gasp of pain.

"Do you have to be so brutal?" she demanded.

He smiled, his face very close to hers. "I'm sorry, but it would be far worse if it got infected. There now, is the stinging wearing off?"

She nodded. "You're enjoying this!" she accused him.

"It makes a nice excuse for getting you back in my arms," he said mockingly. He turned her around to face him and kissed her on the cheek, letting her go with apparent reluctance. "I should have told you who I was," he admitted. "I can't think why I didn't. The quarrel with your father was such a pointless business. It should never have been allowed to bedevil our friendship as it did, but it did, and it's no good crying over spilled milk. I'd like to know who told him about it, all the same!" He went to the door of the tent with the bowl of disinfectant and tossed the fluid onto the sand. "I'll leave you to settle in. I'll have your suitcase brought to you in a few minutes. Okay?"

Victoria thanked him, her voice cooler than she had intended.

He turned his head, pausing for a moment in the entrance of the tent. "Thanks for going on trusting me," he said.

"I don't know that I do," she responded. "But I do trust Omm Beshir and she vouched for you. Besides, I gave you my word, and I take that sort of thing seriously. Do you?"

"I'm learning to." He came back inside the tent. "I didn't know, Victoria, how involved your father was with Juliette. I'd like you to believe that."

She did believe him, but the thought of him with Juliette hurt all the same. "You don't have to tell me about it," she said.

"Your father isn't here to tell," he replied. "If I'd known he'd take it so badly, I'd have thought twice about trying to laugh him out of it. I'm not particularly proud of the incident."

"Juliette is a very attractive woman, though," Victoria observed. "You probably thought it worth it at the time."

He shrugged his shoulders. "She was there, that was all." He gave her a thoughtful look. "There's no malice in Juliette, so I have only myself to blame. I knew she was a hedonist and would take her pleasures where she found them. It didn't mean a thing to either of us. It would have made more sense if it had. But I couldn't persuade your father of that. Whoever told him about us had already twisted the knife in the wound to pretty good effect. He wouldn't listen to a thing I said. He just kept repeating that he wanted me off the site and that I wasn't to come back."

"Perhaps somebody else wanted you off the site, too," Victoria suggested. "My mother always said that once he'd got an idea into his head there was no getting it out again. He probably wasn't liking you much anyway for that article you wrote."

"Well, I'm back now," he said. "This time they may find it harder to get rid of me."

"They'll be too busy trying to get rid of me!" Victoria sighed. "Jim Kerr had already suggested that I get the license put in his or Juliette's name."

"And are you going to?"

She shook her head. "I don't know what I'm going to do. I have the address of my father's lawyers in Cairo. I shall probably take their advice on most things. What else can I do?"

His eyes narrowed. "Did Jim say why he had stayed on?"

"Not that I remember." She pursed her lips, flexing her grazed hands and wincing as she did so. "Tariq, you are still working for the government, aren't you? What is your exact position with them?"

"I'm working for the Egyptian Antiquities Department."

"And that's a fact?"

"Yes, my dear, that's a fact. It gives me the right to ask you to consult me before you do anything, anything at all, here on the site. I'd like to think you'd do that anyway—"

"I've said I will," she murmured.

But still he hesitated. "There's nothing now between Juliette and me," he said abruptly. "Whatever anyone may tell you, and they probably will."

"Tariq, it doesn't matter."

He tipped up her face, forcing her to meet his eyes. "Doesn't it?"

"No."

His eyebrows shot up, making him look more like a bird of prey than ever, and it suddenly mattered very much indeed, and she knew that he knew it, too.

"I should have guessed yesterday you were Torquil Fletcher," she said. "Whoever heard of an Englishman called Tariq? My wits must have been scattered!"

"Or you didn't want to believe it. You didn't want to like someone your father obviously hated."

Her lips kicked up into a smile. "Perhaps I don't like you. Have you thought of that?"

His eyes glinted. "I don't have to," he said. "Look after yourself, Victoria; it's getting so that I can't do without you!"

And he walked out of the tent and away across the sand, whistling.

CHAPTER SIX

VICTORIA OPENED her eyes slowly and for a long moment thought she was still dreaming. Then she remembered that she was in Sakkara and that this was her father's tent. She had thought when she had first seen it that it was beautiful, but it was only now that its full glory was brought home to her. The whole of the inside was elaborately embroidered with appliqué work in brilliant colors, representing patterns and what she took to be texts from the Koran, the sacred book of Islam. The greens, reds and blacks stood out against the white background, a maze of color and design that led the eye from one part to another in the most satisfying way. She wondered briefly if it had all been done by hand and promised herself to ask Tariq about it when next she saw him.

She yawned and stretched herself, glancing at her watch to find out the time. She hoped that today would be better than the day before. It had to be, she thought gloomily, for it could scarcely be worse! Juliette had lost no time in insisting that they should discuss the financial future of the excavation, brushing aside Victoria's suggestion that nothing could be done until they had cleared up the matter of the license to continue to dig. It had proved a long and exhausting session, and in the end nothing had been decided between them.

Victoria was afraid her own ignorance had had something to do with that. Juliette had refused to explain anything on the grounds that Victoria wouldn't understand what she was talking about anyway. In vain did the younger girl point out that she had taken the trouble to read all her father's papers before coming to Egypt, though perhaps they had not meant as much to her as they should. Afterward, she had come to the conclusion that she would have to reread everything and try to learn a little bit more about what had been going on. She had spent most of the evening doing exactly that, making calculations to find out the potential cost of each of the projects that her father had hoped to carry out, and getting into a hopeless muddle as to what was possible and what was not.

That had been when she had decided that the time had come for her to pay a visit to her father's lawyers in Cairo. Her natural instinct was to turn to Tariq for advice, but further thought had suggested to her that that would place him in an intolerable position with the others who already viewed him as little better than a government spy. No, if Tariq was going to direct the excavation, even indirectly through her, he had to be given the powers and the respect that went with the position. So, for the moment at any rate, it had to be the lawyers or no one. She had already asked Juliette if she could borrow the car that everyone involved in the expedition used, and first thing that morning she would call the lawyers and make an appointment to see them.

Through the gaps in the ties of the flap over the tent's entrance she could see the gray light of the predawn morning. If she wanted, she thought, she could go back to sleep for at least another hour, but she had never felt less like sleep, and the strange surroundings outside called to the spirit of adventure within her. Not only that, but she had missed the sunset again the evening before because she had become so involved with her father's papers, and she was determined she was not going to miss a perfectly good sunrise if she could help it.

She pushed back the bedclothes and jumped out of bed, remaking it swiftly before she pulled on her underclothes, jeans and a shirt. When she had dressed, she ran a comb through her long black hair and tied it back behind her head out of her way. She would have to change before she went to Cairo, she supposed, for she was not sure the Cairenes would approve of having trousered young women in their midst, though Juliette had been wearing a pant suit when she had come to the hotel at Giza, and so had many of the women she had seen walking along the streets.

An orange glow spread across the desert from the Nile when she stepped out of her tent. It was also very cold and she was glad she had brought a sweater with her. She climbed to the top of a ridge just outside the camp and looked around her, listening to the astonishing silence. The Step Pyramid took on a rosy glow, and most of the other pyramids looked far more impressive in the half-light than they had in the glare of the midday sun. They rose in majesty, pointing upward to the rose-washed sky. Apart from her, only the animals were taking advantage of the early hour. A young fox chased its own tail in a mad game of its own; desert rats peered out of their holes, making the most of the last few moments of the night before they retired to sleep through the day; and the dogs of the neighborhood, without benefit of pedigree or grooming, met in little groups with waving tails to discuss the events of the night that had passed since they had last seen one another.

The sun rose in a large red ball, changing color so quickly that Victoria felt obliged to keep her eyes firmly fixed on the eastern hemisphere of the sky until the rays grew too strong for her to go on watching. The desert lost its glow of pink mystery and reverted to being stony sand, and the beautiful moment was lost, merging into the eternal silence of the wilderness.

But Victoria was still sitting on the ridge, loath to admit to herself that there was nothing more to wait for, when she saw Jim Kerr coming up the hill toward her. She considered moving before he could see her and engage her in conversation, but she didn't want to be thought unkind. Her first dislike of the man had strengthened into actual aversion the day before when he had spoken to her about his part in the excavation. He had patronized her unbearably, edging toward the idea that she should promote him over Juliette's head because the workers would work more happily for a man than a woman. When she had told him it was unlikely they would be allowed to continue on any terms, he had fallen into a sulk and had accused her of playing favorites. He suggested that she would soon change her mind if he flirted with her and paid her compliments.

"Is that what Tariq does?" he had roared at her. "Where is he now?"

But Victoria hadn't known. She hadn't seen him again after he walked, whistling, out of her tent.

"G'morning, Victoria."

"Good morning, Mr. Kerr."

He sat down beside her, scratching his beard. "Make it Jim, okay, I'm not one to bear a grudge, even if you won't be sensible and let me run things for you. Made up your mind what you're going to do?"

Victoria shifted a few inches away from him. "I have a few ideas on the subject."

"Oh?" He scratched himself some more, pushing his fingers through a hole in his sweater. "Must mend this sometime. I suppose you wouldn't like to do it for me?"

"No, I wouldn't." She saw his wry expression and relented toward him a little. "You wouldn't think much of my efforts if I did. My idea of mending holes is to gather the two sides together and hope for the best."

"Botch it, do you? You're about to make a botch of this job, too, if you don't mind my saying so. You'll never get the men to work for Juliette; she keeps them on far too tight a rein, and they don't understand what she's aiming at. She knows her stuff as far as Egyptology is concerned, but human nature is a closed book to that lady!"

Victoria wriggled a little farther away. "Juliette has her own work to do. My father didn't want her worried by financial considerations. If she can't take control of the excavation, it's up to her to say so."

Jim laughed unpleasantly. "Leaving Torquil Fletcher to reap the rewards. Your father would have loved that!"

"Nobody is going to reap the rewards, certainly not Tariq, and certainly not me. The terms of my father's will don't allow it. My father didn't leave me one penny as his daughter."

"But he gave you the controlling interest in his financial affairs or you wouldn't be here."

"I suppose so. It would have been my husband if I'd had one. But yes, I suppose I can dictate how the money is spent, within certain limits. That's why I'm going to Cairo this afternoon to talk to my father's lawyers. I think it would be better if we all agreed to abide by their professional advice. One day has been quite enough to convince me that I'm no financial wizard!"

"And you won't ask Fletcher to take over?"

"He works for the government, whatever you may think, not for me!"

Jim put a hand on her shoulder. "You don't mind, do you, Vicky?"

"Victoria," she corrected him. "Why should I mind? It's my decision to go to the lawyers and ask their help. At least they know how many piasters go to make up a pound, and the conversion rates between English and Egyptian pounds, which is a great deal more than I do. By the time I've converted figures back and forth, all I have is an absurd muddle!"

"You could get someone to do your calculations for you."

"But that's what I am doing," she stated firmly. She got lightly to her feet and stood looking down at him. "I'm getting hungry," she said. "I think I'll go back to breakfast."

"In your own tent again? Not even your father had all his meals alone. He used to invite Juliette to share most of them with him, particularly—er—breakfast. Are you going to keep up the family tradition?"

"No," Victoria said. "I would have joined you last night if I'd known what time you were eating. Abdul brought me a tray because that was the way my father liked it, but I shan't make a habit of it."

Jim stood up, too. "Pity. You could do worse than stay away from the lower orders. You'd soon get tired of our eternal bickering. Though even that's better than watching Fletcher and Juliette billing and cooing at one another like they did last night! We'll have to give them some competition in that department. That might make them sit up and take notice!"

Victoria barely repressed a shudder, hoping he intended to wash his hands before he appeared at the breakfast table. She wondered if he liked being dirty and, if so, why? If he shaved off his beard and washed his hair, he would have been quite good-looking. Yet she didn't think it was his hairiness that she objected to, but the grimy look of his skin and the distinct odor that came from his body. Other shaggy young men she had both liked and admired. It was only this one she couldn't abide, neither hair nor hide of him!

"What made you work for my father?" she asked him.

"I thought I'd have a free hand to work more or less on my own. I should have known better. Excuse me for saying so, my dear, but he was a self-satisfied prig. He wasn't half as good as he thought he was."

Victoria led the way down the slope toward the camp. "What makes you say that?" She carefully sidestepped a large, rounded stone that had recently been dislodged from higher up. "Didn't he listen to your opinions enough?"

"How well you read me, Miss Lyle," he bowed. "Actually he didn't listen to anyone and I was rather less upset by this characteristic than the others were. Find that difficult to believe? But then I have always lacked ambition. It's the simple life for me—as you can see. That offends you, doesn't it? It offended your father too. I offended his nostrils, he said."

"But you didn't do anything about it?"

"Why should I? He didn't do anything for me, either! Now his daughter is quite another matter! Do you still want to see inside the tomb? I'll show you around after breakfast, if you like. You may as well come with me, as I flatter myself I'll make a better guide than Juliette because I won't expect you to know it all already. I know you'd love to have our Mr. Fletcher for your guide, but I happen to know he has other plans for his morning."

"Thank you," said Victoria, "I'd like to see the tomb."

Jim shot her a swift look, pulling on his beard. "Aren't you curious as to what Fletcher will be doing?"

"Not particularly," Victoria said with commendable calm.

"Then I don't need to tell you that he and Juliette have arranged to catch up on old times in Alexandria. It didn't take them long to get back on the old footing."

"I don't think that's any of our business, do you?"

"If you say not," he grumbled.

Victoria opened her eyes very wide. "I do!" She wished he hadn't told her. She didn't want to have to live with that knowledge all morning, and as Tariq seemed to have taken up permanent residence in her mind, she despaired of being able to forget it. It was a good thing she would have to stretch her mind by concentrating on her father's *mastaba*, and would have to listen to Jim's explanations about the articles they had found there. But her spirits refused to lift at the thought. The inner core of her wanted only Tariq, and the thought of him with Juliette was almost more than she could bear.

If possible, she found the communal tent where the various members of the expedition met for meals and recreation even more beautiful than the one she had inherited from her father. The embroidery was finer and the calligraphy of the texts from the Koran even better executed. Abdul, the cook-*suffragi*, was pleased by her interest.

"Very fine tent this one," he agreed with her. "There is no finer in the Western Desert!"

Victoria chuckled. "What about the Eastern Desert?"

"It is a very little desert on the eastern side of the Nile. I am not knowing about the tents there. I have lived in Sakkara all my life. In the German-English War I was mess boy with the Scottish Regiment. Very fine men! But their tents were not beautiful like this one!"

"Is that when you learned to be a waiter?" she asked him.

"Yes, *madame*. I learn many things. I learn English language and English cooking. Many things. I serve you very well, just like I serve your father. Now I bring your breakfast."

"Thank you." She smiled at him. "Where did these tents come from?"

"Your father bought them when he first came to Egypt. That was a great many years ago." He grinned back at her. "You very little girl, *madame*, but sometimes he would speak of you."

Nobody else came in to breakfast, not even Jim. Victoria ate her solitary meal and then went outside to look for him. She found him nonchalantly leaning on a heavy walking stick.

"Don't you want any breakfast?" she accosted him.

"Never touch it," he answered. "Not at this time of year. I find dinner quite enough to keep me going. Are you ready for your tour of inspection?"

She found him a much better guide than she had expected. The entrance to the *mastaba* was not particularly deep. The original building had been rectangular in shape, but one corner of it had fallen in many centuries before. So far, only the first courtyard had been dug out and the sand neatly piled up outside the opening. The main part of the tomb, containing the sarcophagus and the mummified body of the Second Dynasty Pharaoh they expected to find there, had still to be cleared out and the objects found had to be meticulously recorded and appraised by experts to find out what light, if any, they could throw on this most ancient period in the history of the Two Lands of Ancient Egypt.

"We've been lucky here," Jim told her. "Most of the contemporary tombs in Sakkara were nearer to the Pyramid of Unas over there. There was a bit of trouble—dynastic jealousy, you know the sort of thing—and the winning side tried to set fire to all the tombs of the defeated dynasty. This one seems to have escaped. That's why the gold covering on the walls is particularly fine. D'you see how it's been molded to look like rush mats? There was a whole lot more of it on this side when we got here, but it was one of the things that mysteriously disappeared and caused the trouble with the Department of Antiquities. The other things that went were some rather fine spoons and some gold platters, and a whole lot of other, lesser stuff. The best of the stuff is yet to be uncovered, though, that's my bet. It will be inside there." He jerked his head toward the inner chambers of the *mastaba*.

"Where was the statute of Kha-sekhem found?" Victoria inquired, trying to restrain herself from fingering the ancient patterns on the walls.

"Over there by the entrance. That was one of the things George and Fletcher quarreled about. George claimed the inscription on the statue read that Ka-sekhem came to Lower Egypt in response to some Libyan invasion and took seven thousand prisoners. That would fit in with what is already known about him. But Fletcher maintains that he didn't stay long enough to consolidate his gains—"

"Because he didn't wear the red crown of the North?" Victoria finished for him, glad to show off her own knowledge for once.

Jim clicked his tongue approvingly. "So you do know something about it!" he congratulated her.

"That's the sum of my knowledge," she confessed. "But at least I know I have a lot to learn."

Jim came right up close to her. "You're pretty enough for it not to matter, Vicky. Look, I'm going to stay on here for a while and do a bit of housework to earn my keep. D'you think you can find your own way back to camp?"

Victoria was sorry to have her explorations curtailed, but she went without a word. It was quite hot outside, without a cloud in the sky. She took off her sweater and tied it around her waist by the sleeves to save carrying it, and walked very slowly back to camp. She saw Tariq in the distance and waved to him. His brow cleared at the sight of her and he came running over the sand toward her.

"Where the hell have you been?" he bit out at her. "I've been looking all over the place for you. I wish you'd leave word with Abdul whenever you go out, saying where you're going and how long you're likely to be. You could get lost in the desert going off on your own!"

Victoria was incredulous. "How could I?" she demanded. "I only have to look around until I see the Step Pyramid or even the Bent Pyramid, for that matter, to know exactly where I am!"

Tariq merely looked cross. "I'd like you to leave word with Abdul, all the same. I hear you're going to Cairo this afternoon? Juliette said you were taking the car."

She nodded. "I'm going to see my father's lawyers."

His eyes narrowed. "Do you want me to go with you?"

Victoria thought of where he had been all morning and sniffed. "I wouldn't dream of depriving Juliette of your company," she said.

He jerked her around to face him. "And what does that mean?" he asked her.

Her lips puckered, but she was not going to give him the satisfaction of reading her thoughts. "Let me go! You know I don't like being manhandled!"

He released her at once, running an impatient hand through his hair. "Do you want me to come with you, or not?"

"Juliette—"

"Juliette has gone to Alexandria *on her own*!"

"And I want to go to Cairo on my own! I have to see them by myself. If you came with me, they'd only try to get you fired by the department for overstepping your sphere of influence."

His golden eyes looked into her earnest blue ones. "All right," he said. "What have they been saying about me?"

She shrugged her shoulders. "Nothing much. But I had a hideous time yesterday persuading them that the money was for the excavation only, and not for anyone's personal use."

"I see," he said. "Well, take care, Victoria. Juliette's car is a potential deathtrap. They don't have roadworthy test for cars in Egypt!"

She would have liked to change her mind then, and to have asked him to come with her after all. "I'm quite good at looking after myself," she said. "You don't have to worry about me."

"Sometimes," he said, "you're as stubborn as your father was! Will you call in and see Omm Beshir?"

"If you think she'd like to see me."

His eyes glinted in the sunlight. "You can give her a little something from me!" He cupped her chin in his hand and touched his mouth to her lips. " 'Her hair is black, blacker than the night, blacker than sloes,' " he quoted softly, punctuating each phrase with another gentle caress on her mouth. " 'Red are her lips, redder than beads of red jasper, redder than ripe dates. Lovely are her twin breasts—' "

"Tariq!"

His hands let her go, but the light in his eyes held her fast. "Oh, Victoria," he mocked her.

"Was that an ancient Egyptian poem?" she asked stiffly.

"The way a man describes his beloved doesn't change. Not when she's the love of his life."

She raised startled eyes to his. "Will there ever be a time when you have only one beloved?" she asked him dryly.

He traced the line of her lips with his finger. "You'll have to find the answer to that for youself," he said.

VICTORIA DRESSED with enormous care to go to Cairo. Several times during lunch she had been on the point of asking Tariq's advice over what she should say to her father's lawyers, but Jim Kerr's presence had made her reluctant to discuss her father's affairs in case the fragile harmony of the meal came to an abrupt end. More than once she felt Tariq's eyes on her as she ate, and she wondered what he would say if he could read her thoughts about him.

When they had finished their coffee, he walked with her to where Juliette habitually parked the car.

"Do either Jim or Juliette know the details of what you're going to talk to the lawyers about?" he asked her as he opened the door for her and helped her into the driver's seat.

She looked up at him, a worried crease between her brows. "They know I'm going, but not the details. Should I have talked it over with you first? It's partly that I can't get the figures to add up—"

"Tell me what they say when you get back," he cut her off. His eyes lit with sudden laughter. "And don't forget to embrace Omm Beshir for me! You'll be able to have a nice gossip with her about my misspent past."

"Was it very bad?"

"It was vivid. I don't do things by halves." He straightened his back, a muscle jerking in his cheek. "She's fond of me, and not many people around here are. I think you'll find it reassuring to have a cozy chat with her."

She had no answer to that. She drove off down the track across the sand, leaving a rather wobbly trail behind her. The steering was slack and the stony ground was unstable and made the car slide helplessly from side to side. She was more than glad when she reached the paved road alongside the irrigation canal.

The nearer she got to Cairo, the more traffic there was on the road, honking and edging in and out of the lines of shabby trucks, huge American taxis, the vast multitude of Fiats that were made in Egypt under license, and the horse-drawn wagons that carried both people and produce to and from the surrounding villages. Large bundles of sugar cane, huge cabbages and cauliflowers, bigger than Victoria had ever seen before, caught her attention, and several times she would have liked to stop and take a closer look at the extraordinarily cheap oranges piled up at the side of the road, perhaps even to buy.

She was fortunate to find a place to park in a square not far from the famous bazaar, or *souk*, where the shops huddled together in narrow streets, grouped according to their wares. The street in which the lawyers' offices were was close at hand and she walked along it, congratulating herself on her sense of direction that had brought her there with such expeditious ease.

The offices were announced in English as well as Arabic, and with increasing confidence, Victoria mounted the stairs and walked into the reception room. Two pretty young women, both of them typing letters on strangely marked Arabic typewriters, looked up as she entered. One of them rose to her feet and smiled enthusiastically in Victoria's direction. "Yes?" she said in fairly good English. "Is it that you are Miss Lyle?"

In a matter of seconds Victoria found herself in the rather plush office beyond, seated opposite a gray-faced, gray-haired man, with tired, droopy eyes and a languid manner.

"I fail to see what more we can do for you, Miss Lyle," he said after they had talked for a while. He sat back in his chair, a faint glimmer of interest in the back of his eyes. "The only way out of this tangle for you would be to find a suitable husband, one the Egyptian authorities would approve as a suitable director for this excavation."

Victoria managed a faint laugh. "I don't think I want to get married," she said.

"No, but from our point of view that is a pity. You see," he went on, "my country is no longer dependent on foreign amateurs to dig up her history, no matter how enthusiastic. Your father could not be persuaded to accept this fact and resented everything that the Department of Antiquities tried to do to help him. As a concession the department appointed an Englishman to work with your father—"

"Torquil Fletcher?"

The lawyer nodded. "We sometimes forget he is not one of us, and the arrangement should have worked very well. But there were difficulties, and George Lyle would not allow him to continue at Sakkara on any terms. If your father had lived, there is no doubt the department would have withdrawn his license. As it is, there is absolutely no chance of your obtaining their consent to continue unless Mr. Fletcher has complete control of the excavations. But—and here is the rub—under the terms of your father's will, he can only do this if he is your husband. Otherwise every penny must go to Madame Juliette Mercer."

"But my father wanted the excavation to continue more than anything!" She shrugged helplessly. "What am I to do?"

The lawyer looked rather less languid. "A beautiful woman like you will always be welcome in Egypt. If you wish to see our city, I shall be happy to show you all it has to offer. You will have a happy time to remember when you go back to England. You will have to leave us to worry about our own past, unless you can persuade Mr. Fletcher to change the Department's mind for them, which frankly I don't believe even he can do. And you have to remember that your father didn't either like or trust him, and it will be his money Tariq will be handling."

Victoria felt herself blushing. "He may not want to accept my father's money on those terms."

The lawyer smiled, revealing several gold-capped teeth. "If anyone can persuade him to do so I'm sure it will be you. Tariq has always found it hard to resist a pretty woman, and you have the advantage that he is already very interested in the *mastaba* in question."

"Will you write to him, confirming that my father's estate will be put at his disposal if he can get a license from the Department to go on working?" she asked.

The gold teeth flashed once more. "You realize that if I do this you will have no further interest in the money?" The tired, droopy eyes met hers for a long, thoughtful moment. "But I imagine that will be something of a relief to you. Let's hope we don't receive any objections from Madame Mercer, either. You may find yourself having to persuade her also, but you can always send her to me. As for you, it is better for a woman to have a man to deal with her affairs. Let's hope you need worry no longer, Miss Lyle, and Tariq accepts your solution."

He couldn't have hoped it more devoutly than did Victoria. If only he didn't send her straight back to England! But somehow she didn't think he would do that, not immediately, not until she was good and ready to go.

CHAPTER SEVEN

VICTORIA SIPPED her mint tea with satisfaction. She had been half-afraid that Omm Beshir would expect her to have more of the prickly-pear drink, and she didn't think that even the politeness expected of a guest would induce her stomach to accept it.

"What are you doing in Cairo by yourself?" Omm Beshir asked her, settling herself more comfortably on the rug.

"I came in to see my father's lawyers."

Omm Beshir looked complacent. "When I go out I like to have some member of my family with me. When one's old, one needs to be able to prove that one is still a valued member of one's family. Why didn't Tariq come with you?"

Victoria wished she didn't look so conscious every time his name was mentioned. "I thought it was better to see them by myself," she said.

Omm Beshir searched her face anxiously. "Did Tariq know that?" she demanded with such obvious disapproval that Victoria was hard put not to laugh.

"Yes, he knew," she answered. "I didn't come behind his back. It was he who told me to call in and see you, and—" she took a deep breath "—to embrace you for him. He's very fond of you."

"Of course." Omm Beshir looked a good deal happier. "I should have known you would not come without his consent, but I worry about him still like a silly old woman. Tariq is as dear to me as my own sons, and I knew when he brought you here to see me that you were the one to ease his heart, and I was glad."

Victoria stared at her, wide-eyed. "There's still Juliette," she heard herself say.

"There have been many Juliettes," Omm Beshir returned. "Did you imagine that with a man like Tariq there would not have been? But such women have nothing to do with you."

"But Juliette isn't in his past. She's the here and now," Victoria objected.

Omm Beshir shrugged, completely indifferent to such an argument. "What of that? To Juliette he is a passing pleasure, no more. Will she wish to serve him, to stand beside him in the bad times, to be a part of him? Will she put his good before her own? Of course she will not. Then why should she matter to you? Maybe he will find some pleasures in her for a while, but she will never be important to him as you are. If you are going to resent every pleasure he takes away from you, you had better go away from him now. Tariq has never had any loving for himself, except from me. His father had no time for him. He was left here with us until he was old enough to be sent away to school. After that, he was allowed to come here only once a year. For the rest of the time he went to holiday homes, or to relatives who didn't want him. Naturally there have been many Juliettes. Why should he expect anything more from a woman?"

"But I want to be the only woman in his life!" Victoria exclaimed, shattered.

"Then, for a little while, you will have to accept his affection for Juliette, no?" Omm Beshir said placidly. "You must let him see that his happiness means more to you than your own. It will not be long before he will want to protect you from being hurt by other women, for he is a kind man and he will guard you as closely as you could wish. He is a stranger to love, *yâ bént*. You will have to teach him that he is the breath of life to you. You will not find him ungrateful."

Victoria was silent. She tried to imagine herself having a similarly intimate conversation with her own mother, and knew that her mother would have been as embarrassed as she. And yet she didn't mind this odd, dumpy little woman poking her nose into her innermost feelings—feelings that she had scarcely admitted to herself until this moment.

"You don't know what jealousy is like," she said aloud. "I didn't before—"

"*Alallah*! Leave it to God!" The older woman smiled. "I, too, know what it is to love a man as you do. Our customs are different from yours, but our feelings are not so very different, and all women know how it feels not to come first with the man they love. When I first married my husband I knew him hardly at all, but he made me happier than I had thought it possible to be. But after two years, there were still no children, and I began to be afraid. My husband was rich and handsome and other women would be willing to give him what I could not. Everyone, my own family included, would understand if he were to divorce me and marry again someone who could give him the sons he longed for. I told myself that after a time one woman is much like another in a man's bed, but his children are a part of him. They make him immortal in this world. Yet what could I do? Divorce is very easy for us. A man has only to tell his wife she is divorced three times and the marriage is no more.

"Then came the day when I was abusing him for not coming to me more often, trying to make him notice me. But when he opened his mouth, I was afraid he would send me away from him. I told him that if he wished it, I would accept another wife in the house sooner than have to leave him.

"He was very kind to me. There was still time for me to have a child and he promised to do nothing in a hurry, although he had already been told of a woman who was willing to marry him. At first I was very upset that he would have thought of marrying again, but in time I accepted that it was important to me also that he should have the children he wanted so badly, and I became happier again.

"But God is merciful. He answered my prayers and I conceived my first child, my son Beshir, almost immediately. And my husband put this other woman out of his mind and I have been the only one to enjoy his favors ever since, although I have never been beautiful as she was rumored to have been."

Victoria carefully composed her face to hide the shock she felt at Omm Beshir's story. "In England we are not expected to share our husbands," she said, feeling that some comment was expected of her.

"So I have heard," Omm Beshir smiled. "But is it a good custom, do you think, to cast out the first wife when she is old? I have heard that this frequently happens."

"She may have cast him out first," Victoria pointed out. "Supposing you had wanted to divorce your husband? Could you have done it?"

Omm Beshir laughed at the thought. "A woman may not," she acknowledged. "If she has her husband's consent, she can go to the religious court and make an application for divorce, but without his consent she can do nothing."

"But that isn't fair!"

Omm Beshir laughed again. "You are still a child if you expect life to be fair," she said in fat, consoling tones. "It is God's will that it is as it is."

A sentiment that Victoria found more shocking than all the rest. "Tariq is a Christian, isn't he?" she insisted.

"Of course." The old lady's green eyes snapped with amusement. "But first you must marry him before you can divorce him."

"He may not want to marry me," Victoria said.

"That would be a pity," Omm Beshir conceded. "You are what I have always hoped for Tariq, despite being your father's daughter. Your father was not a loving man. He made use of Tariq and then dismissed him because this Juliette has the morals of a belly dancer."

"Perhaps he was in love with Juliette himself," Victoria suggested gently.

Omm Beshir shook her head. "No, no, Juliette was not the only one with him, either. He had no wish to make a stable relationship with anyone."

Victoria put a hand to her mouth to hide her reluctance to discuss her father when she knew so little about him. "He was unloved too," she said. "My mother wouldn't travel with him out of England and they scarcely ever saw each other. It wasn't a happy marriage." She made a movement to get up. "I must go. May I come and see you again?"

Omm Beshir rose to her feet with surprising grace considering the shape of her figure. "Come whenever you will, *yâ bént*, my daughter." She took Victoria's hand in hers and lifted it to her lips. "It will be as God wills it, and a little bit as Tariq wants it to be. You can do no more than love him. I will call one of the children to walk with you to your car. I would come with you myself, but it is time for the prayer and one must not keep God waiting."

Victoria allowed herself to be smothered in the Egyptian woman's perfumed embrace, sniffing the air appreciatively.

"I like your perfume," she said. "What is it?"

"The essence of the lotus flower. I will give you some for yourself to wear when you are with Tariq." She chuckled happily to herself, pulling Victoria behind her into the bedroom where her prayer mat was already laid out on the floor, facing toward Mecca.

She sat down on the edge of the creaking iron bedstead, and with deft fingers transferred some leaf-green liquid from the larger bottle into a smaller one made from cut crystal. "There! Now you will smell like one of us! Shall I put some on for you? Here, on your wrists, and here, on the nape of your neck. You must rub it in a little so that it lingers on your skin. That's the way!"

Victoria smelled her wrists and smiled. It had a pleasant, sharp tang that stopped it from being oversweet. "I hope Tariq likes it," she said with a touch of mischief.

Omm Beshir's eyes twinkled appreciatively. "He gave it to me! He had better like it! There now, if I put a piece of tape over the stopper it won't fall out. I hope you enjoy wearing it, my dear." She handed Victoria the little bottle with a sly smile. "And now you must be going, but come and see me again whenever you come to Cairo."

Victoria promised she would, kissing Omm Beshir's wrinkled cheek and submitting to a long blessing in Arabic that she thought was probably as well she didn't understand. She clutched the bottle of perfume tightly in her hand and followed the small girl who had been called to show her the way back to the car. Her mind was in a whirl. The thought of

Tariq as a small boy, unwanted and unloved, tore at her heartstrings. Could she make up to him all that he had lacked throughout his childhood? Could she love the child he had been as well as the man he now was? More importantly, did he want her to? Victoria had no means of knowing. She could only try, she thought, and see what happened. *Alallah*. Leave it to God, Omm Beshir had said, but Victoria lacked her faith. She wanted Tariq to love her, and only her, and she wanted it now. She wanted it more than she had ever wanted anything in her whole life.

THE LIGHT was already fading from the sky when she got back to Sakkara. Abdul had started to light the lamps and she stood for a moment in the open doorway of the communal tent, watching him pumping up the flame until the mantle burned bright and very white.

"I'm surprised the light doesn't bring the insects flooding in," she said.

Abdul stood on a chair and hung the lamps, one at a time, on a piece of string that had been tied between the two tent poles over the table. "No, no, *madame*, no insects in here! Ladies dislike insects and there must be none allowed to come in here! I, Abdul, keep them all away!"

She was amused by his earnestness. "How do you do that?" she asked him.

"I spray everything, all the time, morning and evening. All the insects they fall down dead. You have nothing to fear in the desert from them, *madame*."

Victoria wrinkled up her nose. "Good. I'm glad," she said.

He smiled down at her. "You find it nice here when there are no insects? You find it beautiful?"

"It's lovely. And you make us very comfortable, Abdul. I don't know what we'd do without you."

He was pleased, and he stayed on to talk for a little longer, only going when he couldn't delay starting the preliminaries to the evening meal any longer. Victoria was sorry to see him go. She looked around the camp, wondering what the others were doing. Juliette was back, for there was a light in her tent, and Jim was talking to someone over by the *mastaba* but who it was, Victoria couldn't see. Of Tariq there was no sign at all. She would have liked to talk to him about her plan to make him the director of the excavation, before he received the letter from her lawyers in the morning mail, and she had hoped to see him before dinner because the presence of the others would have made such a discussion impossible.

She called out a final word to Abdul at work in his kitchen tent, and went reluctantly toward her own tent to change for dinner, taking one of Abdul's lamps with her to light her way across the stony sand. The guy ropes shone white in the beam of light and she walked carefully around them, remembering her last encounter with them. Did Juliette change clothes in the evenings? She should have asked her before, she supposed, if she wanted to compete in that direction. Juliette was bound to have something French and very chic, whereas Victoria's wardrobe was strictly limited when it came to evening wear. Still, she had Omm Beshir's essence of lotus blossom and unless Tariq had given her some, too, it was unlikely that Juliette would have anything to beat that!

There was an open book lying on her bed. Victoria went straight over to look at it, wondering who had put it there. It was a collection of poems, she saw, culled from the long centuries when Egypt had possessed the greatest civilization in the world. She gave an exclamation of sheer pleasure, and threw herself onto her bed to look at it more closely. Some of the verses had been marked, and to her delight, she recognized them as the "Sycamore Song" that Tariq had quoted to her just after they had met by the Virgin's Tree.

"A letter of love will my lady fair
Send to the one who will happy be,
Saying: 'Oh, come to my garden rare
And sit in the shade with me!

" 'Fruit I will gather for your delight,
Bread I will break and pour out wine,
I'll bring you the perfumed flow'rs and bright
On this festal day divine.'

"My lady alone with her lover will be,
His voice is sweet and his words are dear—
Oh, I am silent of all I see,
Nor tell of the things I hear!"

She read it once silently to herself, and once out loud for the sheer joy of hearing the words spoken. It could only have been Tariq who had left it there, and she loved him for it!

There was a scuffling movement behind her head and she turned quickly to see what it was. A beetle she thought she could dispose of, but what would she do if it were a spider? The scuffling was joined by other noises and her blood froze with horror. There were hundreds of them! Pink and deadly, with their tails in the air—they were scorpions! Victoria shut her eyes and prayed they would go away, but she could hear them coming closer—and closer!

It didn't sound like her screaming. She had never screamed in her life before. But the sound of her own hysteria compounded the panic that gripped her. With a cry of terror, she leaped off the bed and ran for the door, her flesh crawling with fright. She barely noticed when she ran full tilt into someone standing out there in the darkness.

"Tariq!" she yelled.

"No, it's Jim. Whatever's the matter? You were screaming loud enough to wake Ka-sekhem himself—"

She pushed away from him. "I want Tariq," she wept.

"I'm here, Victoria." The tears fell thick and fast, making her quite unintelligible as she sobbed against his chest. He let her cry it out, holding her close until she ran out of tears and breath. "That's enough now, Victoria. You'll feel awful if you go on like this!"

She made an effort to pull herself together. "Oh, Tariq, I didn't know where you were!" Her hands plucked at his shirt. "There are hundreds of scorpions in my tent! I thought they'd kill me—and I wanted to thank you for the poem!"

"Have you ever seen a scorpion?" he asked her patiently.

"Of course I have! I've seen whole films about them!"

She might have know that he wouldn't believe her. She freed herself from his embrace with an impetuosity that unbalanced her. He steadied her with a hand on her arm. "I'll take a look," he said. "Are you all right now, *habibi*?"

She felt foolish that she had made such a fuss, and she nodded quickly, turning away from him. But when he left her to go into the tent, she began to shake with fright again, and went rushing after him, standing in the doorway as he went over to her bed, picked up the light, and held it high as he looked round the enclosed space.

"I don't see anything," he said.

She uttered a stifled gasp. "Over there! In the corner!"

He saw it and stamped on it before she could stop him, looking grimmer than she had ever seen him. He pulled back the bedding on her bed and two more of the creatures crawled out into the light. He stood, staring down at them, his fists clenched. "My God!" he said.

"There were lots of them," Victoria gulped. "They were everywhere!"

He strode out of the tent, yanking her out after him and hurrying her before him across the rough ground.

"What's the matter?" Juliette's voice rang out. "What's happening?"

Tariq paused. "There's a nest of scorpions in Victoria's bed," he said, his voice flat and without any emotion at all.

"*C'est incroyable*! Who would do such a thing, *mon cher*?"

"Perhaps they just came," Victoria suggested, lamely. "I can't believe anyone would deliberately—"

"I should have looked after you better!" he bit out.

"But you couldn't have known—"

"I should have known!" She had never heard anyone sound as angry as he did then. "You can sleep in my tent in future and it will be searched every night before you set foot in it. I'll use the communal tent tonight. I'll go and tell Abdul. He and I can clear out this place tomorrow."

"Yes, yes," Juliette said at once. "Meanwhile Victoria can come to my tent and rest herself. *Mon dieu*, what a terrible thing! Scorpions! It's as well they were not snakes or I would be sleeping in Cairo tonight!"

Tariq went away, taking the lamp with him. Victoria's knees buckled under her and she sat down heavily on the sand.

"But why?" she asked.

Juliette put her arm around her. "It's best not to think of it, *chérie*. Whoever it was will not try that trick again to get rid of you. They'll know that you'll be prepared next time. It was probably only to frighten you into going back to England without starting the excavations up again."

Victoria winced. "Why should anyone care?"

"Your father thought that when we opened up the *mastaba* we would know who the thief is who has been stealing all these things. Of course he thought it was Tariq—"

But Victoria shook her head. "It wasn't Tariq!"

The French girl flung up her hands in a Gallic gesture of fatalism. "How like your father you are! He, too, would believe only what he wanted to believe! Why can't it have been Tariq? He went into your tent earlier, because I saw him go inside myself!"

"He put a book on my bed. But it wasn't him. If he wanted to get rid of me, he has only to say the word to the Egyptian government and I'd be on the next plane!"

"Are you sure you won't believe it because you are a little in love with him?" Juliette countered. "Tariq is mine!"

Victoria shut her eyes, shivering a little as she recalled the scorpions running over the floor of her tent. "Tariq makes his own friends," she said quietly. "I can't imagine him ever allowing any woman to change that, and I wouldn't want him to." She shivered again and Juliette was immediately concerned that she was cold.

"You are tired out," she murmured, "and the night air is bad for you. Come, we must move ourselves before you catch a chill. Tonight I shall give you something to make you sleep, and tomorrow I shall take you myself to see the Pyramid of Unas to take your mind away from these horrid animals!"

"You're being very kind," Victoria thanked her.

Juliette smiled her familiar, jaunty smile. "Me, I am only kind when it suits me, *ma mie*. You are enough like George for me to want to be friends with you, but I think you don't like me enough for that. *Eh bien*, I will try and make you like me a little better tomorrow. Is that so bad?"

Victoria laughed and shook her head. "It's getting better all the time," she said.

JIM KERR was already seated at the table when Victoria went over to the communal tent for her breakfast the next morning. His eyes flickered over her pale, shadowed face.

"Made quite a spectacle of yourself last night, didn't you?" he greeted her.

"What if I did? Scorpions can kill, can't they?"

"Not they! You're not cut out for this sort of thing, my dear. Why don't you cut your losses and turn the money over to Juliette?"

Anger lent a temporary sparkle to Victoria's eyes. She sat down at the table with dignity. "The decision isn't mine to make—and it certainly isn't yours," she told him.

"They're withdrawing the license?" he declared, whistling through his teeth. "Poor Victoria! Didn't I tell you it was unlikely they'd allow you to have it in your own name? You'll have to hand it over to Juliette now, or me!"

"*You*?"

He scratched thoughtfully at his beard. "If you're thinking of getting Tariq to take it on, don't! He's a dangerous man. Who else had the opportunity to put the scorpions in your bed? Have you thought about that?"

He took a swig of coffee and grinned across the table at her, getting slowly to his feet.

"I thought you didn't eat breakfast?" she said.

"I don't, but I sometimes drink it. Good luck to you, girl! May your escapes be many!"

Victoria frowned after him, and she was still frowning when Juliette came in and sat down in the seat he had just vacated.

"Will you be ready in half an hour?" the French girl asked, watching Victoria through her eyelashes. "You look terrible!" she added brutally. "Have you forgotten that I'm taking you to see the Pyramid of Unas? It's only a hundred meters from here and it is something everyone should see. Did you know that the earliest of the Pyramid Texts are to be seen in the burial chamber there?"

"Really?" said Victoria.

"You're not listening!" Juliette accused her.

"Yes, yes I am, but I want to talk to Tariq first. Do you mind, Juliette?"

The French girl shrugged her shoulders. "Mind? No, I don't mind. But Tariq is not here at the moment. You can see him when we come back, Victoria. We shall only be an hour or so."

"Right," Victoria agreed. "I'll be with you just as soon as I've finished my coffee."

The Pyramid of Unas looked rather humble from

the outside. When Victoria remembered the awe she had felt when she had stepped inside the massive Pyramids at Giza, she smiled for the first time that morning. This one was tiny by comparison. She felt quite weak with relief. This time there would be no ramps for her to crawl up, which was just as well as there was no Tariq to support her. The shaft here was not high at all!

Juliette bounced down the catwalk, her feet finding the narrow strips of wood that were nailed across the planks. She moved with an ease that Victoria could only envy. Victoria set off at a great pace behind her and found it much easier going than she had imagined. It was shorter than she had expected, too, and when she found Juliette waiting for her at the bottom, she realized that the worst part of the outing was over and she became quite excited about what she was going to see.

Juliette led the way along a corridor and into the burial chamber itself. At the far end was a stone sarcophagus that had been found empty when Sir Gaston Maspero had first cleared a way into the pyramid. But it was not at the sarcophagus that Victoria found herself looking. This chamber was quite different from the others she had seen. The sloped roof was covered with stars, at least she presumed they were stars, although they looked rather more like starfish. And, more dramatic than anything else she had seen, the walls of the vestibule and the limestone parts of the walls of the burial chamber were completely covered with vertical columns of hieroglyphic inscriptions.

Juliette, very much at home in a place she obviously knew well, positively glowed with enthusiasm as she pointed out the various texts on the walls.

"You see how each hieroglyph has been filled in

with blue pigment to make it stand out clearly against the white background?" she explained.

"Yes, but what do they mean?" Victoria asked.

Juliette jerked her head around to look at her. It had honestly never occurred to her that George Lyle's daughter wouldn't have been reading such inscriptions in her cradle.

"You don't know?" She took in the expression on Victoria's face and had the grace to laugh at herself. "No, of course you don't! They are magical texts. A collection of spells to help the dead king or queen find happiness in the afterlife. There are several pyramids that have them, mostly of the Sixth Dynasty. Altogether there are more than seven hundred spells, but they didn't always choose to have the same ones. In this pyramid there are two hundred and twenty-eight examples. Look, you can see one here!" She picked out the various hieroglyphs with her finger, translating rapidly as she went along. "You see what care was taken to avoid using human and animal signs because they had dangerous magical properties. Here we have only birds and good signs that could do no harm."

"Oh yes," said Victoria, entranced by the different signs. "Is that one meant to be a baby chick?" Juliette's scornful look brought a faint blush to her cheeks. "Isn't it a chick?"

"A chick, yes, but of a quail, not a chicken. It represents the sound of 'w'."

Abashed, Victoria's eye fell on another hieroglyph that looked to her exactly like a pair of sugar tongs. "And that?" she asked faintly.

"A rope to tether things. It makes the sound 'th'. They are all consonants, you see. One has to put in the appropriate vowels oneself so that the words make sense."

"Oh," said Victoria, amazed that anyone could make sense of these strange-looking symbols. "Can Tariq read these spells, too?"

"Of course." Juliette frowned. "But none of us can read them as your father could! George Lyle could make them come alive. He believed them. It was as if he were an ancient Egyptian himself when he was working here. Can you understand that?"

Victoria could not. "You were fond of my father, weren't you?" she said, hoping to gloss over a difficult moment without looking too much like a fool.

Juliette froze. "I was fond of him, yes," she agreed, "but it was not as you are thinking. There were no bones broken between us, as you say in English. I have my work, you understand, but one cannot be working all the time." She shrugged her shoulders. "You think me very hard, no doubt, but I am not half as wicked as you have been told!"

"I don't think you wicked at all," Victoria said impulsively, surprising herself as much as her hearer. "As a matter of fact I was thinking how horrid your husband must have been. He must have hurt you very badly."

Juliette blushed to the roots of her hair and she turned away quickly, leading the way back out of the burial chamber. "He did. How did you guess? You are more acute than you look, *chérie*. Not even your father knew that. He would never listen when I tried to tell him that no one was ever, *ever* going to hurt me again!"

Victoria took a last look at the hieroglyphs on the wall before she hurried after her, afraid of falling too far behind. She rushed blindly up the shaft, doing her best to keep pace with the girl in front of her. The old, paralyzing fear gripped her stomach when she thought she heard a sound behind her and looked back, but she refused to give in to it. Then she felt another body pressed close in behind hers and leaned back with relief, sure that it was Tariq. But the warm security of his strength failed her, giving way as though it had been no more than a figment of her imagination.

She felt herself falling. "Tariq!" she called out, but no one answered.

A blow from an open hand struck her on the diaphragm and she lost her balance completely. Slowly, almost gracefully, she felt herself going over backward and downward, down to the bottom of the shaft. She tried to reach out and save herself, but, just as it had always been in her worst dreams, there was nothing there. It was as she had always known it would be—an endless black pit that had no bottom, and down which she would go on falling forever.

CHAPTER EIGHT

VICTORIA WINCED away from the angry voices that surrounded her. Juliette, sounding shrill and on the defensive, was telling anyone who would listen that it had not been her fault.

"What do you mean, not your fault? Why did you take her there if you weren't going to look after her properly?"

That was Tariq. A warm wave of joy in his presence spread through Victoria and she roused herself and smiled at him. "Don't be angry," she said. "I wanted to go."

Tariq came over to where she was lying on Juliette's bed and stood there, looking down at her. His face was taut with anxiety and suppressed fury.

"Angry? I could knock your heads together! I thought I told you *always* to leave word where you were going?"

Victoria offered him another, if more tentative, smile. "It wasn't exactly a secret," she said.

"No? *I* didn't know where you were, and nor did Abdul."

Victoria shut her eyes. "You'd gone out," she said flatly.

"Who told you that? I was only in your father's tent, retrieving this!" He shoved the book that had contained the "Sycamore Song" into her hands. "I thought you might want it."

Victoria opened her eyes in a hurry and took a quick upward look at him. His expression was as unyielding as ever, but it didn't stop her heart going off into its own ecstatic dance that he would have been thinking about her enough to go and find the book for her.

"As a matter of fact," she said, "I thought it was you behind me, or I would have been more careful." She hesitated. "I mean I would have let him go past, instead of thinking you could keep me from falling."

"Victoria, what are you talking about?"

"But someone was there!" She swallowed. "He pushed me."

"There was no one there," Juliette put in. "You are mistaken, *petite*. It was my fault that you fell. I had forgotten that you are afraid the moment your feet leave the ground. One minute you were there, following me up the ramp, and the next minute you were gone, a huddled heap at the bottom. I thought you were dead!"

"I was pushed," Victoria insisted.

Tariq's eyes held hers in silent accusation. "You thought *I* pushed you?"

She made a shamefaced gesture. "Of course not! But before, when I felt him come up behind me, I thought it was you. I thought you'd know how I'd feel when I saw that ramp, even if it wasn't very high. But it wasn't you, was it?"

"No." The bleak syllable made her wince, but she couldn't think of any way of making it better for him.

"I'm sorry," she said.

"But I don't see how you can be sure it wasn't Tariq," Juliette burst out. "It isn't logical that you should suspect everyone but him!"

Tariq's eyebrows rose into a quizzical expression. "My dear Juliette," he drawled, "I don't have to kill a girl to get what I want from her, as you should know."

"Oh, that!" Juliette dismissed such nonsense with the contempt it deserved. "What has that to do with wanting to take over the direction of the excavation?" She looked curiously at Victoria, and shrugged her shoulders. "But she is not stupid, this one. Did you know that?"

Tariq took Victoria's hand in his. "What makes you say that?"

But Juliette wouldn't answer directly. "Maybe she knows something about you that I do not," she mused. "Is she going to make you director anyway?"

Tariq looked blank. "It's the first I've heard of it." He looked down at Victoria's guilty face and gave her hand a squeeze. "Are you sure, *habibi*, there was someone there?"

"I'm sure," she answered him. "He struck me and I couldn't breathe at all. It knocked all the breath out of me. It was horrid!" She explored her diaphragm tenderly with her free hand. "I wouldn't be surprised if I have a bruise—Tariq! Tariq, don't!"

But she was too late. He had already pulled back the sheet and, letting go her hand, tucked her shirt up under her chin.

"Where? Show me!" he said.

"*Tariq*! I won't have you—"

"Oh, really, Victoria! You're perfectly decent, if that's what you're afraid of—and Juliette is here."

"Much you care!" she retorted, genuinely incensed.

He circled her waist with his fingers, which gave her a queer, breathless feeling, and the fight went out of her.

"Yes, you've got a bruise all right, my sweet, and it was certainly caused by a hand, but it was a smaller hand than mine. It could have been a woman's hand." He caught sight of the scarab he had given her hanging around her neck and gave it a gentle tug. "This didn't do you much good, did it? Perhaps it was too much to expect. From now on I'm not going to allow you out of my sight!"

Victoria touched the scarab, too, her fingers meeting his and darting away again. She pulled down her shirt with determination. "It was a man," she told him. "He smelled like a man!"

He didn't laugh as she had been afraid he might. He turned his head away and she couldn't see what he was thinking at all.

"That settles it!" he said in a voice she had never heard before. "Do you feel well enough to get up? Because I want to talk to you."

"All right," she said. "But can't you talk to me here?"

"No. I don't want there to be any distractions for either of us. I'll see you in the communal tent in half an hour. Okay?"

"Yes," said Victoria.

"But what about me?" Juliette protested. "What am I supposed to do?"

Tariq's glance looked right through her. "Anything you like. Only stay out of my way for the next couple of hours, will you? I want to talk to Victoria by herself!" With which parting shot he was gone, leaving the two girls staring at one another in mutual shock.

"Me, I wouldn't want to talk to him in this mood," Juliette said at last, her eyes wide. "He has a very nasty temper!"

"Hasn't he?" Victoria said. "But he doesn't frighten me, and I don't think he'll do anything very terrible to me, either, do you?"

Juliette gave a significant wiggle to her hips. "He

is not easy to distract when he has made up his mind to something." Her hands trembled. "Shall I tell him you are not well enough to speak with him?"

Victoria was touched by what she saw to be a courageous gesture on the French girl's part. "I'm not afraid of him," she said.

"But—" Juliette began, her eyes dark with memories.

"Tariq isn't your husband," Victoria said gently. "He'd never deliberately hurt anyone, and he knows I know that."

"Yes, you are right," Juliette admitted. "You like him very much, don't you?"

Victoria nodded, fingering her scarab. "I love him," she said.

"That is easily seen!" the French girl retorted. "But what do you know about Torquil Fletcher? Nothing! Do you think you are the first girl to fall in love with him?"

Victoria swung her legs off the bed and stood up, her knees feeling like jelly beneath her. "I'd much rather be the last one he fell in love with than the first," she murmured.

"You are mad!" Juliette exclaimed with considerable drama. "He is one to have fun with, to lose your heart to a little bit, but not too much. These things do not last with someone like Tariq. He is never serious about these matters."

"Perhaps no one has really loved him before."

Juliette gave her a despairing glance. "Do you think he will love you?"

Victoria splashed some cold water on her face and felt a little better. Her head still throbbed, but the sickness had gone and she felt much more like her usual self.

"I don't know," she answered the French girl.

"He may surprise himself when he realizes that he can do as he likes about it. I shall go on loving him just the same."

Juliette hunched up her shoulders, but not before she had given Victoria a respectful look. "You know that Tariq and I—"

Victoria tried to smother the niggling dart of jealousy within her. "Did it mean anything to either of you?" she asked before she could stop herself.

"Less than nothing. He was there, no more than that." Juliette actually blushed. "I preferred your father," she confessed, bringing out the words as though each one hurt her. "George was stupid about many things, but he could make me very happy sometimes. I have good memories of him."

Victoria supposed she should have been resentful on her mother's behalf, but she wasn't. She was only glad that her father had meant something to someone, particularly if it meant that Juliette was giving up her interest in Tariq. She could have anyone she liked, anyone in the whole wide world, as long as she didn't want Mr. Torquil Fletcher anymore.

She looked at herself in the mirror and wished she didn't look so pale. She pinched her cheeks to give them a little color, but they remained obstinately gray in a gray, frightened face.

"I look awful!" she said.

Juliette shrugged. "You never have much color. Tariq will not notice, you can be sure of that!"

But Tariq did notice. He was waiting for her in the communal tent, one eye on his watch, and he stood up with apparent relief when she walked in.

"Those great shadows under your eyes tell their own story," he said. "I suppose you're feeling wretched and not in the least like putting your mind to business matters?"

"I'd rather be doing something," she said. "As a matter of fact, I wanted to speak to you, too."

"I know. I had the letter from your lawyers this morning. But it won't do, Victoria. It wasn't the way your father wanted things—"

"It's the way I want them!"

He shrugged his shoulders. "Do you? I can't think why. I haven't helped you much so far, have I?"

She smiled. "You picked up the shattered pieces last night and again this morning. Do you think I'm not grateful for that?"

"You're easily pleased." He eyed her thoughtfully as she sat down across the table from him. "You can't go on having these accidents, so what are we going to do about it?"

"You tell me," she invited him. "Only I don't want to go back to England—not yet!"

"It depends how much you trust me." He began to walk around the tent. "Do you trust me, Victoria? Do you trust me as Torquil Fletcher, your father's declared enemy?"

"You know I do," she said.

"You see it was a good idea of yours to put the onus on me by making me director here, but it wouldn't work. Juliette would have every right to object, for one thing. And then there would be nothing to stop you from firing me if you felt like it, and so the obvious thing would still be to rid themselves of you. If you went, I'd have to go, too. Do you follow me?"

"But I don't want anything to happen to you!"

The grim look came back to his face. "They won't get rid of me easily." It was difficult not to believe him. He looked as though he could cope with anything at that moment.

"What do you want me to do?" Victoria asked.

He came across the tent toward her. "Marry me," he said.

The silence was like something tangible between them. Victoria hoped she wasn't going to faint.

"Marry you?" she repeated.

He nodded, very much in command of himself and, she was afraid, of her. "Under your father's will, your husband has the responsibility of designating how your money is to be spent. Your father seems to have been unbelievably old-fashioned about such things. If you married me, everyone would know that they had me to deal with in future and we might get somewhere. I think I could persuade the Department to grant me the license and I'd finish your father's excavation for him." He put out a hand and touched her face. "Don't look like that, *habibi*; I won't rush you into anything you're not ready for. You don't have to worry about that."

"I'm not," she denied.

"Look, it won't be a proper marriage. We'll go to the *sharei* court and get married there. We're neither of us Muslims and it won't mean a thing to us. The point is that it's a legal form of marriage in this country and it will give you the protection of being my wife." He smiled wryly. "It has the other advantage that it can easily be brought to an end. Either I can divorce you over a period of three months, or I can consent to your going back to the court and divorcing me." He took a deep breath. "Then we can both start again."

"Supposing we don't want to start again?" she said.

He stroked her cheek. "I shan't take advantage of the arrangement. I promise you that. You'll be my wife by law, but that's all. When I marry a woman for keeps, I'll marry her in a ceremony she can understand and with all my cards on the table."

"My father—" she began.

"Your father will turn over in his grave, but it's that or close down completely, probably without ever knowing who's behind all these thefts, among other things." He turned her face toward him and held her eyes with his. "Do you trust me enough to go to the *sharei* court with me?"

It was an impossible question. Of course she trusted him! But to be legally married to him, and yet not married at all, would be a severe test of both of them. She wanted more than that.

"I'll understand if you can't do it," he went on. "If your father had liked me—"

"Yes, I'll marry you!"

He looked at her in complete disbelief. "Just like that?"

"Yes," she said. "I won't have you thinking that I don't trust you, because I do! I'd trust you when I wouldn't trust myself!" And that, she thought, was what she was doing, because she couldn't trust herself not to want to take advantage of being Mrs. Torquil Fletcher to show him how nice it would be if she could be that forever.

"You'll be trusting me with all your worldly possessions," he reminded her. "I could take everything and leave you to get back to England as best you could."

She managed a rather shaky smile. "They're not my worldly possessions. I haven't any worth speaking of, so if you're marrying me for my money, you'll get a poor bargain."

His eyes searched hers for a long moment. "I hope you know what you're doing," he said at last. "Shall we be off to Cairo, then?"

"I have to change," she murmured. "I hope you don't intend to marry me in my jeans?"

"Not if you hurry. I have a few telephone calls to make, and then I'll pick you up by your tent. Okay?"

It didn't give her very long, but she made the most of the few moments he had allowed her, putting on her best chartreuse-colored dress and an attractive white hat that suited her better than most. When she had finished, she still looked pale and wan and not at all like the blushing bride she felt Tariq deserved.

Her head was still aching when she got into the car beside him, but she summoned up a smile. "Have you told the others?" she asked.

"There'll be time enough for that. Are you sure you're all right?"

"More or less," she said.

"Good." He smiled at her, starting up the engine and driving off down the Cairo road. "By the way, do you know the names of your two grandfathers?"

"Why, yes, Walter Lyle and Henry Babbett. Why?"

"Islam has given a very patriarchal aspect to Egyptian law. The bride's male relatives are as important as her own name on these occasions. It was very different in ancient times. Did you know that?" She knew he was talking for the sake of talking, to take her mind off what she had agreed to do, and she was grateful. She had never felt less like a wedding, with her head hammering and her bruises hurting every time she breathed. "In ancient times inheritance passed through the female line, as in Cleopatra's case, for example. You may have thought she was a much-married lady because she was a noted beauty, but I'm afraid it was politics that made her such a desirable wife. The poor girl was married first to one of her brothers and then to the other, so that each could become Pharaoh in his turn."

"Wasn't one of them a little boy?"

"He was quite a bit younger than she. They both died young, unfortunately for her, leaving Egypt very vulnerable to the attentions of Rome. Julius Caesar got the hang of things pretty quickly and married her himself in order to become King of Egypt. They had a child, a boy called Caesarian. But then Caesar was bumped off on the Ides of March and along came Mark Antony. He wanted to be King of Egypt, too, and so poor Cleopatra found herself with another husband. Their union resulted in two children, a boy called Alexander and a little girl. Mark Antony went the way of all flesh, and along came Octavius. But Cleopatra had had enough and decided not without some justification, that she would sooner be dead than married to him, so she clasped the famous asp to her bosom. Octavius, according to Roman law, had her two sons murdered, thinking that this would make it safe for him to usurp the throne. His Egyptian subjects soon convinced him he'd got it all wrong, that it was the girl who mattered! But for some reason he didn't kill the girl, only married her off to some extremely obscure king on condition he would never hear of her again!"

"Poor Cleopatra," said Victoria. "But perhaps one of them really loved her."

"There speaks the romantic." His tone was mocking. "They married her for what they could get. Most people do."

She shook her head. "Not me," she said. "I'm with Omm Beshir in this. I'd only marry for what I can give."

That seemed to catch his interest, but he only laughed at her. "Like today?"

"Maybe," she compromised. "You'll have to find that out for yourself!"

He looked her straight in the eye then. "Don't flirt with me, Victoria," he warned her. "You may get a great deal more than you bargained for!"

As a reply, she managed a little yawn.

Tariq drove as easily around Cairo as he did his own backyard. When Victoria thought of how nervous she had been trying to find her way the day before, she was doubly glad that it was he who was behind the wheel. Today she wouldn't even have attempted to compete with the jostling traffic, and the noise of the horns hurt her head as they blared away for no reason at all.

He parked the car, giving the crippled attendant a few coins to look after it until they got back.

"You do know I don't speak Arabic," Victoria said to him as he helped her out of the car.

"It doesn't matter," he reassured her. "All you have to do is repeat what the sheikh says to you as well as you can. Most of the time he'll politely ignore you."

"Thanks very much," she said.

The *sharei* court had little to recommend it in her eyes. The building was old and dusty and she couldn't help thinking the law that was administered there could have done with a good spring-cleaning too. There were none of the trappings of a modern state to give the place an official look, such as there would have been at a government office back in England. Here, it was full of old men, dressed in the long robes that were traditional with them, reciting the Koran to themselves in high, singsong voices that she found strangely hypnotic. Their female counterparts, black-garbed and patient, cluttered up the downstairs passages, sitting wherever they could find a space on the floor and pretending not to see the men who walked up and down the corridors between them.

"We go upstairs," Tariq told her. "And for heaven's sake don't speak unless you're spoken to!"

Victoria thought that after this place she would never be surprised again. She hung back a little as Tariq ushered her into a room at the top of the stairs, and she recognized two of Omm Beshir's sons already seated on one side of a desk. On the other side sat an old man she had never seen before, dressed in both turban and robe, with a younger man beside him to draw up the marriage documents.

"Ahlan wa sahlan, el salaam 'aleikum!" the old sheikh intoned.

Not one of the men so much as glanced at her, Victoria noticed with amusement. She felt it was a concession when one of them found her a chair, placing it as close to Tariq's as he could put it. He gestured to her to sit down and she did so, suddenly glad that no one was paying any attention to her. She felt dizzy with the pain in her head and as plain as she had ever looked, and she didn't want them to wonder why Tariq was taking such a poor weak thing as his wife.

Tariq took her right hand in his, holding it so tightly that she wiggled her fingers in protest, but he paid no more attention to her than anyone else did, not even when he began to repeat the long, complicated sentences in classical Arabic after the sheikh.

Victoria's attention began to wander. Was she doing the right thing, she wondered, marrying Tariq in this extraordinary way? But if she had refused him, how else could she have proved to him that it wasn't only her father's money she trusted him with, but her own person, with everything she was?

A sharp dig in the ribs made her aware that silence had fallen over the room. She looked hastily around, but there was no clue as to what was expected from her. The sheikh leaned over the desk and whispered a few words to Tariq.

"Repeat after him—" he translated.

"But I don't understand a word of it!"

His lips twitched. "Just as well!" he said easily.

It was almost impossible for Victoria to get her tongue around the strange words that the sheikh carefully enunciated for her to repeat. It was as well he was a patient man, she thought, to have to listen to her murdering his beautiful language, the only recognizable words being the names of her father and grandfathers—and Tariq's, though that, too, was unfamiliar under the guise of Torquil Fletcher.

However, she finally stammered to a close and exchanged sheepish smiles with the old sheikh, whose eyes slid away from hers as soon as they met, as if afraid that his obvious curiosity about her might be unwelcome to her as a woman.

The younger man, who had sat on the same side of the desk as the sheikh, produced two important-looking documents with a flourish and laid them carefully down in front of Tariq and Victoria. As they were written in the beautiful calligraphy of the Arabic Kufic script, they were as meaningless to Victoria as everything else had been. Tariq picked up a pen and signed his copy quickly in the same script, much to Victoria's obvious admiration. She herself had to wait for the clerk to tell her where she was expected to write her own signature, and she thought it looked far from graceful when she had written it, standing out as it did like a sore thumb on the beautiful parchment.

She signed the second paper with even greater reluctance, accepting it as her own copy, folding it, and putting it away in her handbag. Tariq put his copy in his breast pocket, giving it a little pat as he turned to accept the congratulations of the old sheikh and his foster brothers. No one spoke to her at all.

To her joy, however, Omm Beshir was waiting for them outside the building. She wasn't wearing a veil—evidently she was too emancipated for that—but she had a large, shapeless black cloth over her head and she held it under her chin with one tiny, dainty hand. The other hand was resting on one of her daughter's arms with a certain pride of possession, as if inviting the world to see that she was an appreciated member of a happy family.

"That girl is ill and should be in her bed, not gallivanting around with you," she berated Tariq the minute she set eyes on Victoria. "Are you truly married?"

Victoria, unwilling to be ignored by Omm Beshir as well as everyone else, decided to answer for herself. "*El hamdu Ii'llah*!" she murmured, rather pleased with her carefully acquired Arab sentence.

"Thanks be to God indeed," the old lady retorted. "Are you happy now?" She uttered a long, low chuckle. "Did he say he liked your scent?"

"No," said Victoria.

Tariq bent his head and inhaled gently. "Lotus," he pronounced. "Are you wearing that for me?"

"Omm Beshir gave it to me," she told him. "Please may we go home with her, just for a little while?"

He put his hand on the nape of her neck. "Not now. You'll feel more like celebrating when your head isn't aching and you look a little less like a ghost!"

She made a face at him and Omm Beshir gave her an amused glance. "You must do as he tells you, *yâ bént*, now that you are his wife. We will have a party for you some other time."

But they stood for a while exchanging jokes in Arabic, which Tariq accepted with remarkably good humor, though one or two thrusts obviously embarrassed him and heightened his color. Victoria wished she knew what they were saying. She hadn't thought that *anything* could throw Torquil Fletcher off balance, and she savored the moment, half hoping that one day she, too, would be able to tease him in the same way, and be teased by him in return.

Tariq put his arm around her and she realized she had been swaying where she stood. "Don't you honestly think you'll be better off in bed?" he asked her.

"I suppose so," she admitted. "But it doesn't seem much of a celebration."

He raised his eyebrows. "Have we something to celebrate?"

She refused to be annoyed. "Why not? I might have shone as something in my own light, as *anything*, instead of being virtually ignored by everyone."

"You are tired," Omm Beshir said wisely. "I shall say goodbye to you now before you say something you'll regret."

Victoria suffered her embrace, feeling more lightheaded by the moment. She kissed Omm Beshir's hand, followed by both her daughters, and then allowed Tariq to take her arm in his and lead her away to where they had left the car.

"Feeling better?" he asked her, opening the door for her.

She shook her head. "I'm afraid I'm not feeling very well at all at the moment."

He got into the car beside her and took her firmly into his arms. "All you need is a good night's sleep and you'll be as good as new." He kissed her hard on the mouth and put her back in her seat, starting up the car immediately. "Cheer up, Mrs. Fletcher," he added, "I think you put on a pretty good show. What's more, I think that old sheikh was envying me!"

CHAPTER NINE

VICTORIA TOOK out her copy of the marriage contract and examined it closely.

"I wish I understood it," she said.

"It's written out in English and French on the back," he told her. "You'll find there the Muslim marriage laws as they apply to Egypt."

Victoria turned the parchment over and began to read them for herself. "It is a legal marriage, isn't it?"

He stopped the car at once and took the paper from her, putting it back into her handbag.

"It's legal, yes. Wasn't that the idea?"

She saw that she was being unreasonable. "I know it is," she said. "But I feel so strange, and when I think what my mother will say—" She made a gesture of despair. "You don't know how she goes on about things. She'll never forgive me!"

He looked amused. "Because you haven't married the boy next door! There's a simple answer to that, sweetheart. Don't tell her!"

Victoria was shocked. "But she'll have to know sooner or later. One can't get married and *not* have people know!"

"I don't suppose Juliette or Jim Kerr will ever tell her, or that she will ever meet either of them. By the time you get back to England the marriage will be over, and what will be the point of telling her then?"

"I suppose so," she said, unconvinced.

He pulled off her hat and threw it behind them

onto the backseat. "Won't you leave the worrying to me? I promise you this marriage won't make any difference to you in the long run."

It was impossible to tell him what was on her mind— that she *wanted* to have something to tell her mother about. She shook out her hair, glad to be free of the restricting band of her hat, and then she became aware of him watching her.

"Am I making a fuss about nothing?" she asked him.

He shook his head. "I can't imagine you ever doing that, but it might have been better if you had thought of these difficulties before we took the plunge. It's a bit late now."

"Yes, but I wasn't thinking about anyone else then," she explained. "I was thinking about us—and the excavation, of course!" She had a sudden thought. "What on earth is Juliette going to think?"

Tariq took a piece of her hair between two fingers and began to play with it in silence.

"You'll have to tell her that it doesn't mean anything!" Victoria said quickly. "We can't hurt her like that. Her husband did enough damage—"

"Does it really matter?"

She looked inquiringly at him, trying to read his enigmatic expression. "I thought you liked Juliette?" she said.

"I do, but shall we call it a flash in the pan—for us both! You don't have to worry about Juliette, now or ever. Besides, wouldn't it ruin the object if we tell her we got married in order to deprive her of your father's money?"

"But we didn't!" She thought about it for a while. "Did we?"

"No, we didn't," he agreed. "I went into this as a

rescue operation first, and to nail these thieves before they succeed in damaging your father's or my reputation any further. What your motives were," he added, "I'm beginning to wonder!"

Victoria looked away. "I wanted to help," she told him. "I still do. You will tell me what's going on, won't you?"

"I'll try to." He smiled then, and his eyes lit up. "I'm not used to running in harness, but I won't forget you're there. You have a way of calling yourself to my attention quite forcibly enough without my giving you cause to remind me of your presence."

"But you'd prefer if I kept out of the way?"

"I'd prefer it if you didn't get yourself half-killed again," he said, "and I mean to see that you don't. Now that I'm your husband, it's my duty to protect you from any further accidents or hurt."

"Oh, Tariq, you can't be with me all the time! No one will want to hurt me now, you said so yourself. I'm far more concerned what they'll have to say about our getting married. Aren't you embarrassed at all about it?"

He began to laugh. "Why should I be? They'll offer their congratulations, no doubt, and that will be that." He smiled at her. "I'll see they don't disturb you tonight, don't worry. We'll move into your father's tent, it's bigger than mine—"

"We won't!" she declared. "I'm not going to share any tent with you!"

"It depends what you call sharing," he said. "I'll rig up a curtain between our beds and you can be as private as you like. Will that suit you?"

It would be nice to have him there if the scorpions came back, she thought. It would be nice, too, to know where he was, instead of wondering if he were with Juliette—

"Have I any choice in the matter?" she asked.

"Not much." He laughed and kissed her mouth, taking care not to start her head aching again. "As Omm Beshir said, you must do as I tell you now that you're my wife. You'll scandalize half of Egypt if you don't!"

She knew he was teasing her, that he didn't mean it, but she couldn't be quite sure and she wondered if she minded quite as much as she should. She decided to joke about it, too.

"I don't see how you can make me," she said.

"Don't you? But in a Muslim marriage the man has all the advantages. It is written that those wives 'whose perverseness ye fear, admonish them and remove them into bedchambers and beat them; but if they submit to you, then do not seek a way against them.' "

"But you're not a Muslim," Victoria pointed out.

"No, but they have some good ideas," he said.

She might have argued the matter further, but she was tired and sore from her fall and from all that had happened to her in the past few days. For the moment she was content to sit back and let him take charge of everything. Tomorrow, she thought, would be soon enough to try to sort out her emotions and take in the fact that she was more or less married to the man beside her, not that she had so much as a ring on her finger to show for it.

It was almost dark when they got back to Sakkara. Victoria braced herself to meet Juliette and Jim Kerr, but neither of them was around. The only person who came out to greet them was Abdul, his face wreathed in smiles, alone in his certainty that the wedding was a happy occasion, destined to bring great joy to all concerned.

"*Madame* is going straight to bed," Tariq told him brusquely. "Make up her bed in her father's tent, will you? I'll move my bed in later."

"Yes, yes, I'll be doing that at once." Abdul gave Victoria a kindly look. "*Madame* is not looking well after the fall. What will she eat tonight? Soup? Maybe she would like some little meatballs and rice? That is very good for the strength! I will bring mint tea at once, while she is deciding, no?"

Victoria found she was more than glad to take off the chartreuse dress and climb into her nightgown that was loose enough not to rub her bruises and remind her of her throbbing head. She lay down on the newly made bed and pulled the cotton bedclothes up over her. It was sheer bliss to be horizontal and she was determined to make the most of it, and not worry about a thing until she felt a great deal better.

Abdul brought her mint tea at the same moment that Tariq arrived with his camp bed under his arm. He took the tray from Abdul and put it down beside her bed, pouring a little of the tea into one of the small glasses that shared the copper tray with the painted tin teapot.

"Sugar?" he asked her.

She shook her head. "It's always too sweet already." She sat up in bed and accepted the glass from him. She felt nervous of his presence in what was technically her bedroom and was afraid that he would know it. "Are you going to have some tea?" she asked him.

He studied her face in silence. "I shan't hurt you, Victoria," he said.

"I know," she said at once. "I'm not used to being married, though."

"I should hope not!" He poured himself some tea, still looking at her. "You've never had much to do with men, have you?"

"Not at close quarters," she admitted. "I haven't

had your experience of—of—" She broke off, aware of the hopelessness of what she had been about to say.

"Sleeping around? You should be grateful you're the only wife I've ever had!"

"Am I?"

His reply was impatient. "Stop looking at me as though you expect me to turn into some kind of Bluebeard before your very eyes!" He laughed without any amusement at all. "Though I suppose in a country where they are bidden to 'marry what seems good to you of women, by twos or threes or fours—' "

"Huh!" said Victoria. " 'And if you fear ye cannot be equitable, then only one!' You couldn't possibly treat two wives just the same, could you? Think of the expense when they both wanted identical mink coats at the same time!"

His eyebrows rose, but he ignored her challenge. "More tea?"

She nodded, holding out her glass to him. She thought he had handled the situation rather well. There was something to be said for experience, it seemed, especially if she was going to take it into her head to panic whenever he came near her.

He fetched a chair and began to hang the embroidered curtain across the center of the tent. She watched him in silence, wishing she could tell him she was grateful for his forebearance, without making too much of it.

"Will we have a bit of paper to say we're divorced too?" she asked impulsively.

"Probably. It's quite easy, I believe. We'll go back to the *sharei* court and you can divorce me—"

She sipped her mint tea. "Wouldn't it be better if you were to divorce me? Your foster family might not like it if you take the blame for things going wrong. Besides, it would be easier still for you to divorce me. All you have to do is recite the formula three times and it's done!"

"If I divorce you, it takes three months," he said, looking down at her with a warning look.

"It doesn't say that in the Koran," Victoria objected. "How do you know?"

"I took the trouble to find out. That's how the law stands in Egypt, designed I believe to prevent men from divorcing their unfortunate wives in a fit of ill-temper, which I'm beginning to think must be an ever-present temptation. Look, drop the subject, will you, Victoria? Don't think of yourself as married to me at all, if it's going to nag at you like an aching tooth!"

"I was only trying to be practical about it," she explained.

"Well, don't! This curtain isn't a very substantial barrier and my intentions are usually better than my actions turn out to be." He came down from the chair, looking up at his handiwork. "I'm trying not to think of you as my wife, and you're not making it any easier by continually harping on it—unless you want me to make love to you?"

She pulled the bedding more closely about her in a defensive gesture. "Oh!" she gasped. "I think you're hateful! Just because other women have fallen into your hands like ripe fruit, you needn't imagine that I—"

He turned and looked at her inquiringly, while she was only too aware of the trend of her thoughts. Wasn't that exactly what she wanted?

"I'm sorry," she said, "but you're so conceited!"

He bent down and touched his lips to hers, tucking her sheet in around her shoulders with gentle hands. "Where you're concerned I have reason to be, *habibi.*" He kissed her lightly. "I'll tell Abdul to bring your food at once and then you can sleep through until morning if you want. Good night Mrs. Fletcher."

Her heart pounded within her, and her previous shyness of him washed over her like a wave. "Good night," she whispered back.

IN THE MORNING she woke to the sound of people talking. The voices were strange to her and she lifted her head from the pillow to hear better what they were saying. It was a woman who was doing most of the talking, but although Victoria could distinctly hear the attractive cadences of her voice, she couldn't make out what it was that she was saying. Curious, Victoria got out of bed and went over to the entrance to the tent. A group of people were seated on the ground not far from where the tent was situated, taking shelter from the wind that was blowing up the sand all around the Step Pyramid.

"The Step Pyramid, the first pyramid of Egypt," their woman guide was saying, "was the tomb of Pharaoh Zoser. Its construction has always been attributed to Imhotep, Zoser's architect, the first man ever to have constructed a building in stone. Imhotep's achievement became a legend in later times. He was regarded not only as an architect, but as a magician and the father of medicine. Later on he was deified as the son of Ptah, who was worshipped locally as we have seen, and even the Greeks were filled with admiration for him and identified him with their own god of medicine, Asklepios."

Victoria gave up trying to listen, wondering what time it was. She had the guilty feeling that it was very late indeed, but she must have forgotten to wind her watch, for it had stopped sometime in the early hours of the morning. She must have been asleep for hours! She felt better, though. Her head had stopped aching and the dizzy feeling that she might faint was gone. True, she still felt stiff and bruised, but otherwise she felt ready for anything—even Mr. Torquil Fletcher!

She had almost finished dressing when he came into the tent. "So you're awake at last!" he greeted her, hearing her moving about. "May I come in?"

"Yes, of course," she said.

He came around the edge of the curtain. "You're looking better," he approved.

"I am," she felt self-conscious of him and went on brushing her hair, her face turned away from him.

He sat down on the edge of her bed. "What's the matter?" he asked.

"Nothing."

"Victoria, would you like to go and stay with Omm Beshir for a while?"

And have everyone know that she wasn't married to him at all? How could he even suggest such thing?

"Certainly not," she said.

"You'd be welcome there—"

"I know, but I don't want to go. I love Omm Beshir. She's a lovely person! It would be the last straw to have her thinking that you didn't want me. She'd think there was something wrong with me—" She glanced around at him under arm and was aware that once again he was mocking her. "She would so!" she exclaimed crossly. "She'd never think that it might be your fault!"

"We could explain things to her," he suggested.

"*No*!"

"Darling, don't you think you're being a little bit unreasonable?"

She went on brushing her hair in silence. “Yes,” she said at last. “But I can’t help it, Tariq. Put it down to silly pride if you like, but I couldn’t bear it if she thought I was a disappointment to you. She’d hate me for it! And it doesn’t make any difference that it’s only a marriage contract and nothing more to us. You know she’d never understand how it really is. Nor would she believe it! She’d be quite sure that you at least tried to sleep with me and that I’d been a great disappointment. She wouldn’t see anything wrong in your making love to me, even if you did intend to divorce me the next minute. Well, would she?”

“You seem to know her very well,” he said.

Victoria bit her lip. “I like her, and I want her to like me!”

Tariq leaned back on his elbow, watching her through his lashes. “Juliette is right,” he said. “She is not stupid, this one, is she? You’re probably right. She could well wring your neck for you if she thought you were not fulfilling your wifely duties. I’m surprised that you would know that, though. It doesn’t mean she doesn’t like you, too!”

Victoria smiled at that. “Now, I know. But the whole world has to stop at your command as far as she’s concerned. I don’t mind, in fact it’s one of the things I like most about her, but I don’t want her to think that I’m less—well, you know, less than she is, I suppose.”

“She won’t think that. She knows that your ways are bound to be different from hers.”

“She knows it with her mind,” Victoria said. “In her heart she thinks only her ways are good enough for you. She may be right. She brought you up when you were a child as much as anyone did. You may well think like her about these things.”

"Meaning what?" he drawled. "That I think of women as objects for my pleasure?"

That wasn't what she had meant at all, and she suspected that he knew it, too.

"Meaning that one doesn't always know where one is with you," she retorted. "I might like to give you the world, too, but I don't know if you'd give me a thank-you for it. You'd probably tell me what I could do with it!"

He looked startled and then totally impassive. "Do you want to give me the world?" he asked, not moving a muscle.

"That's not the point."

"Then what is the point? That you don't know if I'd be properly grateful or not?"

She glowered at him. "Not that, either! You're being deliberately obtuse! I don't want your gratitude, but I would like to know where I stand with you as a person. I want to give, too, not just take all the time!"

He stood up and, putting a hand on the small of her back, drew her firmly into the circle of his arms. "I've never doubted your generosity, *yâ habibi*, but I think you're in a bit of a muddle as to what you do want, whereas I'm in no doubt at all as to what I want."

"And what is that?"

"That would be telling," he murmured.

"Tell me!"

"What will you give me if I do?"

She stood still, refusing to commit herself. "Tariq, what's the time?"

"Does it matter?"

"My watch is stopped."

He stroked her back, taking her brush from her and throwing it on the bed behind him. "You're so beautiful," he said. "Are you sure you're feeling better?"

"Mmm," she agreed, "Why?"

"Because I'm going to fulfill an urgent wish of yours."

She shut her eyes, making no answer. She felt him gather her up into his arms and put his mouth against hers. It was a gentle kiss at first, but it changed halfway through and her lips parted beneath the hard, demanding pressure of his, and her arms crept up around his neck and her fingers buried themselves in his hair.

When he broke away, putting her firmly at arm's length and holding her there, she didn't try to hide her disappointment.

"You see why I wanted you to go to Omm Beshir?" he said. "And how much my promises are worth?"

She shrugged her shoulders.

He put the back of his hand against her cheek. "I told you I wouldn't touch you while you were married to me." He let go of her hands, saw her wince, and picked them up again, examining the palms to see how the grazes had healed after her entanglement with the guy rope.

She gripped his fingers in hers. "You haven't hurt me," she said. "What more can I ask?"

"You could ask me to leave you alone." He tipped up her face and looked deep into her navy blue eyes. "Why don't you?"

She blinked. "I trust you," she said.

He turned and left her without another word and she sank back on the bed, holding her head in her hands. She couldn't do anything right as far as he was concerned, she thought gloomily, no matter how hard she tried.

She didn't know how long she sat there but after a while she realized he was not coming back and she wandered out of the tent, wondering what to do with herself. The groups of tourists were leaving the Step Pyramid now. Victoria watched them as they straggled across the blowing sand, making their way to where the camel boys waited. There they would vie with one another for the various modes of transport that would take them down the hill to the Serapeum where the sacred bulls of Ptah had been buried so many thousand years before.

On an impulse, Victoria decided to join them. The sand blew up all around her, stinging her face and legs, but she hardly felt it as she ran to where the tourists were milling around the camels, donkeys and carriages, trying to make their choice among them. She climbed into the nearest chariot and sat down, hoping that no one would challenge her presence, but no one paid any attention to her. Another woman, older than anyone else there, was helped into the chariot beside her and they exchanged cautious smiles of greeting.

"Did you see that nasty gentleman lying on his back at Memphis?" the old lady asked her. "They must have been strange people, with their wigs and false beards! I wouldn't have trusted him with much!"

Victoria smiled. "I thought him quite good-looking," she confided.

"Those are the kind you can trust least of all," the old lady said with decision. "My father was a very handsome man, and my mother soon learned better than to trust him further than she could see him!"

Victoria wondered where Tariq would fit in such a creed. But perhaps the old lady had never trusted any man, handsome or not, her mother's experience having soured her where all men were concerned.

"I suppose Pharaoh could do as he pleased," she said, thinking of Tariq in the same moment.

"Very likely!" the old lady snorted. "Most men do!" She rummaged in her handbag and produced a candy that she popped into her mouth with the first sign of pleasure she had shown. "Strange the care with which they had themselves buried. They did as they liked about that, too! The young lady was telling us they didn't hesitate to pull down somebody else's tomb if it got in the way of their own! No respect, that was the trouble with them!"

"Some of the tombs were burned down by opposing dynasties," Victoria volunteered, glad to be able to offer a piece of information of her own.

"So she told us. She said they're digging one out at this moment. Imagine that!"

"But it hasn't suffered from fire," Victoria murmured.

"It sounded as though it had suffered from everything else!" said the old lady, crunching her candy between her false teeth. "The young lady said that all the above part had been pulled down long ago, and that there was a whole corner missing down below. I suppose another one of them decided to build his tomb alongside and didn't bother himself that there was one there already!"

Victoria made a mental note to ask Juliette if that was what had happened. If Juliette was still speaking to her, that was.

The wheels of the carriage dragged in a pocket of loose sand and the thin horse shuddered with the strain of pulling it free. The driver clicked his tongue against his teeth. "*Yálla!*" he urged the beast forward. "*Yálla bina!*"

AT THE BOTTOM of the hill the animals came to a halt without being told. The camels protested as they were brought to their knees to allow their passengers to dismount, and one or two of the donkeys looked as if they might give their riders a vicious nip with their teeth to help them dismount more quickly. It was a difficult operation and the women modestly tried to pull their skirts back around their knees.

Victoria jumped out of the chariot and began to help the old lady down to the ground. As she did so, she felt a hand on her arm and turned quickly to come face to face with Tariq.

"I've come to parley with you," he said out of the side of his mouth.

She raised her eyebrows. "What about?"

"I put the cart before the horse." He flicked her nose with his fingers. "Three months isn't very long to wait after all!"

She looked up at him in swift inquiry, but the old lady was in front of her, digging Tariq in the ribs with her handbag.

"I don't remember you being in our party, young man!" she attacked him, her eyes frosty with disapproval.

"I'm not," he said. "I came to fetch my wife before she was discovered to be an intruder and realized she hadn't any money with her."

"Your wife, eh?" The old lady unbent a little. "Lucky girl, or I expect you think so!"

"I hope she is," Tariq bowed. "I'm not sure she'd agree with you at the moment!"

"Huh! Had a quarrel, have you?" She rummaged in her bag for another candy, popping it easily into her mouth. "I was just telling her that no woman should trust a handsome man. But seeing you're both here, why don't you come and see where they buried these bulls of theirs? You can have your quarrel afterward!"

Victoria looked uncertainly at Tariq. "May we?" she asked him.

He shrugged his shoulders. "If you want to. I'll wait here until you get back."

She was disappointed, but she didn't try to persuade him. She took the old lady's arm and helped her down the few steps that led into the underground corridor where the tombs of the sacred bulls had been laid out. At the far end the guide began to speak, explaining the characteristics that had been required in any bull before the priests declared it to be the living symbol of Ptah. The Apis bull had to have a triangular spot on his forehead, on his back an eagle, a lump in the form of a beetle under his tongue, and the hair of his tail was double.

The old lady muttered something under her breath. "I suppose they were bred for the purpose," she opined, seating herself on the edge of one of the tombs. "They sound like family characteristics to me!"

Like robbing older tombs that got in the way of one's own! Could that be what it was all about? Victoria muttered an apology to the old lady and ran back to the entrance, ignoring the proffered assistance up the steps by half a dozen eager Egyptian hands. She tore up the ramp and out into the windy sunshine above ground.

"Tariq, I can't imagine why I didn't think of it before! What does Jim Kerr do in the *mastaba* by himself when he says he's doing his housework?" Her voice shook with sudden excitement. "I think he's found a way into another tomb! I think he's robbing it, too!"

CHAPTER TEN

TARIQ CAUGHT HER and held her tightly against him.

"Wait a minute, what are you trying to do? Prove that you're the fastest woman in the west?"

Victoria wriggled impatiently against him. "No, Juliette is that!"

He frowned, unamused. "I thought you were getting along with Juliette quite well?"

"Yes, we do. Please forget I ever said it." She twisted away from him. The last thing she wanted was for him to know that she was jealous of the French girl, but she was. She had seen the way Juliette looked at Tariq and she knew that while the affair might be over for Tariq, it was a long way from being over as far as Juliette was concerned. Oh, yes, she might have preferred George Lyle when he was alive, but George was no longer available to her, and Tariq was!

"If I thought you were worrying over her—"

"I'm not! If anything, I feel a little bit sorry for her. That's all!"

He was still frowning. "Juliette can never take anything from you. You don't want the same things," he told her shortly.

She sighed in despair. "Oh, do shut up!" she begged him. "I was trying to be witty. It's always disastrous when I try to make a joke at someone else's expense. You'd think it would have taught me to keep a charitable tongue in my head. Don't pay any attention to me!"

"I'll try to remember," he promised. "I suppose it was funny—in a way!"

"No, it wasn't. It wasn't at all what I meant to say." She looked frankly up at him. "Only I've had an idea, Tariq. It's important. That's why I came back. I'm sure Jim Kerr is using my father's tomb to get through into another one and that he's systematically looting it for everything he can get!"

His eyebrows rose. "What makes you think that? No, don't tell me now. Open spaces are apt to have more ears than cities have walls. Tell me when we get back to camp!"

"Oh," she said. "I hadn't thought!"

"That's why you married me," he told her. "To do your thinking for you! Do you want to walk back, or shall we commandeer the chariot you came in and ride back in style?"

"Can we?" she said. "What will the old lady do?"

"We'll send it back for her." He swung her easily up into the chariot and followed, smiling at her flushed, breathless face. "It isn't too high for you up there, is it?"

"No," she said rather doubtfully. "But I wouldn't like to be on one of those camels. I know I'd be terrified up there!"

He said something to the driver and they started slowly up the hill. "You have too much imagination," he accused her. "One day I'll put you up on a nice, docile camel and you'll love every minute of it!"

"Never!" she said with certainty.

His smile made her wonder if she was quite so sure. "Not even if I took you up with me?"

She digested that in silence. She wondered what else he knew about her, and whether he was right that she wouldn't blink an eye if she knew herself to be safely in his hands. She thought he probably was, but it gave her an uncomfortable, naked feeling that he should know it, too.

She felt his eyes on her face and pretended to look back toward the Serapeum, lacing her fingers together in a defensive movement that she felt sure must have betrayed her. If it did he said nothing, but looked away again and busied himself with his own thoughts.

"How did you know where I'd gone?" she asked.

"Abdul saw you go."

She remembered that he had told her she was always to leave word with Abdul where she was going. A guilty look spread over her face.

"I would have told someone," she assured him hastily, "but it was an impulse. If I'd missed the group, there wouldn't have been anyone there to tell me about it."

"It doesn't matter as much as it did," he answered. "Everyone knows that you don't have any further say in the excavation. There isn't the same urgency to get rid of you before you poke your nose into something that would send you running to the authorities."

"I see," she said. "By marrying you, I've dropped you right in it, haven't I?"

"That's the idea," Tariq said with an easy smile. "They won't find it easy to keep me from stirring things up. I mean to make it as hot as I can for them."

"But they might try to get rid of you, too!" she said in a small voice.

"They can try. The odds will be against them if they try. I'm not a green young girl suffering from vertigo, my dear."

"But, Tariq—"

He put a finger over her lips. "I know what I'm doing. All you have to do is to stay out of trouble while I settle this mess once and for all. Judging by your past record, it'll take you all your time to concentrate on that!"

Victoria would have said something rude and pungent in answer to that, but at that moment they arrived at the top of the hill. She had no choice but to allow herself to be swung down onto her feet and to stand there, raging inwardly at being treated like a crass idiot, while he paid the driver, exchanging endless compliments with one another, as the Arabs do.

"Now," he said, as the chariot moved off down the hill again, "tell me about this idea of yours. I gather you think another tomb cuts across the corner of the *mastaba*, where it's supposed to have fallen in?"

"Yes," she said in unfriendly tones. "I do."

"Something the matter?"

"*Yes*. Anyone would think that I did nothing but rush from one scrape to another. None of the things that happened to me were my fault!"

"No, they were mine," he said. "I should have looked after you better."

"Oh, Tariq, be reasonable! You can't be with me every hour of the day!"

"That's what you think," he retorted. "My dear Victoria, by the time our marriage is over, you're going to be sick of the sight of me!"

"I may get used to your being around," she said, carefully casual. "I've never had a bodyguard before. It makes me feel quite important!"

"Well? Are you going to tell me?" he asked her.

She nodded. "It was something the old lady said to me that put it into my head," she began, warming to her idea. "She said a lot of the earlier tombs had been demolished by later generations to make room for theirs on the same ground." Her dark blue eyes lit with remembered amusement. "She thought them a ruthless lot, typical of the male sex, I'm afraid! Anyway, when Jim took me into the *mastaba*, he told me one of the far corners had fallen in some time in the past. But, Tariq, couldn't that be why? Couldn't there be another tomb across the corner that Jim has found the way into?" Her voice shook with excitement. "I think it's one of the reasons he keeps himself in such a dirty state, so that no one will suspect what he's doing!"

Tariq stood looking into space, his arms crossed in front of him. His eyes were hidden from her, but she could imagine the sleepy, thoughtful look they would have as he thought over what she had said.

"It's possible, but I don't think it likely. Either your father or Juliette must have come to the same conclusion if there's another tomb alongside."

"I don't see why," Victoria objected, getting fonder of her theory by the minute. "It's an awful mess down there. They've hardly begun digging out the tomb itself, let alone the further passages." She chewed thoughtfully on her lip. "If there are any further passages?"

He threw back his head and laughed. "Oh, Victoria, don't you know?"

"No. I don't know the first thing about it, but I'm sure I'm right all the same! Jim only took me into the first courtyard. He said they hadn't got any further than that."

"They must have done!" Tariq scoffed. "That courtyard was cleared before your father threw me off the site!"

"Then they can't have done a thing since! It

looked blocked from where I was standing, full of sand and muck. You know the sort of thing!" A new thought struck her and she cast him an apologetic look. "How long ago is it since my father asked you to leave?"

His eyes gleamed with mockery at her delicacy. "Three months."

Three months! Was that all? Three months was no time at all, if he had thought himself in love with Juliette only three months ago!

"Perhaps, if my father was already ill then, they stopped work almost at once. He died only two months later." She sucked in her breath, a little on the defensive. "We were told that he died suddenly from a heart attack, but he could have been ill before that, couldn't he?"

"I think Juliette would have told me if he had been." He looked at her disappointed face and made up his mind to humor her. "It's an interesting idea. It wouldn't do any harm if we took a look for ourselves. Do you want to come?"

"Of course, I want to!" Victoria exclaimed in triumph.

"Come on, then. I'll get Abdul to light a couple of lamps for us so that we can see what we're doing. We can find out from him where Jim is, too, as he seems to be suspect number one."

"Does he ever leave Sakkara?" Victoria asked.

"Not since we got here," Tariq said dryly. "But he wasn't around earlier this morning."

When they approached the communal tent, Abdul leaped to his feet, tyring to hide the comic book he had been reading.

"Men fádlak, yâ fândi, yâ sétt!"

It was the first time he had accorded Victoria the status of a married woman and she started at the greeting. Tariq told him that they were going into the *mastaba* and would need lights.

"Have you seen the Sidi Kerr, or the Sétt Mercer?" he asked, as though their absence had only just occurred to him.

"They are gone to Cairo," Abdul responded. "The lady was very angry that you are married, *yâ fândi*. The Sidi Lyle was her friend and she said his daughter had betrayed him. She has gone to see the Department of Antiquities to see if they will transfer the license to her. The other one went with her." He looked at Victoria from beneath his eyelashes, suddenly sly. "They will be away for lunch—all day," he added.

"Thank you," said Tariq. He took one of the lamps, pumped it until the light shone white and even, and handed it to Victoria. "Okay, let's get going!"

Victoria hardly recognized the entrance to the *mastaba*. It had been swept clean since she had last seen it, and the pile of sand by the entrance to the courtyard was gone.

"Do you suppose Jim Kerr meant what he said when he said he had some housekeeping to do? It must have been quite a job to move all that by himself!" Victoria remarked, unable to keep her distaste for the man out of her voice.

"I wouldn't have thought he'd ever cleaned anything in his life," Tariq agreed. He took a first look around and moved across the courtyard, examining every inch of the walls as he went. "Look at this!" he commanded her. "Have you noticed the colors? I'd remembered them as being brighter than they are, but they're still fantastic!"

Victoria came around and stood beside him, adding the light of her lamp to his. "But this isn't brick or plaster, is it?" she exclaimed. "It looks more like matting to me!"

"It is," he answered. "It's more usual to find it inside the burial chamber than in an anteroom like this. Just look at those colors there! Here, you can see how it was done if you look here. They welded these colored mats onto the walls, rather like wallpaper. They're not unlike the heavy hessian papers that are popular nowadays."

They were certainly remarkable. It gave Victoria a funny feeling to think that they had been hidden away there for perhaps five thousand years, waiting to be rediscovered.

"I thought all tombs here were like the one in the Pyramid of Unas, covered with hieroglyphs and magic spells."

Tariq smiled at the image she conjured up of witchcraft and black magic. "More religious formulas than magic spells! They're later than this tomb, which is Second Dynasty at the latest. That puts it into the Archaic Period, when they could read and write, after a fashion, but the symbols they used were few and couldn't convey abstract meanings. What you saw on the walls of Unas's Pyramid is a particularly good example of what are called Pyramid Texts. They antedated the famous *Book of the Dead* by about a thousand years."

"A book?" she asked, confused.

"Not a book in the usual sense. It was written on papyrus at the time of the New Kingdom. It's sometimes called the *Book of Coming Forth Day by Day.* It contained details of how the dead should acquit themselves when they came before the Judgment Seat. Nothing was left out about what they would meet on the way. It was a terrifying ordeal, but these instructions must have fortified them somewhat. To prove they had lived an innocent life, their heart was weighed on the scales against a feather, the symbol of Maat, the goddess of truth. You should read the book sometime. There is a long, negative confession in it of some forty articles that the dead person was invited to recite, each one beginning 'I have not done such and such.' Many people say that the Ten Commandments were directly descended from the principles embedded in it, a code of virtue that had been laid down to regulate the moral life of the Ancient Egyptian, which Moses would certainly have known all about."

"Do you believe that?" she asked, more than willing to take his word.

"Me? I think you can find anything if you look hard enough for it. Ethical codes, whether they are the Ten Commandments or the Code of Hammurabi, are likely to include the same prescriptions, especially as all these were Semitic in origin, or closely related."

Victoria looked at him with new eyes. "Juliette said you could read hieroglyphs," she confided, "but I didn't know you are an expert in these things. You must be a very good archaeologist! Are you better than my father was?"

"Egyptology is my subject. Your father didn't specialize. He wasn't a patient man. He wanted results long before he had unearthed all the available evidence. He was apt to jump to a conclusion and then, when the things he was finding didn't back him up, he'd lose his temper and insist that they didn't alter anything. He'd go on stubbornly maintaining that he was right and everyone else was wrong. Sometimes he was right."

"That doesn't sound very scholarly," Victoria said.

"No, he was no scholar! But he was an intuitive, sometimes brilliant amateur. He made some very shrewd guesses in his career and once or twice he came up with the goods very much against the odds. You don't have to be ashamed of him."

"I'm not!" she said sharply.

He turned and looked at her. "Not as an archaeologist, and not as a man," he insisted.

"I wish he'd been kinder to you, that's all," she tried to explain. "I can accept that he was a stubborn, awkward man, but not that he was stupid! And it was stupid of him to quarrel with you."

"He thought he had cause." He shrugged. "Perhaps he had. Who knows?"

"I know!" she said firmly.

"You, least of all, can know about that. You can't begin to know the pressures that may have been brought to bear on him. Nothing worked out right for him with this expedition. It was strain that brought on his heart attack. And my playing the fool with Juliette can't have helped him to relax."

"I don't think you can be blamed for that!" she declared. She held her lamp up, edging away from him toward the entrance of the burial chamber itself. The light shone on the accumulated rubble of centuries that hid the doorway from her eyes. Despite herself, her hand shook.

"Nor Juliette," he said dryly.

She wasn't prepared to commit herself about that. "Would you ever allow a woman to make a play for you?" she asked him instead.

He took her lamp from her. "Not that it's any of your business, but I chased Juliette. Anything else you want to know?"

Her eyes were wide and very dark in the white light from the lamp. "Yes, as a matter of fact there is, but it isn't any of my business, either, and you might not want to answer."

"Ask away," he invited her.

"If you had a wife—a proper wife, I mean—would you go off and leave her for months at a time while you had fun by yourself digging up something like this?"

He considered the question, his eyes creasing with amusement. "Is that what happened to your mother?"

"Yes, only she didn't want to go with my father, not anywhere!"

"But you wouldn't want to sit at home by yourself?"

She shook her head. "Not me! I'm going to cling to my husband like a barnacle to the side of a ship!" She put her head on one side, wondering if he would recognize the quotation from his own words.

If he did, he didn't let on. "Indeed? Won't he have any say in what you do?" He waited for her answer, and then, when none was forthcoming, he went on, "In my book, it isn't the hen who does the crowing. Wouldn't you listen to his ideas at all?"

"Would you listen to hers?"

"I'd listen, yes," he agreed.

"And then *you'd* decide?"

"That's right!" he said easily.

She tossed her head in the air to show she didn't care. "How long did you live with Omm Beshir?" she demanded.

"Somebody has to make the decisions," he said. "I think it's better when the man does, that's all."

She tried to remember that the whole argument was hypothetical. "I suppose so," she said reluctantly.

He handed her back her lamp after pumping up

the flame to his satisfaction. When she had taken it from him, he put up a hand and pushed her hair back out of her eyes. "I wouldn't be crazy enough to leave you on your own for long," he comforted her. "I'd never have an easy moment, wondering what you were getting up to!"

"My mother was never up to anything. She lives a very tidy life. On the few occasions my father ever visited us, she used to look on him as some unnecessary clutter that had to be shot out of the house as quickly as possible. How do you know that I don't take after her?"

"We-ell," he said thoughtfully. "We haven't had a dull moment since you got here. I wouldn't call that never being up to anything, would you? Perhaps you have less in common with your mother than you think."

That made her want to laugh. "Not very much," she said. She veiled her eyes with her lashes, struggling to maintain a deadpan expression. "We don't even look alike."

"I'd like to meet her some time, all the same."

"Why?" she said. She didn't dare look at him. With his face half in shadows and half lighted by the glow from the lamp, the strong line of his jaw was accentuated and so were the quick, mobile movements of his hands. She was terribly aware of him as his fingers met hers, turning her lamp slightly so that he could see her better.

"I'd like to know the person who brought you up."

"Oh!" She didn't know if she was more pleased or put out that he would be interested. "Why?" she asked again.

"Let's say I have my moments of curiosity, too."

"About me?" She looked at him quickly. "There isn't anything to know!"

"That's what you think!"

She wondered what he wanted to know about her. She couldn't believe she wasn't an open book to him if he cared to read it, so why did he pretend otherwise? Was it an oblique way of flattering her? No, she didn't think so. Tariq wouldn't bother to pander to her vanity.

"If you're curious about me, why don't you ask me whatever you want to know?" she tempted him.

"Because I suspect you don't know the answers yourself!"

"Try me!"

"I'll ask you when we have nothing better to do." He put a possessive hand on the nape of her neck, allowing his fingers to trail down her back. "Shall we go on?"

She would have done anything he told her at that moment. He made it sound as if they had a future together. His touch aroused a delicious feeling of weakness within her that made her blood sing in her veins. If she had never met him, she thought, she would never have known that it was possible to feel so aware of one's own womanhood. She would always be grateful to him for that. It was something that her mother had never known—

"Victoria!"

She started. "I'm sorry. I was daydreaming."

He shone the light on her face. "This is hardly the time or the place 'the dream of your heart to dream,' *habibi*. I said, shall we go?" He turned his light away from her and onto the pile of rubble in front of them. "If we want to get through that door, I'd better go and find a couple of shovels. Will you wait here?"

"Not on my own. Let's look around properly first. Oh, Tariq, look! There are some footsteps in the sand over there. Perhaps they lead somewhere?"

Tariq walked across the courtyard and squatted down, studying the prints with interest. "They don't go anywhere," he reported.

Victoria thought that was ridiculous. It was more likely that the sand had shifted across them and that they would appear again on the other side of the pile of fallen masonry that rested against the wall. She took an impulsive jump upward and forward, balancing herself on the ancient rubble to see what lay on the other side, but her view was obscured by a few jagged bricks that stuck out of the wall at an angle that looked as if they, too, might fall any moment. She took another step upward, putting out a hand against the wall as a loose brick dislodged itself beneath her feet and almost sent her crashing down on top of Tariq.

"Come down," he bade her. "Let me see!"

"No." She raised her lamp above her head, laughing down at him. "I'm the king of the castle!"

"Not for long you won't be if you don't take more care!"

She laughed again. "I like looking down at you for a change. Would you catch me if I fell?"

"Try it and see!" he recommended.

She took another step upward and gasped audibly, frozen where she stood.

"What is it?" Tariq put a sustaining hand on her belt. "There's no need to panic!" He tightened his grip on her. "Oh, no, you don't my girl!" he warned her. "You said yourself that it wasn't very high!"

"But it is!"

He clambered up beside her, holding her so tightly she felt as though she was being cut in two. He pulled her close against him, pushing her face against his shirt. "It's all right, *habibi*. I won't let you go!"

"Look!" she breathed.

"My God," he said, and then in a quite different tone, "It looks as though you were right after all."

"*After all*? Of course I'm right! I knew it all along and—" Her foot slipped and if it had not been for Tariq's hand on her belt, she would have sat down hard on the rubble. "I'm going down there!" she declared.

"No, you're not!" He yanked her back onto her feet. "If anyone goes, I'll go!"

Victoria set her mouth in a mutinous line. She might be afraid of heights, but she was *not* afraid of the dark! She looked with increasing excitement at the gaping black hole in the wall in front of her. It had been totally hidden by the bricks and rubble and the angle of the wall, but it was quite large enough for someone to crawl through, and who knew what was lying on the other side?

"But I found it! Please, Tariq, let me go in first!"

"You don't have to unless you really want to. You don't have to prove anything to me."

"I know, but please let me!"

He took her lamp from her and put it down on the rubble. She held out her hands to him and he swung her down to floor level, right against the large, gaping hole. He followed more slowly, until he, too, could look into it, but there was nothing to see. The silent blackness beyond seemed to be impervious to the light from their lamps.

"I'm going through!" Victoria announced. "Will you pass me my lamp when I'm on the other side?"

He nodded. "Are you sure you wouldn't like me to go first? It may not be safe—"

"Of course it's safe!" she protested. "If it weren't, how would Jim Kerr manage to get in and out?"

She knew Tariq was about to point out that there was no proof that Jim Kerr, or anyone else, had ever seen the hole in the wall, let alone climbed through it. She gave his hand a quick squeeze and pushed her torso through the gap, straining her eyes to see what lay beyond. She paused, blinking, but there was nothing to see but darkness. With care, she balanced herself, pulling one leg behind her and searching for a foothold that would hold her weight, while she turned around and pulled the other leg behind her. For an instant she thought she had found the floor on the other side and she put all her weight on it. Her foot slipped and she jerked downward, holding on for dear life with her hands. There was no foothold, nothing to stand on at all!

Cold with fright, she kicked out, trying to retrieve her position, but her hands lost their grip on the rough edges of the sun-dried bricks and they crumbled into dust between her fingers. Oddly, she wasn't aware of falling. There was no sensation of being pulled from a height and falling over the edge that had haunted her all her life. She was frightened, but she was scarcely aware of falling. All she was frightened of was the unknown beneath her.

It was a long way down. She landed in a heap on some soft sand and was surprised to discover that she wasn't hurt at all.

"Victoria, what happened?"

She tried to laugh, but she thought Tariq would think her hysterical and changed her mind. "I don't know," she said weakly. "I can't see a thing!"

"Are you hurt?"

She drew her legs up under her and tried to stand up, but the sand was more uneven than she had thought, and she sat down again quickly, feeling rather foolish.

"It's a long way down," she said.

CHAPTER ELEVEN

"VICTORIA, ARE YOU HURT? Half the wall has fallen in."

Victoria caught the anxiety in his voice and tried to stand up again. This time she managed it. "I'm quite all right," she assured him. "I had a soft landing on some sand. But don't try to follow me! It's a terribly long way down and I can't see any way out!"

"Shall I pass you your lamp?"

"You'd have to let it down on a rope!" There was a moment's silence. "Tariq, I don't think I'll ever get out!"

"Yes, you will. I'll get you out somehow. You're not afraid, are you?"

"Not yet."

"Cheer up. See if you can reach the lamp if I tie it to the end of my belt—"

Victoria saw the light flash above her and was relieved to see Tariq's face peering down at her.

"I'll never be able to reach it!" she cried out.

"So I see," he said grimly. "Are you sure you're not hurt? For heaven's sake don't move! I'll be gray-haired before my time if you fall down anywhere else!"

"I'm all right, Tariq, I promise you!" She made a play of brushing down her jeans to show she hadn't a care in the world. "I'm beginning to think that Jim Kerr didn't come down this way after all, though."

Tariq's laugh caught in the back of his throat. "I'll have to go and get a rope and some help. I'll try to rig up the light here so that you'll have something to look at, but you took a lot of the wall with you and it isn't very safe."

Victoria achieved a jaunty smile that she feared was wasted on him, for he acted as though he could scarcely bear to look at her.

"I'm not afraid," she claimed. "But you will hurry up, won't you?"

"I'll be ten minutes. Has your watch got a luminous dial? You can time me and tell me what you think of me if I'm a moment longer!"

"Oh, Tariq!"

"I know, *habibi*, but if the wall were to fall it might start a fire. Right, you can start timing me now!"

She hadn't the heart to tell him that her watch was a strictly ornamental affair, pretty, but useless for the practical purpose of telling the time even in strong sunlight, the small gold figures were so difficult to see against the chased gold face. She heard him go, taking the lamp with him, and the darkness reached out to her and enclosed her in total blackness.

She sat down on the sand, pulling her knees up under her chin, and shut her eyes, pretending the darkness was self-inflicted and that she had only to reach out her hand to feel Tariq beside her. She wished she had learned the poem about the sycamore tree by heart, for it would have been comforting to recite it to herself and to remember how he had quoted the first few lines to her when they had only just met, and he had stolen her heart away and called her the sunrise of beauty.

"Papyri green are my leaves arrayed,
    And branch and stem like to opal gleam;
Now come and rest in my cooling shade

The dream of your heart to dream."

Had she dreamed of Tariq even before she met him? It felt like that sometimes. She had looked around and seen him, and she had recognized him at once. But had he recognized her? She sighed, changing her position a little.

Papyri green had the brightness of banana leaves. Sometimes Tariq's golden eyes took on a green tinge, but it wasn't the same green as that. It was more the *eau-de-nil* of the waters of the Nile, when the sun caught the ripples of the waves and turned them into liquid gold; gold and green were then transformed into a single hue. Was it that she had seen in his eyes?

The Nile had always been known as the source of life. It had been navigable long before any other river. Traveling north to the delta regions, the current had carried the boats along; traveling south to the Sudan and beyond, the prevailing wind had filled the simple sails and taken the boats against the stream just as easily. Without the Nile, Egypt would never have been. Without Tariq—but that was a thought she did not wish to continue.

"Eight minutes!" Tariq's voice sounded above her. "Abdul's getting a couple of camels to take the strain of the rope. As soon as he gets here, I'm coming down to join you!"

"Wouldn't it be simpler if I came up?" she asked.

"Probably. But I want to see what's down there, and, as you're already there, I'm sure you'd think it unfair if I checked it out without you."

She managed to laugh. "Yes, I would."

There was a great deal of noise and the explosive sound of a camel protesting against the indignity of being put to work. A few minutes later Tariq appeared in the hole in the wall and came swinging down toward her, carrying one of the lamps in his hand.

When his feet touched the bottom, he lifted the lamp high and studied her face, his expression showing his anxiety more than any words could have done.

"You see," she said. "I really am all right."

He lowered the lamp, saying nothing, but as he did so the glint of gold on her left wrist caught his eye and he lifted her arm, staring in silence at her inadequate watch. Victoria put her hand over his, her heart going out to him.

"I'm afraid of heights, but I've never been afraid of the dark." She thought he would crush the bones in her wrist he held it so tightly. "Besides," she said. "I knew you were coming back."

"And that made it all right? I should never have allowed you to take such a risk. I might have known that something would happen to you!"

She touched her right hand to his cheek in a gesture borrowed from him. "It wasn't your fault, *habipi*."

He shook his head at her, but he let go of her arm and managed a faint smile. "And that makes it all right? I wanted to protect you—to keep you safe, but you seem destined to jump out of the frying pan into the fire every time I let you out of my sight—and even when I don't!"

She buried her face in his shoulder, amused. "But think how much I like to have you rescue me!"

He tugged gently on a lock of hair. "Do you?"

She met his eyes. She did not trust herself to speak and turned away from him, afraid that he would think she wanted more of him than he wanted to give.

She pulled the lamp out of his hand and flashed it all around them. They were standing at the bottom of a shaft that led upward away from the *mastaba* her father had been excavating. It was roughly made, which meant that it had been cut out by robbers, either ancient or modern. It was a steep climb up to the top, and, at the thought of working her way up there, Victoria was gripped by the familiar fear that turned her knees to rubber and her willpower into blind panic.

"You'll manage it all right," Tariq said behind her.

"I hope so." She swallowed, her mouth dry and painful. She clung to the fact that he would be there and some of the unreasoning fear left her limbs. "Anyway," she told herself more than him, "I have to manage it if I want to see what's up there, and I do!"

She found it easier to crawl up the hollowed-out steps on her hands and knees, keeping her eyes firmly on a fixed spot in front of her. Behind her, she could hear Tariq's heavy breathing as he kept pace with her, vying with the sound of the lamp as he pushed it up a step at a time ahead of him.

Then, suddenly, they were almost at the top and she saw that the shaft opened up into a large chamber. Forgetting her fears and the discomfort of her position, Victoria reached back and grabbed the lamp, setting it down on the floor just above her. The room was crowded with objects of every kind, lying scattered around where the rough hands had thrown them while seeking for other things of greater value.

"It's fantastic!" She pulled herself up the last few feet and into the chamber. It was large and solid, the walls covered with hieroglyphs from top to bottom. "Tariq, where can we be?"

He joined her in the chamber, his face white and tense with excitement. If she was thrilled by their discovery, she thought, how much more must it mean to him with his innate love of Egypt's history and the years he had spent learning about it.

"It could be important, couldn't it?" she said.

"Could be."

She recognized the true expert's reluctance to commit himself until he had sifted through every particle of evidence. It was always the same, she thought. They would be as dogmatic as they liked on any other subject, but when it came to their own discipline, they would buttress themselves with ifs and buts as if they feared a single wrong surmise would bring the whole edifice down around their ears.

She wandered off by herself, leaving him to decipher some of the texts in an effort to discover something about the chamber in which they found themselves. She knew better than to touch any of the articles that were strewn across the floor, but nevertheless they were more interesting to her than any number of hieroglyphs. She found a small wooden statue, the paint still clinging to it, and bent down to look at it closer still. She thought it must have been a child's toy, and wondered who could have played with it and what it was doing in someone's tomb.

On the far wall were pictured rows and rows of serving girls, each carrying some article of food. Victoria amused herself by looking at their different expressions, and was surprised, though she admitted she should have known better, by the detail in which the artist had recorded their expressions and actions. Even their hairstyles were varied, depending on whether they wore wigs or their own hair, and whether they had short curly locks, or long straight hair that fell right down to their waists.

"Who are all these women?" she asked.

Tariq came across to her. "The hope was that they would serve the great man in the next world. In very ancient times, his servants would have been buried in person alongside him, to serve him in death as they had served him in life. Look, here was his huntsman, and here a farmer, who probably worked on his estate, bringing the cows home to be milked. By the time this tomb was built, the custom of such wholesale slaughter had fallen into disfavor for obvious reasons, and so they substituted pictorial images for the real thing, which to their mind would have worked equally well. Even today, making a pictorial representation of a living thing is frowned upon by devout Muslims and Jews."

"Much the same idea as making a statue of the dead man for his soul, or *ka*, to return to if anything happened to his body?" Victoria hazarded.

"Right. It's thought that's why so much of Egyptian art is a bit peculiar from the point of view of perspective. They had to show the whole eye, even when the face was in profile, to make sure that the person would be able to see. And both shoulders, so that he could carry as much in death as in life."

"I thought they didn't know about perspective," Victoria said.

Tariq twisted his lips into a wry smile. "No, they knew the principles well enough. There are plenty of chalk drawings, done for fun, that have been found in all sorts of places, and they are as naturalistic as the most modern drawings."

She was intrigued by this and went on looking at the painted figures, amused by the distraught face of one of the cows whose calf was being carried by a man a few feet ahead of her. Victoria didn't notice Tariq move away from her, making his way to the most distant corner of the chamber, and she nearly jumped out of her skin when he made a sudden hissing noise between his teeth.

"I suppose this is how Jim Kerr comes in and out," he remarked in such casual tones that it was a moment or so before she took in what he was saying.

"Where? Let me see!" She rushed over to where he was standing. He pushed at a slab of granite with the palm of his hand and it swung upward, allowing him to pass through to the other side before it slid back into its former position. "Tariq!" she screamed. "Come back!"

He did so immediately, smiling at her. "It goes straight into the burial chamber of your father's *mastaba*, cutting off the corner, just as you said it would."

"And you believe me now? About Jim Kerr?"

"Yes, I think I do," he said. He put a hand up to his head and brushed the dust out of his hair, still smiling. "No wonder he acquired such a dirty image. The tunnel on the other side is falling in places, most of it on the top of my head!"

He pushed the stone into the open position again, changed his mind, and let it swing shut again. "I'm sorry, Victoria, but you realize that I'm going to have to call in the police to deal with this?"

She nodded, blissfully unconcerned, "Has much been taken?"

"It's impossible to tell. Do you want to look into the sarcophagus to see if the mummy's intact?"

She wasn't sure that she did. It was impertinence to intrude into the privacy of the dead occupant, even if he had been dead for a very, very long time. "Won't he crumble or something, if we let the air in?" she objected almost hopefully.

"Somebody has already done that, by the look of

things," he observed. "Still, you don't have to look if you don't want to."

But in the end she couldn't resist. She was shocked to see how little was left of the mortal remains of the mummified body inside. A few wisps of grizzled hair, flesh that looked more like strips of leather, and a great many dirty bandages that had been ripped apart by greedy fingers looking for jewels amongst the folds.

"There's not much left, is there?" she commented, tears in her eyes.

"My dear girl," said Tariq, "he's been dead too long for you to mourn him now. Your crying over him isn't going to help him."

"Perhaps he's a she," she said.

"More likely a man, and an important nobleman at that. But we'll find out as soon as we find the *serdab*—"

"The what?"

"A hidden, yet open, place, built to protect the statue that was to substitute for the body, allowing the *ka* to come and go and be sure of somewhere familiar to return to. Usually it was bricked up, with no more than a couple of holes cut in the wall, allowing the statue to see out and the smell of the incense to greet the nostrils of the dead man. We'll come back and look for it some other time. We ought to be getting back to Abdul."

He pushed open the granite slab again and held it open while she slid past him into the burial chamber of the *mastaba* beyond.

"How are we going to get out of here?" she wondered. "The entrance is still blocked on the other side."

He held up the lamp by way of answer and she saw another crumbling passageway that went straight into one of the corridors that had already been cleared of sand. It was the easiest thing in the world to walk through it, and in a few seconds they found themselves back in the original courtyard of her father's *mastaba*.

Abdul, leaning sleepily against his camel, gave a yell of horror at the sight of them. His relief when he saw who they were brought a flood of Arabic to his lips. "*Bismillah el rahman el rahin!* But you are both safe! I thought you were *djinns* come to frighten me away! Where have you been, *yâ sétt*? The dust! I will run and put the water on to heat for your bath. You will want to wash yourself—your hair, clothes, everything!"

Looking at her Tariq smiled. "Good idea!" he said. "It will give you something to do while I get in touch with the police. I'll have a quick wash myself before I go, in case they mistake me for Kerr!"

Victoria took a deep breath. "Why don't you go after lunch?" she suggested, refusing to meet the mockery in his eyes.

He put out a hand and brushed some of the dust out of her hair. "What a good idea!" he said.

FOR VICTORIA the afternoon passed slowly. She had enjoyed her lunch alone with Tariq. Abdul, sensing an occasion, had chosen not to make any of the European dishes he had learned with such care. He had rushed down to his village and had come back with his wife, carrying so much food in her spindly arms that Victoria had rushed to help her, but Abdul would have none of it. "Leave her alone, *yâ sétt*. She will only drop something or forget what she has brought, if you take her mind off her work." He smiled shyly at her. "You will need the time to make yourself beautiful for your husband. Leave it to my wife to make the meal for you both."

Victoria had not needed his eyes sliding over her filthy appearance twice. She had made the most of the tin bathtub Abdul had brought to her tent, filling it with hot water already perfumed with bath oil, though where that little luxury had come from, Victoria preferred not to inquire. She wanted badly to take down the curtain Tariq had put up between their beds. She looked at it for a long, long time but in the end she hadn't the courage, and she contented herself with giving it a vicious tug as she went from one part of the tent to the other.

After her bath, she had put on a dress and had brushed her newly-washed hair until is shone. She had left it flying free, ostensibly so that it would finish drying in the sun, but really because she thought it made her look more feminine and prettier than when she tied it back. She had been rewarded, too, by the look Tariq had given her when she had joined him at the table. She didn't believe that he had ever looked at Juliette with quite that light in his eyes.

Abdul had served them with his wife's *atayefs*, a kind of cheese pancake that was rolled and fried in oil; followed by *falafels*, little vegetable balls made of chopped beans and onions spiced with salt, pepper and pimentos; together with *bamiyah*, a kind of vegetable served with a tomato sauce. To go with the food, Abdul had opened a bottle of wine and, when they had finished eating, had served them tiny cups of very strong coffee, enjoying their pleasure almost as much as his wife did. Her shy giggles could be heard from the kitchen every time Abdul went in there to tell her how much her cooking was being appreciated.

But after lunch Tariq had gone off immediately, without even bothering to ask what Victoria was going to do with herself all afternoon. She had been strongly tempted to go back to the *mastaba* and take another look around the sad, beautiful tomb that she and Tariq had discovered that morning, but the thought of Tariq's reactions to her doing so deterred her. Instead, she had offered to accompany Abdul's wife back to the village, planning to take a quick look at the ruined Monastery of St. Jeremias on the way.

The Egyptian woman walked ahead of her, her hips swaying as she balanced her pots and pans on her head, leaving her hands free to carry the remains of the vegetables and the other things she had brought with her. From behind she looked like a pretty woman. It was only when one saw the pockmarked skin of her face and the marked squint in her eyes that one realized that poverty could leave a physical mark on the sufferer that no later affluence could ever remove. They had no language in common, but the silence between them was far from being oppressive. Abdul's wife pointed out a nesting heron and a flock of green-backed swallows that dipped over the irrigation channels in their constant search for food. When they came to a pathway that climbed up the hill away from the Causeway of Unas, she made gestures to Victoria that that was where she should go, and with a last fleeting smile, she quickened her footsteps and hurried away into the distance.

The monastery itself was rather disappointing. It had been built in the second half of the fifth century, and had been destroyed by the conquering Arabs around 960. At the beginning of this century it had been cleared of sand and the best carvings and paintings had been removed to the Coptic Museum in Cairo. Now the sand had returned, half burying the few columns and the remaining traces of what had once been an important church.

Victoria retraced her steps back to the causeway, up which the heavy stones had been dragged from the edge of the Nile, along which they had been floated in barges from the quarries, to be heaved into place to form the Pyramid of Unas. Most of the work had been done at the time of the inundation, a season that had infallibly started on the seventeenth day of July, which the Ancient Egyptians had counted as the first day of their year. During the time that the waters from the river had covered the fertile soil of the valley, work on the land had been impossible, and it had been the best time to find the laborers to float the heavy stones down the river and haul them into their final resting place in the pyramid of the Pharaoh.

Looking to the southwest of the Step Pyramid, to where their camp was situated, she could see that Tariq was back and she began to run, wanting to be with him and wanting to know what the police had said, too, and if they would be coming to visit the site themselves, perhaps even to arrest Jim Kerr that very day.

She went straight to the communal tent, bursting her way into it. "What's happening?" she demanded.

Tariq rose to his feet, frowning. "Gently," he warned her. He turned her around and gave her a gentle push in the direction she had come. "We are talking just now. Come back later and serve our tea, will you? Your presence will be more acceptable then."

Shocked at first, she later remembered that the visiting men would be embarrassed and inhibited if they were expected to talk freely in front of a woman. Because they treated Tariq as one of themselves, they would expect his wife to behave according to their customs, too. If she insisted on staying and taking part in their discussions, she would lose their respect and, more important to her, so would Tariq. She went without another word, holding her head high, but there was no way of telling if Tariq was appreciative or not. He sat down again and went straight on with what he had been saying, ignoring the interruption as if it had never happened.

Back in her own tent, she felt even more bored and restless. Finally, she took herself to task for her stupidity and settled down to write a long overdue letter to her mother. She refrained from mentioning the trouble at the dig, concentrating instead on the sights she had seen since coming to Egypt. The fact that Tariq's name cropped up in every paragraph, and practically every other sentence, only occurred to her after she had finished the long account of her activities, and by then it was too late to change what she had written.

She was sealing the envelope when Tariq came into the tent. He stood for a long moment looking down at her, the separating curtain in his hand.

"I thought you were coming back to have tea with us," he said.

"I didn't know when you would be finished talking," she returned, determined not to let him see that she had minded his dismissal of her from the communal tent.

He let the curtain fall. "Do you want to know what they said?"

"If you want to tell me." She was dismayed to hear herself launching into an apology. "I didn't mean to embarrass you," she said. "I'd forgotten they wouldn't want a woman there."

"We're not dealing with the sophisticated citizens of Cairo here," he agreed. "You made quite an impression, nevertheless. They told me they thought you beautiful and that I was a lucky fellow to be married to you!"

"Have they gone?" she said sighing.

"They'll be back tomorrow. We're going to lay a trap for our friend Jim Kerr." He shrugged his shoulders as if he were sloughing off a burden that had been weighing him down too long. "I'll be glad to be done with it all."

"I suppose I shall have to stay out of the way?" Victoria inquired.

"I wish I thought you would!"

She averted her face. "I will, if you say I must, but it was my idea—"

He sat down on the edge of her bed, smiling at her rebellious expression. "I didn't think you'd think it fair. I told the police as much, pointing out that English women don't like being kept in the background."

That brought her head around sharply to look at him. "But I don't want them to think less of you because of me!"

The look in his eyes made a sudden spurt of warm happiness flood through her. "They won't do that," he said certainly. "Even Abdul has nothing but good to say of you."

She was absurdly pleased by his praise. "I suppose you've discussed me with him? Men! How you all hang together!"

"And women don't, I suppose?" he retorted.

She lay back against the pillows, her eyes shut. "What have you decided to do? How are you going to catch Jim Kerr?"

"The police are going to wait for him in the shaft

that we went up this morning. They agree it would be better to catch him in the act because he could quite easily pretend that he had only just come across the tomb himself, and, after what he tried to do to you, he's not going to get away with that!"

There was no escaping his meaning. Victoria wished for the umpteenth time that her father had been less vindictive where Tariq was concerned. "Was it very bad being kicked off the site?" she asked him.

"Bad enough! Largely because it was my own silly fault!"

"But the department believed in you?"

He stood up, going through the curtain to his own side of the tent. "Yes, they did. Largely because Omm Beshir made me go and see them the very next day. It was one hell of an interview and I began to think I never wanted to have anything to do with Egypt again. But then they told me that the thieving was still going on, despite your father's conviction that I was behind it all. I thought I might as well wait it out and see what happened. Then George died, and I was worried about Juliette, but she wasn't interested in me any longer."

Victoria opened her eyes wide. "Some other man?" she asked.

"Not a man, no!" His voice sounded bitter, as though the memory still had the power to hurt him, *Damn Juliette*! "What she wanted was your father's prestige and money without any strings attached. But he thwarted her ambitions nicely by introducing you to the game!" He appeared around the curtain, looking very handsome in a suit and with his hair slicked down against his head. "That was the best thing he ever did!"

"I'm glad you think so," she said, nettled by his tone. "What do you want me to do tomorrow?"

"Will you find Jim Kerr and tell him that digging is going to begin again the next day? I want him to think that I told you in confidence and that you've let it slip out by accident. It's important he should think that no one else knows. Can you do that?"

"Yes," she said.

"Shall I mail your letter for you?" He picked up the envelope and read the address on it. "Your mother?"

She nodded, thinking how much the rather stylish cut of his trousers suited him. "Where are you going?" she asked.

"I'm taking Juliette to dinner. That young lady has a great many questions to answer!"

Victoria sat up, crossing her legs in front of her. Jealousy twisted like a knife within her. Whenever she felt she was getting close to Tariq, Juliette was always there between them. Victoria didn't believe that the French girl would turn Tariq down if he wanted to resume their affair, either.

"Take me with you, too!" she begged him.

He didn't move a muscle. "Not tonight," he said. "I have to see Juliette alone. I want answers, and she won't give them to me with you there."

Victoria turned her back on him, hiding the tears that had flooded into her eyes. "I hope you enjoy yourself!" she said coldly.

"I always try to do that. Sleep well, *habibi*, and don't wait up for me. I'll try not to be late."

But he would be, she thought. Juliette would see to that!

CHAPTER TWELVE

THE URGENCY of the hand on her shoulder started her into wakefulness.

"What is it?" she whispered. She turned over and saw that it was Tariq. There was no mistaking the stocky strength of him, even in the darkness, and her heart leaped within her. "What do you want?"

He cupped her face in her hands. "Victoria, wake up!"

"I am awake!" She retreated a little down into the bedclothes. "What have you done with Juliette?" she asked him nastily, and was immediately ashamed of herself.

He gave her a playful slap. "You sound jealous," he said. "Are you?"

She took a deep breath, preparing to defend herself but at the last moment she couldn't pretend to him, or to herself, any longer. "Yes, " she admitted. She stared at him through the darkness. "What do you want?" she asked again, suddenly breathless.

He stroked her cheek, leaning a little closer to her. "You smell of lotus blossom," he said. "I like it!"

"Abdul put some essence in my bath and I wore some of Omm Beshir's perfume at lunchtime, but I thought it would have worn off by now. You didn't notice it then!"

"I didn't say anything then," he corrected her, "but I noticed all right. I notice almost everything about you." He balanced himself on the edge of her bed. "I woke you up to tell you about Juliette."

"I don't want to hear!"

"Victoria, you have to hear about it. It concerns you, and I don't want you to find out about it from anyone else."

She felt as though he had struck her. She was cold from head to foot, and she knew that the bottom had finally fallen out of her world. "Wouldn't the morning do?" she managed to ask.

"No, it won't!"

She huddled under the blankets, pushing him away from her. "I won't listen!" she defied him, very close to tears.

"Oh yes, you will!" He scooped her up into a sitting position just as if she had been a recalcitrant child. Her shocked gasp drew no more than a mirthless laugh from him. "Victoria, don't be silly, love! Is it likely I'd wake you up in the middle of the night to tell you I'd stolen a kiss from Juliette? If I had, you'd be the last person I'd want to know about it! Now will you listen?"

"I suppose so." She turned her head away to hide her tears. "Why wouldn't you want me to know?"

"That would be telling," he drawled. "But I did tell you that you had no need to worry where that young woman is concerned."

"Yes, but you also told me that she wasn't in love with you—and she is, as much as she's in love with anyone!"

"Which isn't very much." He pulled the scarab he had given her from under the neck of her nightgown and began to play with it. "She told me you'd guessed her husband had treated her pretty badly. Can't you see that she doesn't want to be hurt again? Nobody, but nobody, is allowed that close to Juliette Mercer. Not even your father!"

Victoria sniffed. "Not even you?"

"I was there, *habibi*, and the nights can be cold in the desert. It was no more than that!"

At his words she stopped shivering inside, and managed a rather watery smile. "You didn't have to tell me," she began. "I mean, you're free—"

"Even a *sharei* court wedding gives you some rights. Are you going to listen now?"

"Yes." She nodded. "Tariq, I didn't mean to pry. I know Juliette is a friend of yours and you have a perfect right to see her, only it wasn't much fun here by myself with only Jim Kerr there for dinner. I spent the whole afternoon on my own, too—"

"And you wanted to be with me?"

She put a hand up to the scarab. "It was fun finding the other tomb—and everything, wasn't it?"

"I thought so." He flicked her nose with his fingers, smiling at her. "I don't think Juliette enjoyed her dinner much, either, if that's any comfort to you. She didn't much care for my brand of questions." He took her hand in his, curling his strong fingers into her palm. "You see, when I left the site there was no way into that burial chamber or I would have known about it. Maybe they found it soon after I'd left, or maybe after your father had died, but Jim Kerr couldn't have been the only one to know about it. He couldn't have kept that kind of knowledge to himself! We'll never know if George knew, though I suspect he didn't. Goodness knows, he made enough fuss about the things that were disappearing as it was, and he's never been known as anything but honest. Everybody who's ever worked with him says the same. That left Juliette, and she had to have known! She spent weeks here without much to do, and it wasn't likely that she never went into the *mastaba* in all that time, if only to look around. And of course she had!"

Victoria pulled at her hand "Did you warn her?"

"I suggested that she take the first available flight out of Egypt." He tickled her palm with his forefinger. "It wasn't for old times' sake, at least not entirely, but I wouldn't like to think of any woman languishing for long in the prisons here, and that would probably have been her fate if she hadn't gone."

"Oh, no!" Victoria exclaimed. "How horrible! Poor Juliette," she added softly.

"I hoped you'd feel that way about it—"

"Yes, well, I quite like Juliette as a matter of fact," she cut him off. "I don't believe she'd do anything very dreadful."

"She certainly wouldn't admit that she had had anything to do with ransacking either tomb. She said that everything of value had been taken centuries ago as far as she knew, and that she would hardly be flat broke if she'd been selling odd pieces on the black market. I believe her about that. But she knew what Jim Kerr was up to all right. Apparently he made it his business to find out about her husband, discovered he was in a psychiatric institution, and accused Juliette of putting him there to get rid of him. That was near enough to the truth to hurt, especially as she had never bothered to get a divorce from him and she thought that if George found out he'd have had nothing more to do with her. Your father could be as rigid as the next man about some things, and after he had sent me packing, she was even more afraid that she would be thrown out after me, and she wasn't at all sure that I'd want to take her in. We both knew it had been over between us long before I went."

Victoria made a little sound of sympathy. She felt as sorry for Juliette then as she had felt for herself earlier. "What will she do?" she asked.

"She's going to South America. She had an invitation to join an excavation there some time ago and now she thinks she'll take it up. The snag was they wanted her to put some money into the venture—quite a lot of money." He was silent for so long that Victoria began to think he wasn't going to tell her the rest.

"And?" she prompted him.

"And so I gave her your father's money. Every last cent of it. I gave her a letter to take to your lawyers before she caught her plane." He rubbed the side of his nose and she had a vivid picture of what he must have been like as a small boy. "It seemed the only thing to do. Your father had meant her to have it in the end, and it didn't mean much to you."

Victoria swallowed. "Will they accept your letter?"

"Why not? When you married me, you gave me control of all your possessions according to Egyptian law." He smiled in the darkness. "You gave me all sorts of rights—"

Victoria lay back against the pillow, beginning to enjoy herself. "It hasn't made much difference to me," she complained. "Why don't you show me?"

His arms slipped around her. "Are you angry with me for giving it all to Juliette?"

She put a hand up behind his neck. "Of course not," she whispered. "I don't want to think of Juliette in prison any more than you do. I hope she likes South America very much, and stays there for a long, long time!"

And then his mouth found hers and his kisses, gentle at first, deepened into a vortex of feeling that took her by storm. It was, as she had always known it would be, sheer delight to be loved by Tariq. She abandoned herself completely to his embrace with a sigh of relief. She had no doubts that he wanted her now as much as she wanted him.

"I'm glad I married you," she said.

He sat up, almost throwing her away from him. "That wretched marriage! I wish it were over and done with!" He put a hand on either side of her head, leaning up on his elbows, and kissed her again with a desperation that was echoed in her own response.

"Victoria Lyle, I divorce you for the first time!"

And he kissed her again, his lips warm against hers, while she clung to him, hating him for what he had said, but quite unable to resist the surge of passion that swept through her. But this time when he pushed her away, she knew she had lost, and the knowledge was like a bitter taste in her mouth. He stood for a moment looking down at her, and then he was gone, and the slight movements of the curtain between the two sides of the tent was all that was left to her of his visit.

In the morning he was still asleep when she dressed and went in search of Jim Kerr. She peered around the curtain at him, knowing that his sleep had been as restless as her own. His blankets lay strewn across the floor and she picked them up and tucked them in around him with loving care.

"Divorce me, would you?" she muttered to his sleeping form. "Well, you needn't think you're going to get rid of me so easily. Now that I haven't any visible means of support, I'll build a willow cabin at your gate, *yâ habipi*, and sit it out until I haunt your heart, sleeping and waking, and what will you do then?"

His lips twitched and for a horrified instant she thought he was awake, but he only mumbled and turned in his sleep, and dropping a light kiss on the top of his head, she left him.

She ran into Jim almost at once. He leered at her with heavy humor, patting the sand beside him in an invitation for her to sit down.

"I see the sunrise still has the power to bring you away from the marriage bed," he said. "Or is it that you are still engaged in spying on all your father's old colleagues? What made you decide it wasn't Fletcher, my dear? His *beaux yeux*? Very much in love with him, aren't you? But is he with you? That's the question, isn't it? Didn't I see him departing for dinner in Cairo with our Juliette last night? That must have been a nasty blow to your pride!"

Victoria bit back an icy comment. Her thespian talents were limited and he was no fool, though he might want everyone to think him one.

"My marriage was a business arrangement," she told him. "Only Tariq could get the license to continue from the department, and the only way he could get his hands on my father's money was to marry me." She looked up at him and smiled. "I shouldn't really tell you this, but you have to know soon anyway. Only don't tell Tariq I told you, because he'd be furious with me. He wants to tell Juliette first—you know how it is between them—"

He caught her by the arm and shook her. "They're starting work again soon? Is that what you're trying to tell me?"

She kicked him hard on the shin, forgetting her role in her fury at his handling of her. "I'm not trying to tell you anything! Let me go at once!"

He put a hand over her mouth. "You'll wake your sleeping lord!" he said nastily. "And that would never do, would it? He has a nasty, possessive nature, that husband of yours. He may not want you himself, but heaven help you if he found you in the arms of another man! Now, tell me quickly! When are they starting work again?"

He lifted his hand to allow her to reply and she kicked out at him again. "Why does it matter to you?" she bit out at him.

"I work here, or hadn't you noticed?" he hissed in her ear.

"Tomorrow! They're starting tomorrow!" she spat out. "Tariq is getting the license today. It's all arranged." Her dislike of him was like a bad smell in her nostrils, and then she thought that this was literally true, she could smell something! Her eyes widened with the recollection of where she had smelled that particular smell before. "It was you who pushed me!" she accused him. "But why?"

Jim Kerr let her go, laughing at her. "You'll never prove that, Miss Victoria Lyle. Who would ever believe it? Are you coming to breakfast? I feel particularly hungry now that I've met you, and I think I'll break my rule and eat breakfast with the rest of you. Care to come along and pour my coffee?"

The prospect gave her no pleasure but she wanted her own breakfast, and so she went with him. Abdul greeted her with disapproval. It was obvious he thought she should have waited for Tariq and not pleased herself when she came for her meals. In his own way, she reflected, Abdul was a born romantic!

"How beautiful your camel is looking," she said, hoping to appease him. She nodded her head toward the new covers on the saddle and the brightly colored flag that decorated the rear of the wooden frame that fitted over the animal's hump.

"The Sidi Tariq is riding her this afternoon." He gave her a look that told her he thought it served her right. "He is going into the desert to be alone, away from the chatter of women, and the troubles we have had here!"

Victoria's determination stiffened. She eyed the camel thoughtfully, and nearly died at the thought of being perched up there on the saddle, with her feet at the same level as a man's head.

"I'm going with him," she breathed. "Order me a camel too, Abdul."

"But, *yâ sêtt*, what if the Sidi doesn't wish to take you with him?"

"I'm going, and that's that!" she declared.

The Egyptian shrugged. "I will find another camel for you," he agreed reluctantly. "*Insh'allah*, if Allah wills it." It was obvious that he meant if Tariq willed it, too, and Victoria knew that there would be no camel waiting for her unless Tariq himself ordered Abdul to find her one.

After breakfast, Jim Kerr made no secret of the fact that he was going over to the *mastaba*. Victoria's spirits took a dive as she watched him walk across the sand toward the tomb. It was too early for him to go there! The police couldn't possibly be in position yet. There was no sign of anyone, not so much as a car—and Tariq was still asleep in his bed!

She tore across to the tent she shared with him and found it empty. Perhaps it was not too early after all. She made their two beds, mechanically pushing the bedclothes into place as quickly as she could. When she came out of the tent again, she saw Tariq coming across to her, and waited for him with a nonchalant air.

His face relaxed into a smile as he came up to her. "You did a good job," he congratulated her. "I heard most of it through the canvas."

"I thought you were asleep," she said demurely.

His smile widened. "Oh no! I wouldn't have

missed seeing you kick him in the shins for anything!"

What else had he heard? she wondered. "It was he who pushed me in Unas's Pyramid," she remembered, incensed all over again. "He admitted it!"

"All the more reason for you to keep a low profile this morning," he warned her. "I have your promise about that, haven't I, Victoria?"

"Yes, you have," she agreed. "I don't want to get in the way of justice catching up with Jim Kerr. Not only for me, but for my father too!"

Tariq touched her face. "I have an interest in seeing him nailed myself," he told her. "He won't ever touch you again, I promise you that. Don't fret, love!"

But of course that was easier said than done. She took up her post by the communal tent, trying to see what was happening, but more than an hour later, nothing had happened at all. Later still, a police van drew up, and Tariq came out to greet the occupants, but that was absolutely all.

Disappointed, Victoria turned her attention to Abdul's camel, trying to make the beast look smaller in her mind's eye. The camel turned and stared back at her, chewing its cud, its extraordinary lip protruding in first one direction and then the other, insolently defying her to talk herself into finding the courage to get up on its back.

Then she heard her name being yelled across the sand and she was up and away, running toward the *mastaba* as fast as she could go, her heart pounding in her ears. She had almost reached it when the police emerged, half-carrying Jim Kerr between them, his torn shirt flapping against his ribs. Victoria ignored them, one and all, and ran straight into Tariq's open arms.

"Oh, Tariq," she cried out, "is it all over?"

He kissed her lips. "They caught him red-handed." He ruffled her hair with his hand. "I wish your father could have known."

She kissed him back, smiling. "Perhaps he does know," she said.

VICTORIA EYED Abdul's camel with dislike. She planned to be already mounted when Tariq came out of the communal tent. Feeling slightly sick, she grasped the wooden pommel of the saddle and eased her leg over the camel's back, taking a last, desperate leap into the air to get properly astride. Long before she was ready for it, the camel lurched backwards, came to her knees, and practically flung Victoria over her head as she straightened out her back legs. Another uneasy lurch and she was up. Victoria shut her eyes tightly against the receding ground and hung on for dear life, petrified that the camel might move and she wouldn't be able to stop it.

"Where are you going?" Tariq asked her.

She opened her eyes briefly and shut them again. "With you!" she informed him through clenched teeth.

The camel began to lower herself to her knees again, and Victoria gave a gasp of terror. "*Do something!*" she shrieked at Tariq.

His hands clasped her around the waist, steadying her for the next lurch. "Move up a bit, my sweet. I'm coming up behind you!"

"There isn't room!" she protested.

"Of course there is." His voice was warm and soothing. "There now, isn't that better?"

With his arm holding her tightly against him, she thought perhaps it was, but she had no breath to talk and she was still trembling with fright.

"I told you you'd enjoy it if you were with me," Tariq mocked her, as the camel lurched to her feet again. "Relax, darling, I won't let you fall." He settled his arm more comfortably around her. "Try to feel the rhythm and then you might even open your eyes and see how lovely the desert is!" He chuckled. "You must be feeling brave enough for anything if you would dare to get on a camel!'"

She opened her eyes at last and even dared to relax her hold on the wooden pommel in front of her. "I didn't want to be left behind again," she confessed. She leaned back against him and sighed heavily. "I don't want to be divorced, either," she said under her breath.

She crossed her feet in front of the saddle as she had seen the Egyptians do, and felt very daring. The rocking movement of the camel was better than she had expected and the silence all around them enveloped her in a sense of peace that soothed her ruffled spirits.

He buried his face in her hair, kissing the nape of her neck. "I thought you understood," he said thickly. "I didn't want to hurry you into something you may regret. You have to be free of this legal entanglement before I can woo you as you deserve to be wooed. I want to give you the best, *habibi.* Go home to your mother for three months and give yourself time to be sure that you want to tie yourself up to someone like me."

She sat very still. Three months without him would be an eternity.

"I don't want time," she said. "I want you!"

"I want you, too! But this is different, Victoria. I want you as my wife, not as I've wanted other women. I owe it to you to let you see me in your home surroundings, with your mother there to advise you, and let you make up your mind calmly, without any physical pressures on you. Because there will be no going back once we're married. If you marry me, you'll go where I go, sharing my work, my bed, my whole life! Suppose you're more like your mother than you think and find you want to live in England after all?"

She turned to look at him and very nearly lost her balance. She clutched at his shirt, and felt his heart thumping quite as wildly as her own was against his hand.

"Tariq, don't you know yet that I love you? I loved you yesterday, and I love you today, and I'll love you just as much tomorrow. There'll never be anyone else for me. There never could be!"

His hand tightened against her. "You didn't like it when I took Juliette out last night," he reminded her.

"No," she smiled, putting her hand on his. Omm Beshir was right after all, she thought. Juliette didn't matter, had never mattered, and nor would anyone else like her ever matter. "I'm sorry, I didn't understand," she added. "I should have known you wanted your freedom to have as many Juliettes as you like. But I won't tie you down, *habipi*. All I want is for you to come back to me when you've had enough of the particular Juliette of the moment. I love *you*, as you are, not as you might try to change yourself to please me!"

She felt his anger and was glad of it. "Victoria, if I thought you were serious—" He barked out a harsh command to the camel that brought it to a halt and then, protesting, to its knees. "I want to see more of you than your back while we continue this discussion, *yâ sétt*!" He lifted her out of the saddle and deposited her none too gently on the side of a sand dune, sitting down beside her, his face flushed with temper. "I don't want a complacent wife, my girl, and I won't have you—oh, Victoria!" he groaned. "I love you, too—far too much to want anyone else!"

"Then why do I have to go back to England?" she opened her eyes very wide, presenting him with an innocent face. "If it isn't women you want, is it because you want to have all the fun of finishing my father's excavation by yourself? And *my* tomb, too, I daresay!" A thought struck her and her pose fell away from her. "What are you going to do without my father's money?" she demanded.

"The department has offered to pay—"

Her navy blue eyes met his accusingly "Tariq, you couldn't send me to England while you dug out *my* tomb?"

His face creased into a smile. "No, I'm beginning to think I can't, so you needn't go on about my women any longer." There was a gleam of amusement in his eyes. "Someone should have told you that reformed playboys make the strictest husbands," he went on sternly. He touched her rosy face with a thoughtful finger. "Are you absolutely sure, my love?"

"I was quite sure when I first saw you beside the Virgin's Tree," she said simply.

"I know. You were like a little shy, unbroken filly, wondering if you were going to take to the bridle."

She was shocked that he had read her first reaction to him so accurately. But then why should she be surprised? His knowledge of women was probably much greater than even she had guessed.

"I liked the way you use your hands when you talk, and your falcon's eyes that made me feel like a mouse you'd picked out for breakfast. I *can't* wait three months for you, Tariq!"

He bent over her, kissing her cheek, her eyes, and then finally her mouth, his lips hardening into a passionate demand that took her breath away and sent the wonder of it spinning through her veins. After a few minutes he moved away from her, brushing away some grains of sand that had clung to the back of her hand.

"Three months is far too long," he agreed. "But I mean to marry you first, Victoria. Will you stay with Omm Beshir while I arrange some kind of ceremony for us? Would you object to a Coptic wedding?"

"I'd love it!" she said. "I'll marry you as often as you like! I'd even like to have our marriage blessed by the vicar at home in front of my mother and every one of my friends and acquaintances so that they can see how lucky I am!"

He flushed absurdly. "They might not think so," he murmured.

She laughed. "Oh, Tariq! You know they will!"

"Then you'll go to Omm Beshir?"

She shook her head. "I thought I was legally married to you now," she said. "You've only divorced me once, and that doesn't count, so why do we have to wait? I want to be with you now, darling.

"Fruit I will gather for your delight,
Bread I will break and pour out wine.
I'll bring you the perfumed flow'rs and bright
On this festal day divine."

His eyes lit with love for her. "You must have read the "Sycamore Song" often to be able to recite it?"

"I learned it by heart last night," she told him

with a smile. "While you were with Juliette. It was the only thing of yours I had to hold onto."

"You had more than that! I didn't want to leave you on your own, *habibi*, not then or later. I love you very much!" He reached across and kissed her lightly on the nose. "All right, my darling wife, if you want to bring down the curtain right away, who am I to object to that?"

He sprang to his feet and called the camel to him, helping her to her feet. "Do you care to mount, Mrs. Fletcher, or will you walk?"

Victoria allowed herself to be put up on the saddle and waited for him to climb up behind her, trembling against him as he put his arm around her.

"Love me?" he asked.

She leaned back against him more comfortably, completely unperturbed by anything the camel might do. She had never been more happy in her life.

"Oh, *yes*!" she gasped.

He hugged her more closely to him and began to sing at the top of his voice, with an infectious exuberance that brought a smile to her lips. It was nice to know that he was happy, too.

> Joshua won the battle of Jericho, Jericho, Jericho,
> And the walls came tumbling down!

AUTUMN CONCERTO

Autumn Concerto

Rebecca Stratton

"I think you have the wrong impression of me," Hugo Gerard suggested to Ruth. But she didn't think so. She had read his book and had been fascinated by the life and loves of this handsome Frenchman.

Forewarned in advance, she couldn't see why his reputation should influence her decision to work for him. As a librarian the experience of cataloging his famous collection of old books would be invaluable to her. She was grateful to her friend Jacques for recommending her to his uncle.

But there was nothing avuncular about her employer, Hugo Gerard. Daily contact with him made Ruth realize she was not the levelheaded girl she had considered herself. She was way out of her league in trying to cope with his sophisticated charm.

CHAPTER ONE

FEW BOOK SHOPS IN THE CITY of Oxford looked less impressive than Stoddard's, but few offered a better service to their customers. Stoddard's could be relied upon to supply anything printed from a first edition classic to the latest crime novel—it also had the added attraction of Ruth Colton.

Old Henry Stoddard had not, in the first instance, employed her as an inducement to the student population to visit his shop, but that was the way things had worked out. The only drawback, as far as old Henry was concerned, was that with a girl as pretty as Ruth on his staff, far more young men came into the shop than ever bought books.

He looked across at her now as she sat near the window with the sun beaming in through the ancient pebble glass and turning her dark brown hair to something close to auburn. She had a smooth, heart-shaped face with huge gray eyes and a mouth that was just a little too wide, but smiled readily. She was attractive enough, he allowed, but less of an asset than he had first thought.

Ruth herself was unaware of old Stoddard's scrutiny and his speculation, but she was well aware of Jacques Delange's face peering through the thick pebble glass at her. He lowered one eyelid swiftly in a suggestive wink, then headed for the door, and Ruth awaited his arrival with mixed feelings. Jacques was definitely a distraction and once or twice recently she had noticed Mr. Stoddard giving them discouraging looks.

Jacques came into the shop and straight across to her, as he always did, slipping an arm around her waist with easy familiarity as she got to her feet. There was something quite irresistible about Jacques, although she did her best not to let him know how attractive she found him, for he needed no encouragement.

"Hello, Jacques!" Her greeting was deliberately offhand and she sensed his dislike of it.

She gave him a brief smile, then began sorting out some new stock that had to be put on the shelves, concentrating her whole attention on the job at hand. Inevitably, he disliked being ignored; she often suspected that he was rather spoiled, and he was definitely used to having his own way.

"You do not give me a very warm welcome, *chérie,*" he murmured close to her ear. His hand on her waist squeezed her slimness to him for a moment and she felt the betraying skip her heart gave as she slipped from his hold.

He kept his voice low, but even so Henry Stoddard, in his dim little corner, detected the Gallic lilt in his voice and he frowned his dislike of yet another visit from a young man who was a frequent caller but a far from good customer.

Jacques Delange could be quite devastating, Ruth was only too well aware of it, but she feared for her job if he persisted in coming to see her during working hours. He was not, strictly speaking, good-looking, but he had an air about him that suggested he was the very embodiment of what Englishwomen see as the romantic Frenchman.

His dark brown hair was worn rather long and it curled up over the collar of a velvet jacket, and his deep brown eyes spoke volumes without a word ever being spoken. He was slim and wiry and overwhelmingly self-confident, and she could, Ruth realized, quite easily fall in love with him if she allowed herself to.

"I'm working," she told him, in response to his complaint about her lack of welcome.

"And so you have no time for me!" he said reproachfully.

Ruth smiled, despite herself, but still refused to look at him again, instead she glanced over her shoulder at old Henry Stoddard in his corner. "I haven't time to spend on people who come in here and then don't buy books," she told him. "I have a job to do, Jacques, and apart from Mr. Stoddard not liking you coming in so often and leaving empty-handed, shouldn't you be worrying about your exams?"

He shrugged his shoulders, defiantly ignoring the proprietor's disapproving frown as he seated himself on the edge of the table she was using to sort her books. He covered one of her hands with his own and leaned forward to speak close to her ear, his breath tickling her cheek and starting up the inevitable reaction.

"You are to blame if I do not pass my exams," he told her. "I shall tell *grand-mère* and Hugo it is so!"

Ruth withdrew her hand, her gray eyes meeting his for a moment, mildly indignant. "And I shall deny it," she told him firmly. "In fact, I've half a mind to write to your grandmother and your uncle and tell them how much time you've wasted during the past few weeks!"

"They would not believe you!"

His shrug dismissed any worry in that direction, and yet again Ruth wondered about his family background. He hadn't been very forthcoming on the whole, but she knew he was an orphan and guessed he was wealthy. His education, she gathered, had been decided on and paid for by his grandmother and an uncle who held his money in trust until he decided on a career.

He was the eldest of three children, his twenty-year-old twin sisters being educated in France, and it was not hard to guess that his grandmother doted on him, for he was the only grandson among five grandchildren.

Ruth cast him a resigned look from the corners of her eyes and carried a pile of sorted books across to the shelves. Inevitably Jacques followed her and slid an arm about her waist as she reached up for the top shelf, again drawing a disapproving frown from Henry Stoddard.

"Don't do that!" she told Jacques in an anxious whisper. "At least let me look as if I'm working!" She glanced over her shoulder again at Henry Stoddard, hastily looking away again when she caught his small sharp eyes watching her over the tops of his glasses. "If Mr. Stoddard catches you in here again," she warned, "he'll probably fire me on the spot!"

"What do we care?" Jacques said with a grand air of unconcern and a gesture with his hands that sent the pile of books flying.

Ruth dived swiftly to the rescue, knowing how Henry Stoddard hated to have books mishandled. "*I* care!" she told Jacques in an urgent whisper. "I have my living to earn, Jacques, and I happen to like working among books! You're not making it very easy for me!"

She moved along the shelves, placing books carefully in their right places and moving others to make room for them. No matter how distracted she was, she always managed to do her job properly because she enjoyed it. Attractive as she found Jacques she was not prepared to let him lose her job if she could help it.

"But it does not matter any more, *chérie,*" he told her, and Ruth paused in her task, looking at him curiously.

"What do you mean, it doesn't matter any more?" she asked. "Of course it matters, Jacques!"

"Non, non, ma chérie!" His brown eyes gleamed in the lean dark face and he seemed to glow with excitement as he looked at her. "I have found you another job, Ruth, a much better one than here, and one where I can see you as often as I like!"

"Jacques!" She sat down on the short stepladder just behind her, the rest of the books on her lap, watching him with a certain mistrust. No matter how attractive she found him, there was always, at the back of her mind, a certain wariness. "I wish you'd explain," she said quietly, and for the moment ignored old Stoddard's disapproval as she sat there with a strange sensation of anticipation curling in her stomach suddenly.

Jacques hesitated only briefly, but it was enough to make her suspicious and she wondered what on earth he could have done that sounded so important. Another job, he had said, but it must be more than simply finding another book shop for her to work in.

"You know of my uncle?" he said at last, and Ruth frowned curiously.

"The one who's your guardian?" she asked.

He made a wide, extravagant gesture of dismissal with one hand. "A man of twenty-three years does not require a guardian, *chérie,*" he told her. "Hugo is trustee of my inheritance until I am twenty-five, that is all, also *grand-mère.*" He pulled a wry face.

"Between them they—how is it you say— hold the purse strings!"

"I see." She looked at him questioningly, realizing they had deviated from the subject of his uncle.

"You do not know of my uncle?" he asked, and she shook her head. "You do not know that he is Hugo Gerard?"

Ruth blinked, too stunned for the moment to speak, then she shook her head. "I—I'd no idea," she told him. "You didn't say."

"And you are most impressed, eh?" He smiled somewhat wryly and she thought she realized why he had not mentioned that Hugo Gerard was his uncle. "I gave my uncle your name," he went on. "Hugo needs someone to work for him, to work with his books, and you would serve very well, *ma chérie*."

Ruth said nothing for a moment, it was all a little difficult to grasp and her heart was racing like a wild thing as she considered the idea of working for a man like Hugo Gerard. It was most unlikely he would even consider her for the post, of course, no matter if Jacques had given him her name. There was too much against her, not least that she was no more than a passing acquaintance of his nephew's, although Jacques would have described her as more than that, she had no doubt.

She knew that the books he so casually referred to were, in fact, a very valuable collection of volumes, some of them almost priceless, and the chance to handle them was something she would have given much for. Then there was the man himself, of course; he must be almost as intriguing as his expensive library.

Everyone in the literary world knew of Hugo Gerard, of course, ever since the publication of his book the previous month, a book that had aroused interest and enthusiasm all round the world. It was reputed to be an autobiography, although it was written as a work of fiction, and it recounted the life of an adventurous Frenchman in various parts of the world.

Hugo Gerard had traveled extensively, in the same way his hero did, ready to turn his hand to anything and equally at home digging ditches or gracing some of the most elegant dinner tables in high society. One theme that recurred over and over in the book, and was probably also based on truth, was the absorbing topic of women in love.

The fictional hero had met them, loved them and left them, and Ruth, who had read the English translation, had found the book at once fascinating and intolerant of her sex. It was not difficult to see, reading between the lines, that Hugo Gerard was a man with a very low opinion of the female sex on the whole, despite their fascination for him.

She brought herself back to earth with a shake of her shoulders and smiled wryly at Jacques as she picked up a book and added it to her pile. "It sounds much too pie in the sky for me to take it seriously, Jacques," she told him. "And I'm quite sure Mr. Gerard wouldn't want an *English* girl working for him, I seem to remember that in his book we came very low down on his list of desirables."

"You are wrong," Jacques insisted, taking her hands as best he could for the books she held. "I have told him that you are expert with books, *chérie*, and also—" he leaned toward her until his forehead rested against hers "—I have said how beautiful you are, although I added the caution that you were mine and that he is not to—" An eloquent shrug of his shoulders finished the sentence and brought a swift flush of color to Ruth's cheeks.

"It wasn't necessary to tell him, either," she told him, seeing things getting slightly out of hand and going much too fast for her. "You've probably given your uncle quite the wrong impression, Jacques!"

"How so?" he asked, and she shook her head.

"You know very well how so," she told him, and stood up, holding the books tightly against her as a sort of defense because she was so afraid of letting Jacques persuade her into something she would regret later. "For one thing," she went on as she pushed books into the shelves with much less than her normal care, "he'll almost certainly prefer to employ a French girl for the job, and also I'm not the expert you've made me out to be, as he'd soon discover."

Jacques's brown eyes glowed wickedly and he reached inside his jacket to produce an envelope that he waved triumphantly under her nose. "You are wrong when you think he will not employ you," he told her. "He asks that you go over and see him, that way he can judge for himself how suitable you are."

"Jacques!" She stared at him wide-eyed, the books forgotten again, "I—I don't believe it!"

"It is true," he assured her, smiling at her stunned surprise as if it was what he expected. "We will, of course, pay your fare, and I shall be there myself very soon when the summer vacation begins."

"But—" She sought reasons why she should not go over to France for the interview, why she should simply refuse the offer out of hand and just go on as she was. But there was no reason at all that she could find, and she found herself trembling with excitement at the idea of working for a man like Hugo Gerard, no matter what his reputation was with women. He must be interesting for all sorts of other reasons, if the book was indeed an autobiography.

"You will go?" Jacques pressed, and she nodded almost without thinking, then hastily recalled that she was already employed by Stoddard's, and in the likely event of her not getting the new job she would come back to find herself unemployed.

"No, no, I can't, Jacques!" Her reluctance was evident and she looked at him with a certain wistfulness that betrayed how tempted she was. "I'm—I'm not entitled to a holiday yet," she explained. "And I couldn't simply go off to France for a couple of days when I'm not entitled to it. If I didn't get the job—"

"But you will," Jacques insisted, seeing her weakening.

"Jacques, I—I can't risk it!"

"Then I must force your hand, *ma chérie*!" he murmured, and before she could protest he pulled her suddenly into his arms and held her so close she had no chance of escape before his mouth came down, warm and persuasive, on to hers.

It was a dizzying sensation, being kissed like that, and not at all unpleasant, but the unexpectedness of it took her breath away so that instead of pushing him away, as she would more normally have done in the circumstances, she slid her arms up around his neck and responded in a way that was purely instinctive.

"Miss Colton!"

Ruth brought herself hastily back to earth and blinked for a moment at Mr. Stoddard's red and embarrassed face, his glasses halfway down his nose as he stared at her. She glanced up at Jacques's face and saw his brown eyes glittering darkly in triumph, realizing at last his meaning about forcing her hand. After the response he had induced from her, no one would believe that he had caught her unawares, or that she was an unwilling partner.

She lowered her own arms from Jacques's neck and tried to wriggle free of the hold he still had on her, hastily seeking a reasonable explanation. Mr. Stoddard was very firmly outspoken about the laxity of morals among young people and he would definitely not tolerate such behavior on his own premises. "I'm sorry—I'm very sorry, Mr. Stoddard," she said, wishing her apologies did not sound so ineffectual, or that Jacques looked less pleased with himself.

"I cannot allow such conduct on my premises," the old man told her sternly. "You know my feelings in these matters, Miss Colton, I simply cannot allow it."

"A kiss," Jacques said with a short laugh. "How can you object to one small kiss, *monsieur*? Is it that you have no heart?"

Mr. Stoddard's round plump face flushed, as much with embarrassment as anger, and he looked again at Ruth, his head shaking slowly. "I am disappointed in you, Miss Colton, I had thought you interested in your work here, but lately—" He sighed and shook his head over the decline. "I feel I cannot continue to employ you, much as I regret it."

Ruth felt suddenly quite sad, and she did not look at the old man, but down at her hands, her face half hidden by the thick curtain of her hair as she bowed her head. "I'm very sorry, Mr. Stoddard," she said, and quite genuinely meant it.

The old man looked at Jacques over the top of his glasses and frowned. "As for you, young man," he told him, "I have watched you for some time now. The number of times you have visited my premises have not proved very profitable, for I have seen you make only one purchase. I must ask that you do not come here again."

"Do not fear, *monsieur libraire*," Jacques told him with an impudent grin and a wink at Ruth, "now that you are no longer the employer of Mademoiselle Colton I will have no desire to visit your premises!"

It seemed unduly harsh of him to be so unkind to the old man, Ruth decided, and she looked genuinely regretful as she shook her head. "I can only repeat that I'm sorry it happened, Mr. Stoddard," she said. "I'll be very sorry to go. I've—I've really enjoyed my work here."

For a moment it looked as if Henry Stoddard would offer to take her back, and Ruth was very unsure whether she would have been pleased about it or not. But he was given no chance to say anything, for Jacques was making sure he had his way, and he was smiling at the old man confidently.

"*Mademoiselle* already has another job," he informed him, and the old man looked startled, his eyes fixed questioningly on Ruth.

"Oh, it isn't definite by any means," she hastened to assure him. "But Mr. Delange has spoken to his—his uncle about my possibly working for him in France. Hugo Gerard," she explained when he looked puzzled. "The man who wrote *Life and Truth*."

Henry Stoddard's thin brows rose and he looked from her to Jacques with a look of understanding, as if something was suddenly clear to him. "Ah! Now I see," he said, rubbing his chin with one hand. "I am well aware of the identity of Hugo Gerard, Miss Colton, as I am also aware that the gentleman has something of a . . . reputation. A clever writer, no doubt, but are you sure of what you are doing, Miss Colton? Have you spoken to your stepfather about this?"

Long ago he had known her stepfather, Ruth remembered, and she supposed it made him feel as if he had some kind of obligation to look out for her. It was touching in a way, and she appreciated his concern, but she felt well able to take care of herself, should she be lucky enough to land the job with Hugo Gerard.

"I've only just heard about it myself," she explained with a rather wry smile, and glanced at Jacques. "Mr. Delange has only just broken the news to me."

"Ha! Hence the—" He waved vague hands to express something he found himself unable to put into words, and Ruth nodded.

"That's right," she said. "Of course it isn't settled yet, I have to go across and see Monsieur Gerard—"

"But there is little doubt that you will get it, *chérie,*" Jacques interrupted, and smiled at the old man confidently. "And please do not fear for *mademoiselle*'s reputation, *monsieur*. I will personally take care of her when the summer vacation begins."

Henry Stoddard's misgivings, Ruth thought wryly as she saw herself with little option now but to go, were no more deep than her own. Hugo Gerard might have a reputation for his dealings with women, but she hardly saw his nephew as an ideal guardian for her own reputation.

TWO WEEKS HAD PASSED so quickly that Ruth found it hard to believe that it was so long since old Henry Stoddard had decided to dispense with her services and given her notice. She would have preferred to delay her departure until the summer vacation began and Jacques could have accompanied her, but he had decided that she should go as soon as possible in case his uncle grew impatient and found another girl for the job of cataloging his valuable collection.

It was really quite exciting to be going so far for an interview, and she wondered if it wasn't all some strange dream as the plane landed at Orly Airport and she stepped onto French soil for the first time in her life.

Cleared through customs by a short, plump but appreciative official, she came out of the terminal to be met by an elderly man in chauffeur's uniform who inquired in very broken English if she was Mademoiselle Colton. Admitting as much, she was led to a huge gleaming black Mercedes and ushered in as if she was a visiting celebrity.

Jacques, she felt sure, must have been behind such a grand reception, for even Hugo Gerard would surely not send a chauffeured limousine for an applicant for such a humble post. Not that she had any objection to being cosseted in that way, for she had not been looking forward to traveling on her own on a foreign train.

Her chauffeur spoke little, and she suspected that his English was as limited as her French, but she had no special desire for conversation, and quite enjoyed the journey. She marveled at the prettiness of the rural route and was surprised how quickly they came upon it after the city itself. Paris was somewhere she had always hoped to visit, and she made up her mind to try and make it before she went back, for she was quite expecting to be rejected for the job she was applying for.

The long, dusty country road twisted and turned tortuously through lovely woodland scenery and gave occasional glimpses, through breaks in the trees, of distant views across the deep dark sweep of the forest that covered acres of this part of France, so Jacques had told her.

A château seen only briefly behind its guardian trees reminded her of something in a fairy tale, with its rounded towers soaring above the trees and set in the serene beauty of its own parkland. A winding river, hemmed around with poplars and the sweeping green of willows, looked cool and inviting as she sat in the car, and she found herself smiling, less reluctant suddenly and feeling vaguely pleased with herself.

Then she noticed a metal signpost that named the approaching village as Vallée des Arbres and bit her lip anxiously as she realized they were almost there. The château that was Jacques's home lay a little south of the village, he had told her, and she almost wished they need not have come upon it quite so soon, because all her former misgivings were returning tenfold.

She leaned forward and spoke to the chauffeur, not sure if he would understand her very well or not. "Are we nearly there?" she asked, and sought for the right French words to repeat the question, breathing a sigh of relief when he answered her without a translation.

"Mais oui, mademoiselle!" He gave her a brief but speculative look over his shoulder and his seamed face creased for a moment into a smile, as if he sensed her nervousness. "You are to be the employee of Monsieur Gerard?" he asked, and Ruth laughed uneasily, wondering what was going on in his mind. He had probably given rides to many other young females in his time and was speculating on her true role in his master's household.

"I'm—I'm not sure yet," she said, realizing too

late that she had said nothing to establish herself firmly as a possible member of the staff and not . . . whatever else he had in mind.

"Ah, oui, mademoiselle!" The lined face split into a wide and knowing grin and Ruth felt the color in her cheeks as she hastened to put him right, a bright, determined gleam in her eyes.

"I'm coming here for an interview for the position of—of cataloger," she explained. "Making a list of Monsieur Gerard's collection of books."

"Ah, oui, mademoiselle!" He made the same reply without the suggestive grin this time, but Ruth wondered still if he actually believed her. There were obviously going to be a great many more drawbacks to the job, if she got it, than she had anticipated.

She made no more attempt at conversation but sat back in her seat and once more speculated on the wisdom of having come at all. There were a good many advantages, no doubt, and it was a privilege to have the opportunity of working for a man as well known as Hugo Gerard, but there were obvious disadvantages too and she wondered which would outweigh the other, if she was ever allowed to find out.

Speculation gave way abruptly to another wave of nervousness when the car turned into a long, tree-lined driveway and picked up speed. At the far end, half-concealed by more trees and the broad, stone balustraded elegance of a courtyard, she caught her first glimpse of the castle.

At first it looked very little different from one of the larger châteaux they had passed along the road, and she felt vaguely disappointed. Expecting the same rugged squareness that characterized so many of the old English castles, she was surprised to see this one more smooth and round-looking, with a tall, pointed-roofed tower at each corner and neat flat windows.

Huge square stone erections enclosed the base of neatly aligned, umbrella-shaped trees skirting the courtyard, and a stone staircase led up from the courtyard to the tall wooden door set back under an arched canopy. It looked tremendously impressive and at the sight of it Ruth's heart sank, for she felt sure she would never feel at home in a place as grand as that.

The chauffeur helped her from the car and for a moment looked down at her and smiled, as if he realized how she felt and sympathized. Then he bobbed his head in a brief bow and prepared to leave, but Ruth put a hand on his arm, her eyes wide and uncertain.

"How do—who do I see?" she asked, and he shrugged.

"Madame Rousseau will attend to you, *mademoiselle,*" he told her. "If you ring, she will come."

"I see . . . thank you."

Taking her courage in both hands, Ruth started to climb the stone staircase, her heart thudding heavily in her breast as she neared the tall, impressive doorway, and she started nervously one hand to her mouth when someone spoke from below in the courtyard.

"Bonjour, mademoiselle!"

The voice was quiet and held a note of curiosity. Whether it was cultured or not, she was too inexpert to tell, but judging by his clothes the man was an employee of some kind, so it was unlikely. He was quite tall and had a lean, rangy look, like a man who has spent most of his life in the open air.

He had light brown hair, almost fair, and light gray eyes that were looking at her in a way that brought a flush of resentment to her cheeks as she met their gaze. His features were rugged rather than handsome and they had a strong, confident look that dared her to object to his scrutiny.

"*Bonjour!*" She replied to his greeting simply because she saw him as a possible source of assistance, if he spoke any English, of course. From his looks he must be a gardener or something of the sort, so he probably didn't.

"Can I help you, *mademoiselle*?" The lightly accented voice brought a sigh of relief from her, and she instinctively smiled.

"I was told to see Madame Rousseau," she told him doing her best with the very French-sounding name. "I was about to ring—"

"You are Miss Colton?"

He came up the stone stairs two at a time and she noticed how quick and agile his movements were; he was not at all out of breath when he stood beside her. One hand was thrust into the pocket of some very shabby slacks that nevertheless looked as if they had once been expensively tailored, and were probably castoffs, and a faded, pale blue shirt looked as if it might have come from the same stable.

"I'm Miss Colton," she said, unconsciously putting on a slight air of superiority. "Perhaps you'll tell me where I can find Madame Rousseau, will you?"

He stood looking down at her from his superior height and seemed to be amused about something, for there was a definite glitter in the light gray eyes that she found annoying under the circumstances. She felt nervous enough without being accosted on the doorstep by one of the staff and cross-questioned.

"You must *see* Madame Rousseau?" he asked, and Ruth looked at him uncertainly for a moment.

"I'm—I'm sure that was the name the chauffeur said," she told him. "Isn't it right? I'm afraid I don't even know who she is."

"Madame Rousseau is the housekeeper," he informed her, and walked past her to open the door, standing back to allow her to enter. "But I don't think we need trouble her in the circumstances."

Ruth's head was spinning with confusion and she hung back, declining to follow the invitation of the hand that gestured her inside. "I—I don't know—" she began, and shook her head, at which a deep frown drew his brows together impatiently.

"If you will please come into the hall at least, *mademoiselle*," he requested shortly. "I do not like standing on the doorstep!"

Ruth's cheeks flushed angrily at the temerity of the man and she stuck out her chin as she swept past him into the vast echoing space of a hall—a hall like nothing she had ever seen before with an enormously high ceiling and its walls hung with tapestries that must have been there for centuries past. Its floor was wood, laid in an intricate design of different shades of brown and gold, and it gleamed richly in the sunlight that came in through high slim windows.

A huge staircase swept upward from each side and a long gallery ran along the far end, richly embellished with gilt balustrades. It was easy to realize that one was inside a castle, no matter how disappointing the outside might have been, and she looked around her with undisguised amazement.

"You are impressed, Miss Colton?"

The quiet voice jolted her from her reverie and she looked again at her guide, frowning slightly because he seemed so out of place in such splendid surroundings dressed as he was. A second look, however, gave her second thoughts, and she found herself curious to know who he was. Obviously he was an employee of some kind and yet there was an air about him that denied servility, and an aura of strength and confidence that did not go with those shabby clothes he wore.

"I'm impressed," she told him, still with that slight air of superiority. "But I'm quite sure Monsieur Gerard wouldn't take kindly to my being taken on a conducted tour by one of his staff when I have an appointment with him. If you'll please do something about finding Madame Rousseau for me—"

"I have told you it will not be necessary for you to see Madame Rousseau," he said, so firmly confident that she again frowned and looked at him with the first glimmerings of suspicion stirring uneasily in her.

"But I—" She stopped short when a door opened at the far end of the vast hall and a woman appeared, coming swiftly across toward them, and Ruth sighed her relief. This must surely be Madame Rousseau, judging by her appearance, and at last she would discover who this rather forceful character was.

"Ah! *Monsieur!*" The woman's rather gaunt face relaxed into a hint of smile when she saw him, and she spared no more than a brief, inquiring glance for Ruth, but spoke in such rapid French to the man with her that it was no more than a gabble of sound to Ruth. She advanced no farther into the hall either, but seemed content to leave Ruth in his care.

He replied in the same tongue, then immediately turned to Ruth and smiled, inclining his head as if in apology. "You do not speak French, Miss Colton?" he asked, and she shook her head somewhat dazedly. "Not at all?" He wore a slight frown, as if the knowledge displeased him. "That is a pity," he said.

Ruth was almost sure she knew his identity now, although she found it hard to believe that this shabbily dressed man could be the one she had come so far to see. "*Monsieur,*" she ventured a little breathlessly. "Who—who are you?"

For a moment the light gray eyes looked down at her, and again she caught a glint of amusement in their depths as one brow rose and a hand slid under her elbow, turning her towards one of the many doors that led off the vast hall. "Do you not know who I am?" he asked, and Ruth blinked uncertainly as she looked at him.

First at the strong, confident face whose eyes regarded her so steadily, and then at the shabby old clothes he wore. "I—I'm not sure," she admitted, unwilling to hazard a guess in case she made a fool of herself.

"I am Hugo Gerard, *mademoiselle*," he told her in a quiet, confident voice, and led her, unresisting, across the hall. "And you, I believe, Miss Colton, are one of those people who judge a book by its cover, hmm?"

His obvious amusement did nothing to put her at ease, and again she realized just how rash she had been to think she could cope with working for a man like Hugo Gerard. But it was too late to turn back now—she was committed to an interview at least.

CHAPTER TWO

THE ROOM INTO WHICH Hugo Gerard led her struck Ruth as quite unlike any office she had ever seen before, not that she had been into too many, but they had always been plain and strictly functional. This room was as beautiful in its way as that vast hall she had seen first.

A thick pile carpet in dark green gave the big room a somber but restful air and complemented cream walls that were generously gilded on friezes that ran all around it for about eighteen inches below an ornately molded ceiling.

A few somber portraits occupied wall space and a big dark rosewood desk shone richly in the sun from partially shaded high windows at the far end. A couple of exquisitely fragile-looking armchairs against one wall contrasted sharply with the solidity of the desk and its accompanying leather chair, and it was one of those that Hugo Gerard set for her, on the other side of the desk.

He sat down facing her, and for a moment regarded her across the intervening space with a steady gaze that she found much too disconcerting to meet. With her hands in her lap and still holding onto her overnight bag, she looked up at a beautiful crystal chandelier that hung suspended almost over their heads. Everything she had seen so far seemed much larger than life, and she had seldom felt so small and inadequate in her life before.

Being unsure of what she ought to wear for this

somewhat unusual interview, she had finally decided on a neat, dark dress in navy seersucker with a small white collar and a full flowing bow at the neck. Navy shoes matched it well and to complete the air of businesslike efficiency she had done something to her hair, something Jacques would never have approved of.

Normally it hung loosely about her shoulders, thick and silky and with just a hint of curl, but today she had wound it into a loose knot and pinned it on top of her head—and she was beginning to wish she hadn't. It was not only uncomfortable, it threatened at any moment to come down altogether, and that would do nothing for her businesslike image.

"Now, Miss Colton!" Ruth started almost guiltily and looked at him at last, her heart skipping rather fast as if she was afraid of him. The gray eyes had a cool speculative look, but they were not exactly unfriendly and she took heart from that. He leaned back in the big leather armchair and one elbow rested on the arm, the hand in turn supporting his chin. "You would like to work for me, now that you have assured yourself that I am not the gardener or the handyman?" he asked.

The allusion to her first impression was both pointed and inescapable and Ruth sought wildly for words for a moment before she answered. The temptation was to be as rude to him as he had intended to be to her, but she did not have the courage to say what she thought, much to her dismay. Instead she found herself apologizing.

"I—I'm sorry I mistook you for—for someone else," she told him. "I didn't realize—"

"Do you always put on that . . . ladylike air with the more poorly dressed staff?" he asked without giving her time to finish, and she looked at him uncertainly.

"I didn't know I was putting on an air," she said in a small tight voice, and he laughed shortly, shaking his head.

"Judging by my own experience, you most certainly do, *mademoiselle*!" he assured her. "Did Jacques not tell you that I like to do manual work sometimes as a means of keeping fit?"

She should have remembered, of course, Ruth thought wryly, that the so-called fictional hero in his book had been a very physical man. With all the advantages of education and social training he still liked to turn his hand to more earthy tasks for the sheer satisfaction of exploiting his muscular strength to the utmost. And beneath the veneer of polished civilization was the deep, primeval ruthlessness that showed itself to some extent in his dealings with women.

"Jacques said very little about you, *monsieur*," she said, and noticed the faint hint of smile that touched his mouth when she told him.

"So?" He flicked one brow upwards in question and fixed her with a steady eye that she found much too disconcerting to meet for very long. "But you still wish to work for me, *mademoiselle*?"

"I—I think so." The longer she was with him the less sure she was that she would be able to do justice to the work that would be involved. He made her feel quite appallingly inadequate and it was unnerving. "Jacques said that you needed someone to catalog your books."

"And you would like to do that? You know what is involved?"

"Oh, I'd love to do it!" Ruth agreed without hesitation. "Your collection is well known, Monsieur Gerard."

Again, for a moment, his wide mouth was

touched by a faint smile and he elevated a brow, apparently surprised at her enthusiasm. "You know of my collection?" he asked. "I had not thought its fame so wide-spread, *mademoiselle*—except of course among the more elderly and scholarly. I had not foreseen it being of interest to a young girl."

Although he had not openly derided her in any specific way, Ruth had the impression that he was making fun of her, and she instinctively thrust out her chin as she looked across at him on the other side of the big desk.

"I have worked with books for my living, ever since I left school, Monsieur Gerard," she said in as cool a voice as she could manage. "I'm a trained librarian, so you need have no fear that any harm will come to your valuable collection. Also there is no age limit at which one begins to appreciate beautiful books, *monsieur*!"

It was quite a little speech when she considered how uneasy and nervous she felt, but she thought her argument impressed him, although she could not be sure how well he took to her jumping to her own defence so readily. He was not a man who took kindly to opposition, she guessed, and waited to see how he would react with a strangely apprehensive feeling in her stomach.

"Indeed not, *mademoiselle*!" He regarded her for so long in silence that she began to feel she could not stand it much longer, and she wondered what was going on behind that rugged, impassive exterior.

"You met Jacques at your place of work?" he said quietly.

Ruth nodded. "I did—Stoddard's in Oxford, it's—"

"Yes, I know it." He smiled at her look of surprise and shook his head. "I, too, had the advantage of several years at your famous university, Miss Colton, and so did my elder brother— that is why I wanted Jacques to go there, too."

"Oh, I see."

"I have visited Stoddard's many times," he went on, and smiled wryly. "But that was well before your time, of course."

Ruth looked at him curiously for a moment through the thickness of her lashes, speculating. He was not as old as she had expected him to be, being Jacques's uncle, but he was possibly the youngest of his family; Jacques had not explained that. He would be, she decided after a quick scrutiny, about thirty-five or thirty-six, no more.

"Jacques didn't say anyone else in his family had been there before him," she said, and a brow flicked upward curiously.

"Non?"

He spoke softly and she was aware that he was studying her with much more intensity than she had him, and with less reticence too. He made no secret of his scrutiny and she felt her heartbeat rapping nervously at her ribs as she bore it.

There was something about him that she was beginning to find strangely disquieting, and unconsciously she tightened her hold on the handle of her bag when he moved and leaned forward in his chair. Both elbows rested on the desk in front of him and the open neck of the faded blue shirt fell open, revealing a length of tanned throat and a glimpse of broad chest that she found alarmingly evocative in the circumstances.

She recalled old Henry Stoddard's warning, and the supposedly autobiographical adventures featured in his book. Despite her trying to think of him only as Jacques's uncle she was finding it much more difficult than she had anticipated. There was something about him that destroyed any avuncular impression and made the idea laughable.

Jacques was attractive, but his attraction was more easy to define. He was charming and lighthearted, and he put himself out to be irresistible, but Hugo Gerard was different altogether. He was more mature, of course, less extrovert and certainly less anxious to please than his nephew was, but his very arrogance was a large part of his attraction, and Ruth recognized it ruefully.

He wouldn't care whether women liked him or not, and contrarily, she guessed, most of them would. There was an air of ruthless masculinity about him that was much more potent than any charm of Jacques's, but it alarmed rather than enthralled Ruth and she could not see herself being able to work for him without, sooner or later, quarreling bitterly with him in sheer self-defense.

Realizing how long she had been silent, and that he was still watching her with curious eyes, she hastily jolted herself back to sanity, meaning to apologize for not anwering. "*Monsieur*—" she began, but was allowed to go no further.

"Just how much *did* Jacques tell you, *mademoiselle*?" he interrupted quietly, and Ruth blinked for a moment, wondering what was in his mind.

"About what, *monsieur*?" she asked, and he shrugged his broad shoulders lightly.

"About my books—myself, perhaps."

Ruth shook her head. "A little about both, *monsieur*," she told him frankly, and once more one expressive brow rose in speculation. "Jacques didn't often discuss his family."

"So," he said softly, the gray eyes glinting, "I ask

myself, *mademoiselle*—was it the Gerard collection that made you want to come and work for me, or the reputation of Hugo Gerard, hmm? It is a reasonable question, you will agree?"

"It's nothing of the sort!" Ruth denied swiftly and angrily, her heart thudding wildly at her ribs and her hands tightly clenched on the handle of the bag she held. She felt the color flood swiftly and warmly into her cheeks, and she looked across at him angrily. It was only with a great effort that she resisted the temptation to get to her feet and stalk out of the room, but common sense prevailed. After all, she had no job at the moment and having come so far she should at least try to last out the interview.

"The idea of working for you, Monsieur Gerard," she told him in a dismayingly unsteady voice, "was Jacques's, not mine. I didn't even know you *were* his uncle until the other day."

"Non?"

There was a hint of disbelief in the soft-voiced inquiry and she resented it. *"Non!"* she echoed fiercely. "And you can believe me or not—I don't really care!"

Her anger, she suspected, amused rather than disturbed him and she hoped she could control it better from now on. "Why should I not believe you?" he asked.

"Because you seem to think—" She bit her lip trying to remember that he was not only a prospective employer that she should have been trying to please, but also Jacques's uncle. "I have the feeling that you suspect my motives for coming here, Monsieur Gerard," she said more quietly. "But in fact it was Jacques who insisted I come for this interview and apply for the job. In fact," she added ruefully, "he made sure I had to try for it by getting Mr. Stoddard to fire me!"

"Indeed?" There was a kind of tense suspicion about him now and he looked quite dismayingly stern as he leaned closer, so that she wished she had not been so frank about Jacques's part in her being there. He rested his arms on the desk and she felt the effects of that forceful character more strongly than ever as he sought and held her gaze. "And how did he achieve that, Miss Colton?" he asked.

It was not easy to explain, and Ruth guessed he would find it difficult to understand a reaction like old Henry Stoddard's. A kiss taken in the comparative privacy of a quiet book shop would probably strike him as no reason at all for dismissing an assistant.

"He—he kissed me," she said, in a small and strangely husky voice, and waited for the sound of scornful laughter, or at least a snort of derision, but neither happened.

Instead he still regarded her steadily across the desk, his gray eyes curious. "So I would hope, *mademoiselle*," he said quietly, and so matter-of-factly that she stared at him for a moment. "He would not be worthy of either his race or his family if he had *not* kissed you."

"But not in full view of my employer!" Ruth retorted.

"And against your wishes?" he suggested softly, and Ruth nodded, almost without thinking. He shook his head, his frown impatient. "*Zut!* He has much to answer for, that young fool!"

He once more leaned back in his chair, his hands clasped together, so that she could see how long and strong-looking his fingers were, and his arms tanned and sinewy as if he was no stranger to hard, physical work. She wanted to say something, perhaps to deny that Jacques had been one hundred percent to blame for her being fired, but somehow it wasn't easy to find the right words.

"Did Monsieur Stoddard not realize the fault was not yours?" he asked, after a moment or two, and Ruth glanced up briefly, trying to be fair.

"I—I think he was already annoyed about Jacques's coming in so often without buying anything," she told him.

"Because of you?"

She nodded, feeling suddenly embarrassed, although he seemed unaware that there was any reason for her to be. "I—I'm afraid so," she admitted.

The gray eyes made a swift, intense survey of her from the smooth, glossy rich brown of her head to the soft curves visible above the edge of the desk. "Whatever his faults," he observed quietly, "Jacques has excellent taste for his age!"

Such a frank appraisal was both unexpected and disturbing and Ruth tightened her fingers again on the handle of her bag, as she coped with a suddenly increased heartbeat. "Monsieur Gerard," she said, "I'm not sure I'm right for you—I— I mean for your collection," she amended hastily, and realized in sudden panic that she was getting in deeper all the time. To make matters worse that hint of laughter was again in his eyes as she struggled to make sense of what she was trying to say.

"You refer to my collection of books, of course, *mademoiselle*?" he said softly, and Ruth bit her lip. She knew how pink-flushed her face was and felt convinced that he must see her very silly and gauche.

"Of course, *monsieur*!" she said in a tight angry little voice. "I can see I made a mistake in coming all this way, I knew it wouldn't work and I told Jacques so. I'm not the sort of assistant you're looking for at all!"

"You are not?" That quizzical brow questioned her certainty, and she shook her head.

"No, I'm sure you'd much rather have one of your own countrywomen—you're not very impressed with Englishwomen, are you?"

"Ah!" The gray eyes gleamed at her across the desk. "You have read *Vie et Vérité, n'est-ce pas*?"

"I've read the English translation," she admitted, and prayed he would not ask her for her opinion. She had found the book intensely interesting and exciting, if a little earthy in parts, but she fought shy of telling him so to his face.

"So?" he prompted, after a long moment of silence, and Ruth played for time, seeking some way of evading a firm answer.

"I'm sure my opinion can't interest you, *monsieur*," she said.

"Ah, but it does, Miss Colton!" The light gray eyes held a glint of challenge as they looked at her across the desk, and she knew she was not going to be allowed to get out of answering.

Still she hesitated, then, when she answered at last, made it deliberately offhand, even shrugging her shoulders lightly. "It's good," she told him.

For a moment he said nothing, but there was a glittering disbelief in his eyes, resenting the hint of condescension she had unwittingly put into her voice, and she felt a strange and disturbing curling sensation in her stomach as she hastily avoided his gaze.

"I am humbly grateful for your appreciation, *mademoiselle*!" he said quietly, and Ruth flushed.

She took an ever firmer grip on the overnight bag and decided she wanted nothing so much as to leave, before she got in any deeper. She got to her feet, suddenly determined not to prolong the charade any longer.

It was obvious from his attitude so far that he would never consider employing her; the impression he gave in his book had evidently been true of the author as well as the character he created—he was not impressed by Englishwomen. It was even less likely he would consider her, now that she had seemingly been so patronizing about his book.

For a moment she stood there in front of the big rosewood desk and tried to think of suitable words that would end the situation and enable her to leave without further adding to her embarrassment. Her hair, as she feared it might, had come loose from its captive bun and straggled down on to her neck in wispy strands that tickled, and she felt very small and woebegone now that it was all over.

"I—I won't take up any more of your time, Monsieur Gerard," she told him in a rather unsteady little voice. Both her hands clasped the handle of the bag and she held it in front of her defensively. "I'm—I'm grateful to you for seeing me, and for paying my expenses, but I told Jacques it was a waste of time and money, my coming."

"So?" Again that brief, soft query disturbed her senses and she shrugged her shoulders in a gesture of helplessness.

"I—I wasn't denigrating your book," she said. "I—I enjoyed it." Again she shrugged. "Thank you for seeing me."

He still sat behind the desk, his hands clasped and his eyes half concealed by lowered lids and a fringe of quite feminine-looking eyelashes for that strong, rugged face. "You do not want the work, *mademoiselle*?" he asked quietly, and Ruth hesitated.

She did not even know the answer to that herself, but she could hardly tell him that, and she could hardly believe that he was not simply sighing with relief to see her go. Instead he was watching her steadily, and apparently the question was quite serious and he was waiting for an answer.

"I—of course I want a job," she said, her heart doing a hard and fast tattoo against her ribs as she looked down at him uncertainly. "But I thought—"

"You gave me no opportunity to decide, Miss Colton," he told her quietly. "Do you always rush in and out of things this way?"

"Not always," Ruth admitted in a small shaky voice. "But you can't mean—"

"If you wish to catalog my collection, *mademoiselle*," he interrupted, "you have the opportunity. If you would rather not work for a man of my reputation then you will of course return to your own home and find something more suitable."

There was no other way, Ruth thought, suddenly sure what she wanted. Even if that hint about a man of his reputation had been meant as a warning, she could not resist the idea of handling all those beautiful books and she nodded, without realizing she was smiling too.

"I'd like to take it," she said, sounding slightly breathless. "Thank you, Monsieur Gerard."

He, too, got to his feet then and came around the big desk to stand in front of her, and once more she felt herself small and uneasy. He was much too strong a personality to make anyone feel at ease, she thought, and wished with all her heart that Jacques could have been there too.

He looked at the small overnight bag she still held on to as if her life depended on it, and a hint of smile touched his mouth again. "Do you have all your worldly possessions in that valise, *mademoiselle*?" he asked softly, but gave her no time to answer. "You cling to it so fervently."

"It's my overnight bag," Ruth explained, a flush in her cheeks because she suspected he was laughing at her. "I believe Jacques booked me a room in the village."

"Jacques asked that we accommodate you here for the night," he told her, and stretched out a hand for the bag. "I should have relieved you of this when you arrived, I apologize for not doing so, but you seemed to cling to it as if it was not to be surrendered at any price."

He *was* laughing at her and she resented it, but there was little she could do about it without jeopardizing her newly acquired job, and she gave him the bag reluctantly. "I didn't realize I was expected to stay here," she said, and sounded so doubtful about the idea that again that expressive brow rose and the gray eyes looked at her steadily.

"Did Jacques not explain that the position was a resident one?" he asked, and she blinked for a moment, her mind racing off at all sorts of wild tangents as she faced the possibilities an arrangement like that could give rise to.

"He didn't," she said, then pulled a wry face when she saw the light at last. "I should have known of course—he'll be home here for good after this term and he said he would be on hand while I was working."

"And he will also not invade your working hours," Hugo Gerard told her in a voice that left no doubt he meant to stand no nonsense from his nephew. "If you are employed by me, Miss Colton, I hope you do not expect to merely use it as a cover for a prolonged *vacance* in Jacques's company."

"Of course I don't," Ruth denied indignantly. "I don't see—"

She stopped short and looked beyond him to the

door, which, after a preliminary knock, opened to admit a woman. She was perhaps in her middle sixties, Ruth guessed, and immediately decided that she must be Madame Gerard, Jacques's grandmother and joint holder of the purse strings until he reached the age of majority.

Brown eyes, like Jacques's twinkled with good humor and a small brown face grimaced apologetically at her son, but the apology was superficial, Ruth felt sure; she had come in with the express purpose of taking stock of Ruth herself. Her suspicion, she thought, was shared by Hugo Gerard, for he, too, pulled a face as he smiled at his mother.

"Maman," he said in a resigned voice. "What may I do for you?"

"*Pardonne-moi*, Hugo," she said, still coming across the room toward them and smiling at Ruth expectantly. "I did not know that you were . . . busy."

Hugo Gerard sighed, but he smiled as he put an affectionate hand on her arm and introduced Ruth. "I think you knew I was with Miss Colton, *maman*," he told her, mildly reproachful. "That is why you came, *n'est-ce pas? Permette-moi de te présenter* Mademoiselle Ruth Colton—*mademoiselle*, my mother, Madame Gerard."

A small but strong hand clasped hers eagerly and Ruth smiled in response to the enthusiastic greeting, so different from the one she had experienced on arrival. "Tell me, *mademoiselle*," she said, in an accent that was much more pronounced than her son's, "how is *mon cher* Jacques? You have seen him lately?"

"I saw him yesterday, *madame*." Ruth smiled as she passed on the message she had been given. "He sent his love and says he'll be seeing you very soon."

Madame Gerard's small face crinkled happily and she nodded her heard. "*Ah, oui!*" she said softly, "It will be good to have him home again, *n'est-ce pas*, Hugo?"

If Hugo's response was less enthusiastic than her own it was doubtful if Madame Gerard noticed it, for she was too wrapped up in the thought of having her beloved grandson home again and she smiled at Ruth with the air of a conspirator. "Jacques has told you that he is the favorite in the eyes of his *grand-mère, eh, mademoiselle*?"

Ruth smiled agreement. She liked the old lady and she was grateful, too, for her appearance, for having her there made her feel less inadequate. "I suspected it, *madame*," she told her, and the bright brown eyes regarded her curiously for a moment.

"You are very—close to Jacques, *mademoiselle*?" she asked, and Ruth, for some inexplicable reason, glanced first at Hugo Gerard before she answered.

From the expression she saw in his eyes, she suspected that he too was interested in her answer, and she hesitated briefly before committing herself to an answer. "I—I think we're friendly, *madame*," she said at last. "Not as close as you might be thinking, seeing all the trouble he went to to get me this appointment, but—yes, we're good friends."

"No more than good friends?"

It was Hugo Gerard who asked the question this time and despite the softness of his voice she felt his insistence was done with a purpose. She took a second to consider, then nodded her head. "That's right," she said. "No more than good friends."

"Ah, I see!" She frowned at him curiously, and saw the way Madame Gerard's eyebrows rose as she looked at her son. "Then it is curious, is it not, *mademoiselle*, that he tells us he is thinking of marrying you when he returns?"

Ruth stared at him for a moment in disbelief, her eyes wide and startled, and she sensed that Madame Gerard waited for her answer with some anxiety. "I—I know nothing about that," she said at last in a small, husky voice. "It must be some scheme that Jacques thought up to embarrass me."

"He would do such a thing?" Madame Gerard asked, looking as if she doubted it. "Surely not, *mademoiselle*!"

"It is possible, *maman*." Hugo's quiet voice forestalled Ruth's own opinion, and she looked at him in some surprise. She had not expected support from that quarter. "Miss Colton has already told me that Jacques contrived to lose her the job she held in Stoddard's so that he could have her come over here and work for me." He pulled a wry face. "Not for my sake, of course, but for his own because he thinks to have *mademoiselle* here at his pleasure."

"Oh, Hugo!" She looked at him reproachfully, and it was easy to see that she preferred not to believe anything about her grandson that was not to his credit.

"It is true, *maman*!" The light gray eyes looked at Ruth, seeking her confirmation. "You would not lie to me, would you, Miss Colton?"

"I certainly didn't in this instance," Ruth assured him. "Jacques *was* determined I should come over here, and he made sure I lost my job by—well, by behaving as he did."

Hugo Gerard's lower lip curled derisively and he laughed shortly as he explained to his mother what had happened. "Jacques kissed *mademoiselle* in the shop of Monsieur Stoddard, *maman*," he said. "It was sufficient to make the good Stoddard so angry that he dismissed Miss Colton out of hand!"

"Ah, *mais non*!" Madame Gerard looked appalled at such lack of understanding, and she put a gentle hand on Ruth's arm, her bright brown eyes sympathetic. "But such a thing is impossible. Has this Monsieur Stoddard no soul that he can behave so?"

"Actually he's rather a nice old man," Ruth told her, unwilling to have Henry Stoddard the complete villain of the piece just so that Jacques could be exonerated. "He frowns on public displays of—of that sort, and Jacques knew it, that's why he kissed me when and where he did."

"I find the whole idea utterly ridiculous," Hugo said in that firm, unarguable voice, "but at the same time I have to blame Jacques for deliberately acting in a way that would cause Miss Colton to lose her position."

"You could blame him?" Madame Gerard said, her eyes on his reproachfully. "How could you, Hugo, when you have been his example?"

For a moment Ruth wondered how he would react to the accusation, but after a second or two he merely smiled down at the old lady and cocked a brow in Ruth's direction. "Is there not a saying in England, Miss Colton," he asked softly, "about—Do As I Say, Not As I Do?"

CHAPTER THREE

IT WAS, IF ANYTHING, more nerve-racking to come back to the castle at Vallée des Arbres than it had been arriving for the first time, and Ruth already had misgivings. It had been so startling to hear that Hugo Gerard was still ready to give her the job of cataloging his collection of books that she had accepted without really realizing she had done so.

One thing consoled her as she sat behind the same ancient chauffeur being driven along the narrow, tree-bordered lanes, and that was the thought of Jacques coming to join her in less than two weeks' time. She had found Madame Gerard friendly and pleasant, but she was still very much a stranger to her, and Jacques would be someone she could turn to if she needed moral support.

He had been delighted when she told him of her success in getting the job with his uncle, but with his customary impulsiveness had announced that he would skip the last few days of the term and return with her when she went to take up her new position. It had been difficult to dissuade him, but finally she had made him understand that it would not help her relations with his uncle if he thought she had been the cause of his skipping the rest of his term.

The countryside looked fresh and bright in the summer sunshine, and it had a prettiness that once again struck her as unexpected. She could picture herself walking with Jacques beside that deep, cool river that meandered across the lush meadows, shaded by groups of willows and tall plumes of poplars. She must find time, too, to explore the depths of that cool, dark forest, and she must certainly get Jacques to drive her into Paris one evening for a glimpse of the famous Paris nightlife.

There was so much she wanted to see and do, and Jacques would love to show her the countryside and the sights of Paris. And then it struck her suddenly that there would probably be little opportunity for her to go sight-seeing with Jacques. Hugo Gerard had warned her, during the interview, that he expected her to work and not to look upon her being at the château merely as an excuse for a holiday with Jacques.

It was not beyond him, she thought ruefully, to make sure that Jacques did not interfere with her work by sending his nephew off on some other pretext—perhaps on a worldwide tour such as he had done himself, traveling and turning his hand to whatever offered itself in the way of work or pleasure.

She was jolted back to earth suddenly, when the car turned into that long, tree-lined driveway that led to the château, and her heart gave a violent leap in her breast before setting up a quite alarming tattoo against her ribs. The prospect of meeting Hugo Gerard again filled her with a nerve-racking anxiety, and she bit her lip in vexation with herself for being so foolish.

Instead of driving up and around onto that wide, flagged courtyard this time, she was taken around under an arched opening and into a cobbled yard. Compared to the expanse of parkland and the warmth of the sun they had just left the yard was cramped and chill, and the windows had a tight closed look. The sight of it gave Ruth a strangely uneasy feeling and she gazed out somewhat apprehensively.

The chauffeur got out and came to open the door for her, helping her out with something of a flourish. *"Entrez par ici, aujourd'hui, mademoiselle,"* he said, giving her a broad amiable smile that did a little to dispel the gloom of her surroundings.

Ruth took the proffered hand and stepped out, looking around her curiously. It was obvious that she had been brought to the equivalent of the back door of the château and it suddenly occurred to her for the first time that she was to be considered an employee, rather than a friend of Jacques. Recalling how she had been abandoned to find her own way the first time she came, she looked at the little chauffeur anxiously as he took her luggage from the trunk of the car, and felt even less happy about her situation.

"I'm—I'm not quite sure where I have to go," she told him. "If you could—"

"Mais oui, mademoiselle!" he assured her cheerfully, and picked up her two suitcases with surprising ease for such a small man. "You will please to come with me!"

Feeling more nervous every minute, Ruth did as she was bid and followed his short, thin figure across the cobbled yard. The blank stares of all those small windows had a strangely unnerving effect, she found, and she could not help the shiver that ran along her spine as her heels click-clicked on the smooth cobblestones. There was an air about this stark, quiet part of the château that was not noticeable in the more sumptuous comfort of the building itself.

The chauffeur made for a dark painted door set low in the huge stone wall and kicked it open with one booted foot, inviting her in with a wide grin while he stepped aside. It was cool and dim and there was barely room for her guide to squeeze himself past with her cases and take up the lead once more.

She had half expected to find herself in the kitchen, but once she had her bearings she realized that they must be heading in the direction of the vast hall she had seen the last time she arrived. Sure enough, after a few moments, she could see the huge, lighted hall ahead of them, and it was almost with relief that she heaved a small sigh.

Her guide, however, stopped just short of the hall and outside a closed door, putting down her cases and rapping smartly on the wooden panels. "Clotilde!" he called out loudly, and rapped again even harder. "Madame Rousseau! *Êtes-vous occupée, madame?*"

The door opened suddenly and the housekeeper Ruth had seen before looked out, her rather gaunt-looking face wearing a frown of dislike for the din. "*Chut*, Robert Toulée!" she told him sharply. "*Attendez un moment!*" Her expression changed when she saw Ruth, and she smiled, shrugging resignation for the impatience of men. "*Bonjour, mademoiselle!*" she said, much more quietly, "*Vous êtes* Mademoiselle Colton, *n'est-ce pas?*"

"I'm Ruth Colton," Ruth admitted, and looked at her anxiously, "I'm sorry, *madame*, I don't speak French."

"*Ah, mais naturellement!* But I forget—I am sorry, *mademoiselle*!"

Ruth shook her head, and responded to the smile readily, for the housekeeper could prove a valuable ally in the future. "I really must make an effort and learn," she said. "I haven't even tried since I left school!"

For a moment the woman's dark eyes regarded her, kindly but speculative, then she smiled again. "And *mademoiselle* is not long from the schoolroom, I think," she said softly. "You are very young, *mademoiselle*." She said it almost wistfully, as if it was cause for regret, and Ruth was puzzled.

"Not too young," the old chauffeur opined quietly and with such a wicked glint in his faded old eyes that Ruth felt her cheeks color.

He received a discouraging frown from Madame Rousseau, too, "You will bring *mademoiselle*'s *bagages,* Robert," she told him. "If you will please to follow me, *mademoiselle*, I will show you to your room."

The housekeeper led the way into the hall and across that beautiful wood floor to the stairs. It was a grand, sweeping staircase that had impressed her on her first visit, and Ruth felt herself very grand to be living, for some time at least, in such surroundings.

The chauffeur followed, carrying her cases, but they had gone only a few steps upward when another door into the hall opened suddenly and all three turned to see who it might be. Ruth, who half expected it to be Hugo Gerard, felt her heart rapping hard at her ribs again and instinctively tightened her hands into curled fists as she turned.

But it was Madame Gerard who came across the hall, smiling and nodding to Ruth, a look of genuine welcome on her face as she looked up at her. "*Bonjour*, Mademoiselle Colton!" she said. "I am so pleased you have arrived safely—did you have a pleasant journey?"

"Yes, thank you, Madame Gerard."

Ruth was uncertain just what her next move should be, whether she should go down again or stay where she was, but she was not long in doubt. Madame Gerard indicated to the chauffeur that he should take the suitcases up, then smiled again at Ruth.

"Will you not speak with me for a little while before you go to your room, *mademoiselle*?" she asked. "You will tell me of Jacques, hmm?"

"Yes, of course, *madame*!"

She came down again and the housekeeper took it as her cue to return to her own quarters. She bobbed her head to her employer as she passed. "I will show *mademoiselle* to her room when she is ready," she murmured.

"*Mademoiselle* is in the same room as before when one night was spent here, *n'est-ce pas*?" she asked, and when the housekeeper noddingly agreed, she smiled at Ruth. "You must be at home here, Mademoiselle Colton," she told her. "You know where is your room, yes?"

"I—I think so," Ruth said, grateful for the welcome, but wondering if she would ever find the same room again among the huge number of doors on the same landing.

"I did not hear your arrival, *mademoiselle*," Madame Gerard told her, her fingertips just lightly touching her arm as she led the way back across the hall. "Generally I hear *l'auto* and I cannot imagine why I did not do so this time!"

"Oh, it was possibly because we went around the back way, *madame*," Ruth explained with a smile, and was startled to see the expression of dismay on Madame Gerard's face.

"You were taken to the rear door?" she asked, apparently scandalized. Her brown eyes were glinting in a way that Ruth had seen Jacques's do more than once, and she realized that she had probably made things difficult for the chauffeur, quite unintentionally.

"Oh, but it didn't matter in the least, *madame*," she hastened to assure her. "I assumed the staff came in that way."

"The staff!" Madame Gerard echoed with scorn. "You are a close friend of my grandson, Mademoiselle Colton, and I will not have you conducted to the rear entrance of his home when you arrive! I will not allow it! And what would Jacques have to say of it, eh?"

Her vehemence surprised, almost startled Ruth, and she wondered just whose decision it had been to have her brought in via the back door, since it was obviously not Madame Gerard's. As yet she was unsure just who was the current owner of the castle, but she had assumed Madame Gerard was—now it seemed she could be wrong. On consideration, she thought, it was just the kind of instruction she could imagine Hugo Gerard issuing.

"But I do—I shall be working for Monsieur Gerard," she explained as mildly as possible. "Perhaps it was on his instruction that I was taken that way—anyway, it really doesn't matter, *madame*."

"Most certainly it matters!" Madame Gerard argued, and her accent became stronger as she became agitated. "If Hugo gave such an instruction then I shall speak of it to him! You will be treated as a friend of Jacques's, *mademoiselle*, I will have it no other way!"

It was very satisfactory, in one way, to be so considerately treated, but Ruth was afraid there would be difficulties in store if she was to be looked at in the light of being Jacques's girl friend rather than his uncle's employee and she wondered how she was going to set matters right, without causing too much of a disturbance. Madame Gerard sounded so adamant, and she could, Ruth guessed, be almost as strong willed as her son if she once made up her mind.

"You're very kind, Madame Gerard," she murmured. "But perhaps Monsieur Gerard—"

The old lady's brown eyes sparkled determinedly when she looked back over her shoulder as she opened the door. "Hugo is master in his own house," she said with a wicked smile that reminded Ruth of Jacques, "but he still does not like to displease his *maman, mademoiselle*!"

Ruth smiled and felt suddenly more able to cope with whatever came her way. If she knew that Madame Gerard was on her side, it would make things a lot easier. "I'm sure you're right, *madame*," she murmured.

The room they entered was quite up to the standard of anything she had seen so far, and she looked around her with pleasure. She remembered coming in there briefly during her overnight stay last time, but she had been much too nervous for anything to leave a lasting impression, and she came to it as new.

A luxuriously thick carpet in deep blue was complemented by walls papered in cream and gold as far as the deep frieze that ran round the room about a foot below the molded and gilded ceiling. Deep scrolls and ornate roses decorated the frieze and were gilded like the ceiling, while two huge crystal chandeliers shone and glittered, even without the benefit of artificial light.

There were paintings here too, like the ones she had noticed in the room where she had been interviewed, but most of these were of ladies in the style of dress that had disappeared with the French Revolution, and Ruth wondered if they could possibly be ancestors of the present occupants.

The furniture was of a later period and chosen for its comfort rather than its daintiness, but even that had a brocaded elegance that spoke of expensive and impeccable tastes. Noticing her interest, Madame Gerard smiled and indicated with one hand that she should sit down, then used the same hand in a wide sweeping gesture to encompass the whole room.

"You like this room, Mademoiselle Colton?" she asked, and Ruth nodded unhesitatingly.

"It's beautiful," she said truthfully. "Each part of the château I've seen so far has been quite beautiful. I'd no idea that people still lived in such places."

"Very few do," Madame Gerard said, shaking her head. "Most are either museums or some other form of public exhibition. The Gerards have been fortunate, *mademoiselle*, they still are. Alas, the men of the family do not always appreciate it as they should until they are old enough to take more interest in things domestic than in—" expressive hands spread wide "—other pursuits."

It was all too easy to guess what those other pursuits were and once more Ruth was reminded of the warnings she had been given about working for a man like Hugo Gerard. Even his mother, it seemed, recognized his shortcomings, but accepted it as a matter of course. Perhaps, she thought ruefully, Jacques would be expected to follow the same path.

"It's an—an ancestral home?" she asked, and *madame* smiled, nodding her head slowly.

"It has been in the Gerard family for a very long time," she said, "but not always in happy circumstances, *mademoiselle*. I fear many marriages have been arranged in the past for the sole purpose of saving the estate from ruin, you understand. But—" again she shrugged and smiled ruefully "—even when others lost such homes as this, the Gerards managed to hold theirs by choosing sides carefully." For a moment her bright brown eyes rested on Ruth shrewdly. "The Gerard men have always been ruthless, I am afraid, *mademoiselle*. Very—how is it you say—certain of themselves."

Just like Hugo, Ruth thought, and guessed Madame Gerard had no illusions about her son, although she loved him dearly. If the present generation was any guide, their dispositions did nothing to detract from their appeal to women, and no doubt they always made the most of the fact.

Again the brown eyes were regarding her with a look of speculation, and she hastily brought herself back to earth, smiling apologetically. "You think you will enjoy to work with my son?" Madame Gerard asked, and Ruth took a moment to answer.

She looked down at her hands in her lap instead, and sat straight and upright in the deep-seated brocade chair. "I hope so, *madame*," she said, trying not to allow the doubt she felt sound in her voice.

She realized she had failed when Madame Gerard spoke again, her own voice soft and gentle as she leaned forward in her chair, touching her hand and trying to draw her gaze. "You are—how is it—wary of Hugo, hmm?" she asked softly, and Ruth looked up, startled to have her feelings so accurately diagnosed.

"I—I don't really know," she confessed. "I would never have dreamed of applying for a job like this if Jacques hadn't forced my hand, and Monsieur Gerard's, too, I suspect."

"But why should you not?" the old lady insisted. "You do well at your work, I think, or the Stoddard would not employ you. I know of him," she added with a wry laugh, "both from my son and my grandson. Such a man would not employ a fool, I think you have nothing to fear that you will not be able to do this work, *mademoiselle*!"

It would not do, Ruth thought, to tell the old lady that she had been warned about taking the job, nor could she very well tell her that her first contact with Hugo Gerard had scarcely been a roaring success, despite the fact that he had given her the job. "I suppose not," she said.

Again that gentle hand reached out to her and the brown eyes smiled at her warmly. "You will enjoy it here, *mon enfant*," she said softly. "You will soon become accustomed to us and—" she rolled her eyes expressively and smiled, "—soon Jacques will be here and you will like it then, hmm?"

It seemed that her denials on the day of the interview had not impressed Madame Gerard, Ruth thought. She apparently still thought that there was more between herself and Jacques than there was. "*Madame*," she ventured, not looking at her as she spoke, "I—I think you have the wrong impression of my—my relationship with Jacques."

"Have I so, *mon enfant*?" the old lady said softly.

"I—I know nothing about his wanting to marry me," Ruth insisted. "He's said nothing to me about it, *madame*, and I wouldn't have come over and taken this position if he had."

For a moment she imagined that the brown eyes hardened, as if something displeased her, but she smiled again a moment later and shook her head. "You do not like Jacques?" she asked, and Ruth hastily denied that, too.

"I like him a great deal, *madame*," she assured her. "But not enough to marry him—even if he'd asked me."

"Ah, but now you are in the same house, *n'est-ce pas*?" the old lady reminded her. "Now you will see much more of one another, and—" She tapped her nose and smiled knowingly. "Who knows, hmm?"

Ruth, remembering another moment of that day, smiled ruefully and pulled a face. "I don't think that's going to be very easy, either, *madame*," she told her. "Monsieur Gerard warned me that I would be here to work and that I would not be allowed to treat it as a holiday with Jacques."

"Oh, he is a *tyran*, my son!" Madame Gerard declared indignantly. "Of course you must see Jacques and go out with him while you are here, *mademoiselle*! I will not allow that—that driver of slaves to keep you at your work for all day and night, too! Do not fear, *mon enfant*, I will see that you are not enslaved!"

It was rather an exaggerated term to use, Ruth thought, but she did not bother to argue, merely smiled, then looked up swiftly when the door opened. The color came warmly to her cheeks when the man they had been discussing came into the room.

The light gray eyes went straight to Ruth and he frowned as if he found her presence there not to his liking. For a moment a silence hung in the air like a pall and then Madame Gerard held out a hand to him, smiling and encouraging him to come and stand beside her. Although he came across the room to her he did not smile in response, and Madame Gerard made a wry face as she took his hand in hers and looked across at Ruth.

"You see that *mademoiselle* has arrived safely," she told him, and he inclined his head briefly, while Ruth coped with an unexpected flutter in the region of her heart.

"I see also that *mademoiselle* has made an ally, *maman*," he said in a quiet, cool voice. "I did not even know that you had arrived, Mademoiselle Colton—I was not told."

"I'm sorry."

Ruth's apology was almost overridden by Madame Gerard's protest. "Because that imbecile Robert took *mademoiselle* to the rear door, *mon cher*," she told him, determined to have her say before the matter was overlooked.

Still those gray eyes were watching Ruth and she felt as if she should perhaps stand up, show some deference to her new employer; it was the effect he had on her and she despaired of her own weakness. He also had the effect of making her heart hammer so hard at her ribs that she could scarcely hear what was being said for the clamor of it.

"And did *mademoiselle* object?" he asked softly, as if he saw that as the reason for her being there with his mother.

"I did not!" Ruth denied swiftly, and saw a hint of laughter in his eyes as he squeezed his mother's hand.

"Then you have no need to take up arms, *maman*," he told her.

"Indeed I have!" Madame Gerard insisted. "Mademoiselle Colton is a very dear friend of Jacques's, and as such she is not to be delivered to the rear door!"

"And you think I gave such instructions?" he asked her gently, shaking his head before she had time to answer. "I did not, *maman*, it was simply that Robert knew *mademoiselle* was to join the staff here and he assumed she would be treated in the same way as the other staff are." Again he turned his gaze on Ruth and there was a speculative glint in his eyes. "If *mademoiselle* has been offended by her treatment," he said softly, "then I will see that Robert apologizes. Is that what you wish, Mademoiselle Colton?"

"Oh, no, no, of course not!" Ruth said hastily.

The gray eyes still watched her until she felt she wanted to sink through the floor with embarrassment. "You did not complain to my mother about your treatment?" he insisted, but before Ruth could answer, Madame Gerard intervened again.

"Certainly Mademoiselle Colton did not complain, Hugo!" she told him, "*I* did!"

He smiled at her with a kind of tolerant affection, and shook his head, squeezing her hand before he released it and went to sit in a chair next to her, facing Ruth. "You are so ready to take up causes, *maman*," he told his mother. "And I am quite sure Mademoiselle Colton has no need of your protection— am I not right, *mademoiselle*?"

A warm pink flush colored Ruth's cheeks, and she felt sure he was trying to embarrass her deliberately. She lifted her chin and there was a bright, defiant look in her own gray eyes as she looked across at him. "I'm perfectly capable of taking care of myself, *monsieur*," she said in a small, tight voice, while Madame Gerard smiled with approval. Evidently it was a new experience for her to hear someone stand up to her formidable son.

"*Bon!*" He held her gaze for a moment longer and she thought he was smiling to himself, but it appeared only as a deep, dark glint in his eyes. Then he turned to his mother again. "I have booked a telephone call for you this evening, *maman*," he told her. "I have done my part to help, now you must hope that Jacques will not be out for the evening when the call goes through."

"Oh, *merci, mon cher*!" Madame Gerard said, her eyes bright with anticipation. "It will be *merveilleux* to speak with him again!" She looked at Ruth and nodded her head eagerly. "You, too, will speak with Jacques, *mademoiselle*!" she told her, and Hugo looked disapproving, a small frown drawing at his brows as he shook his head.

"I do not think that will be necessary, *maman*," he said coolly. "It is possibly no more than hours since Jacques was in the company of Mademoiselle Colton."

"But, *chéri*, if they are to be married, *mademoiselle* and—"

"*Mademoiselle* has denied any knowledge of such an arrangement," Hugo interrupted firmly. "And Jacques is far too young to consider marriage—he is not yet out of the schoolroom, *maman*. Also," he added with a glint in his eyes as he looked across at Ruth, "he is not the most stable of characters, I am sure Mademoiselle Colton will agree."

Angry at the slight, on Jacques's behalf, Ruth curled her hands and glared. He had no right to belittle Jacques, especially in front of someone who was virtually a stranger, and since he was not there to defend himself, she would do it for him.

"Jacques isn't the fool you make him sound, Monsieur Gerard," she told him in a tight, angry voice. "He's kind and gentle and—and very nice. He's intelligent, too, or he wouldn't be at university!"

Her reaction seemed to surprise him and for a moment or two he sat looking across at her steadily, his elbows resting on his knees, his big muscular hands clasped together in front of him. "The latter will be proved when we have his examination results," he said coolly, and his mouth tipped briefly into a hint of smile. "For the rest, *mademoiselle*, you speak with such authority that I hesitate to disagree with you."

It was all much too tense and meaningful, Ruth thought desperately, wondering why he always seemed to arouse feelings of defensiveness in her. She scarcely knew the man and yet he could make her angry more quickly than anyone she had ever met. It did not promise well, she thought ruefully, for their future association as employer and employee.

Seeing her at a loss for the moment, Madame Gerard leaned across and again touched her hand lightly, as if to reassure her of her support. "I too find Jacques kind and gentle, *mon enfant*," she told her softly. "And soon he will be here, hmm? Then we will both be very happy." She glanced at her son from the corners of her eyes with a sly smile, and Ruth thought she detected a trace of the girl she might once have been many years ago. "You will not then have too much your own way, *mon cher Hugo*, hmm?"

For a moment the gray eyes held Ruth's steadily and again that hint of smile touched his wide mouth as he answered his mother's question. "Perhaps not," he said softly, and Ruth hastily averted her gaze, her hands tightly clasped together.

RUTH LAY IN HER BED the following morning looking across at a streak of sunlight that was slowly making its way across her bedroom wall, and pursed her lips thoughtfully. Today she was to commence her task of cataloging the famous Gerard collection, and deep down inside her she had far too many doubts to be entirely happy about it.

She could find no fault with the room she had

been given, and it was clear that she was indeed being treated as a friend of Jacques's rather than a member of the staff, for the rest of the staff surely did not sleep in such luxurious surroundings. Probably in comparison to some of the rooms in the château, it was not large, but it was comfortably and expensively furnished.

A deep cream carpet allowed her to walk barefoot about her room, it was so deep and soft, and the walls were the same cream and gold that seemed to be repeated throughout the château as far as she had seen. There was even a smaller replica of one of those crystal chandeliers overhead, although a more up-to-date lamp stood on a table beside the tall, narrow, four-poster bed.

Two of those innumerable long, flat windows she had noticed from outside gave a view of the château's own grounds and also of more distant vistas, where the surrounding trees allowed it. She could even catch a glimpse of that dark, cool forest if she looked far enough to her right.

No matter what doubts she had about the job she was to do, or the man she was to work for, she had none at all about her good fortune in being able to spend some time in such surroundings. Briefly, the night before, Hugo Gerard had shown her into the library where she was to work and she had been astounded by its size. The room itself was huge, and the walls on three sides were lined with books from floor to ceiling. At first glance it would seem that the task before her was so enormous it could take a lifetime to complete.

Another glance at the bedside clock convinced her that it was time she got up, and she threw back the covers and sat for a moment swinging her bare feet above the deep softness of the carpet. Several times she had heard sounds of movement out there on the gallery, and wondered if it was the staff or her employer who was around so early.

With the château so thoroughly modernized as far as comfort was concerned, there were more than enough bathrooms to go around, and Ruth had been allocated a small but quite luxurious one next to her bedroom. She slipped into a brand-new robe of pink and white candy-striped nylon and tied the sash at her waist, taking a moment on her way out to admire the effect in the dressing-table mirror.

With her brown hair tousled from sleep and the flimsy striped robe covering her only as far as her knees, she looked much less than her twenty-two years, and realizing it, she pulled a face at herself in the mirror, then laughed as she turned and walked across to the door.

She could hear no sound on the gallery, and she nodded her satisfaction, then opened the door and went out onto the long, carpeted walk that seemed to stretch for yards on either side and overlooked the hall. All the other doors on either side of her own were closed, and once again she nodded her satisfaction at being apparently the only one around.

Curiosity got the better of her as she emerged from her room and she slipped across to the opposite side of the gallery and peeped over the ornate gilded balustrade at the vastness of the hall below, her slippered feet making no sound on the carpeted floor. There seemed to be no one around down there, either, and she spent several seconds looking down and admiring the intricate and beautiful patterned inlay of the wooden floor and the hanging tapestries that reached almost as far as where she stood on the gallery.

It was like being in another world and, for a while

anyway, she was to be part of it. To live in a château, surrounded by luxury and working with books she would never otherwise have the opportunity of seeing, let alone handling! The thought sent a quite pleasurable shiver along her spine and she smiled, suddenly less apprehensive, as she turned back to make her way to the bathroom.

Unprepared, she let out a small cry of alarm when she was suddenly and unexpectedly thrown into contact with a broad, hard masculine chest, and arms went around her swiftly, strong as steel and as unyielding, holding her briefly against the smooth coolness of a cotton shirt.

"Bonjour, mademoiselle!" A deep, soft voice spoke close to her ear and it took her a moment or two to realize the fact that she was in Hugo Gerard's arms.

"I'm sorry!"

Her own voice sounded small and breathless and she dared not look up yet, but tried to free herself from that unyielding embrace. It had not occurred to her before quite how tall he was, although compared to her own lack of inches he need have been no more than six feet for her eyes to have been level with the opening of his shirt as they were now.

There was a warmth and a strange, disturbing aura of sensuality about the hardness of his body, and she did her best to prize herself away from it, her hands flat on his chest and conscious of the steady, throbbing heartbeat under her palms.

He let her go at last, but only to the length of his arms, and Ruth could feel the steady gaze on her as she kept her own eyes fixed on the base of his throat and the strong, steady pulse that beat there. His big, work-strong hands held her upper arms and felt warm through the nylon robe, the fingers almost gentle but still holding her captive.

"Did you sleep well, *mademoiselle*?" he asked, and Ruth nodded.

"Yes, thank you, *monsieur*."

"Bon!" For a moment neither of them spoke or moved and Ruth had the strangest feeling that she was on the brink of something new and infinitely disturbing, although heaven knew what it could be. His dark tan was emphasized that morning by a white shirt, and but for his light, almost fair hair and the gray eyes, he might have been of some darker race as he stood there in the shadows of the long gallery looking down at her. Then his hands slid down her arms and lingered briefly on the slim curve of her waist before he released her, leaving the warmth of his touch still tingling on her skin.

"Are you lost?" he asked softly, and Ruth hastily shook her head, her pulses skipping with alarming rapidity, and very aware of her disheveled hair and the flimsiness of her robe.

"Oh, no," she told him. "I—I was just looking down at the hall, that's all."

A brief glance through her lashes at his face revealed that elusive hint of laughter in his eyes again, and she wondered why it was that she always seemed either to anger or amuse him. "You are very impressed by it all, are you not?" he asked, and his mouth smiled briefly as he quizzed her. "Did Jacques not tell you about his home, *mademoiselle*?"

Ruth felt convinced he was making fun of her, mocking her susceptibility to such grand surroundings, and she resented it bitterly. Never before had she been made to feel so gauche and vulnerable. "I'm glad it amuses you, Monsieur Gerard," she told him in a voice that trembled despite her efforts to sound cool and distant. "I'm afraid that contrast with a small suburban house in England is rather too much to absorb without showing *some* reaction. I've no doubt you find it rather naive of me!"

She intended to give him no time to answer, but brushed past him, making her way again toward the bathroom. She had taken only a step or two, however, when strong fingers encircled her left arm again and brought her to an immediate halt, her breath caught in her throat as she looked up swiftly into his eyes.

"You do me an injustice, Miss Colton," he said quietly, and as precisely as he always pronounced her name in English. "And yourself, also—I had no intention of mocking you."

It came as a surprise that he had even troubled to say or do anything more than simply shrug, then walk off and leave her, and she looked up at him again, her pulses tapping wildly at her temple when she met his eyes. "You don't have to apologize, Monsieur Gerard—" she began, but was allowed to go no further.

"I was *not* apologizing, *mademoiselle*," he assured her brusquely. "I have no reason to and you have no reason to expect me to!"

Ruth gazed at him wide-eyed for a moment, his manner beyond her comprehension. "But you—"

"I was merely explaining, not apologizing," he told her in a cool voice.

Ruth wished the floor would open up and swallow her, for she knew how pink-flushed her face was and she wished with all her heart that she had known he was around so that she could either have stayed in her bedroom until he was gone, or gone straight into the bathroom without stopping for that admiring look at the hall below.

"You don't like me, do you?" she asked, without

quite knowing why she should ask him such a question.

One brow rose, as if the question surprised him too, and his mouth had a firm, straight look she didn't like at all. "You will do well to remember, *mademoiselle*," he informed her in a cool voice, "that I am your employer, no matter if Madame my mother chooses to regard you as my nephew's . . . friend. As long as I find your work satisfactory it matters little whether *I* like you or not. The moment your work fails to satisfy me I shall dismiss you, no matter whose friend you are." The gray eyes swept over her in a brief but devastating scrutiny. "When you are more suitably attired, *mademoiselle*, I will see you at breakfast, since you are to join us for meals."

The slight, curt inclination he made with his head was more Teutonic than Gallic, and Ruth had never felt more chastened in her life as she watched him with wide, unblinking eyes, turn on his heel and stride swiftly along the gallery to the stairs. Her hands curled into fists as she fought with any number of new and disturbing emotions, of which anger was the only one she clearly recognized.

Thank heaven Jacques would be home in a few days now, and she would not feel quite so alien, or so unwelcome. Madame Gerard had made it clear that she was delighted to have her there, but even her support could not compensate for the way her son had behaved towards her just now. It would take very little for her to go right back to her room and pack, telling Hugo Gerard that even the pleasure of working on his wonderful collection could not compensate for working for a man who made her feel as ineffectual as he did.

CHAPTER FOUR

IT WAS FIVE DAYS since Ruth started on her marathon task and even working steadily, as she had been, her efforts seemed to have made only a small impression on the thousands of books around her. She was, in fact, quite pleased with the progress she *had* made, considering the immensity of her task.

Although she could not translate the titles of most of the books she was cataloging, what she had to do was basically so simple that a knowledge of French was not really necessary. She was required merely to list them in alphabetical order and eventually restore them to the shelves in their order, not allocate them to their different subjects.

Some of the books were very old, with exquisite leather bindings and pages that smelled of age and the strangely musty scent of early print, their edges rich with gold leaf. Some of the first editions were priceless and it occurred to her more than once that the whole collection must have been worth even more than she had first realized. In fact it sometimes gave her a moment of panic when she stopped to think what could happen if she should accidentally damage one of them in handling.

She was enjoying herself so far, she had to admit, and the fact that she had seen very little of her employer during the past days was an added bonus that she accepted gratefully. Hugo Gerard keeping a careful eye on her would have been a distraction hard to cope with.

Except for the first morning, when he had given her a brief but thorough summary of what was required of her, Ruth saw him only at mealtimes. She took her meals with him and Madame Gerard and she thanked heaven more than once that *madame* was an easy conversationalist. With the subject of Jacques of mutual interest, she and Madame Gerard were never short of a topic of conversation, although Hugo, Ruth suspected, found the subject of his absent nephew rather wearing after a time. Several times she had noticed a frown appear between his brows and he withdrew into a solitary silence.

It was during the morning of the sixth day, when she was busy taking the books from the shelves prior to listing them, that she had visitors. Madame Gerard came into the library accompanied by a man who reminded Ruth so strongly of Jacques that she had to believe he was Madame's other son, even before he was introduced to her.

Of medium height, he had dark brown hair and a broad friendly face, with brown eyes that smiled readily at her. There was also the same appreciative warmth in his eyes that she had noticed often in Jacques's.

"Ruth!" The old lady led the way across the huge library. "May we disturb you for just a moment, *ma chère*?"

Madame Gerard had insisted on using her Christian name from the first day, although Hugo still stuck to the more formal 'Mademoiselle Colton' or just '*mademoiselle*,' with the intention of keeping her firmly in her place, she suspected. She put down the books she was moving on the desk behind her, and turned to smile at them.

"I don't mind in the least, *madame*," she told her. "I'm getting on quite well so far."

"Bon!" Her bright brown eyes twinkled mischievously. "Hugo will be pleased with you, hmm?"

"I should think it's unlikely!" Ruth said, and her wry face brought a soft understanding laugh from Madame Gerard.

"I would like you to meet my other son, Bruno," she told her, confirming Ruth's suspicions. She put a hand on her son's arm and smiled rather archly at Ruth. "Bruno, *mon cher*, this is Mademoiselle Ruth Colton, who is such a very good friend of Jacques's!"

The expressive rolling of her eyes and long-drawn-out vowels lent a great deal more meaning to the simple words, and Ruth felt the color warm her cheeks as she took Bruno Gerard's proffered hand. She would like to have denied that there was any reason for those meaningful implications, but it was difficult to know how to do so without putting Madame Gerard at fault.

"Mademoiselle Colton!"

The strong pressure of his fingers reminded her of Jacques, too, and it was the only thing about him that was reminiscent of his brother. There were no other similarities as far as she could see. His accent was much more pronounced, and that puzzled her rather, for she distinctly remembered Hugo telling her that his elder brother had also gone to Oxford.

"Bonjour, monsieur." She politely murmured the greeting in French, and Bruno's brown eyes regarded her with even more approval.

"Ah—vous parlez français!" he said with satisfaction.

Ruth hastily shook her head. "No, I'm afraid I don't, Monsieur Gerard," she told him. "I'm sorry."

"But your accent is . . . *très bon, mademoiselle*!"

He used his eyes to lend meaning to his words and laughed, shrugging his shoulders resignedly. "Ah, well, then it seems you must suffer my English, *mademoiselle*, and I am not so good as Jacques or my brother, for I have never visited your lovely country!"

Ruth looked at him curiously for a moment, wondering how she could have misunderstood. "I'm sorry," she said after a moment or two and still looking puzzled. "I thought—I must have misunderstood, but I thought Monsieur Gerard, Monsieur Hugo Gerard, told me that you'd been to Oxford, too, like him and Jacques. He said his brother and I thought—"

There followed a brief, taut silence that hung in the air around them for several seconds, and then Madame Gerard shook her head, a small, sad smile on her face that did not touch her eyes. "Hugo speaks of Philippe," she said softly. "No one else ever does now, but Hugo—" She shrugged eloquent shoulders and Bruno put a hand briefly on her arm and shook his head.

"*Maman*," he said softly, and to Ruth it sounded oddly like a warning.

Madame Gerard's brown eyes looked at him briefly, then she turned again to Ruth and there was a hint of defiance in her expression that startled Ruth and puzzled her, because she could think of no reason for it.

"There were once three sons, Ruth," she said quietly, and Ruth did not for the moment question her way of wording it, but she did notice Bruno's frown of disapproval. "Philippe was the eldest," *madame* went on in the same quiet voice, "but—"

"He died young, *mademoiselle*," Bruno intervened at last. "It is a painful matter, you will understand." He touched his mother's arm again lightly. "*Maman*," he said softly, "I am sure that Mademoiselle Colton does not wish to hear of our tragedies, hmm?"

For a moment it looked as if the old lady would disregard his advice, but after a second or two she merely nodded her head slowly, and once again her shoulders lifted in a shrug of resignation. *"Tu as raison,"* she murmured, and Ruth could almost have sworn that she heard Bruno sigh with relief.

"You admire Hugo's collection of books, *mademoiselle*?" he asked.

"It's magnificent," Ruth said readily, and laughed, a short and oddly nervous sound because the brief air of tension had somehow touched her. "I feel quite guilty about being paid to do something I enjoy so much!"

"Then perhaps you would care to give your services for nothing, *mademoiselle*!"

Ruth had no need to turn to identify the speaker, and she felt her hands curl involuntarily when he came into the room towards them, his long legs striding out as they always did whether indoors or out.

Thin cotton pants that had seen many years' wash and wear, she suspected, made his legs look even longer, and combined with a faded navy blue shirt that was open almost as far as his waist, gave him a stirringly piratical look that she found disturbing.

Madame turned when she recognized the voice, a smile on her face that banished all trace of her earlier sadness. "If you are going to be angry because Ruth is not doing her work," she told him, pulling a face that brought a smile to that stern expression, "you must be angry with me, *mon cher*, not with Ruth, for it was my fault completely—you must blame me!"

"You speak as if I am such an ogre that I do not allow *mademoiselle* to lift her head," Hugo accused. "You do me an injustice, *maman*."

"Ah, mais non, mon cher!" Madame Gerard denied with a laugh. "It is simply that I am to make sure you do not drive poor Ruth like the slave! I promise her that I will—how is it you say—keep the eye on you, huh?"

Immediately the gray eyes were on Ruth again, curious and slightly narrowed, as if in suspicion, and the wide mouth was crooked wryly at one corner. "Has *mademoiselle* complained of my treatment of her?" he asked softly, and Ruth was the one swift to deny it, strangely disturbed by that steady scrutiny as always.

"I haven't complained, Monsieur Gerard," she told him. "I have no reason to complain, in fact I was just saying that I feel almost guilty about being paid for something I enjoy doing so much."

"And I suggested that you might care to do the work for nothing," he reminded her, his gaze still fixed on her as he perched himself on the edge of the desk, one foot swinging, his light eyes narrowed against the smoke that rose in front of his face when he lit a cigarette.

He did not offer a cigarette to his brother, Ruth noticed, and wondered whether it was because he did not smoke or if there was some other reason. On reflection, she realized he had not even spoken to Bruno since he joined them.

"I'd willingly do the work for nothing if it wasn't necessary for me to earn my living," she said. "Just for the pleasure of handling these lovely books."

"You really enjoy it so much?"

The softly spoken question had an oddly intimate sound and it seemed to Ruth that, for a few seconds, there might have been no one else in the room but the two of them discussing her work and her love of beautiful books.

"I enjoy it so much," she agreed quietly.

She vaguely sensed that Madame Gerard was watching them, although she saw her only from the corners of her eyes, and Bruno Gerard shifted his feet impatiently, as if to recall them. For a moment longer Hugo held her gaze, then he shook his head and began to swing that booted foot again, as if he deliberately set out to break some indefinable rapport that had existed between them briefly.

"For how much longer, I wonder, *mademoiselle,*" he said quietly. "Once Jacques is back here, I doubt the books will hold your interest as easily."

Ruth would have denied it, however true she knew it to be, but Madame Gerard, reminded of the prospect of having her beloved grandson home, laughed delightedly and clasped her hands together. "But of course the books will not be of such interest when Jacques is home, Hugo," she told her son. "How could it be so, *mon cher*?"

"It was foolish of me, I suppose, to hope that someone I pay to work for me will continue to do so when Jacques arrives!" Hugo said sarcastically, and even Madame Gerard looked at him in some surprise.

"But, Hugo," she said, and shook her head reproachfully, "you would not part the young people, for sure, *mon cher*. You could not be so cruel!"

"I shall be as cruel as I have the right to be, *maman*," he said, and once more the gray eyes quizzed Ruth from behind the screen of blue smoke.

Madame Gerard shook her head in reproach, then made a grimace of sympathy at Ruth and put a hand on her arm. "We will go and leave you to your work, *ma chère* Ruth," she told her. "If we do not this... *brute* will make you pay for speaking with us, hmm?"

Hugo raised no objection either to their going or to the denigration of his character. He kissed his mother lightly on her brow and murmured a few brief words of parting to his brother, then perched himself on the edge of the desk again as the door closed behind them, while Ruth went back to work.

For several seconds he sat there, one booted foot swinging back and forth, his body half turned toward her, quietly smoking his cigarette while Ruth took more books from the shelves and put them down carefully on the desk behind him. Her hands were trembling, although heaven knew why, except that possibly some of the nervous tension that seemed to emanate from him, despite his quietness, communicated itself to her.

She was also uneasily aware that behind that haze of blue smoke the gray eyes were watching her, and adding to her discomfort. "Do you also fear that I mean to keep you and Jacques apart, *mademoiselle*?" he asked suddenly, and Ruth looked up, a little dazed at having the question sprung on her so unexpectedly.

The rising smoke hid his expression from her, but she could see the glitter of his eyes and sensed the air of tension about him, despite his seeming calm and quiet. "I—I don't know," she admitted at last. "I can't see any reason why you should."

"Précisément!"

She looked at him for a moment, then shook her head slowly. "I—I think perhaps Madame Gerard thought, as I did, that you have some objection to Jacques taking me out, *monsieur*," she ventured, and he shrugged.

"Not at all," he denied. "I merely wished to remind you, and my mother, that I am employing you to work for me, not to chase around the countryside with Jacques when he is here."

"Of course I realize that," Ruth insisted.

She resented the suggestion that she was likely to lose interest as soon as Jacques came home, and immediately abandon her work to go out with him. Of course Jacques was a distraction, she knew that only too well, but she would be firm and he could not take her away from her work by force.

"You will not expect me to free you to go with Jacques?"

Ruth shook her head. "No, *monsieur*, of course not!"

A faint smile touched that wide, expressive mouth briefly. "I am very pleased to hear it," he said, and narrowed his eyes again against the rising smoke. "Because the temptation will be there, *mademoiselle*—I know Jacques!"

"And I know how to say no!" Ruth insisted.

Again that hint of smile tugged at his mouth. "But apparently not always to good effect," he said quietly. "You informed me that Monsieur Stoddard was driven to dismissing you because of your inability to say no to Jacques!"

It was an unfair gibe and Ruth flushed pink, her hands curling tightly when she remembered his remarks about the incident. After what he had said then he could scarcely claim to take a less tolerant view now—or could he?

"You said then that Jacques had only done what you would have expected of him," she reminded him, watching his face through the thickness of her lashes. "You seemed to think that old Henry Stoddard was a—a puritan for objecting to my being kissed against my will, so you could hardly make a fuss if he did the same here." She could not explain what made her look at him the way she did, daring him to change his view. "Could you?" she asked softly.

She could feel the heavy, thudding beat of her heart against her side as she did her best to hold that steady, intense gaze and he said nothing for a moment. One foot swung slowly back and forth in an almost hypnotic rhythm and she found it so much easier after all to follow its movement than to look at him direct.

"If you imply that I will allow Jacques to come in here while you are working and kiss you whenever the fancy takes him," he told her quietly, "you are quite wrong in your estimation of me, *mademoiselle*!"

He would be quite ruthless, Ruth realized with a sudden sense of panic. Even his mother had said as much to her, and he seemed bent on proving it. She had not expected him to give her unlimited time to go about with Jacques, but she had secretly suspected that he might allow some relaxation—now, it seemed, she was wrong.

"I don't expect you to tolerate his being in and out of here all the time," she said. "That wouldn't be reasonable, but after what you had to say about poor old Henry Stoddard you—" She shrugged, looking at him again through the length of her lashes, her heart thudding wildly. "But then I suppose it's a different matter when you're calling the tune yourself, isn't it, *monsieur*?"

The silence that followed could have been cut with a knife and his gray eyes had a chill look that made her shiver involuntarily when he looked at her, his mouth tight and thin. "You will decide for yourself, *mademoiselle*," he told her coolly. "I warned you that I would not consider paying you to work for me simply so that you could take a holiday with Jacques. When he arrives you will either continue to work as you have for the past five days or I will engage someone else—it is your choice!"

"Oh, no, please!" She was surprised to find herself pleading with him, but she felt she had so much to lose if she allowed him to goad her into leaving now, when she was so happy with what she was doing. It was the kind of job she had long dreamed of and she hated to think of losing it so soon. "I—I don't want to leave," she said in a small husky voice, and looked at him appealingly. "I—I really *want* to stay."

He said nothing for several seconds and Ruth found the waiting almost intolerable. She stood there in front of him holding a beautiful leather-bound copy of an early Tolstoy novel between her hands, trying to stop them from trembling, and her eyes were still unconsciously appealing as she glanced at him again.

"Then stay," he said softly, at last, and the breath she had been unconsciously holding left her body in a great sigh.

It was quite incredible, she thought, that it could matter so much to her, but somehow it did, and now he must realize it too. "You—you won't mind if I see Jacques when—"

"When you have completed your work for the day," he interrupted, shrugging his broad shoulders as if it did not matter to him either way, "Jacques may kiss you all night long, *mademoiselle*—it will not concern me!"

"Well, it would concern me!" Ruth objected, a bright, warm flush on her cheeks as she faced him indignantly, the book still held tight against her breast. "You have the wrong impression of me altogether, Monsieur Gerard!"

Briefly the gray eyes regarded her steadily and one brow rose quizzically. "As I think you have the wrong impression of me, *mademoiselle*," he told her quietly. He got to his feet, strong brown fingers crushing out the cigarette with an oddly savage motion, and looked at her again through the acrid smoke from the smoldering stub. Then he put both hands into the pockets of his pants and she thought there was a hint of a smile on that wide, straight mouth. "Let us agree to misunderstand one another, *mon enfant*, huh?" he suggested softly.

He was striding across the room before Ruth could find a suitable answer and she wondered just why he had come in in the first place. Whether he had wanted to make sure that his mother and brother did not waste too much of her time, or if there had been some other reason that had been forgotten in the ensuing exchange.

When he reached the doorway he turned and looked back over his shoulder at her. "You will not go too far on that ladder," he told her, indicating the library steps just behind her. "When you require books from the higher shelves I will arrange for Robert or one of the other servants to assist you."

"Oh, but I can—" Her objection was instinctive, but he dismissed it even before it was voiced.

"You will do as I say," he informed her coolly. "When you reach the higher shelves you will inform me and I will make arrangements to find you some assistance." He would have left it there and gone out of the room, but when she did not answer he turned again and looked across at her. "Do you understand me, *mademoiselle*?" he asked sharply.

Ruth looked down at the book in her hands, her emotions playing odd tricks on her. There was no earthly reason why she should feel the way she did, an odd sense of elation that was quite inexplicable, but her hands were trembling and she could feel the strong steady beat of her heart as she sought to control her voice.

"Oui, monsieur," she said meekly, and caught a brief look of surprise in his eyes before he turned and went out.

It was several moments after he had closed the door behind him that she realized she had forgotten to mention a find she had made that morning. While taking some very old and precious volumes from the lowest shelf, she had discovered a reel of recording tape tucked away behind them.

She had no idea what it contained, but judging by its condition it had been there at the back of the shelf for some time undisturbed, and the fact that it had been put there with the object of concealing it added to her mystification. She even wondered if Hugo Gerard was the one it had been hidden from, but that was a passing speculation and she would tell him about it as soon as she saw him again.

THE WHOLE OF the following day passed without Ruth even giving a thought to the reel of tape she had found, and it was only by accident that she remembered it at all. Two days after Madame Gerard's visit to the library she opened a drawer in the desk and discovered it again.

The metal case was old and dusty, and her curiosity was again aroused as she turned it over in her hands. She should have reported its discovery to Hugo before now, but somehow it had slipped her mind, and she excused herself by deciding that it was unlikely to be anything important anyway.

It was most likely a recording of some music, for there was a label stuck on the protective metal case that read *Concerto d'Automne*, and even Ruth's basic knowledge of French could make that *Autumn Concerto*. The puzzle was why it had been hidden and for a while she toyed with the idea that Hugo Gerard was a secret music lover, but then that would not explain why the tape had been so thoroughly hidden—and anyway, she could not imagine him caring who knew what his likes and dislikes were.

There was a very modern tape recorder over on a table near the window, in one of the alcoves, and she looked at it from a distance for several minutes while she debated the ethics of playing back the discovered tape. Eventually she decided that if it was a piece of music then it could do no possible harm to play it and see if she recognized it. From its title she thought it promised to be a classical piece, and she enjoyed classical music, but she did not recognize the title and the label gave no clue as to who the composer was.

It was difficult to discover how the machine worked at first, but finally she managed to get it right and switched it on. To begin with there was nothing but vague rustling noises in a void of scratchy silence, but then suddenly a man's voice spoke, so clearly and distinctly that he might have been in the room with her, and she started visibly.

"Hugo, *mon frère* . . . " it began, and she listened closely, for although it sounded like the voice of a young man, it had such a deep intonation of sadness in it that she experienced a strange curling sensation in her stomach when she heard it, and her heart began to flutter as if in panic. She recognized only the name Hugo, but that was enough, and after a pause the voice went on. "*Ici* Philippe—"

Ruth sprang forward swiftly and clicked off the switch, hand to her mouth, her breath caught in her throat. Philippe Gerard was the brother that Bruno was so reluctant to have mentioned, and the son that Madame Gerard had spoken of so sadly, the eldest son. He had died young, Bruno had said, but without specifying how, and now his voice rang sad and clear in the big sunny room, making Ruth shiver.

She stood there for a moment or two by the machine, her heart pounding heavily in her breast as she looked down at the silent tape. It was foolish to be so afraid of a young man who had died tragically many years before, but some of her fear, she recognized, was for being caught listening to something she had no right to hear.

Nevertheless, after a moment or two, she reached across again and clicked on the switch. She had no right, of course, to hear any more and she could not understand the words, only recognize the names, but something about that voice was irresistible, despite its air of sadness. The rest of the message was short, just a few slow, careful words, that was all, and then it was silent again.

About to switch off, she drew back when the music started suddenly and unexpectedly and she put her hands to her face as she listened to it, vaguely disturbed for no reason that she could think of, but finding it irresistible, like that sad voice. Indeed, it had quite a lot in common with the voice.

It was a piano piece, a sweet but impressive melody, and despite a certain lack of skill in the pianist, she found herself swept along by it. There were grand, sweeping phrases and softer, more gentle passages between, but the whole piece had that same indescribable sense of sadness she had heard in the man's voice.

She was engrossed in it, so completely captured by it that she heard nothing of the door open behind her, and did not realize she was no longer alone until the music ended and, in the scratchy silence that followed, Hugo Gerard spoke from behind her.

"Ruth—where did you get that?"

She spun around swiftly, smothering a cry of surprise, her eyes wide and her teeth biting hard into her lower lip. Following the emotional impact of the music, his sudden appearance shocked her and for a moment she felt quite dizzy.

"I—I'm sorry," she whispered at last, reaching over to switch off the machine.

He reached out and picked up the dusty metal case bearing the title. "Where *did* you get this?" he asked again, and Ruth sought hard for words to explain.

"It—it was hidden," she said huskily. "In the bookcase, behind the Voltaire on the first shelf. I—I found it the other morning—a couple of days ago."

"And you did not consider telling me about it?"

There was a steely hardness about him; in the strong, rugged features and most of all in the gray eyes that now looked as chilling as ice as he gazed down at her. As if he suspected her of heaven knew what. She wanted to explain to him, to tell him that she had had no idea what the tape contained when she found it, or that it was so important to him—and it obviously was, judging by his reaction.

"I—I meant to tell you," she said in a small husky voice. "I was going to tell you the same morning, but somehow—Madame Gerard and your brother came in and—"

"You said nothing to them of this?"

She shook her head, startled by his harshness. "No, there was no time to tell anyone anything, even if it had occurred to me. Madame Gerard introduced me to your brother and then you came in."

"Ah!"

She looked at him cautiously through the thickness of her lashes. "I—I made the mistake of saying that I thought *monsieur*—your brother had been to Oxford," she said. "He and *madame* corrected me."

"I see!" He eyed her coolly. "So you are learning more about us, *mademoiselle*, are you not?"

When he had first come into the room and found her playing the tape, she realized, he had called her Ruth, but perhaps shock had momentarily put him off his guard, for he was now back to that formal '*mademoiselle*' again.

She said nothing, for there seemed little she could say in the circumstances and, after a moment, he leaned across her to take the tape from the machine. His lean hardness was suddenly and heart-stoppingly close as he brushed against her, and although he seemed unmoved by the contact it had a disturbing effect on Ruth.

A brown sinewy arm touched her with warmth and a strangely disquieting sensation that fluttered her pulses alarmingly, and in the brief time their bodies were in contact she felt oddly breathless. For a while he held the reel in his big, work-hard hands and she saw an expression there that she had never seen before—a warm, gentle look of tenderness that stirred a response in her she could not fully understand.

"Do you know what this is?" he asked suddenly, and Ruth shook her head, too disturbed by inexplicable things to find words. *"Concerto d'Automne,"* he said softly. "My brother's music."

It took Ruth a moment or two to realize his meaning, and when she did she gazed at him in wonder.

"You—you mean he *wrote* it?" she asked, and he nodded. "But—it's beautiful!"

"It's beautiful," he echoed softly. "I thought so when I heard it first, many years ago." He looked down at the reel of tape as if he could not quite believe in its existence. "I never knew he made a recording of it."

"He made it for you, I think," Ruth said, and instantly responded to the look of sharp curiosity he gave her. "There's a message at the beginning," she added hastily. "Before the music starts."

"And you have listened to that, too?" There was a hint of iciness in his eyes again which she found incredibly hard to bear, and she hastily shook her head.

"I—I didn't understand it—except the names," she told him. "Your name and then—and then Philippe."

The icy gaze still held her. "You know of Philippe, too?"

Ruth nodded, her voice sounding small and uncertain and echoing the sense of regret she felt in her heart. "I know that he was your elder brother, *monsieur*, and that—that he died young, that's all."

"That is quite enough, *mademoiselle*!"

She looked up at the dark, rugged face shadowed in the alcove of the sunny room, and saw bitterness and regret in the wide tightness of his mouth and the icy lightness of his eyes. "I—I didn't mean to pry when I played the tape, Monsieur Gerard," she said, wishing her voice could have sounded less shaky. "I—I don't really know why I put it on."

"Curiosity!" The gray eyes sought and held hers again, and she felt the rapid tap-tapping of her heart against her ribs. It was possible there was a less icy look there now, but he still radiated an air of tautness that did not relax even when the firm mouth tilted briefly into a smile. "It is a failing of your sex, *mademoiselle*, and I cannot blame you for something over which you have no control."

It was difficult to know how to reply to that, and so she said nothing but stood beside him for what seemed like and interminable time, with her heart tapping steadily away like the ticking of a clock. "I'd—I'd better get back to my work," she said at last, finding the silence too overbearing.

She would have turned away, but he put out a hand and the strong fingers curled over her bare arm with a touch that startled her. "Please leave me for a while, *mademoiselle*," he said quietly, and lifted the reel of tape in his other hand. "I would like to hear that message."

"Yes, of course!"

She understood perfectly why he wanted to listen to the message alone. Hugo Gerard was not a man who was used to betraying his feelings to strangers and she guessed that hearing his dead brother's voice would have a shattering effect even on his iron self-control. She had already seen a hint of it when he had recognized the music, and they must have been very close, she guessed, for the message and the tape to have been left for Hugo and not for his mother.

She opened the door and was on her way out when he called after her. "Mademoiselle Colton!" Ruth turned and looked over her shoulder, startled. "You will not find it necessary to tell . . . anyone, of this," he said, and she shook her head instinctively.

"No, Monsieur Gerard, of course not."

"*Merci!*" When she turned again to close the door behind her he was already winding the tape back on to the machine and as she pulled the door to she heard the faint snick of a switch.

CHAPTER FIVE

JACQUES ARRIVED QUITE EARLY the following day, and when Ruth heard the car she momentarily forgot about everything else and half rose from her seat at the library desk to go out and welcome him. She heard Madame Gerard hurry across the hall, calling excitedly to him, and a few moments later she heard them come in together.

Their voices sounded oddly echoing and unreal in the vastness of the hall, with Madame Gerard chattering away excitedly and the deeper tone of Jacques' voice and the sound of his laughter. There was a great deal of laughter and Ruth smiled to herself when she heard it. The quiet old château would take on a new life now that Jacques was home again.

When, after a few seconds, she heard Hugo's voice added to the general hubbub, she knew she had been wiser not to go out and join them. Madame would probably not have minded and Jacques would have welcomed her appearance, but she doubted if Hugo would have approved of her joining the family welcome.

Keeping her entire attention on the job in hand proved quite difficult, however, and she was reminded of Hugo's anticipation of the situation. Jacques would detract from her interest in her work, he had forecast, and he was already being proved right.

She sighed and hastily altered an incorrect entry, then looked up swiftly when the door opened suddenly and Jacques stood in the doorway. His arms were spread wide in one of those extravagant gestures she had come to expect of him, and his brown eyes were sparkling wickedly as he looked across at her. Then he laughed and came hurrying across the room, pushing the door to only carelessly behind him.

"Ruth! Oh, Ruth, *chérie*!" He took her in his arms, his eyes glitteringly dark, and kissed her so fervently that she had little breath left to protest, even had she felt inclined to. There was something comfortingly familiar about his embrace, and she knew she was smiling as he pressed his lips to her smooth neck and throat, murmuring all the time, endearments in his own tongue.

"Jacques!" She found breath at last and laughed up at him.

"Oh, *chérie*, it is so good to see you again!" He held her at arm's length for a moment, his eyes slightly narrowed and still glittering with his unquenchable high spirits. "How have they been treating you, *mon amour*?" he asked, and Ruth smiled.

"Very well!" she told him. "How else?"

He hugged her close again, his arms tight about her. "I have been breaking my heart for you, *ma belle*!" he whispered against her ear. "Thinking of you here with Hugo, and wondering—" He shrugged expressive shoulders and Ruth felt the warm flush that colored her cheeks at the implication he was making.

"Jacques!" she said in a voice she wished could have sounded more steady. "You have no reason to make suggestions like that, especially since I've been here only a little over a week!"

His dark eyes scorned her objections, but he was smiling as if he knew her protests were true. "Hugo has been known to make a conquest in much less than a week, *ma chérie*!" he told her, and laughed, kissing her mouth lightly.

"I work for Monsieur Gerard, that's all," Ruth insisted. "You've no call to start making remarks like that the minute you're here!"

"Oh, Ruth! *Ma belle!*" He lifted her chin with one hand and looked down at her for a moment steadily, then he bent his head and kissed her slowly and lingeringly on her mouth. "You should not scold me so angrily, *chérie*," he murmured against her lips. "I do not suspect you of anything, but Hugo—" He flicked one brow into the flop of dark hair on his forehead and made a wry grimace at her. "Hugo is Hugo, and you are a very beautiful woman, *chérie*!"

"I'm also English," Ruth reminded him, producing the best argument she could think of for his being wrong, but wishing she could do something about the way her heart was rapping at her ribs. "Your uncle doesn't see Englishwomen in the same light as other females, and being English means I'm rather too levelheaded to be swept off my feet by a—reputation!"

"Oh, Ruth! *Chérie!*" He rested his forehead against hers and looked down at her, his breath warm on her cheek as he spoke. "Does that also mean that you are not—how is it—swept off your feet by me?"

Ruth laughed. She simply couldn't help it, it bubbled up inside her and she put back her head and laughed aloud, and it was as if some weight had been lifted from her. She had not realized until now, but in the little over a week that she had been there she hadn't laughed, not really laughed, once, and the sensation it gave her was indescribable.

"You're different," she told Jacques, and put her

arms up around his neck, smiling up at him. For a moment she looked at him, her eyes taking in the familiar features and the bright, dark mischief in his eyes, then she tiptoed and kissed him lightly on his chin. "It's going to be wonderful having you around again," she told him.

"You are right, *chérie*!" Jacques's dark eyes rolled heavenward. "You do not know how I have longed for you!" He kissed her forehead lightly and smiled down at her. "Have you also missed me, *ma belle* Ruth? Or has Hugo had you so busy that you have not even noticed I was not here?"

"I've noticed!" Ruth assured him laughingly. "It's been very peaceful until now and I got through a lot of work!"

"Belle et cruelle!" he scolded, and kissed her again. "I will lighten your life, *mon chou*! You shall no longer be at Hugo's—how is it—beck and call, huh?"

Ruth shook her head, thinking suddenly that Hugo and Madame Gerard were in all probability still within hearing, out in the hall where Jacques had left them. She thought she could catch the murmur of voices and it was probably Hugo supervising Jacques's luggage.

"I can't just drop everything and take time off to come with you, Jacques," she told him, and eased herself from his arms. "I work for Hu—Monsieur Gerard, and I still have a job to do."

"And I will not tolerate you changing the situation, Jacques." Hugo's voice sounded adamant as he came striding into the room, followed more slowly by Madame Gerard, who looked slightly unhappy about something.

"The situation?" Jacques was already looking at his grandmother with a mildly speculative eye, counting on her support, Ruth guessed wryly.

"Mademoiselle Colton works for me," Hugo reminded him. "You may have her company whenever I do not want her—there will be no argument!"

It was an autocratic, imperious statement and Ruth found it strangely disturbing. He spoke as if he owned her but was prepared to let someone else have her when his own needs were served, and she found the air of possessiveness oddly satisfying, instead of annoying as she would have expected. Jacques looked as if he was prepared to argue about it, but then evidently thought better of it, and he shrugged resignedly then bent and kissed Ruth beside her left ear.

"We will see," he murmured, his voice muffled by her hair, and Ruth thought she heard Madame Gerard chuckle softly to herself, but she couldn't be sure.

"Jacques." She put a hand on Jacques's arm, but then her gaze met the cool determined look in those gray eyes, and she shook her head. "You'd better go and get yourself settled in," she told him quietly. "I'll see you later."

MOST OF HIS FIRST DAY at home Jacques had spent with his grandmother, since Ruth was working, although he quite blatantly transferred his attentions to Ruth during lunch and dinner and the old lady did no more than smile benignly at them. Despite Ruth's own plain speaking, and his uncle's, she suspected, about his avowed intention of marrying her, she thought Madame Gerard would not be altogether averse to the idea.

The old lady adored him, and he certainly wasn't the schoolboy his uncle designated him, he was well past the age when many young men marry. But at twenty-three Jacques was much less mature than she was herself in a lot of ways. He had the sophisticated tastes of a practiced philanderer, it was true, but that was bred in him rather than acquired through experience, she suspected.

It was odd, she thought as she sat at the desk in the library the following morning, how much more youthful he seemed now than she remembered him only a couple of weeks before. It was quite a jolt to realize that she was, in fact, comparing him with Hugo, which was hardly a fair comparison. Jacques was fresh from university, young and carefree and with nothing to cloud a promising future, while Hugo Gerard was a much traveled, well-matured sophisticate who could surely have few illusions left, if his writing was anything to judge by.

Once again it startled her to realize that she had grown used to the more mature sophistication of his uncle, even in such a short time as she had been there. There was a lot about Hugo Gerard that mystified her still, and some things that angered her, but she could not forget that look of indescribable tenderness she had seen on his face as he held the recording of his dead brother's music in his hands.

Hastily she dismissed Hugo Gerard from her mind and dwelt instead on the pleasure of having Jacques's company again, no matter how distracting it was. It was almost as if thinking about him had brought him to her, for she had been carefully listing books from a pile at her elbow when the door opened suddenly and he was smiling across at her.

"*Ah, bon*! You are alone!" he said in such a conspiratorial tone that she laughed.

"I'm also busy," she told him, getting up from behind the desk and walking across to the shelves. "You'd better go, Jacques; your uncle doesn't like people coming in here when I'm working."

"Ha!" He dismissed Hugo's dislikes with a careless shrug and came across to join her, taking her hands in his and so preventing her from taking any more books from the shelf. "It is a beautiful day," he murmured, his voice muffled by her hair as he kissed her ear. "You should not be shut up in here like a prisoner, *ma belle*!"

"I'm working," she insisted, and tried hastily to move aside when she realized they were not alone any more.

Hugo strode across the carpeted floor undetected by Jacques, who had his back to the room and was much too engrossed in trying to persuade her, to notice anything else. Standing at the desk she had just left, Hugo seemingly took not the slightest notice of them, either, although Ruth found it hard to believe that he was as unconcerned as he appeared to be. Not when he had been so adamantly firm about Jacques taking her away from her work.

She tried again to break the hold on her hands and there was a bright pink flush on her cheeks as she looked across at the tall figure at the desk. "Jacques, please!" she said anxiously.

Still unaware that they were not alone, Jacques looked at her reproachfully. *"Chérie,"* he whispered. "Are you not pleased to see me?"

"Yes! Yes, of course I am!" She looked up at the dark face with its reproachful brown eyes and smiled. "Of course I'm glad to see you, Jacques, you know that."

"Then why do you try to hold me away, hmm?" His mouth brushed lightly, teasingly on hers and he drew her close into his arms, laughing softly. "You will come with me, *mon petit chou*, and we will drive for a long way, huh?"

Again Ruth glanced uneasily at the man beside

the desk, seemingly unaware of them as Jacques was still unaware of him, and she shook her head. "I—I can't, Jacques, you know that," she told him. "Not during the day."

"Oh?" He looked less sure of himself suddenly and frowned. "You do not want to come with me, I think, *chérie*!"

"Oh, but of course I do—" Ruth began, and a quiet voice interrupted her before she could explain.

"Mademoiselle Colton is doing the work I pay her to do, Jacques." Hugo told him coolly. "Must I remind you that you yourself recommended her for the position?"

Jacques spun around swiftly, startled to discover his uncle in the room, but refusing to be disconcerted. "*Mais oui*, of course I know that," he said, and there was a hint of sulkiness about his mouth, expressing his dislike of the situation. "But why cannot Ruth come with me for just a little while?"

"Because I need her here!" The quiet voice was adamant and she sensed Jacques's inner conflict as he decided whether it was worthwhile trying to bend what he must know to be an indomitable will.

"You *need* her?" he asked, and laughed shortly.

Hugo looked up and his gray eyes were glistening with that hint of amusement Ruth had seen before, as if he enjoyed the challenge of an argument. "Very well," he said softly. "I *want* her here—does that satisfy you, *garçon*?"

Used as he used it the word became a studied insult, a gibe at Jacques's comparative youth, and Ruth caught her breath at the deliberate harshness of it, for it would have stung the younger man's pride and he must know it. She knew from her own experience that it did not pay to try and cross Hugo Gerard, but she had thought his ruthlessness confined to his dealings with strangers— she had hardly expected him to put his nephew so firmly in his place, and particularly in front of her.

Jacques's dark face was flushed angrily and there was a resentful glitter in his eyes as he looked at his uncle. "It is not so much to ask that you spare my fian—"

A swiftly arched brow prevented him from referring to her as his fiancée, and again Ruth noticed that hint of amusement in the cool gray eyes as Hugo perched himself on the desk and regarded his nephew steadily.

A dark green shirt fitted closely to the broadness of his chest and was smarter than anything she had seen him wearing yet, even though it was open to about halfway down and revealed the smooth tanned skin beneath. Fawn slacks clung just as closely to his lean hips and long legs, and he swung one foot carelessly as he perched there, offering a provocative challenge to the younger man and seeming to revel in the certainty that he could outface him.

"Ruth knows my feelings about her going with you during working hours," he told Jacques, and Ruth's own pulses leaped at the use of her Christian name, used as if that, too, was part of the challenge. "Since she has already refused to go with you why do you not leave her to her work, hmm?"

"Ruth has refused to come with me because she is afraid of angering you!" Jacques declared belligerently, and Hugo smiled, not in the least offended by the suggestion.

It was a slow, meaningful smile and his gray eyes were looking at Ruth inquiringly. "Is that so, *mademoiselle*?" he asked softly. "Are you afraid of angering me?"

The question, despite its content, had a strangely disturbing intimacy about it, and she felt her pulse quicken again as she hastily lowered her eyes. "No, no, of course not!"

She had answered without thinking and she knew as soon as the words were out of her mouth that it wasn't true. She was not exactly afraid of making him angry, but she was reluctant to do so, and she doubted if Jacques would appreciate the difference.

"So you refused the offer because you prefer not to go?"

The quiet voice was insistent and she bit her lip in her uncertainty before she answered. "Of course I'd *like* to go with Jacques," she said at last. "But—well, I do work for you, Monsieur Gerard, and I remember you told me before I started that I couldn't expect to have a holiday when Jacques arrived. Not that I think I'm entitled to it," she added hastily, and caught her breath when he got up from the desk with one of his quick, sharp movements and stood looking at the two of them for a moment, his hands in his pockets and a strangely taut look on his rugged features suddenly.

"Oh, go with him, for the love of heaven!" he said harshly, and strode across to the door, banging it shut behind him.

It was so unlike him to lose control that for a moment or two neither of them said anything, although Ruth's heart was banging away heavily in her breast and she found herself regretting his angry departure without quite knowing why it should matter so much.

Jacques, however, was quite unconcerned about anything but having his own way, and he looked at her and laughed, lifting her off her feet and into his arms, whirling her around and around until she clung to him breathlessly. "He gave in!" he laughed exultantly, still not believing it. "Hugo surrendered, Ruth—I never thought to see the day!" He put her back on her feet and kissed her, holding her by her arms and looking down at her for a moment with a bright quizzical look. "You have worked *magie, mon amour*!" he told her. "Come, let us go before the spell wears away and you are brought back!"

Ruth felt oddly reluctant to go now, although heaven knew why when she had been given an unexpected day off, and Jacques was ready and waiting. Her hesitation both puzzled Jacques and made him slightly impatient and he looked at her curiously.

"I really shouldn't go when I've work to do," she told him in a small uncertain voice, and he took her arms firmly and looked down into her face.

"I think that Hugo has also put a spell on you, *chérie*," he told her seriously. "What is wrong with you, Ruth? Hugo has said that you may go and yet you hesitate... why, *mignonne*?"

She did not answer for a moment, then suddenly shrugged and smiled up at him a little ruefully. "Maybe my conscience is bothering me," she suggested. "But since I *have* been given an unexpected break it would be a pity to waste it, so where are you taking me?"

"Where would you like to go?"

Ruth had no hesitation in naming her choice and she looked up at him and smiled, her head to one side. "I'd love to go to Paris," she told him. "Is that too far?"

"*Mais non!*" He put an arm around her shoulders and drew her with him across the room. "If you wish to see Paris then you shall, *ma chérie*!"

PARIS WAS EVERYTHING that Ruth had expected of it. Mellow buildings, countless statues, beautiful avenues and noisy, excitable traffic tearing about as if the drivers were bent on self-destruction. Ruth favored leaving the car and walking in the sun, so that was what they did, and despite several close calls with the traffic, she managed to see much more than if her view had been cramped by the confines of a car.

She picked on a familiar name and asked to go to the Place de la Concorde, finding it every bit as lovely as she had been led to believe. Jacques seemed not to mind in the least acting as guide and taking her to the tourist places because he could see that she was enjoying it.

She loved the fountains and the gardens and was thrilled to be able to see so much just by standing near the river by one of the fountains. He pointed out the trees that were part of the gardens of the Tuileries and the golden dome of the Invalides, where he told her Napoleon lay in his last resting place. And most exciting of all, although much more distant from their vantage point, she could see the skeleton shape of the Eiffel Tower, looking slightly unreal in the sunny haze.

The impressiveness of the Place de la Concorde itself delighted Ruth, too. A huge square so beautifully planned that it pleased the eye wherever she looked. Tall trees, casting welcome shade as well as beautifying their environment, artfully arranged groups of statues, and an endless impression of people and sunlight and mellow buildings. It all seemed to fit together so perfectly that she was lulled into a wonderful sense of well-being.

Eventually they found their way to one of the little street cafés and sat outside drinking coffee accompanied by the most delicious pastries Ruth had ever eaten. She was uncertain how the subject of Hugo arose, but judging by his frown it was plain that Jacques disliked having him mentioned.

"I'm wondering if I'll be expected to make up for this time tomorrow," she said. "Monsieur Gerard may extract vengeance by making me work harder!"

Jacques's dark eyes glittered as he rested his elbows on the little white table, a cup of coffee cupped in his hands. "It would be like him to do something like that," he agreed, and Ruth looked at him in surprise. She had seen Hugo Gerard as a hard man, ruthless at times even, but always scrupulously fair and certainly not given to extracting petty vengeance. Jacques being so ready to agree with her facetious suggestion puzzled her.

"He surely isn't like that, is he?" she asked, and met his curious look with a headshake. "I mean he wouldn't be petty about letting me come with you today. It doesn't sound like him, somehow."

"Non?" He found her opinion of his uncle unexpected, too, she guessed. "You are a champion of my uncle already, *chérie*, perhaps I was not so wrong in my first suspicions, hmm?"

"You were *quite* wrong," Ruth said firmly, a faint warm flush seemingly giving lie to her insistence, something that Jacques did not miss.

He reached out with one hand and with a finger gently touched her warm cheek. "Am I?" he asked softly.

Annoyed that she should be giving the wrong impression altogether, Ruth knocked his hand away sharply and shook her head. "I wish you wouldn't automatically assume that I'll join your uncle's apparently limitless queue of lovers," she told him, deliberately frank with her language to try and shock him into believing her. "I shan't, Jacques, and I wish you wouldn't keep harping on the subject!"

"Chérie!" He took her hands in his, hastily putting his coffee out of harm's way. "You are angry again and I did not want to make you angry with me!"

"I'm not angry," Ruth denied, already prepared to forget the matter if he would. "And I'm certainly not going to lose my temper and spoil my lovely day in Paris!"

"Amie!" He kissed her hands gently, and looked up at her with earnest brown eyes. "I was concerned only that Hugo should not—how do you say—bully you, and I said all the wrong words. I am sorry, *ma chérie*!"

"He doesn't bully me," she said quietly, and looked at him through her lashes. "I'm quite surprised you think he might," she added. "Don't—don't you get on very well with him, Jacques?"

"Pretty well!" He shrugged his shoulders and released her hands to take up his coffee cup again, emptying it before he put it down and folded his hands carefully on the table in front of him. "I used to think that he was *merveilleux* when I was a little boy," he said soberly, and went on, almost as if he was talking to himself. "When my mother and father died he was—" Expressive hands said more than words, and it was as serious as Ruth had ever seen him. "He is very good with children," he went on. "You should see him with Bruno's *enfants*—they adore him, as I did!"

"I met Bruno," she said, remembering the meeting clearly and the mistake she had made in thinking he had been the one who had been educated in England.

Jacques flicked an expressive brow. "Now there is someone who does not meet with Hugo's approval," he said, and Ruth nodded, her own suspicions confirmed.

"I thought that might be the case," she said. "Although I didn't know why, of course."

Jacques shrugged, and she thought he was uneasy. "It's an old story," he said.

For a moment Ruth resisted the temptation, but she could not get the mystery of Philippe Gerard out of her mind and she had an opportunity to discover just what had happened to him now. "I—I also learned about your other uncle," she told him. "The one who died—Philippe."

Jacques's dark eyes looked at her for a second as if he could not believe her, and even in the bright sunlight his face had a curiously shadowed look suddenly. "It was more than just . . . died," he said quietly, and Ruth felt her heart give a great leap in her breast as she clenched her hands tightly together on the little table.

They were both so tense and serious suddenly, sitting at a small table in the middle of sunlit Paris, and so out of tune with their surroundings, not fitting into them perfectly as they had only a few moments since.

"He wrote some beautiful music," Ruth said softly.

Ruth had intended only to let him know that she knew how talented his uncle had been and she genuinely forgot for the moment the promise she had made to Hugo not to tell anyone about the tape she had discovered. Jacques was looking at her with an expression that both surprised and startled her, and he reached across and took her hands again, his eyes dark and glittering, as he leaned towards her.

"What do you know about his music?" he asked. "I cannot believe that Hugo—no!" He dismissed the idea with a firm shake of his head, and it was then that Ruth remembered the promise she had made.

"I—I discovered it by accident," she said, seeking words that would cover her mistake.

"Discovered it?" He looked puzzled. "You discovered some of Philippe's music?" he asked. "Where, Ruth, how?"

It was inevitable now, she could see that, and she shrugged her resignation of the unavoidable. "I promised I would tell no one," she said in a small, husky voice. "Please, Jacques, don't let Hugo know that I told you about it."

The brown eyes were looking at her again in that curious and slightly suspicious way. "Does it matter?" he asked, and she nodded.

"I don't like breaking a promise," she said.

His hands squeezed hers gently. "Tell me about the music," he coaxed softly.

Ruth looked up at him and for a long moment tussled with her conscience. "I don't know why Hugo wants it kept quiet," she said at last. "But it can't hurt to tell you, if you promise to—"

"I won't let Hugo know that you broke your promise," he assured her. "What was this music, Ruth?"

"It was called *Autumn Concerto*," she said, not attempting to say its French title. "I found a tape recording behind some books in the library and Hugo—he caught me listening to it the other morning. There was a message for him at the beginning, too."

"Yes, there would be," he said, nodding slowly. "Hugo was the only one who ever believed in him."

"I—I guessed they were very close," she said softly, remembering again that look of gentleness on Hugo's rugged features. "Jacques . . . how did he die?"

For a moment Jacques said nothing, then he looked at her and half smiled, a wry little smile for him, his hands still holding hers. "You must know now, eh, *chérie*?" he asked, and did not wait for her to answer, but looked down at her fingers as he spoke. "Philippe was . . . how is it you say?" One hand made circling motions beside his head. "He had the uncertain mind, you understand?"

"Oh! Oh, poor Philippe!" Her sympathy seemed to please him, for he leaned across and kissed her lightly.

"At the same time he was clever," he went on. "He went to Oxford, as Hugo and I did."

"Yes, I know."

Jacques frowned at her curiously. "You know that?" he asked, and Ruth looked down at her hands.

"Hugo told me," she said. "Although he didn't say it was—he didn't say which brother it was and I automatically assumed he meant Bruno."

"Ah, oui!"

He nodded understanding, but Ruth shook her head, remembering again the embarrassment of that moment, and the taut, uneasy silence before Madame Gerard had explained. "I—I spoke to Bruno about being at Oxford," she explained. "And—" She spread her hands helplessly, still regretting the trap she had fallen into. "I had no idea another brother had ever existed. Then Madame Gerard told me about Philippe—that there had been another son."

"He is never talked of," Jacques said. "But Hugo

never forgets him. Hugo knew just how clever he was and he believed he could do well, but no one else took Philippe seriously and Hugo was too young then to help him."

The shock Ruth felt showed in her eyes and she looked at him in stunned surprise. "But surely Madame Gerard—" she said. "His mother?"

"His stepmother," Jacques corrected her softly. "*Grand-mère* was a second wife, you understand, although Philippe was only very small when she married *Grand-père* Gerard . . . and she was newly a widow when Philippe . . . died."

"Oh, I see!"

It explained so much, Ruth thought. For one thing why the tape had been left to Hugo and to no one else, and having heard the sad young voice of Philippe and the beautiful music he had created, she felt a strange sense of affinity with Hugo Gerard suddenly.

"When it was found that Philippe was a little strange," Jacques was saying, "no one troubled to take him seriously, except Hugo, who adored him as a big brother. My *maman* was the first child of *grand-mère*'s marriage and for a long time it was feared that there would be no other son, but then, five years after *maman*, Hugo was born and then Bruno the following year."

"And the name was safe again," Ruth said softly, remembering her conversation with Madame Gerard.

Jacques shrugged expressively. "*Precisement!*" he said wryly. "I think they all felt a little guilty when Philippe—did what he did, but it was a relief too." He sat for a moment holding her hands tightly in his, and they were both completely unaware of the sunny, peaceful scene around them for the moment.

"He—took his own life, Ruth," he said softly, as if he feared a reaction. "In the *cour* at the rear of the château, he took his own life, *chérie*."

As he spoke Ruth could see again that shadowed and chill courtyard where Robert, the chauffeur, had taken her when she arrived to take up her post, and she shivered. All those blank, closed windows like sleeping eyes, and the echoing cobblestones—no wonder it had struck her as a chill and unfriendly place when the unhappy spirit of Philippe Gerard still hovered about it.

Then she looked across at Jacques's solemn face, so unlike his normal bright and cheerful expression, and felt guilty for having brought such tragic memories into the open. She put her hands over his and squeezed his fingers gently. "I'm sorry I've made us both so sad," she told him softly. "Will you forgive me, Jacques?"

For a moment he still had that sad and lost look, and then he smiled, slowly at first but soon with his more customary air of impudence, and he leaned across the table and kissed her mouth lingeringly. "I will forgive you," he said, "if you will promise never to mention Philippe again. It was—oh, *mon dieu*—twenty-one years ago, and much too long ago to hurt us, so . . . we will forget, eh?"

Twenty-one years ago, Ruth thought, when Hugo could have been a boy of no more than fifteen; no wonder he had been so affected by his brother's death, and so soon after his father's, too. Jacques might think it was too long ago to hurt them, but it would, she guessed, hurt Hugo Gerard for a long time.

She realized suddenly that Jacques was frowning at her in mock disapproval, and she smiled, shaking her head and echoing his words. "We will forget," she said.

CHAPTER SIX

IT SEEMED MORE DIFFICULT SOMEHOW, now that Ruth knew how Philippe Gerard had died, to settle down to working in the room where she had listened to his music. She found herself constantly wondering about the young man whose shadow now seemed to have so much more substance.

She frequently looked across at the tape recorder in the alcove by the window and wondered if anyone else would ever hear that beautiful music, or if Hugo had hidden it away again for good. It was out of the question that she could ask him about it, and yet she would love to have listened to it once more.

During the next week or so Jacques scarcely came near the library at all and she guessed, despite his denial of the fact, that Hugo had far more influence on him than he was prepared to admit. There was a certain rapport between the two men, uncle and nephew, that not even that almost primitive air of challenge could destroy.

She saw little of Hugo, either, and wondered if by some chance Jacques had held him to some kind of promise that if he stayed away from the library, Hugo would, too. It was a little presumptuous of her, perhaps, but whenever they were both with her she had the strangest feeling that some sort of tussle of wills existed.

The work was going well, and she was quite pleased with herself for having got as far as she had in the time, even though she had spent some time dwelling on the subject of Philippe Gerard and his unhappy ending. The first two shelves on one side of the big room were already stripped of their contents and her lists were growing rapidly.

Several days before she had spotted a familiar title on the next to top shelf and decided to attempt to read a French copy of Dumas. Not that she expected to have much success, but she would like to try just for the mental exercise, and she had no doubt that Hugo would raise no objection to her borrowing it.

Climbing the tall stepladder presented some difficulties because she had a not very good head for heights, but if she was careful she would come to no harm, and she certainly had no intention of asking for help, as Hugo had suggested.

The worn wooden steps felt less safe as she went higher and the structure moved slightly on its smooth-running wheels, making her grab at the support bar tightly. From where she was she had an excellent view out into the gardens, and she spent a few precarious seconds looking out of the window before reaching for her book.

It was higher than she realized and she was obliged to go up another step before she could even get her fingers on it, another step that proved her undoing. She was standing on tiptoe, stretching upward for the book, when someone opened the door and she lost her balance when she looked down to see who it was.

The mobile steps seemed to run away from her and she let out a sharp scream of alarm as she toppled sideways, her arms flailing helplessly and her feet slipping off the worn step. It was a long way to the floor, and although it was carpeted, it would make a hard landing from that height.

Before she hit the floor, however, someone

caught her and held her tightly for a moment while she caught her breath. She was breathing shortly and unevenly in her alarm and her eyes were closed as she clung to her rescuer without, for the moment, knowing or caring who it was, her face buried against the warm, sensual smoothness of bare skin.

Then, without raising her head, she realized who it was who had caught her so deftly. The shabby blue shirt open to the waist could only belong to Hugo, and so could the hands that held her so tightly. Strong, hard hands that held her pressed against him as if he feared she might fall again if he let her go.

Her face was pressed against the expanse of bare chest exposed by that open shirt, and she could feel the steady drumming of a strong heartbeat under her ear. Her own heart set up an incredibly wild tattoo against her ribs and for a moment she resisted her initial instinct to draw hastily away. There was something infinitely comforting about being where she was, no matter if she did realize what a fool she was for feeling that way.

After a second or two the hands were smoothed gently over her back, and she realized with a leaping pulse that the light weight that suddenly rested on her head was his chin. "Did I not forbid you to climb those steps?" he asked in a deep, quiet voice that caused a strange curling sensation in her stomach as she listened to it.

She nodded, but still did not move, and her eyes were shut again, her hands laid flat against his chest. "I wanted a book from the top but one shelf," she explained in a small, husky voice that she scarcely recognized.

"So you climbed the steps for it?" His voice had an oddly muffled sound, as if it was muffled in the thickness of her hair. Again she nodded, and heard him sigh deeply. "Are you always so disobedient?" he asked.

She raised her head at last and looked up into the strong, rugged features with eyes that sought some expression she was not sure of. Some expression that would give her a hint as to how she should react, but there was still no more than the customary slightly stern look, with a hint of amusement in the light gray eyes, and she looked away hastily, down at her own hands now curled against that expanse of chest.

"I didn't think it was worth bothering anybody for one book," she said, and his hands moved around to hold her by her upper arms, the gray eyes looking down at her with exasperation as well as amusement now.

"I do not give instructions without good reason," he told her, sounding rather as if he was lecturing her. "You are not to use them again," he added, indicating the steps with a nod of his head. "You see what happens when you do!"

"It was only because you came in and I looked to see who it was," she told him, and she saw a small frown draw at his brows for a moment.

"Ha! So it is my fault, hmm?"

"I didn't say that," Ruth denied hastily. "It wouldn't have mattered who it was."

"But if it had been *maman* she could not have broken your fall," he said, and Ruth never knew what prompted her to say what she did next.

"But Jacques would have done," she said softly, and kept her eyes firmly fixed on her own curled fingers, suddenly conscious of a desire to spread them out over the golden tanned skin where her face had lain.

Briefly the hands holding her stiffened, and she wondered if he would lose his temper, but when she glanced up at his face again she saw that his mouth was crooked into a faint smile. "And no doubt he would have taken advantage of the situation, eh, Ruth?"

She was sorry now she had been so provocative, but some involuntary imp of mischief had prompted her and he would now no doubt make the most of her rashness. "I—I don't know what he'd do," she said, and attempted to draw away from him at last, pulling against the hold of those strong hands that held her arms so tightly.

"Do you not?" he asked softly, and instead of letting her go, the fingers tightened their hold and she was drawn even closer to him.

There was a strong, sensual air of masculinity about the lean body she was pressed against and she felt her senses spinning chaotically out of control when he put his arms right around her again and held her even closer, one hand reaching up to twine his strong fingers in the thick brown hair and pull back her head.

"No!"

There was a hint of panic in the small-voiced cry she gave when he bent his head over her, and she heard him laugh softly just before his mouth took hers. Not even Jacques had kissed her like that and she felt as if she was being drawn along into a dangerous whirlpool and was unable to draw breath.

She struggled to begin with, her hands trying to push him away from her, to release her mouth from that hard, ruthless assault, but it was no use, and after a while she simply let herself go along with it. Spreading her hands over his broad chest, she struggled no longer, but yielded to the demands he made.

It was the opening of the door again that brought her back to sanity, and she had no breath even to free herself for a moment, but stood there, still in the circle of his arms, her breathing erratic and her eyes still half-closed.

"Hugo—oh, *mon cher*!" It was not Jacques's voice, as she had half feared it would be, but Madame Gerard's gently scolding tones that she heard, and Ruth turned swiftly from the arms that now let her go, and went across to the desk, her back to the room, and especially the newcomer.

There was silence for a moment, and she could guess that Madame Gerard was looking across at her, wondering, trying to guess if this was the first time that such a thing had happened. If it was likely to hurt her beloved Jacques.

"There is nothing to worry about, *maman*." Surprisingly to Ruth, Hugo spoke in English; she had somehow expected him to make his explanations in his own tongue.

Apparently Madame Gerard needed confirmation of that and Ruth bit her lip when she called across to her softly. "Ruth, *mon enfant*!"

She turned slowly, her eyes still downcast and a violent thudding beat in her heart that almost deafened her, aware that those light gray eyes were watching her too. "Monsieur—Monsieur Gerard's right, *madame*," she said in a small husky voice. "There's nothing—nothing serious."

The old lady came across the room to her, and Ruth felt suddenly as if she wanted to run away, away from that big sunny room and into the open air. Gently Madame Gerard put an arm around her and hugged her for a second, her eyes gentle and understanding.

"You are . . . all right, *chérie*?" she asked softly,

and and from somewhere behind her Ruth heard a short, impatient sound, an angry sound.

"Ruth has been kissed before, I have no doubt!" Hugo said shortly. "There is no need to fuss, *maman*!"

Chancing a brief glimpse at him, Ruth saw that he looked much more angry than embarrassed. It was unlikely of course that he could be embarrassed in such a situation, but she could not quite understand why he was so angry. It was quite by accident that she met his eyes and for a brief moment she saw something there that startled her so that she let out a small sound, like a sigh. Then he turned on his heel and was gone, leaving the two of them standing there in silence.

Then Madame Gerard touched Ruth's arm gently and her brown eyes regarded her for a moment before she spoke. "I will not say anything of this to Jacques," she said softly, and Ruth, without thinking, shook her head.

"It doesn't matter," she said, and realized even as she spoke that she had said quite the wrong thing in the circumstances. *Madame*'s first concern would be for Jacques and the way he would feel about the scene she had just witnessed.

"But Jacques would be hurt, Ruth," the old lady told her. "You do not wish such a thing, *mon enfant*, hmm?"

Ruth hesitated, her mind's eyes still seeing that strange disturbing look in Hugo's eyes just before he strode off out of the room. "No, *madame*," she agreed, but so absently that she looked at her curiously. "But—well, Jacques and I have no special relationship, you know, *madame*, I don't have a—conscience about—what just happened."

"No conscience perhaps, *ma petite*," the old lady

said gently, her fingers exerting a gentle pressure on her arm. "But perhaps a broken heart if you allow it to happen again."

WHETHER OR NOT she had a conscience about being kissed by Hugo Gerard it was certain that Ruth found it incredibly hard to forget the experience and, despite her assurance to Madame Gerard that the relationship she had with Jacques was no more than a close friendship, she was glad that the old lady had promised not to tell him. A quarrel between Hugo and Jacques was the last thing she wanted and she was afraid that Jacques would take a far from tolerant view of the incident.

During the next day or two, in fact, he showed an increased tendency to act much more possessively toward her, as if she was indeed his fiancée, although he was careful to stay away from the library during working hours. Even Jacques, she thought, knew where to draw the line where Hugo was concerned.

It was while they were walking in the gardens one evening that Jacques made the first positive move toward establishing a more settled relationship between them, and although it was not altogether a surprise, Ruth wished she could have done something to avert the situation. She was not yet ready for it.

The evening was cool, cooler than it had been yet since her arrival, with some dark gray clouds lying low over the tall poplars and billowing before the red evening sun like smoke from a fire. There was a tense expectant feeling in the air, as before a storm, and they said little as they walked through the neatly laid out beds of roses and geraniums, boxed and bordered in the classical style that Ruth found less attractive than the more abandoned confusion of the English country garden.

The shadowy bulk of the château rose behind them as they walked down the geometrically laid paths, its hundreds of flat, straight windows reflecting the evening sun like red and gold lights, winking from among the surrounding trees. It had been a busy and somewhat unsatisfactory day for Ruth, for she had found herself less able to concentrate in the tranquillity of her surroundings than usual, and she blamed the threatening storm for her uneasiness.

Jacques had an arm around her slim waist and his head was inclined toward her as they walked, going slowly, for it was the kind of atmosphere that induced lethargy. He bent his head closer suddenly and kissed her ear, murmuring her name in a voice that was muffled by her hair.

"You know that I wish to marry you?" he asked softly, and Ruth did not immediately answer. "Ruth? *Mon amie?*"

She turned her face and looked up at him for a moment, then shook her head. "I know you say you do, Jacques." It seemed difficult to find the right words, to know how to explain to him that, although she liked him a lot and she enjoyed being in his company, she was not fond enough of him to consider him as a husband. Also she was not at all sure that he fully realized what marriage would involve, he was in some ways much more immature than she was herself, although he was a year older.

"But I mean what I say, *chérie*, why should you doubt me?" He brought them to a halt suddenly and turned her to face him, his eyes dark and glittering in the fading light, his hands on her arms in a grip that felt at once firm and caressing. "You do not think me serious, Ruth?" he asked quietly, and Ruth, despite her misgivings, felt touched by his obvious anxiety to be taken seriously.

She traced the outline of his shirt collar with one finger and did not look at him while she spoke, but her heart was fluttering uneasily as she sought for the right words. "I—I don't doubt your sincerity, Jacques," she said in a small soft voice, "but I don't think you realize just what getting married would involve."

He laughed softly and kissed her forehead, just brushing her with his lips, his breath warm on her skin when he spoke. "I understand perfectly, *mon amour*," he whispered. "I love you and I want to marry you and, despite the fact that Hugo still looks upon me as a schoolboy, I assure you I am not!"

"I know." She looked up at him again, at the dark face with its crown of dark brown hair, the dark eyes that looked so warm and alive that they sent a little shiver along her spine with the promise they held.

"Then will you marry me, Ruth?"

It was much more difficult than she had ever anticipated, trying to find words to refuse him, and she knew at the back of her mind that she was a fool to even consider refusing him. He was fond of her, perhaps he was even in love with her as he claimed, and he was wealthy and very, very attractive. There were a dozen reasons why a girl like her should accept his proposal instantly and think herself lucky to have been asked. But she couldn't—she couldn't bring herself to accept him when she knew deep down that she would not be putting her whole heart into the promise.

She said nothing for a long moment, and he stood with his dark head bent over her, his eyes seeking some clue in her face as to what her answer would be. "I—I can't, Jacques," she said at last, and the words seemed to have a strangely breathless quality that caught in her throat.

"Ruth?" He lifted her chin with one hand and she thought as she raised her eyes and looked at him that he had never looked quite so mature as he did now, and for a moment she felt herself almost in love with him. His mouth brushed gently against hers and his voice did not rise above a whisper. "Is it that you do not love me?" he asked. "Or that you love someone else?"

"No!" The answer was swift and certain and she did not stop to question who it was he suspected of having her affection. She felt her heart rapping hard at her side and her head was shaking firmly, convinced she was right and anxious to convince him too.

"Is that true, *mon amie*?" he asked softly, and again she nodded her head insistently.

"Quite true," she said. "It's just that—I'm sorry, Jacques, but I just don't love you enough."

His sigh was deep and, she thought, genuine despite its hint of exaggeration, and she instinctively put a hand to touch his face, her eyes soft and shining, because she really was fond of him, although not fond enough. He took the hand in his and turned the palm toward him, pressing his lips to the soft warmth of her skin.

"Then I cannot take you with me," he said, and Ruth glanced up swiftly, wide-eyed and not quite believing. "You are not, I think," he added softly, "a girl who would come without the protection of marriage."

"Take me with you?" she said, ignoring the latter implication for the moment. "Take me where, Jacques?"

He shrugged, but even before he said any more she knew in her heart that it was something to do with Hugo, and that it was something she had half expected. It had, she remembered, crossed her mind as a definite possibility that Hugo would send Jacques away on some long trip if he foresaw him becoming too serious about her.

Jacques kissed her palm again gently, and smiled down at her, pressing her hand to his cheek as he spoke. "I am going away for a long time, *chérie*," he said softly.

"Abroad?" She knew, of course, but she needed time to think, to take in the fact that it was possible she might not see him again once he went.

"Many places," he said, and from the way he shrugged it was evident that he was resigned to the fact—perhaps even looked forward to it, how could she know? "It was always to be, of course," he went on. "The men in our family always take this . . . *grand voyage*, when we have completed our formal education. One travels the world a little and learns to live, *comprenez*? It is a big opportunity, *ma belle*!"

"And you really want to go?"

It was silly of her to ask, she thought, for of course he wanted to go, but being Jacques he had thought to have his cake and eat it too, and the realization made her smile. "I want to go," he agreed. "But I would like to have you with me, *chérie*, as my wife."

"Oh, Jacques!" She tiptoed and kissed him lightly on his cheek, one finger gently stroking his chin. "I'm very flattered and I don't for one minute doubt your sincerity, but—" She shook her head, wondering if she could find the right words to explain, one finger again tracing the outline of his collar. "I've read Hugo's book," she said slowly, hoping to make him understand. "You're going on the same kind of—of adventure that *he* wrote about, and a wife wouldn't fit into that kind of trip at all."

"But I am not Hugo," he insisted, and again Ruth shook her head.

"But you're very like him," she said softly. "Perhaps more than you realize."

Looking up again at that dark, attractive face with its brown eyes that could look so wickedly suggestive, and the mouth that kissed as readily as it smiled, she could in fact see him as Hugo all over again. Doing the same things, taking everything in his stride, getting the last ounce out of everything that came his way. Definitely a wife was not what he needed on such a trip, and she was ready to accept that Hugo had known exactly what he was doing when he had organized it—as he undoubtedly had.

"Are the arrangements all made?" she asked, and Jacques shrugged.

"They are," he said. "I had not expected to leave so soon, but Hugo has arranged for me to go with a friend of his on the first leg of the journey. I am to leave for Africa in three weeks' time."

"Hugo!"

She sounded reproving as well as resigned and he looked down at her curiously, his brown eyes questioning the tone of her voice. "But of course, he knows about these things." He apparently saw nothing untoward in the trip having been arranged so soon, and Ruth began to wonder if she was, in fact, being a little unfair in suspecting Hugo of an ulterior motive.

"Yes, yes, of course he does!" she said, and he smiled.

One hand lifted her chin and he looked down at

her again, his gaze fixed on her mouth with an intensity that did stirring things to her pulse. "Will you not come with me, *ma belle chérie*?" he asked softly.

Ruth shook her head again, but at the back of her mind was the temptation to say she would go, just to see what Hugo would do about it. If he had arranged that journey so quickly just to get him out of what he considered harm's way, it would have been interesting to see what he did about trying to stop her.

"I couldn't, Jacques," she said gently. "It wouldn't work, and I'm certain you'd regret it before very long if I did come with you."

"Non, non," he denied earnestly. "I want you to come with me!"

Ruth was still shaking her head, a small wry smile on her mouth as she visualized just how much he would regret it when the whole world opened up before him and he found himself bound by a wife. His natural predatory instincts curbed by having her always there and unable to follow his uncle's footsteps as closely as he wanted to. She tiptoed and kissed him lingeringly on his mouth, her hands either side of his face, cool fingertips touching the lean angular cheekbones that gave his face such character.

"You go alone," she said softly. "I'll still be around when you come back, though not here I don't suppose. Then, if you want to, you can come and find me."

"Ruth—"

"Have fun!" she whispered, and turned in his arm to walk on down the straight formal pathway between the beds of roses.

IT WAS THE FOLLOWING MORNING, when Ruth was just getting down to writing up her latest lists, that the door of the library opened and she looked up and saw Hugo. It was unusual enough at that hour of the day to see him for her to blink her eyes in surprise and watch him as he came across to the desk.

He said nothing for the moment, but took a cigarette from the box on the desk, sending a cloud of pungent smoke drifting in front of his face and concealing his expression for a moment. Then, inevitably, he perched himself on the edge of the desk, with one foot swinging and the cigarette making a blue haze about him. A cool, aloof figure that looked somehow very discouraging.

"You know that Jacques is to go away?' he asked, so abruptly that for a moment she stared at him uncomprehendingly.

"Yes, I know," she said at last. "Jacques told me."

"Yes, of course!"

Her heart was hammering wildly at her ribs and she was uncertain just what was causing so much disturbance, only sure that it gave her a strangely breathless feeling. Since the day she had taken a fall from the library ladder and he caught her, since the disturbing results that followed, she had not been alone with him, and she felt quite alarmingly nervous.

Whether it was remembering that occasion, or whether it was because she resented the almost certainty that he was going to question her about her attitude to Jacques's departure, she couldn't tell, but she experienced a feeling close to panic as she sat there overshadowed by that tall figure perched on the edge of the desk in front of her.

He always looked so much darker when he was wearing a white shirt, as he was this morning, and the contrast it made to that deep, golden tan was something she always found irresistibly fascinating. He looked so much more the popular conception of the typical Frenchman, despite his fair hair and those light gray eyes, and there was something so undeniably basic and masculine about him that her femininity responded to it despite any effort she made to resist it.

Dark slacks hugged his lean hips and fitted taut over his long legs as he sat there, swinging one foot with a rhythm that beat like a metronome each time his heel thudded against the wooden desk. The white shirt was pulled tight across his back and showed the dark shadow of his body through its thin texture. It was certain that he knew what effect he could have and in all probability he reveled in the fact.

Although it was much cooler he wore no jacket and there was something evocative about those strong, bare brown arms and hands as he impatiently ground out the cigarette after only a few seconds. A simple gesture, but he somehow managed to make even that look ruthless and a little shiver slid along her spine as she watched him.

"You will not, of course, go with him!"

She had expected him to question her, to ask if she imagined that she was going with Jacques, but such a firm, autocratic statement took her breath away, and she felt the color flood warmly into her cheeks. It made her feel so small and inadequate to be sitting down at the desk while he hovered over her, so she got to her feet and faced him, her eyes bright and angry.

"I don't see what you could do about it if I *did* decide to go!" she declared firmly, and he cocked one brow at her, apparently not even disturbed by her anger.

"Has he asked you?"

She found it difficult to face those light eyes and tell an outright lie, so she looked down instead at her hands clenched tightly together on the top of the desk. "Jacques asked me to marry him," she said, and saw that that, at least, was unexpected, for he looked at her for a moment as if he suspected her of lying.

Then he made a wry grimace and shrugged his broad shoulders. "That was a very foolish thing for him to do," he said coolly. "I expected that he would have told you he was going and I thought that possibly he would suggest you go with him as—" His shrug said so much that Ruth felt herself coloring furiously and clenched her hands even tighter. "I had not expected him to be so rash as to suggest you marry him," he went on. "You have refused him, of course, *mademoiselle*!"

The formality of the "*mademoiselle*" told her that he meant to keep her firmly in her place, and she toyed for a moment with the idea of telling him that she had accepted Jacques's proposal, but that would have meant that she was committed and she was not prepared to go that far simply to cross Hugo. She looked at him for a moment through the thickness of her lashes, the temptation still there in the back of her mind.

"What would you say if I told you I'd accepted him?" she asked, and he smiled.

It was a small, tight disbelieving smile that showed her he was not deceived for one minute by that bit of bravado. "You have not, *mademoiselle*," he said with certainty.

"Oh?'

He was shaking his head, a trace of that smile still on his mouth as he watched her steadily. "I know you too well, *mon enfant*," he said in a surprisingly soft voice, and started a strange curling sensation in her stomach. "You are too—too honest! A romantic—you could not marry a man you do not love! And do not tell me that you love Jacques," he added, before she could say anything. "You do not!"

Ruth clenched her hands tightly, her cheeks burning. She felt strangely light-headed, despite her anger, and wondered how on earth he could claim to be so knowledgeable about her. "How do you know what I feel?" she demanded, determined not to be browbeaten.

The gray eyes glittered darkly across the desk at her and their gaze swept over her from the curves that showed above the edge of the desk to the top of her head, a gaze that took in every minute detail and left no inch unexplored. "I know women," he said softly.

"So you claim!" The retort was instinctive and defensive, and something inexplicably disturbing stirred her pulses and hammered relentlessly with her heartbeat in her breast.

Swiftly that telling gaze swept over her again and he laughed softly, sending a soft shudder down her spine. "Little girls like you are very easy to read, *ma petite*!"

Ruth's eyes blazed. She was so angry she could not find words, angry enough to strike out, and her hand swept back before she even realized what she was doing. It caught him sharply across his left cheek and left a mark that made her gasp in alarm and dismay when she realized what she had done.

Before she could say a word of apology, however, he was on his feet and his right hand reached across the desk for her, his long fingers encompassing both her wrists easily and tightly. In one of those swift, sudden movements he came around the desk, and without giving her time to realize what he meant to do, he had pulled her roughly into his arms and was crushing her against his chest.

Anger made him hard and unyielding and his mouth on hers had the same harshness as the body that strained her to him and at the same time pressed her back against the edge of the desk so forcibly she could have cried out.

It was as she imagined the sensation of drowning to be, and her head spun dizzily as she fought to control her response to the assault. She began by pushing with her hands at his chest, but her palms met only the hard resistance of his anger and he tightened his hold, straining her even more closely to him until she was unable to do anything but yield to the traitorous demands of her own instincts.

When he eventually released her, she stood for a moment trying to clear her brain, her eyes closed and her head spinning with the rapid thud of her heartbeat. The hard, bruising strength of his hands still held her and she could almost feel the glittering gaze that was fixed on her, and then suddenly he let her go.

She felt strangely bereft for a moment without the harsh demands of his hands and his mouth, and she put out a hand to the support of the desk behind her, while he moved away, half turning his back to her. His shoulders were bowed and one hand brushed backward through his hair as he spoke in a strangely husky voice that did not sound like his at all, and was much more strongly accented than usual.

"Je regrette beaucoup, mademoiselle," he said, and the formality of it fell harshly on her ears after the previous few moments. "I should not have lost my temper with you!"

So that was it! He had simply kissed her as a way of giving vent to his temper, no doubt thinking to punish her, if she was an unwilling partner. She chanced a glance from beneath lowered lids and saw only the profile of the strong face turned to her. The expression in his eyes was hidden by those quite ridiculously long lashes that always seemed far too feminine for such a rugged face, and for a moment she almost smiled.

"I—I was the one who lost my temper," she said in a small voice. "I should—I think *I* should apologize."

It was almost as if he sensed her instinct to smile, and he turned his head, looking down at her over his shoulder for a moment, his gaze glitteringly disturbing. "Then let us agree that we both lost control for a moment, hmm?" he asked softly, and Ruth willingly nodded agreement.

They stood with only inches between them in the big, book-lined room and she felt the silence almost as a tangible thing. She had never in her life felt so unsure of herself, nor so strangely elated as she felt at that moment, and she could see only one explanation for it.

Being kissed by Hugo Gerard was an experience that she found increasingly acceptable, no matter what his reasons were. She was, she realized, being extremely foolish to imagine that he had meant anything more by it than a means of appeasing his anger, but her heart refused to accept that as his only motive.

He shrugged his shoulders suddenly and turned again to face her, so that she caught her breath audibly. He frowned and shook his head. "I will not touch you again against your will, Ruth," he said quietly. "Please do not run away!"

Ruth said nothing for a moment, then she looked up and for a moment met his eyes, although it did disturbing things to her pulses when she saw the deep, dark glitter in them. "I wasn't going to run away," she said huskily.

"You trust me?" She nodded, her heart leaping like a wild thing when he took her hands gently in his and stood looking down at her. "I was afraid I might have spoiled everything, and there is something—" He hesitated, and uncertainty about anything was so unlike him that Ruth looked at him curiously.

"Something you want me to do?" she asked, and for a second his wide mouth tipped into a wry smile that glistened in his eyes.

"In one way," he said. "I wish you to come out with me one evening soon, Ruth. Will you come?"

For a moment she stared at him without speaking, not quite believing she had heard him rightly. Then she shook her head slowly, though not in refusal, merely in bewilderment. "I—I don't understand," she said, and knew as she said it that it would sound incredibly naive to him.

"You like music, I think?" She nodded, unable to find the right words, and he appeared satisfied with that. "*Bon*! Then you will enjoy yourself, as long as you do not judge your enjoyment by the luxury of your surroundings."

She flushed, suspecting a gibe, although she was possibly being a little too sensitive. It was too soon after that violent scene only minutes ago to be discussing music as if nothing had happened. Evidently her emotions took longer to readjust than his, and she still felt strangely out-of-this-world, as she stood there listening to him.

"I—I seldom bother where I am if the music's

good to listen to," she told him, trying to sound as normal as possible. "Is—is it anything special we're going to hear?"

It sounded strangely intimate to say 'we' like that, but again she realized she was probably making too much of what was to him nothing extraordinary. His smile was curiously enigmatic and his eyes half hidden by those long lashes again as he looked down at her.

"You will see," he told her quietly, and briefly one hand reached out and touched her cheek with its fingertips, caressingly, sensuously gentle so that she shivered and half closed her eyes on the sensation it created.

He turned away then and, without a word, strode across the room with his usual swift and sudden decisiveness, leaving her standing there beside the desk, small and very uncertain, her hands clasped tightly together and her eyes following him to the door. Then he turned in the doorway and looked back at her over his shoulder, one brow raised.

"I hope you will not find it necessary to say anything to Jacques or to anyone else about—our arrangement," he said, and once again Ruth felt the color in her cheeks, sensitive as ever to his meaning.

Her chin thrust out and she looked at him with bright, defiant eyes. "If you fear for your reputation by taking out your—one of your employees," she said in a small, tight voice, "please don't bother taking me, Monsieur Gerard!"

For a moment she thought he would lose his temper again and her heart was already rapping anxiously at her ribs, but after a moment he smiled and shook his head. "You do yourself an injustice," he told her softly, "and, not for the first time, you do me one also. I have a very good reason for asking you to say nothing of where we are going, Ruth. I have no objection at all to you saying that you are spending an evening with me, although I think Jacques will not find the idea very palatable!" That was quite true, of course, and Ruth faced the fact for the first time as he closed the door behind him.

CHAPTER SEVEN

JACQUES NOT ONLY FOUND the idea of Ruth spending an evening with his uncle unpalatable, he voiced his objections in no uncertain manner. Madame Gerard, too, Ruth suspected, took a not very favorable view of the proposed outing because it affected Jacques. They both let their feelings be known the following evening after dinner, when Hugo had left them to pursue some activity of his own.

All day long she had been debating the wisdom of saying anything at all to Jacques about going, but then realized that he would have to know, there was no way it could be avoided, and she really had no need to feel guilty about it.

"But why did you say that you would go with him, *chérie?*" Jacques insisted, a dark unhappy look in his eyes as he watched her face.

They sat together on a divan in that long, beautiful room that Ruth loved so much, and she was aware that Madame Gerard too was watching her as she sought for a reply. If only Hugo had stayed and shared the questioning, but then of course there would have been no questions. No one questioned Hugo's movements—least of all Jacques.

It was difficult to find the right answer and her hesitation no doubt gave quite the wrong impression to the waiting listeners. The truth she was bound to recognize was that she rather looked forward to an evening with Hugo, but she could hardly say so without being misunderstood. She was fully aware too that she was being very foolish to anticipate it with such pleasure, for it could lead to nothing but trouble if she let herself become involved with a man like Hugo Gerard.

"Had you no choice, *mon enfant*?" Madame Gerard inquired gently, and Ruth looked up hastily.

"Oh, yes, of course I had, *madame*!" she assured her.

A glance at Jacques showed that he was still far from satisfied and she sighed inwardly at the prospect of trying to appease him. "Then why did you consent to go, *mon amour*?" he asked.

She knew the signs well from past experience. There was already a hint of sulkiness around his expressive mouth, a sulkiness that she had become familiar with during their days in Oxford, when he had wanted his own way and meant to have it. Ruth took a deep breath, almost a sigh, trying to make him see it from her point of view, although she suspected it was already a lost argument.

"I—I suppose the truth is I didn't stop to think," she said, remembering how stunned the invitation had left her at the time. "Hu—Monsieur Gerard asked me to go with him and I just accepted."

"He had no right!" Jacques declared vehemently, his eyes bright with anger. "Why can he not—oh, *mon dieu*! I knew this would happen—I should not have sent you here, Ruth, I should have left you in England where he could not see you, where I could have come and found you again! Idiot that I am, I should have known!"

"Jacques, *mon cher*," Madame Gerard murmured gently, a hand on his arm, sympathizing with his mood. But Jacques was in no mood to be pitied and Ruth was not prepared to have a simple invitation for an evening out turned into a major disaster.

"You're making a mountain out of a molehill," Ruth told him, while he impatiently shook his head over his grandmother's sympathy. "I'm spending an evening with my employer, Jacques, not eloping with him, it's quite idiotic to make so much fuss about it!"

Madame Gerard looked at her reproachfully, but Jacques she could see took her words more reassuringly. His brown eyes looked at her for a moment, narrowed and curious, then he took her hands in his and bent his head to press kisses into her palms.

"Am I really such a fool, *mon amie*?" he asked, and Ruth smiled.

"If you imagine for one minute that your uncle looks upon me as anything but a rather youthful librarian," she told him lightly, "you are!"

For a moment Jacques's eyes searched her face, still seeking reassurance, then he raised her hands to his lips again. "I cannot understand why he has asked you to go with him, *ma chérie*, so suddenly like this! Where is he taking you?"

That was something that Ruth could answer without evasion and she smiled ruefully as she admitted it. "I honestly don't know, Jacques," she said. "He's being very mysterious about it!"

"He is?" He glanced at his grandmother briefly as if speculating on the likelihood of her knowing, and Ruth realized that the old lady was still watching her closely, alert as ever to anything that could upset Jacques. "But why should he not tell you where he is taking you?" he asked, and Ruth shrugged.

"I really don't know."

"It is most unlike Hugo to be... vague about such things," Madame Gerard remarked quietly. "I cannot imagine why he is behaving so... unlike himself. My son has many faults, but he is usually a forthright man."

"He—he simply didn't tell me," Ruth said, and wished she could at least tell them that she knew it was something to do with music, but Hugo had stressed that she did not tell them anything beyond the fact that she was going out with him for an evening. He really had made things difficult for her, but it was doubtful if the fact would worry him much.

"*When* is this event to be?" Jacques asked, and looked at her wryly. "Do you at least know that, *mon amour*?"

"Not exactly," Ruth admitted. "But one night next week, I think."

Jacques stared at her curiously. "You do not know for certain when or where you are to be taken?" he said. "And yet you consent to go with him?"

Put like that it did sound all rather vague and uncertain, Ruth had to admit, but it had not struck her as in any way untoward until now. "I suppose I didn't stop to think," she admitted. "He—Monsieur Gerard asked me and I said I'd go."

Jacques narrowed his eyes and regarded her for a long time without speaking. "Why?" he asked softly at last. "It is not like you, *chérie*!"

"I—I suppose it isn't," she allowed, and laughed a little shakily. "But there's nothing I can do about it now. I promised I'd go so—I'll go!"

"Then I, too, will go!" Jacques declared firmly, and Ruth stared at him.

"Jacques, you can't!"

"I will go alone somewhere and perhaps we will—" His shrug conveyed his meaning plainly enough. "Since my uncle is stealing my girl from me I will spend a lonely evening wondering if *ma belle* Ruth is missing me or if she is so swept away by the presence of the great Hugo Gerard that she does not even notice that I am not here!"

"Oh, no, Jacques!"

The idea of him discovering where Hugo was taking her and actually following them was not impossible, she guessed, and the thought of it did not appeal at all. For one thing if he did find them and joined them, Hugo was bound to think that she was the cause, that she had done exactly as he had asked her not to.

"You do not wish to perhaps accidentally meet with me?" Jacques asked, and Ruth almost let him see how much she disliked the idea. Instead she merely shrugged her shoulders and half smiled, as if it mattered little to her.

"I don't think your uncle would quite believe that it was an accidental meeting," she told him.

"And would that matter?"

She nodded, wary of making too big an issue of it. "I—I wouldn't like it, either, Jacques," she said quietly. "I don't like the idea of being followed. It looks as if you suspect me of... heaven knows what! As if you think it's far more than a simple evening out with my boss!"

Jacques said nothing for a moment, then he kissed her fingers and shook his head, his face grave as he looked at her "I only hope that it may prove to be no more than a simple evening out with your boss," he said softly.

IT WAS SOMETHING of a surprise to Ruth when Madame Gerard came into the library a couple of days later, looking oddly surreptitious, and she looked up curiously when she came in. Obviously Madame Gerard had not come merely to indulge in idle gossip, for she knew and respected Hugo's views on visits during her working hours and, despite the fact that she got on so well with her son, Ruth thought she would hesitate to break the rules he had imposed.

"You are alone, *ma chère*?" she asked, before coming right into the room, and her hasty glance around the library to confirm the fact was almost comically secretive. When Ruth nodded she smiled her satisfaction and came right in.

"I think Monsieur Gerard's out somewhere," Ruth told her. "I think I heard his car going out earlier."

"I did not know if I would find Jacques with you," Madame Gerard said. "Evidently he does not know that once again Hugo has driven into Paris! He is taking many trips to Paris recently, that wicked son of mine, huh?" She laughed, affectionately tolerant of her son's activities, whatever they might be, and rolled her eyes as meaningfully as Jacques ever did.

Ruth did not know quite what she was expected to reply to that, although she had a strange feeling that in some way the allusion to Hugo's activities was meant as a warning to her, "I—I don't know where Monsieur Gerard goes, *madame*," she told her, and Madame Gerard shrugged expressive shoulders.

"I know only that he goes to Paris very often lately," she said. "One does not question, of course, the reason for such visits, although one would have thought the evening—" Again she shrugged and there was a hint of resignation in the expression on her small brown face. "Always I hope that one day Hugo will find for himself a suitable wife and become the family man, for already he is in his thirty-sixth year and as yet no wife and no grandsons."

Ruth felt vaguely embarrassed by these confidences and she felt sure that Hugo himself would have been furious if he had known he was under discussion on such a personal level. She did, however, manage to smile encouragement at the old lady as she got up from the desk.

"Oh, I'm sure it'll happen one day, *madame*," she said.

"Mais oui," Madame Gerard agreed with Gallic gloom, "but when, *ma chère*, when?"

With no special reason in mind other than to reassure the old lady, Ruth shrugged and smiled. "Who knows?" she said lightly. "Maybe sooner than you think!"

In a moment those shrewd brown eyes showed her alert, anxious to learn more, and Ruth realized how rash she had been. "You think so, Ruth?" Madame Gerard asked, and when Ruth looked at her, startled, "Do you perhaps know of something, *mon enfant*? Of someone perhaps?"

"Oh, no, *madame*, I know of no one!" she said hastily. "I—I was only speculating!"

"Ah!" The old lady looked disappointed, she thought, then she sighed. "Ah well, *ma chère*," she said after a second or two, "while Hugo is away we can talk in safety, *n'est-ce pas*?"

Her choice of words rather startled Ruth. "I—I don't understand, *madame*!"

Madame Gerard smiled ruefully, walking across to one of the armchairs and patting the seat of the one next to it for Ruth to come and sit beside her. "We can talk without fear of Hugo's anger, huh?" she suggested. "Although you will think that I am possibly—how is it you say in English—making the mountains from the molehills, hmm?"

Ruth sat herself, rather uneasily, on the edge of the chair and was disturbed to find that her hands were trembling. At the back of her mind was a suspicion that Madame Gerard was about to deliver a lecture on the unsuitability of her going out for an evening with her son, and she was surprised to find herself ready to argue the point.

"I can't imagine what it is you want to speak to me about, *madame*," she said. "Have I done something wrong?"

"*Mais non*, not you, Ruth!" She reached over and patted her hand comfortingly. "And do not look so upset, so . . . apprehensive, *mon enfant*, I am not angry with you. But I am so with Hugo for putting you into such a position that you cannot refuse him."

"Madame!"

"I mean that you cannot refuse to go—wherever it is he is to take you," Madame Gerard explained.

So her guess had been right, Ruth thought ruefully. It was to be about her spending an evening with Hugo, and she sighed inwardly at the prospect of displeasing the old lady. Of course Jacques would have complained bitterly to his grandmother about it, possibly even more bitterly than to Ruth herself, and the old lady would feel bound to try and do something about it.

"Madame—" She hesitated, not wanting to give Madame Gerard any wrong impressions, but unwilling to be talked out of her evening with Hugo, which she admitted she was looking forward to. "*Madame*, I wasn't put into a position where I couldn't say no, as I explained to you and Jacques the other night. Monsieur Gerard invited me to go with him to—to go somewhere with him for the evening, and I said I'd like to go."

Her insistence seemed to puzzle Madame Gerard, she could see that, and she guessed that it was Jacques's insistence also that had given his grandmother the impression that Ruth was an unwilling partner. "You wish to go?" she asked, and Ruth nodded. "Even when you know—" She shook her head and looked as if, momentarily, things were beyond her comprehension. "My son is an older man, Ruth, and also very . . . *expérimenté*. You understand?" she added anxiously, and again Ruth nodded, a faint pink flush betraying her embarrassment.

"I understand, *madame*," she said as quietly as her racing pulses would allow. "And I appreciate your concern for me, but it's quite unnecessary. There's nothing like . . . nothing like that at all. I work for Monsieur Gerard and he's asked me to go out with him one evening, that's all; there's nothing meaningful in the invitation at all."

For a few moments Madame Gerard looked at her steadily in almost that same disconcerting way that her son sometimes did, then she shook her head slowly. "Do you forget, *mon enfant*," she said softly, "that I saw you together in this room one day?"

Ruth had indeed forgotten for the moment. Not the fact that Hugo had first saved her from a fall and then kissed her, but that Madame Gerard had come into the room while he was still kissing her, she had, she remembered, been extremely anxious for her. Then there was that other time, when she had been so angry with him that she had slapped his face and again found herself in his arms and being kissed in a way no one else had ever kissed her. She bit her lip and said nothing for a moment while Madame Gerard still watched her, then she shook her head.

"That—that was my own fault, *madame*," she said in a small voice. "I . . . provoked Monsieur Gerard until he was so angry that—well, he lost control for a moment. It meant nothing more than that."

"Such anger," Madame Gerard said softly, "is dangerous, *mon enfant*. If you can provoke my son to such passion, your relationship is not merely a business one, as you would have me believe."

"But, *madame*—"

"Ruth, *ma chère*—" the old lady put a gentle hand on her arm "—I know my son. You should take care, and also you should think sometimes of Jacques, hmm?"

This, Ruth thought, was going to be the hardest part of all and she wondered for a moment why Jacques had not told his grandmother about her refusing his proposal, as he obviously hadn't. "*Madame*, Jacques asked me to marry him," she said at last. "Did you know that?"

"Ah!" She looked as if a suspicion had been confirmed, and also as if she found the next words barely credible. "You have said no?" she asked.

"I had to, *madame*," Ruth told her gently, finding it almost harder than refusing Jacques himself. "It wouldn't have been fair to do anything else."

"You do not love Jacques?" That too she found hard to believe, Ruth thought, and felt quite cruel when she shook her head.

"I'm very fond of Jacques," she said. "But no, *madame*, I don't love him—I'm sorry."

"*Mon cher enfant*, it is for Jacques that you should feel pity," Madame Gerard told her quietly, then sighed and reached out for one of her hands, patting it understandingly. "You are very honest, Ruth," she told her. "Many young girls in your position would have seen Jacques as a—" She sought for the right words and Ruth, following her meaning all too easily, came swiftly to her aid.

"Jacques *is* a good catch, Madame Gerard," she said softly. "He's also a very nice person, and I couldn't cheat him by pretending something that doesn't exist. Also," she added making a wry face,

"I suspect that Jacques will be following in his uncle's footsteps in more ways than one, and I'm sure you'd agree, *madame*, that a wife in such circumstances would prove a definite drawback!"

"Oh, Ruth, *ma chère*!" Impulsively Madame Gerard took both Ruth's hands in hers and smiled at her affectionately. "I would so like to have had you in our family, you are so . . . *sympathique*! If not Jacques, perhaps—" She shrugged. "*Mais non*! But you must stay with us as long as possible, hmm?"

"I will!" Ruth promised with a smile, and wondered just how long it was possible to make her work on Hugo's collection last.

IT WAS THE FOLLOWING MORNING, when Hugo was again safely out of the way, that Jacques came to the library, and this time Ruth looked less encouraging at the interruption. "Jacques, you have no business being—"

"Ssh!" he interrupted, coming across swiftly and kissing her before she could complete the sentence. "Hugo is off again," he told her with a conspiratorial smile, "we are safe, *mon amour*!"

"I'm working," Ruth insisted, smiling despite herself. "And you know how angry Hugo gets when you come in here while I'm busy, Jacques."

"But he will not know," Jacques said blithely. "*Grand-mère* thinks he has gone again to Paris." He tapped the side of his nose and winked knowingly. "He is—how is it—otherwise engaged, *n'est-ce pas*?"

"You don't know what he's doing!" Ruth declared, and was quite surprised to hear how sharp her voice sounded, as if she did not like the insinuations he was making about Hugo's reasons for visiting Paris.

Jacques looked at her, a little startled, too, by her tone, and one dark brow was elevated to the dark hair over his forehead. "We can guess," he told her. "With Hugo it is not difficult to guess that there is a lady somewhere who has his undivided attention!"

"Not undivided, surely," Ruth said with a shrug, and smiled when he looked puzzled. "He's taking me out one night this week."

Jacques frowned, his dark face looking quite cross as he took her hand in his and spread out her fingers over his chest, pressing them there with the flat of his own hand. "*Grand-mère* says that you have not changed your mind about going with him," he said, and Ruth looked up at him curiously.

"Did you expect me to?" she asked softly.

"Oh, Ruth!" He bent his head and kissed her hard, his mouth more desperate than gentle, and she pushed against him, trying to turn her head. His arms were too tightly around her, though, and he looked down at her, still holding her in the same iron grip, his eyes glittering darkly. "You do not truly wish to go with Hugo, do you?"

Her face was pink flushed with a mixture of emotions that she could not identify and she spent some time looking at the tip of her finger as it traced the outline of his shirt pocket. "I don't see quite why you and Madame Gerard are so sure I'm being shanghaied against my will," she said quietly. "I—I accepted an invitation to go out with my employer, who also happens to be a very famous man, and I don't see why everyone seems so anxious to warn me off."

"Oh, *chérie*!" He looked down at her, scornful of her apparent innocence. "You know what kind of a man Hugo is! How can you be so—so willing to be led to the slaughter, huh?"

"I'm *not* being led to the slaughter, as you so graphically put it!" Ruth denied, growing angry with his persistence. "I'm simply going to listen to some music with him, that's all!"

"Music?"

Ruth bit her lip, realizing that she had said far more than Hugo would have wanted her to, and it would be difficult now to convince Jacques that his knowledge was now as great as her own. "That's all I know," she said lamely, and he stood for a moment looking down at her, his eyes speculative.

"So," he said softly, "you are going to listen to music? That is a new departure for Hugo, and quite significant, too, *mon amour*!" He shook his head. "I do not like it!"

"I don't understand you," Ruth said, frowning. Her heart was hammering at her ribs at the suggestion that there was anything even slightly untoward about Hugo's choice of entertainment for her. "Why—why shouldn't we go to a concert or something? Thousands of people do!"

"Not Hugo—not with a woman," Jacques said as if he was quite sure of his facts. "He loves music and he never allows a distraction when he goes to a concert or *l'opéra* never a woman on his arm then, *mon amour*! Now do you see why I am so surprised?"

"But—" Ruth hesitated, uncertain herself now that he had explained. "I don't see how you can be so sure," she said uneasily. "You don't follow him every time he goes out, Jacques, so how can you know?"

"From his own word," Jacques replied promptly. He looked down at her for a moment, then kissed her gently on her mouth. "Perhaps because you are so very special, *mon amour*, hmm?"

"Not to your uncle!" Ruth declared hastily, and he smiled.

"For very little, *ma chérie*, I would make a fuss and say that he could not take you." He shrugged and pulled a wry face, his expression making Ruth laugh. "But I will not," he said. "Hugo is no more than thirteen years older than me, but, *ma foi*! I feel like the schoolboy when he loses his temper!"

His honesty, his frankly schoolboy fear of his uncle amused her, partly, she supposed, because she suspected it was less fear than respect that made him wary of quarreling with Hugo. "Then don't make him lose his temper!" she suggested laughingly. "I might have to pay for it as well, if you make him bad tempered, and I can do without that!"

"You are beautiful when you laugh," he whispered softly, brushing his lips against her forehead. "Are you quite sure you will not come with me when I go away, *mon amour*? I shall miss you so very much."

"And I shall miss you," Ruth said, truthfully enough. "But I can't come with you, Jacques, and eventually you'll thank me for saying it."

"Very well, heartless creature!" He kissed her again much more fervently, on her mouth, then buried his face in her hair, his voice muffled in its softness. "Then I will make love to every beautiful woman I meet on my *grand voyage*," he said. "I will seek them out and—how is it—sweep them off their feet, huh? I will be a much bigger devil than Hugo even! You will see!"

"Oh, Jacques!" She leaned back against his arms, her eyes bright and misty, her heart very tempted to do as he wanted and go with him. Only she was so certain that he was not the man for her, despite the fact that she was so fond of him and would miss him terribly. "I *shall* miss you!" she said softly, and lifted her face to be kissed.

Jacques's kisses were exciting and there was no doubt that he would prove, in time, to be a worthy successor to his uncle, but Ruth was appalled to find herself comparing him with Hugo even as she put her arms up round his neck and closed her eyes. She found herself wishing that Jacques, too, could arouse all the wild and chaotic emotions that Hugo did when he kissed her, in anger or not, and the significance of it refused to be subdued.

The library door banged shut with a violence that shook the room and Ruth let out a startled gasp when Jacques released her and she hastily turned her head. She should have known, of course, she thought ruefully, but she had heard nothing until that violently banging door, and now Hugo was standing there his feet apart, hands on his hips and a tight, angry look on his face.

Her own reaction startled her almost as much as the banging door had done, and she put up a hand to her throat where a pulse beat wildly out of control like the heart that hammered at her ribs and made her breathless. If Hugo had ever been to Paris he was too soon back, and she knew that a quarrel was inevitable when she saw his face.

Those light gray eyes could be as cold and hard as ice and they glittered at her and Jacques now while the wide straight mouth had a stern, cruel look that dismissed any chance of his being placated. His first words were in French and violently abusive, Ruth guessed from Jacques's expression when he heard them. Then he looked at Ruth with the same glittering iciness, sweeping a gaze over her from head to foot that brought a swift flush of color to her cheeks.

"You have a saying, have you not, *mademoiselle*?" he said in a cold hard voice. "When the cat is away, the mice will...play, *oui*?"

His meaning was obvious and Ruth's anger was swift as she faced him, her face brightly pink and her eyes glowingly indignant. "You have no right—" she began, and he raised a hand as he took another step nearer, but only to silence her, she realized too late.

Her gasp of dismay and the backward step she took seemed to surprise both him and Jacques. Hugo lowered his hand slowly and Jacques reached out to put an arm around her shoulders, his voice whispering briefly and urgently against her ear as he bent his head over her protectively.

"Cry, *mon amour*," he whispered. "For the love of God, be tearful!"

"You have no need to blame Ruth, Hugo," Jacques said with far more bravado than he could have felt, Ruth knew. "*I* was the one who came into the library, and *I* was kissing Ruth, it is my fault!"

"Have no fear, *mon brave*," Hugo told him shortly. "I know well who is to blame for you being here, but *mademoiselle* was not protesting very much when I came in!"

"Oh, you're not being—" Again Ruth tried, and again his raised hand stopped her from saying more, but this time she did not flinch from it.

"I pay you to work, *mademoiselle*," he told her coldly, "and I will not tolerate you taking advantage of my absence to indulge in secret meetings with your lover!"

"Oh, you've no *right* to say that!" Ruth cried, desperately anxious to be believed. "You've no right at all, it simply isn't true!"

The gray eyes glittered icily and he showed only contempt for her denial. "I saw for myself, *mademoiselle*," he said coldly. "And I have every right to object to your behavior! Apart from my being your employer, this is my house and I say and do as I please here!"

It was all rather incredible, Ruth thought hazily. He was making far too much fuss about something he had more or less dismissed as not worth bothering about when old Henry Stoddard had objected to the same thing in his shop. Just why he was behaving as he was she could not imagine for the moment, but Jacques was looking at him narrow-eyed and once more attempted to intervene.

"Hugo, it was my—"

A large hand waved him to silence again. "You may do as you please," Hugo told him shortly, "but not during the hours that Mademoiselle Colton is working for me!" Again the gray eyes turned on her and Ruth felt her stomach curl inside as she met them briefly. "You also may entertain who you will, *mademoiselle*," he said, "but only in your free time. Is that understood?"

"Yes, of course, *monsieur*." She had no need to pretend tearfulness, for the tears were already rolling down her cheeks as she stood there in the curve of Jacques's arm and looked at his uncle appealingly, a fact he seemed not to notice for the moment.

"If you do not care for my ruling," he went on, coldly insistent, "then you must leave my employ—the choice is simple and it is yours, *mademoiselle*!"

"You—you'd send me away?"

It was perhaps a strangely naive thing to say to him in the circumstances, and of course he *would* send her away if she did not comply with his rules. In his present mood he was capable of anything, she thought, and the tears flowed even more freely.

The pressure of Jacques's fingers on her arm told her that he took her tears for a deliberate ploy to soften his uncle's anger, but in fact she felt very unhappy that the situation had got so out of hand. She expected him to be angry about finding Jacques there with her, but not quite so unreasonably so.

The way he was looking at her now, she realized he had only just noticed that she was crying. "Ruth!" His face through the haze of her tears looked so dismayed she found it hard to believe. "Ruth, please, do not cry!"

He came across and stood close to where she was still snug in the curve of Jacques's arm, and one large hand reached out to touch her bare arm, gently and soothingly, while Jacques bent his head and buried his face in her hair. "Ssh, *chérie*," he murmured softly against her ear. "That is enough—do not cry anymore!"

"I—I wish I hadn't—I wish you hadn't been here!" she said in a small shaky voice. "And I can't think why—why I'm so weepy! I wish—"

"There is no need to be so upset, Ruth!" Hugo's voice was quieter now, and it had lost most of its icy hardness as he again reached out and touched her soft skin with his fingertips. "I lost my temper and you were here!" He lifted her chin with one finger and smiled at her ruefully, ignoring Jacques as if he was not there, and again Ruth had that strange sense of isolation, as if they were indeed alone. "You have borne the brunt of my anger before, hmm?" he reminded her softly, and she hastily looked down again.

Jacques hugged her close for a second, then dropped a light kiss on her head. "I, too, am sorry, *chérie*," he said. "If I had not come in to see you, you would not have been upset like this."

Hugo turned on his heel and walked across to the desk, his tall, slim body still tense with the passion that had exploded when he came into the room first, the dark shape of his back shadowy smooth in the thin shirt that stretched across it.

"You have wasted enough of our time, Jacques," he said in a cool hard voice. "Perhaps now you will leave Ruth to go on with her work."

"*Mais oui*, of course!" Now that his uncle was safely out of earshot on the other side of the room Jacques put his mouth close to Ruth's ear again. "You did well, *mon amour*," he whispered huskily. "Hugo cannot bear to see a woman cry—not one he is fond of; with some he can be ruthless, but—"

"Jacques!"

From across the room Hugo's voice was sharp and imperious and Jacques moved away from her as if he had been forcibly propelled so that she had no chance to explain that her tears had been genuine, or that there was no reason to suppose that his uncle was in any way fond of her, as he suggested.

"Au revoir, mon amour!" He turned in the doorway and winked broadly. "I will see you later, huh?"

"Allez!" Hugo called sharply, and the door closed quickly behind Jacques, his footsteps rapidly disappearing in the direction of the room where he knew he would find his grandmother. Hugo looked across at her and one brow lifted in query, setting Ruth's heart rapping anxiously at her ribs again as she faced him alone with that strange sense of anticipation curling in her stomach again.

"Are you quite recovered, Ruth?" he asked quietly, and she nodded.

"Yes, thank you, Monsieur Gerard."

He waited there, perched on the edge of the desk, one foot swinging as she came across the room and she had seldom felt more vulnerable or uneasy in her life before. When she got close enough he reached out a hand and brought her to a halt, then with one finger gently smoothed away the last tear from her cheek.

"Do I frighten you, *petite*?" he asked softly, and Ruth said nothing for a moment, she was finding it very hard to control her feelings and her shaking limbs.

"No, *monsieur*," she said at last in a small and very husky voice.

"But I made you cry," he said.

"I—I was silly," Ruth declared hastily, looking up at him and then as hastily looking away again when she saw the gentleness in his eyes. Hugo Gerard was an enigma she would never fully understand, and yet she felt she wanted to try. "I—I suppose," she went on in a shaky voice, "I was feeling slightly guilty for being caught—for you coming in when you did and—"

"I should have known better than to blame you," he said quietly. He laughed shortly and got up from the desk, standing tall and straight and much too close beside her. "And I should not grudge Jacques what time he has with you," he said. "Soon he will be gone and then there will be no more secret meetings in the library when I am away, hmm?" He lifted her chin, gently, with one hand and looked down at her for a moment in silence. "Does it make you sad to think of Jacques leaving, Ruth?" he asked softly.

She nodded, then immediately qualified the impression she might have given. "I shall miss him very much," she told him, sounding oddly breathless. "But I'm not sad for the reasons you think, Monsieur Gerard!"

Still that firm hand supported her chin and she knew that at any moment she would be obliged to raise her eyes and look at him again. "And what reasons are those?" he asked.

Ruth hesitated, wishing she was more sure of herself, less aware of that strong, warm body so close beside her and less clearly able to remember the way he had kissed her in this same room. "You—you think I'm—I think you probably think I'm—in love with Jacques," she said breathlessly, and he was shaking his head before she had even finished speaking, so that she looked at him in surprise.

"I know you are not in love with Jacques," he said, quietly confident. "But I am not so sure about Jacques, and that is why I will be thankful when he is on his way."

Ruth evaded that gentle hand at last, disliking the implication she thought she detected in the words. "So that he'll be safely out of the way of temptation?" she suggested reproachfully, and he shook his head.

"Non, ma petite," he said softly. "So that you will not be persuaded into something you will regret later!"

CHAPTER EIGHT

FOR THE WHOLE OF the following day Ruth gave much less of her attention to her work, and she was startled to find how often her thoughts dwelt on the prospective outing with Hugo. She saw nothing of him, except at mealtimes, and she gathered from Jacques that he had been yet again to Paris, something which she viewed with quite amazing dislike.

The next morning he put his head around the door of the library and cocked a quizzical brow at her. "You have not forgotten that you will be in town with me tonight?" he asked with a brief smile, and Ruth shook her head.

"No, Monsieur Gerard," she said. "I haven't forgotten."

"Bon!"

Before she could say anything else he was gone and she was left still with the problem of what to wear. She had never before spent an evening in Paris and she felt strangely trembly and wildly excited as she dressed.

Her mirror showed her that the deep yellow chiffon she had chosen did wonders for her brown hair and made it look definitely auburn, while her skin had a soft, creamy look that was enhanced by a soft pink flush of excitement on her cheeks. Her eyes looked huge and brilliant and much darker than their usual gray.

She had started her preparations early and for a while had toyed with the idea of putting up her hair in a more sophisticated coiffure on top of her head, but had decided against it eventually and left it long and silky about her shoulders. She looked very young with it like that, but it suited her as well as any other way and she wanted to look her best. Picking up a small evening purse, she took a last hasty look in the mirror and went downstairs.

Coming downstairs in the château was never a simple matter as it was elsewhere; Ruth always felt so very grand as she made her way down the wide, curved stairway with its gilded balustrades and marble steps. The companion stairway on the opposite side of the big hall made her think of stage or film settings and she always had the sensation of stepping out of reality as she walked down, like an actress on stage.

The chandeliers in the hall gave a beautiful rich glowing look to the inlaid floor and yet detracted somehow from the more mat colors of the tapestries, but still it never failed to impress her even after more than a month there. Below her, in the hall, she saw that Hugo was speaking to Madame Rousseau, and for a moment her heart stopped in sheer panic.

One hand to her breast to seek the reassurance of a heartbeat, she came on down the stairs and when she was no more than halfway he looked up and smiled. Madame Rousseau, too, smiled and there was a hint of suggestion in the brow that she briefly flicked upward, her rather gaunt face showing approval.

"Ruth!"

Hugo came across to meet her at the foot of the stairs and she felt the color that warmed her cheeks when he took her hand and swept those light gray eyes over her from head to toe in evident approval.

Never in her life had she felt so small or so anxious to be approved, and she smiled a little anxiously up at him.

"Will I do?" she asked as lightly as she was able for the tremor in her voice, and Hugo nodded.

"You'll do," he said, but with so much less warmth than she had somehow expected that she felt a chill of disappointment.

He was wearing evening dress himself and she thought how much it suited him. Such a contrast to his more usual rather shabby clothes and yet both suited him in their different ways. Tonight he was very definitely Monsieur Hugo Gerard, the well-known author and traveler, and for a minute she felt slightly overawed at the very idea of going out with him.

A frilled shirt gave him an almost romantic air and fitted him perfectly as his clothes always did. The black jacket and pants made him look somber, but there was a rakish look in the close-cut style of both that dispelled any impression of mundane sobriety.

"If you think this dress is too—" She made vague signs with her hands, and he smiled, shaking his head. "You don't think I should change it?"

"No, of course not," he told her, and smiled again. "You look very much like a little girl, but my pride will allow me to escort you without fear of my reputation, I think."

Ruth frowned and looked up at him reproachfully, her eyes bright with the excitement she could not subdue. "I hope you don't intend treating me like a favorite niece, *monsieur*!" she told him pertly, and he flicked one brow in comment.

"How would you have me treat you, *mademoiselle*?" he challenged softly.

Realizing how rash she had been and what a wrong impression she had given, Ruth flushed. "I'm sorry," she said, "I shouldn't have said that."

"It was rather provocative in the circumstances," he agreed blandly. "Especially when I have given Jacques my solemn oath to be on my best behavior with you!"

"Oh, no!"

She put her hands to her burning cheeks and could have curled up and died when she saw the amusement in his eyes. She should have known, of course, Jacques would never be able to resist issuing a warning to his uncle, and Hugo was bound to find the idea amusing.

"He does not approve of my taking you anywhere at all," he told her, apparently unperturbed by his nephew's disapproval, "and the fact that neither he nor you know where we are going seems to make him even more suspicious!"

Ruth looked at him through the thickness of her lashes, her heart doing a wild and breathtaking tattoo against her ribs as she registered every rugged, piratical feature of his face and the glitter in those light eyes as they looked down at her.

"I—I'm sorry if he made too much of it," she said, not quite knowing what to say for the best. "He—he didn't—he doesn't like me coming with you at all and he's got quite the wrong idea about it. I mean," she added hastily when that expressive brow flicked upward yet again, "he thinks that—"

"Jacques was brought up on a certain reputation I have acquired," he said calmly. "I do not blame him for feeling as he does, but I have no intention of letting his dislike of the situation deter me from enjoying my evening with you, and you should do likewise, *mon enfant*!"

Ruth stood for a moment in front of him, her hands curled, her eyes bright with determination and a flush on her cheeks as she stuck out her chin. "Until you promise not to call me 'child' again, Monsieur Gerard," she said firmly, "I won't budge a step from this place—I mean it!"

His laughter did wild and disturbing things to her pulses and she wondered for a moment if he was going to call her bluff, but then he shook his head, and put one large hand over the region of his heart. "I will not do so again, *mademoiselle*!" he vowed, then reached for her left hand and raised it to his lips, pressing them briefly to her fingers. "Shall we go?" he asked softly, and Ruth nodded, unable at the moment to find words.

DINNER, OF COURSE, CAME FIRST, and to Ruth the whole concept of dining French fashion in one of the big restaurants was a revelation. Food in these palaces of rich smells and fantastic decor was treated with reverence, and she had never seen such a menu. It was impossible for her to choose for herself, so she left the choice to Hugo, which, she suspected, was the way he preferred it.

Strange and marvelous things had been done to the duckling that she was served and she made no pretense of doing anything other than thoroughly enjoy it. There were wine and spices somewhere in its composition and it was so delicious that she was almost reluctant to follow it, even with the delicious *baba au rhum* that she eventually succumbed to.

Hugo, she thought, found his enjoyment in her own, and once or twice she looked at him across the table to find his eyes on her and a disturbing, glittery look in them that made her look away again hastily. The wine had done something toward making her feel as light and happy as she did, but there was something else, too, a sense of anticipation that she did not quite understand.

As they sat with the last of the wine she again felt his eyes on her and this time tried to hold his gaze without turning away. The light gray eyes were deep and glowing and she felt her heart do a skip of pleasure when he smiled across at her.

"You are enjoying it all, are you not, Ruth?" he asked softly, and she nodded.

"I'm thoroughly enjoying it, thank you, *monsieur!*"

He pulled a wry face and then for a moment the smoke from his cigarette hid the expression on his face as he spoke. "I have kept my word and refrained from calling you 'child', have I not?" he asked, but gave her no time to answer. "It would be more appropriate, then, do you not agree, if you called me by my name instead of that very formal '*monsieur*'?"

"I didn't know—" She bit her lip, her heart rapping at her ribs in anxious anticipation. "I wasn't sure if you'd like me to do that," she said, and he raised a brow.

"Why not?" he asked.

Ruth shrugged. "I don't know," she confessed. "I—I suppose because I work for you—you're my employer."

There was a hint of laughter about his mouth for her explanation and he sent a spiral of smoke into the air again before he answered. "And do English employers never allow themselves to be called by their first names?" he asked.

"It—it depends." Suddenly she felt as if the whole character of the evening was changing and she was being swept off into something she was not at all sure about.

"I see." He answered her seriously despite that hint of laughter. "And on what does it depend, Ruth?"

For a moment she sought for an answer, feeling much more out of her depth suddenly. "Oh, you know!" she said at last, and now he was laughing openly.

"On whether or not *le patron* sits the lady on his knee, *eh, mon adorable*?" he asked, and shook his head. "But then I qualify, do I not?"

"Monsieur Gerard—"

He was still laughing and still shaking his head at her and she pouted reproachfully. Leaning across the table, he reached out and gently touched her lower lip with one finger. "Smile, Ruth," he said softly. "I am teasing you, huh?"

"Monsieur—Hugo—" She did her best to control the breathtaking beat of her heart and the sudden wild sense of elation she felt. "You're laughing at me," she accused, and he shook his head slowly.

"Non, ma belle petite fille," he denied softly, and she wondered when she had ever heard him sound so very French before. He seldom did as Jacques did, and sprinkled his conversation with phrases in his own tongue, and she suspected that the wine had possibly had some effect on him, too.

"I don't speak French," she reminded him with another hint of a pout, and he laughed softly.

"And I do not mean to translate *that* for you, *ma belle*!" he told her.

Ruth felt strangely isolated, as if they were alone somewhere, a sensation that she remembered experiencing before when she had been with him. They seemed to have the knack of isolating themselves, a sense of rapport that she had never known with anyone else and for a moment its existence startled her.

"Hugo," she ventured, and liked the sound of it, "where *are* you taking me?"

The gray eyes studied her for a moment and she realized that he was suddenly more serious. There was a distant kind of look there, as if he was thinking about something he found less amusing than present company and she barely restrained the impulse to reach out and touch his hand, bring him back to her.

"When you are ready to go, *ma chère*," he said softly, "we will leave and you shall find out."

Outside it was still warm, but there was a threat of rain in the air and Ruth glanced up at the scowling black clouds above the bright lights of the shop windows. If it rained she was bound to get very wet, for she had no wrap of any sort, but somehow the prospect did not trouble her as it would have done in other circumstances. Paris was not a place to worry about such trivialities, and she would much rather walk if her companion had no objection.

"We're going to walk, aren't we?" she asked as they left the restaurant, and Hugo looked at her questioningly.

"I will get the car," he offered, but something in his manner gave her the impression that he, too, would as soon walk to their destination.

Ruth shook her head. "I'd rather walk," she told him, and he nodded agreeably.

"*Bon!*" he said briefly.

The streets were bright, despite the overcast sky, and the lighted shops and cafés excluded and ignored the threatening rain. Even the noisy, honking traffic seemed to do its share toward the evening air of excitement. It was not late by any means, and in the country the sky would probably have appeared much lighter, but here among the lights of the city it retreated early into a glowering blackness that hovered over the rooftops.

They took their time and walked along the crowded streets almost in silence, and it was a situation that Ruth was quite happy with. The touch of Hugo's fingertips on her arm was the only reassurance she needed that all was well.

After a while they turned off the busier streets into a quiet boulevard and her heart gave a sudden skip of anticipation when she realized that they had reached their destination. Before them was a small, stone-front theater with a printed banner spanning its facade and below, in flickering neon, the name Théâtre Honoré.

Ruth glanced up at Hugo and he nodded even before she could form her question, his fingers on her arm tightening their hold slightly as he led the way into the small and brightly lighted foyer. Surprisingly, to Ruth, there were quite a few people waiting to go in, standing about and talking, and she noticed that most of them seemed well dressed and looked opulent enough to be able to afford the Opéra, yet seemed quite at home in this curiously shabby little theater.

Hugo looked around him for a moment, then Ruth saw him smile and a moment later a short, stockily built man of middle age joined them. He greeted Hugo enthusiastically, shaking his hand and embracing him at the same time, chattering excitedly.

"Speak English, Honoré, *s'il vous plaît*," Hugo told him with a smile. "Mademoiselle Colton does not speak our language."

"Ah, *mais oui, mademoiselle*!" The little man did not wait for Hugo to introduce him properly, but grasped her hand and raised it to his lips. "We owe you so much, *ma chère mademoiselle*! Such a discovery! It is—it is *formidable*! Forgive me, *mademoiselle*, but at such a moment, my English deserts me!"

He chattered on in his own tongue at some length, in much the same vein, she gathered, and she knew that Hugo was watching her, waiting to see her reaction. When she looked up at him at last and was about to ask him what on earth the little man was talking about, he pointed to a poster just behind her.

Most of it was in French, but she could read enough to understand that it announced a concert of music and that it was presented by Honoré Bellair, the man she had just met. What finally caught her attention, however, was another name part way down what was presumably a program of pieces to be played. *Concerto d'Automne*, it read, and opposite, the name Philippe Gerard.

"Hugo!" She looked up at him with shining eyes, so moved she could not find words, and he smiled.

"I thought you would like to hear its first performance," he told her softly.

She nodded, still finding it difficult not to cry, she was so touched. It was evident that Honoré Bellair was a friend probably of long standing, and obviously Hugo had told him all about her discovery of the hidden tape, hence his delight in meeting her. It was touching, too, to think that Hugo had gone to some trouble to have his brother's music given a public hearing, hence all those visits to Paris.

"Shall we go in?" Hugo suggested softly, and she nodded.

The theater was quite small, but the acoustics were excellent and the place was packed, every seat filled with people who obviously loved music, for there was not a sound while the first two items were played and warm applause at the end. Surprisingly Ruth found herself quite nervous when the baton was raised for the beginning of Philippe's concerto and she could feel Hugo tense and anxious beside her.

Instinctively she looked at him, his face shadowed in the darkness of the theater, his eyes hidden by those long lashes, and only a small pulse beside his mouth betraying visible signs of his tension. The conductor led the orchestra into the first melodic bars of the piece and Ruth held her breath.

If it had sounded impressive in the big sunny library with only Philippe's own inexpert playing it now sounded far better with a full orchestra and the intent interest of a theater full of people. The soft passages flowed from violins and piano and the full-throated sadness of the sweeping phrases between had the voice of the full orchestra. It was incredibly beautiful, and Ruth was even more moved by it than she had been the first time she heard it.

When the final notes died there was a moment of silence, and then suddenly it was broken and all around them people were clapping their hands. The applause went on for a long time and as she listened to it Ruth did nothing to stop the tears that coursed down her cheeks, but she reached over and took Hugo's hand in hers, squeezing the strong fingers gently as she smiled.

"They liked it!" she whispered.

For a moment he said nothing, but his eyes had a dark and distant look so that she realized he was thinking about his brother and wishing he could have been there to hear the applause. Then he turned his head and looked down at her for a moment in silence, his mouth just touched by a hint of smile.

He reached over and took her other hand and raised it to his mouth, pressing his lips to her palm. "They liked it!" he echoed softly.

FOR SOME TIME after they left the theater neither Ruth nor Hugo spoke. The evening was cooler now and the first drops of that threatened rain fell onto the sidewalk like dark coins, and cooled Ruth's bare arms. After several minutes during which it grew heavier, Hugo looked up at the sky and then at Ruth.

"Will you stay here in a doorway while I get the car?" he asked, and she shook her head.

"No," she said with a smile. "I don't mind the rain, and it's beautifully cool."

He smiled. "Are you not afraid of becoming drenched?" he asked. "I would not like you to end your evening catching a cold, Ruth. I am sure Jacques would have something to say about that!"

Mentioning Jacques like that was almost like slapping her, Ruth felt, and she said nothing for several seconds but walked beside him ignoring the increasing downpour. "If you want to hurry," she told him, "please don't wait for me. You can go and get the car and I'll walk along and meet you."

Something in her voice must have told him that she was not happy about his change of mood, and he looked down at her for a moment curiously. "Now you are angry with me, hmm?"

"Not angry," Ruth denied. "I—I didn't like having you spoil my mood, that's all."

"And Jacques—the thought of Jacques could spoil your mood?" he suggested softly.

"No, no, you know I didn't mean that, Hugo!" She looked up at him, her face small and shining with the raindrops that spattered them both. "I've enjoyed tonight," she said in a small soft voice. "I really have, and I—I'm glad you did something about Philippe's music."

"It was not difficult," he said, an edge on his voice. "It was something that could have been done many years ago if only someone had listened then."

"You know Monsieur Bellair—he's a friend?" she asked, and he nodded.

"I have known him for many years, and I knew that if anyone could do anything about giving Philippe's music a hearing it would be him."

It was curious, Ruth thought, pushing back the wet hair from her forehead, how easily they talked of Philippe, as if she had known him as well as his brother. It was one more evidence of that strange rapport that seemed to exist between them and it gave her a strange sense of comfort.

"You'll—you'll tell Madame Gerard and Jacques about it now?" she ventured, and he did not answer. Instead he took her arm in a firm grasp and pushed her into a convenient doorway, squeezing in beside her, so that their bodies were packed close in the confined space.

Ruth felt her heart hammering away wildly as she reached up a hand to brush back her hair, and when she would have put her arm down again he took it and laid it across his shoulder so that her fingers touched the hair at the back of his neck, and the temptation to curl them into the thick thatch was almost irresistible.

"If you will not stay here while I get the car," he said in a quiet voice that warmed her cheek with his breath, "I will stay with you."

As he spoke he reached down for her other arm and put that, too, around his neck, then put his own hands on her slim waist and drew her closer to him.

"Now the *gendarme* will think we are lovers," he whispered, and laughed softly when she shook her head.

"Hugo—"

"I can feel your heart, *petite fille*," he said softly. "Are you afraid of me, Ruth?"

"No, of course I'm not afraid of you," Ruth denied, but wondered if in fact it was true. She was afraid, or at least half-afraid of what her own reactions could lead to. She could not deny that she found Hugo every bit as attractive as his reputation had led her believe he would be, and she had had firsthand experience of the way he could kiss her. It was something she both feared would happen again and feared it would not.

There were people still hurrying by in the rain, much too intent on making their own way to give them more than a passing glance, not that any Parisian worthy of the name would have dreamed of disapproving, she felt sure, but the gendarme Hugo had mentioned might just come along, and be curious.

There was something so blatantly and irresistibly masculine about him, about the body that pressed so close to her own and the strong hands that held her there. It was not fair of him to take such advantage of the situation the way he did, and she wished she had agreed to wait alone while he went for the car.

The pavements were shinily wet now, and the tires of the cars hissed and shushed over the wet road, so that she felt as if they were tucked away in a dry little world of their own, and that too added to the chaos of her emotions.

A hand slid upward to her neck and he moved aside her wet hair with gentle, caressing fingers. "Ruth?" His voice was little more than a whisper and he looked down at her with a hint of smile on his mouth. "If we are to be prisoners in this doorway, *ma petite*," he said softly, "can we not be less... apart?"

"Hugo!" She shook back her hair, bringing an end to that seductive caress. Her heart was thudding violently hard and her limbs were shaking as if she had no control over them at all, and she dared not look up at him. Instead she kept her eyes on the white, frilled front of his shirt. "Please—please don't—play with me!"

"Play with you?" He sounded genuinely puzzled by her terminology. "I do not understand you, *petite*."

It was difficult to put into words and she was quite sure he would never understand her objections. Possibly no woman had ever objected to his attentions before, but she was thinking more of her own feelings at the moment rather than any injury to his pride. She was not averse to his caresses, nor to his kisses, but she was very unsure that she could simply let it happen and then shrug it off as simply part of an evening's amusement. Her own feelings for him were already too deep for that.

He would probably treat her reasons with scorn and decide that she was the little girl he had dubbed her after all, but she could not help that. She put her arms down at her sides again and raised her eyes as far as the straight firmness of his mouth, her heartbeat wild and uncontrollable suddenly.

"I'll stay here alone if you'll fetch the car, Monsieur Gerard," she said in a small husky voice.

She felt his body stiffen and the hand that now lay against her neck curled its fingers until it felt hard and cruel and no longer caressing. Then he drew back from her, leaving a coolness where before there had been warmth, both his hands at his sides, and she could imagine the icy look of contempt in his gray eyes as he looked down at her.

Then surprisingly he laughed, and Ruth looked up swiftly at the dark shadowed face, her eyes wide and unbelieving. He was shaking his head and his mouth had a slight crooked tilt at one corner as he looked down at her. "Oh, Ruth, *ma petite* Ruth, what ideas you have of me!"

Ruth's stomach crawled with embarrassment. Anything but laughter would have been acceptable, even anger, the anger that had threatened when she first spoke, but to have him standing there in the middle of a Paris street laughing at her was unbearable. "Don't laugh at me!" she said, much more loudly than she had meant to, and he shook his head at her, still laughing.

"You wish the whole of Paris to hear you berate me, *mon chou*?" he asked.

Her cheeks were brightly pink and her eyes blazed with anger, as much for her own gullibility as for any other reason. "I don't care who hears me!" she declared, although she lowered her voice a little. "You just have to make me look small and foolish, don't you?"

The light gray eyes glittered wickedly at her in the shadowed doorway and she felt a flutter of excitement as well as the anger that consumed her. "I did not do anything, *mon chou*!" he denied blithely. "Nature has made you petite and if you look foolish then it is your own doing, not mine!"

"Oh, you—you—" Words failed her for the moment, and she only just resisted the temptation to hit him, hard, only she remembered in time the outcome of the last time she had done that. "And don't call me names," she added breathlessly.

"Mon chou?" He cocked a brow at her, and smiled broadly. "Very well, Ruth, I will not call you names, either—there, are you quite happy again, hmm?"

He was still teasing her, she knew, but she was not really anxious to openly quarrel with him, so she accepted the proffered peace move by leaning back againt the brick doorway. "I suppose you think I make a fuss about nothing," she guessed, and he said nothing for a moment, leaning against the opposite side of the doorway, although that still meant that contact was inevitable in the little space available.

When he smiled again it was without that teasing quality, and there was a hint of his former gentleness in his voice when he spoke. "I should not tease you, Ruth," he said. "I just find that doing so is almost—irresistible to me!"

Neither of them said anything more for several moments and the rain still came down steadily, hissing on the pavements and the road, diffusing the lights from shops and cafés and making dazzling yellow patches under the passing feet.

Then, quite suddenly, Hugo reached out a hand and she put hers into it without hesitation. "Shall we risk the rain and go home?" he suggested softly, and Ruth nodded.

As they turned into the long driveway sometime later she turned and looked at him in the almost dark, her eyes searching that strong, stern profile as if she found it irresistible. "Will you—will you tell Jacques and Madame Gerard where we've been?" she asked, and remembered that he had not given her an answer the last time she asked the same question.

"I will tell them," he said quietly, and loosed one

hand from the wheel reaching out to cover hers where they lay on her lap. For a second the strong fingers squeezed hers gently and her heart fluttered as it always did in response. "I am glad that you were with me, Ruth, to hear Phillipe's music. You—understood how I felt, did you not?"

"I understood," Ruth agreed softly, and realized as she said it that Jacques would never understand why it was her that Hugo had taken and no one else. It was that strange and somehow exciting rapport again. Something special that she had never yet found with anyone else but Hugo Gerard, and that in itself was very hard to understand.

CHAPTER NINE

IT WAS NOT really late when they arrived back from the concert, but Ruth was strangely reluctant to face either Jacques or Madame Gerard, and especially Jacques. It had been a strange and exciting evening, disturbing at times, but one she would not have missed for anything, and she did not want to have to answer questions about what they had heard. Best leave that to Hugo—he could explain why he had excluded his family from hearing the first performance of his half brother's music.

She had said good-night without even taking off her coat, and thanked Hugo, rather formally, catching her breath when he raised her fingers to his lips and murmured, *"Bonne nuit, chérie,"* in such a soft and deeply seductive voice that Jacques had scowled his dislike.

She awoke the next morning with a strange feeling of anticipation fluttering in her stomach, which she did not attempt to find a reason for. Bathed and dressed, she found the sensation undiminished and her heart was fluttering as if with excitement as she left her bedroom.

"*Bonjour*, Ruth!"

Her indrawn breath was sharp and audible as she spun round to find Hugo standing just behind her. The morning sun from the high windows showed him tall and dark clothed against the background of gilded balustrades and the curiously glowing light reflected from the vastness of the hall below. On either side of them the wide, sweeping staircases curved gracefully downward, and once again Ruth experienced that sense of isolation, the feeling of being alone in the world with him. She was reminded of the first day she began work at the château, when he had similarly accosted her when she was far less formally dressed, and because of that she smiled, a small, slow smile that lent a glow to her gray eyes.

"*Bonjour*, Monsieur Gerard," she said.

Her use of his full name seemed not to please him and he frowned briefly, shaking his head. "Are we to be—distant again today, *petite*?" he asked softly, and Ruth bit her lip, mostly on the effect of that soft deep voice using the endearment.

"I—I thought perhaps during working hours," she ventured.

"Ah! You do not wish me to be the kind of *patron* who sits the employee on his knee, huh?" His smile teased her, reminding her of their similar conversation last night, and she shook her head, trying to control the increasing rate of her pulses and finding it alarmingly difficult.

"Now I know you don't mind," she said, trying to sound matter-of-fact and ignoring the question, "I'll call you by your Christian name. I always refer to you as Hugo anyway."

Briefly those faintly disapproving brows drew together again. "When you talk about me to Jacques?" he guessed, and Ruth looked uneasy.

"You make it sound as if I do nothing but gossip about you," she accused. "And that's far from the truth, *monsieur*!"

"Hmm?" He raised a brow over the title, and she half smiled, unwilling to have him angry with her.

"Hugo," she said obediently.

"That is better!" Light gray eyes searched her face for a moment, warmly quizzical, and there was a hint of smile about his mouth that did incredible things to her self-control. "You *did* enjoy last night, did you not, *ma petite*?" he asked softly, and Ruth nodded.

"I enjoyed it enormously!" she assured him with a smile. "It was so—so exciting hearing Philippe's music really played by an orchestra! And the audience loved it too, it wasn't that we were prejudiced!"

She had not realized until she heard her own words just how intimate they sounded, and that warm, gentle look was still in his eyes as he stood close beside her, his fingertips just touching her arm and sensuously caressing. There was something different about this morning and it had all to do with that sense of anticipation she had when she woke, she felt sure.

"And afterward, Ruth?"

He asked the question softly and her heart leaped in response as she remembered how they had stood together in that sheltered little world in the center of Paris. How she had begged him not to play with her, to amuse himself at her expense, as nervous as a silly schoolgirl, which was probably how he saw her.

She kept her eyes on that strong tanned throat above the collar of his dark shirt. "I—I was probably very silly," she admitted in a small husky voice.

"You were very sweet, *chérie*," he argued softly. "But you still do not trust me, do you, *petite*?"

"Hugo, please! I may have been—silly, childish perhaps, but I—I know what I'm doing and I have to be—to be sensible!"

"Sensible!" He gave it a French pronunciation and laughed softly. "Poor little Ruth! What are you afraid of, *chérie*?"

She looked up at him reproachfully. "Hugo, please don't laugh at me, I—" The sound of a door closing somewhere below checked her sharply and she instinctively stepped back from him and turned her head in the direction of the sound.

It was as if a spell had been broken and she thought he regretted it as he took her arm, his fingers gently persuasive, guiding her along the gallery to the stairs. "Let us go and breakfast, *petite*," he said softly. "I will speak with you again when you have eaten and perhaps feel less like treating me as if I meant to eat you, huh?"

JACQUES FOLLOWED HER to the library when she went in to start work, and she would have discouraged him, seeing Hugo's swift frown, but Jacques was not in a mood to be dismissed. He closed the door carefully behind them and stood for a moment, saying nothing but looking far more serious than she had seen him for a long time.

He had his hands in the pockets of his slacks and his shoulders were hunched in a curiously defensive attitude as he stood on the opposite side of the desk. "So," he said at last, "I have really lost you, *chérie*!"

Ruth, in the act of sitting down, remained standing and looked at him for a moment uncertainly. "I—I'm not quite sure I understand you, Jacques," she said.

"Oh, Ruth, *mignonne*!" His brown eyes, regarding her across the desk, were faintly reproachful, and he was shaking his head slowly. "Can you not see the way things are going? Did Hugo not take you to listen to Philippe's music? Philippe, who was almost sacred to him! Oh, *mais non, chérie*, you cannot pretend that such a thing has no significance!"

Ruth's heart was thudding mercilessly hard at her

ribs and her head felt strangely light and dizzy as she stood there facing Jacques across the desk, her hands almost automatically picking up books which she gazed at unseeingly. "But I told you how I found the tape with the music," she said in a small, husky voice. "Monsieur Bellair wanted to meet me and—and Hugo wanted to thank me, in a way, for discovering the tape. You're making a mountain out of a molehill, Jacques, if you think it's any more significant than that!"

"Ruth!" He came around the desk and for a moment stood with his hands on her arms looking down at her with a curiously anxious look. Then he shook his head and pulled her closer, bending to kiss her lips gently. "I have made no mountains," he said softly, "but Hugo has built many hopes, *chérie*, and he, I think, will not be such a good loser as I am!"

"Jacques!"

Her heart was beating so hard and fast that she felt quite alarmingly breathless and she saw again in her mind's eye that gentle quizzical warmth in Hugo's eyes when they stood on the gallery earlier, his promise to talk to her after she had breakfasted. It was futile to suppose that there was anything beyond a passing affair on his mind, and she felt an upsurge of panic suddenly when she realized that her own feelings went much too deep for her to endure that.

Jacques must do something to help her; he must get her away, back to England before she became any more deeply involved. Before she was badly hurt by something she couldn't control, no matter how sensible she tried to be. Hugo, she recalled, had laughed at the idea of her being sensible.

She had always thought herself a sensible and levelheaded girl, well able to take care of herself in any eventuality, but Hugo Gerard was a mature and experienced man with little regard for any but his own desires, and she realized too late how vulnerable she was. Her sudden realization that she was in love with him made her even more vulnerable to hurt and she had to do something about it before it was too late.

"Jacques!" She reached out for him, meaning to take his arm, beg him to do something to help her, but he was already halfway across the room and out of her reach.

"Someone is coming," he said, a wry smile tilting his mouth. If it is Hugo I must be gone when he comes or there will be—*mon dieu*! I go!"

"Jacques, please!"

He raised one hand to his lips and blew her a kiss from the doorway. "*Au revoir, ma belle* Ruth!" he whispered.

He did not close the door behind him, but left it ajar, and Ruth kept her eyes on that narrow opening, standing as if transfixed, the books she hugged tightly to her breast defensive and anxious.

Hugo said nothing when he came in, only looked across at her curiously with those light gray eyes, and quietly closed the door. Her heart was thudding wildly and she could feel it like a deafening drumbeat that made her head spin. The dark shirt and close-fitting dark trousers seemed to give him a menacing look suddenly, and she heard her own breath catch in her throat as he came across to her in long swift strides, silent on the sound-deadening carpet.

"Ruth?"

She realized then how wildly fearful she must look, and she tried to restore normality to her reeling senses by shaking her head and putting down the books she held. Only then was she conscious of the way her hands were trembling.

For a moment he said nothing, then he reached out his hands and took hers, small and trembling, enclosing them in the comfort of his strong fingers. "Jacques has said too much," he said softly. "He had no right!" He drew her closer until the sensual, virile strength of his body warmed her and at the same time a shiver along her spine like an icy finger.

"Hugo, please don't—"

"Oh, Ruth! *Ma petite amie*!" The deep, seductive voice and those strong hands, now at her waist and drawing her closer, made her shudder violently with emotions she could not control. "Why are you so afraid of me, *ma chérie*?" he asked softly, and brushed his lips lightly across the smoothness of her forehead. "Is it that you think I mean to harm you?"

"I don't know *what* you mean to do!" Her fear of being drawn into something inescapable lent panic to her voice and she fought with other more urgent desires that wanted her to respond to him in quite a different way. "Please, Hugo—please don't—don't make me just another—"

"Ruth!" His hands restrained her when she would have pulled free of him and he held her where he wanted her, close in his arms, her heart thudding wildly at her breast. Then he looked down at her steadily for a long moment, his eyes deep and with a curious glow in their depths that did wild things to her senses. "Is that what you think, *ma chérie*?" he asked softly.

"What else can you mean?" Ruth whispered huskily. "You—"

"Oh, Ruth!" he whispered softly. "Did you not realize last night how I felt about you, *mon amour*? Did I not make it plain enough?" He smiled, a gentle, teasing smile that glistened in his eyes. "You speak of being sensible, *mignonne*, had you not sense enough to see that I love you?"

His arms completely enfolded her, drawing even closer and, feeling the urgent pressure of his body, her own betrayed her, curving into his as if to make them one as his mouth sought hers. Her lips parted and she lifted her arms to encircle his neck, everything forgotten in the ecstasy of being in his arms.

After a long moment his gray eyes regarded her again, deep and glowing, while his arms still folded her close to him. "You think perhaps I should not fall in love with such a *petite fille*?" he asked, and he was, she suspected, more than half-serious although he was smiling. "Little girl," he explained when she looked puzzled, and she shook her head.

"I keep telling you I'm not a little girl," she told him, her voice huskily breathless. "But, Hugo—" She looked up at him, her eyes glowing softly and her mouth begging to be kissed again. Never in her life had she experienced such a confusion of emotions at one time. She was at once deliriously happy and light-headed and yet still not completely sure he meant it as seriously as she prayed he did. "You—you're not playing with me, are you?" she begged.

She had asked that same question once before, she remembered, and he had queried it then, as he did now.

"Such a curious phrase!" he smiled, and kissed her lightly on her mouth. "Why do you insist that I am playing with you, *mon petit chou*?"

"Because—because you— Oh, I don't *know*! That wretched book of yours, I suppose!" She put her arms round that lean, sinewy body and hugged against it as tightly as she could get, her eyes closed, her heart beating with an urgency that threatened to deafen her. "Oh, please, Hugo," she begged in a breathlessly husky voice, "don't let me go on like this if I mean no more to you than that! Tell me now and let me go away as far as I can get from you so that it won't hurt so much!"

"Ruth, *mon adorable*," he said softly, and took her face between his big, gentle hands, his head bent so that his breath warmed her mouth as he spoke. *"Je t'aime beaucoup, ma chérie."*

His mouth silenced her asking for a translation and for a second passion trembled between them, would not be checked, and unleashed itself in a desire so fierce that it obliterated everything else from her mind. Again and again they kissed, holding one another close, exploring each other's nearness, like dreamers, unwilling to awake.

Ruth laid her head against that broad, strong chest, turning her face to the smooth tanned skin, her lips pressed to its vibrant warmth. "Ruth!" He buried his face against the softness of her neck, his voice muffled by her hair. "Can you forget that I am Jacques's uncle, that I wrote that book? Can you forget what I am, what I have been, *mon amour*, and say you will marry me?"

"I love you," Ruth said simply, and stretched up on tiptoe to kiss his mouth. Her eyes were huge and shining, and there was a soft pink flush on her cheeks as she looked up at him. "I don't care what you've been," she told him softly. "I only know what you are and that I love you enough to want to spend the rest of my life with you."

For a moment he raised an expressive brow and there was a hint of gentle amusement in his gray eyes as he looked down at her. "Do you trust me at last, *mon amour*?" he asked, and Ruth nodded, her eyes shining as she lifted her face again to be kissed.

"With my life," she said softly.

BEWARE THE HUNTSMAN

Beware the Huntsman
Sophie Weston

"You shall go with Claire," her grandfather had ordered. Susanna was horrified. It was none of her business what her cousin did with her life and she had no wish to become Claire's watchdog.

Nevertheless that was the role in which she eventually found herself: sharing an apartment with Claire, who considered her a spy, and living in the city, which she hated. She blamed Giovanni di Montefiorino for her dilemma. He must have encouraged Claire in her shameless pursuit of him.

But Susanna, with her ready-made prejudice against him, was not prepared for the impact his devastating charm would have on her....

CHAPTER ONE

THE DOOR SLAMMED SHUT. Stuart Shaw stared at it blankly as if he could not believe that his favorite granddaughter could have flung so noisily out of the room.

"Well!" he said foolishly.

His other granddaughter regarded him thoughtfully from her window seat. He was flushed, and his handsome gray mop of hair was wildly disarranged. It was a long time since he had been in such a temper. Not, she reflected, since her own father had delivered her fourteen-year-old self on Stuart's doorstep and left in his turn for London. And now Claire wanted to do the same thing, although not, admittedly, depositing any offspring before doing so, she thought wryly. And Stuart was furious.

"Well, what, Stuart?" she said.

Her calm tones had their usual effect and he relaxed, running his hands through his hair. Some of the ugly color left his cheeks, she noted with satisfaction.

"Well, I've made a fool of myself, I suppose," he said ruefully. "I certainly never thought I'd find myself playing the heavy guardian. Certainly not with Claire. She's always been so reasonable. What's got into her, Sue?"

He looked so bewildered that Susanna nearly laughed.

"She wants to take a job in London," she replied patiently. "She doesn't think that's unreasonable, and neither do I. After all, she's not a child. She's eighteen and she's just spent the best part of a year in Florence. You not only let her go there, you actually encouraged her. She can't see what's the great difference between Florence and London. I sympathize."

"So you're against me, too," he said moodily.

"No, I'm not. I just think in this case you're being more unreasonable than Claire is."

He paid no attention to this. Flinging himself back in a chair, he said abruptly, "Claire's changed."

Hearing the disquiet in his voice, Susanna replied soothingly, "She's grown up a lot. It was bound to happen."

But it was more than that. While Stuart lit his pipe in silence she thought uneasily how very much more than that it was.

They had all had such high hopes for Claire when she set off for Florence a year earlier. It had been Stuart's idea really. It had become painfully obvious that Claire was bored at school and was not going to pass any of her important exams.

Claire herself was blithely unconcerned. "Not to worry, lamb," she would say when Stuart remonstrated over a particularly damning school report, "my talents simply aren't academic."

He had blustered, of course, and threatened horrible reprisals if Claire did not start to work, but secretly he had not been altogether dismayed. She was fully aware that he continually hoped that the artistic talent that had missed his son and daughter would emerge in the second generation of the family. Claire and her art instructor could both have told him how unfounded was that hope, but he consulted neither. He simply plotted to send her to live with an old Italian friend to study art. That the friend was also a sculptor and Claire would find herself in the middle of an exclusive club of artists was, he assured Sue, purest coincidence.

"And, anyway," he had added darkly, "you don't know what talent Claire may have hidden away. It'll never come out in a family environment. She needs to get away from you and me, Sue. We protect her too much. You may not care to develop your own talents—" a long-standing bone of contention, this "—but that's no reason to deny Claire her chance."

She had sighed. As she well knew, Claire's talents ended with her accomplished game of tennis. She was decorative and sweet-natured. She had been a philosophical child, accepting her grandfather's moods uncomplainingly. Both her parents had been killed in an airplane crash when she was only a few months old.

Immediately Stuart had taken her to live with him in his ramshackle home on the edge of the Sussex marshes. Little Claire had been alternately cosseted and ignored. When he was working he was likely to forget everything, a habit she had caught from him. When Claire was concentrating nothing distracted her. And when she was not concentrating, she still held an unshakable conviction that everything would turn out for the best, which gave her an attractive air of serenity.

Even when another cousin had arrived in her sheltered world, she had not been disturbed. With another child there would have been jealousies and arguments, but not Claire. Sunnily she had accepted the glowering Susanna, warned her about their grandfather's fluctuations of temper and left her to accustom herself to the strange household at her own pace.

In gratitude Susanna had constituted herself housekeeper and general administrator. She was six years older than Claire, and there was much she could do to make her cousin's life easier. They had become very close.

And now the intimacy was gone, and in its place was—what? Hostility, almost.

Stuart broke into her reflection. "Of course, it must be a man."

"A man?" queried Susanna, lost.

"The change in Claire," explained her grandfather impatiently. "She's done more than grow up."

"You mean she's in love?" demanded Sue incredulously.

Exasperated, he snorted. "That's not the way I would have put it. A child of her age! Claire," he said darkly, "has been sowing her wild oats."

Her protest was instinctive. "Oh, really, Stuart!"

He regarded her with a curious smile. "I should have thought of it at once. Or you should have. Most women would have recognized the signs instantly. But not you." Then as she still looked doubtful he snapped. "Look—tell me what's different about Claire."

"Different?" Sue marshaled her thoughts. "Well, she's quieter I suppose and she doesn't tell things as she used to do. She seems as if she's gone away from us...."

"No, no. I meant physically."

"Oh!" She pondered it. "Well, I don't think she's changed physically at all, has she?"

"Sue, I despair of you. She comes back looking like a fashion model, and you say she hasn't changed. She's lost weight, discovered makeup and learned to sit still. When she went away she bounced like a puppy. Now she has grace."

Sue was startled. His voice was quite objective. He might have been discussing any stranger. She stared at him, wondering.

In a way it was true. Claire had become an elegant wraith, fashionably slender, with an expensively contrived pallor and huge shadowed eyes. Her soft blond hair was beautifully cut. Stuart of course would notice such things.

"I suppose you're right." Amusement crept into her voice. "I didn't notice. I just thought she looked ill."

"Sue, you're unnatural!" He considered her from under thick brows. "If Claire weren't such a problem, I'd worry about you."

"No, you wouldn't. You'd go into your studio and forget all about it. And a good thing, too. I'm quite happy."

"Sweating in a solicitor's office," he said bitterly. "Wasting a good education and a perfectly respectable brain.

She sighed. "I've told you, I'm perfectly happy. I don't want a career—I never have done. If I can live here peacefully in the country and grow roses, I shall be quite happy."

"Changeling!" he accused, half-angry. Then, "What am I going to do about Claire, Sue?"

After a pause she countered with another question, "Why are you so worried about her going to London? It's not as if she hasn't been away from home before."

He gave her a pitying look. "Sure. She was staying with old friends of mine. If anything went wrong—say, she ran out of money or something—there was help at hand."

"But if she ran out of money in London she could telephone us," she objected.

"Yes, but she wouldn't." He stood up and began to move restlessly about the room. "Look, Sue. She turned up here out of the blue. No warning, nothing. Says she left Italy, isn't going back, and is moving on to London—just like that. But she's got herself a job to go to and an apartment. How did she get them? And when? She more or less told us she'd come straight home from Florence. If she stopped off in London where did she stay? And why didn't she tell us?"

He stared out of the window, his hands clasped behind his back. "Face it, Sue. She's off to London to be with this man, whoever he is."

She did not exclaim. He swung around on her impatiently.

"And if she is?" Sue said softly. "Isn't that her business?"

"For God's sake!" he exploded. "A child of eighteen. Are you out of your mind?"

"I thought you wanted her to be independent?"

"Don't be mischievous. I did. I do. But I never said I wanted to throw her into the arms of some—some—"

"Vile seducer?" she offered. "Rake?"

He smiled unwillingly. "Don't be ridiculous."

"Well," she said reasonably, "you can't tell Claire that you want her to be independent and then withdraw her charter the moment she does something you don't like."

Stuart frowned. "Whose side are you on?"

"Nobody's. I'm trying to be sensible."

He looked at her narrowly. "Are you crowing over me, Susanna? You never thought I should have let her go in the first place, did you?"

"What does it matter now?"

"It does. You have every right to say I told you so."

"Poor Stuart," she commiserated, her eyes twinkling. "I simply thought it was a bit unwise to push Claire. She would have found what she wanted to do in the end."

"And now it looks as if she has," he commented wryly.

"And she'll work it out without any interference from you," she soothed.

"Yes, I know."

He wandered over to the mantelpiece and took a cigarette from a teak box. It was a sign that he was very disturbed, she knew. Normally he detested smoking and only offered guests cigarettes with dire predictions of disease.

"But she might get badly hurt in the meantime," he went on, following his own train of thought. "She's not happy."

"She's tired," Sue said flatly. "She's just had a blazing row with you. You can't expect her to be cheerful on top of that."

"It's deeper than that," he insisted obstinately. The dangerous color was rising in his cheeks again. It was some months since the family doctor had warned him about overtaxing his heart. Stuart habitually ignored Dr. Kenton, and it had been left to Sue to see that nothing came his way to annoy him. Recently he had been working a good deal in his studio, and it had not, until now, proved a difficult task. But now he was worried and, as always on these occasions, promptly lost his volatile temper.

"You may be right," she said diplomatically. "Give her time and she'll probably tell you all about it."

"Time!" Cigarette ash spilled down his sweater, and he brushed it carelessly onto the floor. "There isn't any time. You heard her say it. She wants to go back to London tomorrow."

"Yes, I know. But I'm sure she'll stay at least until the weekend if we ask her. She'll probably be glad of the country air. But not," on a rising note as he appeared about to interrupt, "if you shout at her. I'll talk to her."

Susanna stood up, thinking compassionately that for once he looked his sixty-eight years.

She said gently, "You'll have to get used to the idea, though. You can't make a cocoon around her now, Stuart. And you can't live her life for her."

He waved her away. "Spare me the homespun philosophy! Go and talk to the girl. God knows, I can't."

And because she knew that this was his saddest disillusionment, Susanna went without further comment.

CLAIRE WAS SITTING motionless in front of the mirror in her room. She looked up as Susanna came in but did not turn around.

"Yes?" she said into the glass. "Come to mop me up, Sue?"

She was oddly out of place in the room surrounded by stuffed toys and her old school books. Sue hesitated. The pale, perfect features regarded her calmly in the mirror.

After a moment she said, "I think Stuart's more in need of mopping up than you are. He isn't used to being shouted at."

Claire smiled. It was a mere stretching of the lips that left the eyes steady, unmoved. "Whereas you and I are all too, too used to it. He doesn't like his own medicine, does he?"

"Claire—" Sue sat on the bed and spread her fingers on the patchwork coverlet. When they were children it had been a game to stretch a different finger into each patch. Today it was easy. Looking at her own neat hands, she said, "He isn't well, Claire. I should have written to tell you, I suppose, but there didn't seem to be anything you could do about it and—well, I just didn't bother." She looked up quickly at the impassive stranger's face in the mirror. "I'm sorry," she finished lamely.

"So you think you can blackmail me with Stuart's health?" Claire sounded amused. "What's the matter? Does he have spasms?"

"A weak heart," Susanna said stiffly. "He should avoid excitement."

"Really?" Claire swung around on her stool. "And how do you intend to control his filthy temper, his insatiable curiosity, his vanity, his gluttony . . . in short his whole life? Be realistic, Sue. Stuart could no more live without excitement than he could without air. This whole stupid fuss is of his making, not mine."

Sue bit her lip. "I know," she acknowledged. "But if you could only be a bit more understanding. . . ."

"Understanding? How? Of what?"

"Of Stuart?"

"But I already understand Stuart perfectly." Claire was airy. "He's a cunning, selfish man. He sent me away for a year—not to study, oh, no. Who should know better than the master sculptor that I haven't an atom of artistic talent in my soul? He knew and he didn't care. Because it wasn't for *me* that he sent me away at all. I was to go to Florence and see all his old friends and come back and live the rest of my life in this miserable place amusing him with anecdotes about them."

Her face was not impassive now. Her eyes were gleaming with fury while her hands twisted and twisted in her lap. She glared at Sue almost as if she held her responsible, Sue thought.

"Were you unhappy?" she ventured.

Claire gave her a contemptuous glance. "Unhappy and more. Much, much more. You have no idea. They soon found I couldn't paint, of course, and after that they treated me as if I weren't quite human."

Shocked at her bitterness, Sue said bracingly, "So why didn't you come home?"

"I have."

"Have you?" Sue raised her eyebrows. "One night under our roof and off to the fleshpots of London?"

"Hardly the fleshpots," Claire murmured. The passion of temper was over. "I have a perfectly respectable job in a perfectly respectable bank. It isn't as if I was going to sit under the statue of Eros and wait for the call. I don't see what Stuart is so mad about. Unless," she added wryly, "he thinks a bank is *too* respectable."

Sue considered her thoughtfully. Her defenses were up again. There seemed to be no trace of the old Claire in the carefully made-up face. In spite of her superficial calm she seemed tense and ill at ease. There was an unnerving distance between them.

Choosing her words carefully, Sue said, "Rather the reverse, I think. Stuart is a little—concerned—about the nature of this job and how you found it. You weren't," she said excusingly, "very clear."

Claire sighed. "It's quite simple. I can use my Italian. I imagine I shall hop about from department to department and translate. I don't know any more than that yet. It's quite a small bank, and this is the first branch outside Italy. As for how I found it—it's a family concern run by some people I met in Italy."

"And the apartment?"

"The apartment belongs to them. The son who's going to run the London branch has been over here for some time working for one of the merchant banks. Now that he's moving up in the world he gets a house. Hence one spare apartment. Satisfied?"

Stuart would have apoplexy.

"I suppose—as he's been living in London—you won't have met the son you'll be working for?" Sue said casually. She met Claire's eyes defiantly.

"You don't suppose anything of the sort." Suddenly Claire sounded very tired. "Rightly. Italian families are close. He goes home at least once a month. This job was his suggestion."

"Oh." In spite of her six years' superiority Sue found herself feeling infinitely younger than her cousin and rather helpless. "That won't help your case with Stuart."

Claire shrugged, her mouth wry. "I know. He's a sharp old bird, isn't he? He knew the minute I walked in. It—threw me rather. I didn't know I had Giovanni branded on my brow for all to see."

"You haven't," Sue said comfortingly. "I didn't see it. But you and Stuart are so very alike."

"He probably expected it," Claire said bitterly. "He just wasn't prepared for a banker."

Sue hid a smile. "He'll get used to it. Especially if you marry."

"Marry?" Claire gave a harsh little laugh. "No chance, my dear. If my grandfather didn't stop it, his old dragon of a mother would. Rich Italian young men don't marry penniless English girls. In fact, they don't marry any girls at all that don't come already stamped with mamma's seal of approval."

"But that's outrageous!" gasped Sue, forgetting to ask why Claire did not win his mother's approval.

Her cousin shrugged fatalistically. "I knew what would happen. They were all quite open about it. There's even some sort of marriage in the air—a distant cousin, I believe. They negotiate it like an international treaty." She stirred her suitcase with her foot. "Besides," she added tonelessly, "he doesn't want to marry me. I must unpack."

Helpfully tucking her legs out of the way, Sue watched a sophisticated wardrobe emerge from the battered case. Long dresses, short dresses, tailored trousers and jewel-colored sweaters. And quantities of silk. Raising her eyebrows at some cobwebby underwear, Sue said, "That looks like very expensive confectionery."

For a moment, laughing, Claire was her old self. "It is," she admitted. "A good deal of it was given to me one way and another, but Italian prices are crippling."

"Which can't be said for Italian clothes," Sue retorted, running a silken petticoat through her fingers.

"No, indeed. That was given to me by a friend whose father owns a silk mill. A petticoat like that is supposed to be fine enough to go through a wedding ring."

"Really?" Sue was intrigued. "But doesn't it crease frightfully, er, en route?"

Claire laughed at that, a cheerful schoolgirl peal. "I don't suppose you *do* it. You just ought to be able to. Anyway," with a return to misery, "I haven't got a wedding ring to try it."

There was a silence. Back turned, Claire folded her clothes and put them carefully in the drawers of her old, white-painted dressing table. Again Sue was struck by a sense of incongruity.

"The drawers will be dusty," she said, getting off

the bed. "Not expecting you, I didn't do anything about them." She looked around the pretty room guiltily. "To be honest, I haven't touched this room for weeks."

"Not to worry." Claire's voice was strained, but she was obviously trying to behave normally. "Stuart or no Stuart, I won't be staying long. After all, I am of age."

Looking at her flushed face, Sue demanded, "Then why did you bother to come back at all?"

Claire straightened. "I'm not sure. It seemed—appropriate somehow. Anyway, I'm short of cash."

"I see."

"Only for the time being. The airfare took everything left of my allowance. Once I start work I'll be all right. It's just the next five or six weeks. . . ." She broke off. "But I'll get it from somewhere," she said with resolution. "If I have to sell mother's engagement ring. Or I suppose I could borrow it from Giovanni."

Sue regarded her with misgiving. "Wouldn't you mind? Taking money from him, I mean."

"How sweetly old-fashioned," Claire said affectedly. She met Sue's clear eyes with a faint smile. "You think I ought to have more pride, don't you?"

"Well, I—" Sue murmured uncomfortably.

Claire sank down on the bed, head bent. "Look. I'm in love with the man. I don't have any pride where he's concerned." She looked up a little blindly, a sour smile twisting her mouth. "If I had any pride I would have left him alone a long time ago. I wouldn't have crawled for this job in the first place."

Suddenly she raised her eyes to Sue's shocked face. She stood up violently.

"You don't know what I've been doing, Sue. Manufacturing excuses to see him, maneuvering my friends just to spend an hour with him. Asking myself to lunch with his family every Sunday, just in case . . . . Letting his damned old mother insult me. You wouldn't ever behave like that."

Appalled, Sue said nothing.

"So what's a little thing like asking him for money?" Claire demanded bitterly.

"If Stuart knew you felt like that . . . ."

"He'd have me locked up."

"No. No, I don't think he would. I don't say he wouldn't be upset, because he would, but he'd survive that. But he'd help, I'm sure of it. Even to the extent of giving you the money you want to go to London."

"Then you'd better be my ambassador. I can't ask him myself, I can't face any more arguments," Claire said on a rising note.

"All right," Sue said reluctantly. "I'll ask him for you if that's what you really want."

"It is."

The tone was definite, forbidding further discussion, but Sue hesitated.

"Are you sure? I mean, it seems to me that it's an awful lot of effort and—well, humiliation—for not too much result. Is it worth it?"

Claire knuckled her eyes. When she looked up her face was pale again, and she looked exhausted.

"You don't understand, do you, Sue? No, in your terms, it's not worth it. It almost certainly won't get me anywhere. But I've got to try. Can't you see that?"

The window frame began to rattle. Wind had been blowing off the marsh all day, and now the clouds had come over and the little room darkened. Huge raindrops the size of a penny appeared on the windowpane. With a harassed look at the rain Sue searched for words.

"Not really," she said apologetically. "In your place, I'd probably stay here and try to forget him. But I always was more of a rabbit. Now, I must go and rescue Stuart's shirts. Mrs. Rose insisted on washing them and they're outside. They'll get soaked." At the door she turned back. Claire was a sad little figure in the storm-shadowed room. "I'm sorry," Sue offered awkwardly.

"Don't be. I'd rather have it this way than not to have known him at all," she said with a faint smile. "I doubt if you'll ever understand. You haven't the temperament." Amazingly, Claire sounded almost compassionate. "But believe me."

"Of course. I'll speak to Stuart," Sue murmured as she escaped.

Outside it had not properly begun to rain. Under the heavy clouds the landscape was lighted with an odd sulphurous light. The wind bit. It was salty and carried the scent of seaweed from the coast twenty miles away. In the midst of unpegging shirts, Susanna sniffed pleasurably. It was a smell that always stirred her blood.

She stood in the gathering dark listening to seabirds wheeling in the sky, crying a warning to their fellows still at sea. It was not cold when the wind dropped. Great splashes of warm rain fell on her face and she turned it up to the sky, laughing. Somewhere in the distance thunder began to roll.

The house stood at the end of a rutted lane on a slight rise overlooking the marsh. The road was hidden by the hedge, and from the garden it looked as if the house was entirely surrounded by flat, damp fields. They had terrified her when she first came, those fields. They had seemed like an uncrossable waste imprisoning her in her grandfather's house. Later they had turned it into a fortress in which she could shelter. But just that first week they had frightened her.

Standing on the doorstep she surveyed the scene, her mouth quirking. She had been a city child—London, Milan, Turin, Manchester. Halfway across Europe and back again in the wake of her mercurial father. Her mother would say bravely that travel was good for children, but all Susanna could remember of the mind-broadening experience was a succession of dingy rented apartments and battered cars. This time her father was really making a career for himself. This time they could put down roots. But of course he never did, and in six months he would be off again in search of brighter prospects or a more amusing job.

Amusing! It had been one of her father's favorite words—still was, for that matter. He had not found it amusing to have a growing daughter or a wife, either, in the end. Susanna always suspected that secretly it had been something of a relief to him when that depressed lady died.

Simon Shaw had promptly abandoned his only child and started work as an interior decorator in London. Ironically this time he seemed to have found himself and was still there ten years later, mildly successful and sufficiently prosperous to live the life he wanted. He and Susanna met two or three times a year, got on very amiably and parted without the slightest desire ever to see each other again. On each occasion Simon was accompanied by a different, beautiful woman. It was noticeable that the women got younger, Susanna thought tolerantly. The last one would have been younger than herself.

She walked indoors thoughtfully. The wind was rising. She slid the bolt across the stout back door and closed the shutters in the kitchen before bringing out two, old oil lamps. Stuart had had a generator installed, but it was an uncertain thing and temperamental in storms. She put a box of matches beside the lamps on the scrubbed wooden table. If the light went out while Stuart was working, he would scream for lamps intemperately.

Although it was still only three o'clock it was as dark as if it were late evening. Listening to the wind howling, Susanna felt a great satisfaction with her life. She added some wood to the boiler and filled a kettle to make tea. The water was clear, and she took a gulp of it when she had put the kettle on the range. It tasted different from the water in London and Milan. She had noticed that at once when she was fourteen and told Stuart, and he had been almost offended.

"Of course. It's good water, not that chemical muck you get in London out of reservoirs full of fluoride and suicidal businessmen."

And Claire was actually choosing to go there. She shuddered. Of course Claire had never lived anywhere but Sussex, and she might have some rosy illusions about London, but even she would not expect it to be tranquil. Surely, thought Susanna, eyeing the kettle balefully, if one were as unhappy as Claire clearly was, one would want to recover in tranquillity. She shook her head, lost. For her own part, having found her haven, she was not to be prized out of it. Not for any of Stuart's grandiose plans to turn her into a prodigy. Not for any of her father's moneymaking schemes to take her into the business.

I have peace, she thought smugly, *and I know how to value it.*

Of course, the cottage was less peaceful when Claire was in it. She was too like her grandfather to live peacefully with him. And like her Uncle Simon, thought Sue ruefully. There was a pronounced strain of self-will in them all. And if Claire lacked the family vanity, she more than made up for it with her ability to ignore facts and people she found inconvenient. Claire was as good as Stuart at making herself comfortable and ultimately as careless of other people's feelings.

For a moment Susanna had a vision of Giovanni's mother enduring Claire week after week willy-nilly because Claire wanted her son. There was resolution there and, more, a sort of ruthlessness, the kind of ruthlessness that Stuart had when he used people. But he at least only used them for his work. That, in his eyes, justified everything, and he only cared about his sculpture. While Claire only cared about—what? This Giovanni?

It was deplorable, of course. Susanna disapproved, naturally. And yet—thinking of her own placid romance—she was aware of a faint dissatisfaction stirring. Roger Thornfield had already asked her to marry him. He was the new junior partner in the solicitors' office where she worked. She had known him for nearly two years. They shared—surely they shared—the same values. He was not vain or sly or evil tempered. He did not use people or play underhand tricks on them. Marriage to him would be a peaceful thing.

And yet she had hesitated. It had not surprised Roger. It was a big decision to make. He had even rather approved of her caution, and that, unreasonably, had annoyed her. Certainly he would never oppress her as this Italian seemed happy to oppress Claire—and she to let him.

The kettle was whistling.

She would never understand Claire. Perhaps it

would be best if she went to London as she wanted and worked out her own salvation. If only Stuart could be reconciled to it.

She was warming the earthenware pot in her hands when the kitchen door opened.

Stuart peered around it, like a squirrel. "Tea?" he said hopefully.

"Of course. It's a grand storm brewing. Do you want some toast?"

"Treacle sandwiches," he said promptly. Like cigarettes they were traditionally consolatory.

"Very well," she sighed. Stickiness all over the kitchen table seemed inevitable. Stuart took his pleasures exuberantly.

"Have you told Claire that tea's made?" he asked.

"No. I thought she'd probably have a snooze. She looked very tired."

He watched her slicing bread. "Have you, er, talked to her?"

She chuckled. "She talked to me. It seemed more to the point. I think you'll have to let her go, Stuart. If she doesn't get your consent, she'll go without it. And then she won't come back."

"I have thought of that," he said with dignity. He dribbled a thoughtful finger in the pot of syrup. "We have to be subtle."

"We?"

"You care about Claire, don't you?" he said limpidly.

"Too much to interfere," she said firmly. "Can I have the butter?"

As she daubed it on the thick slices of fresh bread he watched greedily.

"I've thought of the answer," he said at length.

"What answer?"

"To our problem."

She sighed and pushed the plate of thick sandwiches across the table to him.

"*We* haven't got a problem. Claire has."

"Ah!" He pounced on it. "So you admit it."

"Admit what?"

"That Claire has a problem."

"That's hardly a secret."

"Did she tell you about it?"

"A little," she admitted. She poured steaming tea into thick mugs and added milk from the jug on the table.

"There you are."

"Will she tell me about it?"

Susanna took a gulp of the too hot tea. "I don't know. How could I? Possibly not. I don't think she has any particular urge to confide."

"There you are," he said triumphantly. "She's bottling it all up. She's too young to be left on her own to do that."

"Oh, yes?" She was suspicious. "So what do you propose to do about it?"

"It's obviously impractical to order her to stay here."

"Obviously."

"She'll probably even be happier in London."

"Probably."

"You're not being very helpful," he complained.

"You're a devious man, Stuart. What do you want?"

"She ought not to be on her own," he said, wheedling.

There was a pregnant silence. The kitchen door opened and Claire appeared looking sleepy-eyed and, with the makeup washed from her face and her freckles in evidence, more like the child who had left for Florence.

"I heard the kettle," she said, yawning. "I was asleep. Oh, beautiful, beautiful English tea, how I missed you!" She unhooked another mug from the range and began pouring steaming tea into it.

"Did you sleep well?" Sue began, but her grandfather interrupted.

"I've been thinking about this scheme of yours," he said importantly. "Perhaps it's not such a bad idea after all. In fact, I think it will be good experience, widen your horizons. I have been," he was lachrymose, "a selfish old man. You both ought to get away. There's Sue who can draw like an angel dwindling into a country solicitor's wife under my very eyes. Well, before you do, my girl, you shall have a term at art school. You shall go with Claire. It will," he concluded blandly, looking from one horrified face to the other, "be good for you!"

CHAPTER TWO

IT WAS A MONTH LATER, and Susanna was living in a state of uneasy truce with Claire. The apartment was large and quiet and there was plenty of room for both of them. So much so, in fact, that Susanna often wondered how a solitary man had managed to fill it. He had apparently left, to her unexpressed relief, before Claire returned to London. Most of his possessions had been cleared away, although occasionally Susanna found odds and ends that he had clearly discarded. She was putting them all in a box that Claire was to return to him when he reappeared in London. At the moment, apparently, he was attending to business at home in Italy.

Odd, thought Susanna, how that little collection of his possessions haunted them as if he were somehow still in the apartment. The sensation was not dissipated by the fact that a good deal of mail still arrived for him. Up every morning before Claire, she would gather it up with a heavy heart. Almost always there were three or four letters addressed to the Marchése di Montefiorino.

"The mailman must think we're entertaining the Count of Monte Cristo's brother at the very least," she had said, startled, when she first saw the name in florid writing scrawled on a purple envelope.

Claire had shrugged indifferently. "No London mailman would notice," she said. "Anyway, the title is meaningless. I doubt if he even knows where Montefiorino is—if it's anywhere. He's no feudal baron."

"You disappoint me," Susanna said drily.

But Claire did not laugh at her teasing. In fact, Claire laughed at very little these days. Susanna did not see a great deal of her, for most of her days were spent at her new job, but what she did see was not encouraging. Claire looked tired and was bad tempered. Although she never seemed to lack friends and was out nearly every evening, there was a look of strain about her as if very few of her amusements were relaxing.

By tacit consent she and Susanna avoided each other as much as possible.

Stuart had, by devious means known only to himself, contrived to get Susanna a place at St. Daniel's School. It was already full to overflowing, and she found that most of her classes were in the evening. Her instructor, a sympathetic, harassed man, had made time to see her after these late study groups until she had suggested in desperation that he come to the apartment during one of his weekly lunch hours, when he could eat and study her work at the same time.

She had managed to turn what had obviously been the master bedroom into a very passable studio. It had plenty of light, and with the bed pushed into a corner and the other furniture banished to other rooms, there was enough room for her to set up three or four easels at a time if she should ever want to. At the moment she was still tentative with paint and most of her work for school was done in charcoal or pastels.

"We lead a funny existence," she had remarked to Claire, amused. "I'm here all day while you're at the bank, and when you come home I'm off to class. It's as good as living on one's own."

"Not quite," Claire had said resentfully, and Susanna sighed. She did not relish the watchdog role thrust upon her by her grandfather, but Claire refused to accept it. To Claire she was a spy—almost a traitor—and was treated as such.

Between Claire's hostility and her own dislike of cities Susanna might have expected to be very unhappy. And it was true that she had some uncomfortable moments trying to avoid Claire and her friends. But somewhat to her own surprise, she found she enjoyed renewing her studies. She missed Sussex, of course. She missed being able to slip out onto the marsh for a walk before anyone was up. Above all she missed the sounds of the country. *No spring cuckoo for me this year,* she thought resignedly.

On the other hand there were things to do in London that she had not remembered from her childhood. Not just the art galleries and museums but the actual city and its people. She became attached to some of its crazy architecture, and on Sundays, when Claire seemed for once to want to stay at home, she would take her sketchbook and wander around some of the little back streets.

The apartment was in a luxurious new complex built on the site of old docks. The river ran almost under its windows, and Susanna would sit for hours cross-legged on the windowsill in her studio, drawing, or sometimes simply looking at the river and its traffic, until her muscles complained and she fell off her perch.

She was drawing well, Susanna knew. There was a certain excitement in finding out for herself how far her neglected talent would stretch. Claire was frankly uninterested, so it was almost a secret between herself and her tutor, for Stuart of course was by far too concerned about Claire to ask after Susanna's studies.

Relieved of the responsibility of looking after Stuart, she reveled in her freedom. It pleased her deeply to be able to wander unobtrusively and sketch unnoticed by passersby. It was interesting to be an observer of life. Her detachment was precious to her, and she resolved to take good care to remain uninvolved in Claire's troubled existence, no matter what her grandfather had to say on the matter.

In pursuance of this policy, she seldom met Claire at breakfast, but bathed and took her own sustenance when her cousin had left for the office.

One particularly dreary morning Claire rushed out late leaving the percolator still boiling and a trail of toast crumbs from the kitchen to the front door. Susanna, who had been pottering for a couple of hours, emerged from her studio. She turned off the machine, glared at the toast crumbs and went to fetch the mail.

As usual, most of it was for the absent Giovanni. She made a face and thrust it into the pocket of her jeans. Claire had been promising to unload his possessions on his secretary at the bank but so far had forgotten to take them every morning. Susanna turned over the motley collection of objects: a couple of paperbacks in Italian, a roll of color film, a cigarette lighter. They were anonymous things, she mused. You could tell nothing about their owner from them.

But his mail, that was a very different matter. Some of the envelopes held bills, of course. No less obviously a good many were invitations. She wondered briefly if the absent Giovanni were popular or whether they were duty invitations from other stuffy bankers. Was he stuffy? Claire had said virtually nothing about him.

She rifled through the half-dozen or so private letters in the collection. Apart from the purple envelope there were two airmail letters from South America and some interesting script in the addresses. In particular, an express letter from Italy was written in a flowing italic hand that Susanna would have sworn to be feminine and fierce. The dominant mamma, perhaps.

Absentmindedly she took an apple and sank her teeth into it reflectively. She would be happier when all his stuff was gone. At the moment it was like being haunted. It was as if they were sharing the apartment with someone they never saw but nevertheless knew was there.

Susanna shivered. Pure fantasy, she reproached herself, and took another heartening bite of her apple. She straightened her shoulders and went back to the kitchen. Splashing some of Claire's coffee into a mug, she switched on the radio and perched on a kitchen stool.

The kitchen was full of dirty glasses and plates of curling sandwiches. Claire had obviously had some sort of party last night. After she was in bed, Susanna thought. Claire had not been home when she returned from class, and the kitchen had been perfectly clear then. And she had read until past midnight. No wonder Claire had been up late that morning.

She wondered if Stuart would be worried if he knew that Claire was entertaining in the small hours and came to the rueful conclusion that he would regard it as perfectly normal. It was only her infatuation with Giovanni that concerned Stuart.

Irritated, she stood up and turned off the chirping music. Well, it did not concern her, she thought defiantly. She took her coffee and apple into the bathroom and began to run a bath, singing to herself.

It was while she was soaking happily, her hair pinned carelessly on top of her head, that she heard the front door slam. Obviously Claire had left something vital behind in her speed. She grinned to herself and took another substantial bite from the apple. It occurred to her that she could ask Claire to take the *marchese*'s mail to work with her. She clambered out of the bath and wrapped a towel around her before padding out to the living room, the apple in her teeth as she knotted the towel in front.

"Claire, don't forget—" she began thickly through the fruit—and stopped dead.

Sitting in the middle of the Montefiorino Persian carpet with the insides of the stereo strewn around him was a young man. As she emerged he looked up, bright-eyed. For a moment his eyes widened, and then they began to twinkle irrepressibly, and he gave a long appreciative whistle that was purely mischievous.

"Ugh!" Susanna made a sound between a gasp and a snort and choked on her apple.

Instantly he was beside her in a lithe movement, thumping her solicitously between her damp shoulder blades.

"Who are you?" managed Susanna, and sneezed.

He produced a large and surprisingly white handkerchief from his denims. "Blow," he said professionally. As she did so, he surveyed her. "For that matter, who are you? I thought the lady tenant was a Miss Claire Hamilton and guaranteed to be out at this time of day."

"Yes, she is," she nodded, drawing soothing air into her lungs. "I'm her cousin. I didn't know you were coming. I'm sorry."

"Don't be," he urged. "Look on it as a unique experience."

She eyed him frostily. "I meant," she said with precision, "that if I'd known you were coming I would have been around to open the door. How did you get in?"

Again he fished in his pocket and brought out a ring full of keys, which he dangled negligently under her nose.

"You mean Claire gave you a key?" She was outraged. "But good heavens, I could have been doing anything. . . ." She spread her hands helplessly.

"Could you?" he said interestedly. He sat down again cross-legged on the carpet and looked up at her inquiringly. "What sort of anything?"

"Oh—" She searched for horrifying situations and found them impossible to turn into words. "Well, it was very inconsiderate of her," she finished weakly.

He smiled on her kindly. "She didn't know exactly when I would be coming. You mustn't blame her. I wouldn't like you to quarrel on my account."

"We won't," said Susanna with dignity. She bestowed a cold look on the scattered screws and wire. "Don't let me interrupt you."

"You're not," he assured her blandly. "I've gone about as far as I can go with this contraption."

She was retreating, but she spun around at that, her towel swirling dangerously. Gathering it in firm hands, she came back to him. "What?"

He waved a hand at the ruins of the *marchese*'s no doubt priceless instrument. "I give up."

"You—you mean you can't repair it?" she gasped, horrified.

"Well," he temporized, "not without a spot of research and a soldering iron."

"Have you broken it?" Susanna demanded.

"No. No, it isn't any worse than it was when I started."

"Except that when you arrived it was in its box and now it's all over the floor."

"True." Head on one side, he studied the remains. "Perhaps the air will do it good?"

"Thank you," she said sarcastically. "That's very comforting. It isn't even ours."

"Oh? It belongs to your landlord?"

"Yes. And I suppose he'll throw a Florentine fury when he hears about it."

The young man shook his head. "They're an unreasonable lot, landlords," he remarked. "I'm sorry. Of course, I could always have another try. Coffee," he ruminated, "might aid my concentration."

Susanna shrugged. The towel slipped again and she caught it. "Help yourself." He gave a chuckle and she fixed him with a cold eye. "To coffee. It's in the kitchen—in the percolator. It will need heating. You'll find milk and sugar on the table. Now, if you don't mind, I'll finish my bath."

While he murmured deprecatingly she stamped into the bathroom and locked the door smartly behind her.

Her bath water was, of course, tepid by now and she washed quickly and tumbled back into her clothes in the shortest possible time. Unpinning her hair, she went into the kitchen to find her visitor calmly helping himself to a large wedge of cheese.

For a moment surprise held her still, her hands in her hair and her mouth half-open. Very deliberately he put his elbows on the table and surveyed her. His mouth twitched. Slowly an appreciative smile grew. He gestured to a stool.

"Sit down?"

"Thank you," she said blankly. Her hands fell and a shower of pins scattered over the floor among last night's crumbs. Conscience-stricken, she looked at the unsavory collection. "What a mess this is!"

"Never mind." He passed her a coffee. "It's still abominably early. You'll be inspired to tidy all this up later."

"Oh, will I?" Susanna was militant. "And I suppose I'll be inspired to tidy up all those bits and pieces of metal in there, as well?"

"With that," he said graciously, "I will help you."

She swallowed. "How kind," she said faintly.

He chuckled. "Have some cheese. It's full of protein for energy."

She stared at him. At first she had thought him just a boy, but he was clearly older than that. The bright eyes were surrounded by laughter lines, and sitting opposite him, she could see that there were flecks of gray in the dark hair. His expression was that of a wicked schoolboy, but though she did not doubt the teasing, she was sure he was no schoolboy. The breadth of his shoulders owed nothing to the tailoring of his denim shirt. And now she came to think of it, wasn't that shirt too well cut to suit his role?

Narrowing her eyes, Susanna said suspiciously, "How long have you been repairing record players?"

"Oh," he said airily, "since I was ten or eleven."

"I mean professionally."

"Well—" he hedged.

She leaned back, her eyes snapping, and drummed her fingers on the table. "Well?"

"Well, it's more of a sideline," he confessed.

"A sideline to what?" said the inexorable Susanna.

"Oh, this and that."

"Enough!" She slapped her hand down flat on the table. "I think you're a con man."

"Well," he debated, "I suppose in a way, you might say. . . ."

"*Might* say!" The telephone began to ring. She rose to answer it. "I *have* said," she flung at him vindictively. "Hello?" she said into the telephone.

It was Claire. She sounded flurried and more human than she had for weeks.

"Oh, Sue, I'm sorry to bother you, but I'm in a mess. Well, not really, it's just a bit awkward. You see, Giovanni kept asking me for his letters. I told him the stereo needed fixing and he could have his mail if he came and did it and he hasn't, and I thought he would have to and. . . ."

"Try taking a breath," said Susanna unsympathetically. "Someone's here about the stereo thing."

"Yes, I know." Claire was impatient. "That's what I'm trying to tell you. . . ."

"In fact," said Sue, warming to her theme, "he walked in when I was in the bath. You could have told me he was coming, Claire."

"But I didn't know!" Her voice was rising frantically. "Will you *listen*, Sue? I got here this morning to find a note on my desk saying Giovanni was going to collect his mail if I wouldn't give it to him."

"Oh." Susanna digested it, remembering the purple envelope. "I can't say I blame him. He's waited a long time for some of it. I thought he was still in Italy."

"That's what I wanted you to think, so you could report to Stuart with a clear conscience. I told you, Sue, love makes you do nasty things like lie and cheat."

"Is that what you want me to do?" Susanna was intrigued. "Bar the door against him and hide his letters?"

Claire giggled. "I wish you could. No, I just wondered if you'd tidy the place a bit. I left it in a bit of a mess."

"You did," Sue said tranquilly. "And it's worse now. Your mechanic has disemboweled the machine all over the living-room carpet."

Claire moaned. "Oh, God! And his mother always has everything beautifully in order. But at least he can't blame the mechanic on me. I haven't asked anyone to come. Why should I? I kept hoping he'd turn up to do it himself. Giovanni must have sent him. Didn't he say anything when you let him in?"

"I," said Susanna with commendable patience, "did not let him in. He walked in by himself, with a key."

There was a shriek from her cousin. "But, good heavens, that must be him!" she said ungrammatically with great feeling.

Susanna turned slowly around to face the object of their discussion. He was still cheerfully eating cheese at the kitchen table. Sensing her eyes on him, he glanced up and waved his knife at her companionably. With gestures he asked if she wanted her coffee. Slowly, stunned, she nodded.

"Sue? Sue? Are you there, Sue?"

Sue cleared her throat. "Him?" she said huskily.

"Giovanni, of course. Sue, what's the matter with you? Did he give you a fright? He's perfectly respectable, you know."

"I know nothing of the sort." She almost snatched the coffee from the offender's hand. "What's he doing barging in here?"

"Well, it is his apartment, after all. He owns it, Sue."

"You mean he still has a key?" Sue demanded in slowly gathering wrath.

Giovanni grinned unrepentantly and settled himself at her feet.

"Of course. Sue, don't be stupid. Have you been upset? Have you," she said anxiously, "been rude to him?"

"Not," said Susanna sweetly, "yet."

"You'd better let me talk to him," said Claire, alarmed. Susanna looked down at him. "It's for you. The lady tenant, Miss Claire Hamilton."

He looked a little guilty as he took the phone from her and began to talk to Claire in his own language. Susanna left him alone with the telephone and pointedly closed the kitchen door. She found she was trembling.

As a professional confidence trickster—or even an unprofessional mechanic—she had found him amusing. As the object of Claire's romantic aspirations there was nothing remotely entertaining about the man.

The door opened behind her.

"I'm sorry," offered Giovanni disarmingly.

"Yes?" She was distant. "I should perhaps warn you—if you intend to make a habit of talking about me to my cousin in my presence, I mean—that most of my formative years were spent in Milan—a disgusting city, but they do speak Italian there. I'm not as fluent as Claire, but I can understand most of what's said to me. Or," with brittle self-mockery, "what isn't."

Before she had closed the door she had heard too clearly. "Claire my love," he had said, "we have met at last, the dragon and I."

Now he had the grace to look a little confused. "I didn't think. I always talk to Claire in Italian—it's natural. Forgive me?"

"It's unimportant. Why didn't you tell me who you were?"

He sat down, facing her across the table, his chin

on his hands. "I'm not sure," he admitted. "Claire had, er, told me so much about you and how your grandfather sent you to guard her. I wondered what you were really like, discounting the advance publicity."

"To discover what sort of dragon I was, in fact?"

He should have been embarrassed. Instead he laughed with real enjoyment.

"I'm sorry about that," he said, not sounding in the least sorry. "Would it help if I said that I was referring to your, er, function rather than your character?"

"Not in the least." She looked at him coolly. "I take it you were hoping I'd make a fool of myself, not knowing who you were. It amused you, didn't it?"

There was a pause while he considered her.

"Didn't it?" she insisted, a little breathlessly.

"Oh, naturally." He sounded bored. "It was quite irresistible. Don't you ever do things on the spur of the moment?"

She flushed. "Of course I do. But I don't tell lies."

"Nor do I." He thought about it. "Quite."

Exasperated, Susanna gave a furious squeak. "Well, you've had your fun. The show is quite definitely over. Take your electrical garbage and whatever else you want and go!"

Ostentatiously she swept the kitchen table clean of crockery. He tipped his stool back at a dangerous angle and his eyes gleamed.

"That's very kind of you," he said with deceptive politeness. "*Anything* else I want?"

"It's yours, I believe." She gave a comprehensive glance around the kitchen. Susanna had a brief vision of him marching out of the apartment weighed down by vacuum cleaners and electric egg whisks. Her mouth twitched. "Feel free."

She strode past him, but he put out a hand and hooked a negligent finger into the belt of her jeans. Astonished, she found she could not move. He laughed and she looked down at him, baffled. His eyes were the color of sherry, brilliant and wickedly teasing. Susanna blushed. Stretching a lazy arm above his head, he held her briefly while she struggled fruitlessly and then, still laughing, stood up and kissed her in a smoothly professional style that infuriated her.

Eventually he let her go and stepped back. "Thank you," he said outrageously.

She fought with the desire to kick him. Only the reflection that her bare feet would probably hurt themselves more than him prevented her. Seething, she strove for dignity, but with her hair in her eyes and her cheeks furiously pink it was hard to achieve.

Abandoning the unequal struggle, Susanna said between her teeth, "Out!"

He looked reproachful. "That's not very civil. After your charming generosity, too."

She was puzzled but suspected an unpalatable meaning. "Generosity?" Under frowning brows she dared him to further insults.

"It was you who offered me anything I wanted," he reminded her.

Susanna was speechless. "*Oh!* Oh, how dare you! I meant anything of your own, as you very well know."

The corner of his mouth lifted, though his face remained solemn. "That wasn't what I understood. You should make yourself clear."

Breathing deeply, she snapped, "I see. When I said 'out' I meant you. Perhaps I should have said, 'will you please go?' "

"Much better," he approved. "No room for doubt there."

She was nearly dancing with exasperation. "Then *will* you go? Leave. Get out. Vanish. *Now!*"

He shook his head. "I can't imagine how you manage to get on with Claire. She's been trying to decoy me here for weeks, and now you want to throw me out."

"Claire," she said crushingly, "has some odd tastes." His eyes lighted up again with undisguised laughter and his brows rose. She held his glance for a defiant moment. Obviously he was enjoying himself. The advantage was his, she thought resentfully. Head high, she stalked past him into the living room.

"Perhaps it would be more sensible, then, if you came back when Claire was here and I was not."

"Would you call it sensible?" he demurred. "I should have thought it highly inflammatory. What would grandfather say?"

"I don't give a damn!"

"Tut," he said mildly. "Isn't this an admission of failure? You can't leave Claire without a chaperon just because you don't like the company she keeps. In fact," he pondered, "I suppose that would be when she needs a chaperon most."

"When she's with you?" Susanna offered sweetly.

"That," he said appreciatively, "is not kind. When I've been going to such great lengths to be good."

"Really?"

"Really." He sat down uninvited on the arm of a huge leather chair and smiled across at her. "Your helpless little cousin," he said grimly, "has been doing her best to blackmail me. She knows perfectly well that my brother and I built this stereo, so she sabotaged it in the hopes that I would be too worried about it in her hands to keep away. I trust she hasn't done any lasting damage. Anyway, I'll call around for it this evening and take it away so she can't do it any more harm. And I'll have my mail, please. Claire isn't very good at bringing it to the office."

"I see." Susanna frowned. She knew that Claire could be ruthless in pursuit of what she wanted, but she was surprised that her cousin could get the better of this self-confident demon. On the other hand, Claire had not behaved well, and the glow of admiration faltered. "Perhaps I should apologize. Your things are there, by the door in that box. I kept reminding Claire, but she always forgot to take them with her in the morning." She stopped and bit her lip. "I thought—I'm sorry. If any more come I'll readdress them. Oh." She fished in the pocket of her jeans and brought out the crumpled envelopes. "These came this morning."

In the steamy bathroom the ink had run somewhat. Noticing their blotted state, he sighed.

"Thank you."

"I hope—" she stood on one leg, scraping her bare foot up the back of the other. It was a childhood trick that returned to her when she was embarrassed. "I hope none of them is—was—urgent."

"I hope none of them is illegible," he replied ruefully. "But at least I've got them now. Thank you, Miss Hamilton."

"Shaw."

He looked bewildered. "My name," she explained, "is Shaw. Like my grandfather."

"Oh, I see. What sort of Shaw? Prudence?" he hazarded.

"Susanna," she said shortly, turning away. "Goodbye."

"Susanna," he repeated softly. For the first time she detected the un-English inflexion in his voice. It was more a matter of emphasis than actual pronunciation, she thought confusedly. And it was very attractive.

He looked around at the devastated living room. "Leave this," he ordered. "I'll come back this evening and take it all away." He inclined his head courteously enough, but there was still, she was sure, that gleam of mischief in his eyes. "Goodbye—Susanna!"

AFTER THAT ENCOUNTER, of course, the rest of her day was spoiled. She prowled around the apartment restlessly. Now she had met Giovanni she found that she could picture him there, sitting in the great leather chairs that drowned her. Cooking with all the kitchen gadgetry she had left severely alone. Drinking from the lovely smoky Finnish glasses. Sleeping on that bed now shrouded with dust covers in the corner of her studio.

It was quite impossible to settle down to work. Susanna tried to sketch but tore up the results impatiently. She washed up and tidied the kitchen, but the living room remained as it was, an intrusive reminder of the man.

She made herself endless cups of coffee and listened impatiently to the radio's uninspired offerings. Fiddling with the controls, she managed to tune into a series of foreign stations ending up with an excitable news bulletin. In Italian.

"Damn!" screamed the normally sweet-tempered Susanna.

Clearly the day was jinxed. Trying to regain her sense of humor, she thought how she had burst in upon Giovanni in her bath towel. He must have been quite as disconcerted as she, but he had recovered sooner. Experience, she thought dourly. And natural impertinence. The man was quite unsquashable. What Claire could see in him she could not imagine.

Except, of course, that she could. The man was totally arrogant, of course, but he had style and even a certain charm. You would need a thicker skin than Susanna's to endure his teasing, she thought. But Claire had shown no signs of a thin skin. And she did not seem to resent his cavalier manner. Susanna decided that she resented it very much indeed and frowned quickly.

Really she must put him out of her mind. She could not spend untold time dreaming of retorts she could have made if she had thought of them at the time. She must put him out of her mind.

Two hours later, full of coffee and with a headache, she decided to telephone her father. They had met briefly when she first arrived in London and had not spoken since. If he was in his office he would at least distract her from thinking about her unsatisfactory interview with Giovanni di Montefiorino.

Not only was he there, he seemed, for once, to want her company and invited her to lunch. Relieved to have something to do, she changed out of her jeans and sailed out to meet him.

HE WAS AT a small corner table, his head buried in a glossy magazine sporting photographs of eighteenth-century furniture. As always, when she saw him from a distance, Susanna was struck by his elegance. He did not look like anyone's father, she thought ruefully.

"Hello, daddy."

Simon Shaw looked up, his eyes welcoming.

"Sue." He stood up and took her hands. He was an affectionate father when he remembered. "How lucky you could come. I hate eating alone."

"Deserted by that beautiful secretary, daddy?"

Not in the least put out of countenance, he grimaced. "She's getting herself married." He took a menu from a hovering waiter and handed it to her. "Just as well, really. A decorative creature, but too stupid. God knows what the files are like. I haven't dared to look. Next time we'll have to have somebody who can do simple filing." He sipped gin. "Would you like something to drink now or wait till the fodder?"

She shook her head. "I don't think I could. I've about five gallons of coffee slopping around inside me."

He raised his eyebrows but ordered another drink for himself without comment. When it came he settled himself comfortably back in his seat and looked at her over the top of his glass.

"So how is St. Daniel's?" he said when they had ordered.

Susanna smiled. "Tolerant. They have to keep me because Stuart has promised them a memorial sculpture or some such thing, but there isn't really room for me."

Simon Shaw knew his daughter. "At a bit of a loose end?" he said sympathetically. "You could always come and work for me."

A smile lighted her eyes. "And perform major surgery on the filing system?"

"Of course not!" He was indignant. "Come in as a trainee and you'll be a partner in a year. You have a feeling for line."

She shook her head. "No, thank you, daddy. I'm drawing a lot and my instructor is very helpful. If I were on my own I'd be perfectly happy."

"Aha—the fair Claire. That child," said Simon, who did not like children, "is a pain."

"Well," temporized Susanna, feeling ashamed of herself, "she's not very happy at the moment."

"And making a big production of it. You don't have to tell me. She's just like her mother was." He snorted. "Parasites," he said comprehensively. "Whose damned silly idea was it that you two should live together?"

"Stuart's." She took a cashew nut and nibbled it thoughtfully. "He thought she needed—oh, a shoulder to cry on, I suppose."

"And Stuart proposed yours. It's diabolical," Simon said self-righteously. "Stuart's a selfish old devil, but I never thought he'd do anything like this."

She looked at him in amusement. "He didn't drive me from his house with whips," she said gently. "I agreed to come. In some ways I'm rather glad. But Claire can be a little trying."

"Like her mother. Kate was unbearable at her age. She went from bad to worse. Stuart was so worried he couldn't work. And then she found that boring man....."

"Claire's father?"

"Yes." He helped himself to a nut. "Don't you know the story?"

Susanna shook her head.

"I suppose Stuart didn't want to upset Claire," he said. "It's ancient history. But it rocked Stuart. It's the only thing I've ever seen turn him off his work. Kate was a pest. She used to go around with a crowd of Borstal boys—they were called teds in those days. You wouldn't remember. Then she took up with this older guy."

Warming to the cold scandal, he leaned forward conspiratorially. "They went off to Spain—love's idyll. Stuart was relieved. He thought he'd delegated Kate to someone else. We didn't hear any more until he got a phone call in the middle of the night, from Kate. She was pregnant. Hamilton had gone back to his mother, and she was going to kill herself."

He finished his drink. "Calamity!" he said indifferently. "Of course Hamilton, poor devil, didn't know she was as mad as a hatter. As far as he was concerned it was the end of an interlude, and he was going home to take up the family business. If he'd known what a parasite Kate was going to be he'd never have got involved in the first place. But she was a devious girl, Kate.

"Anyway, Stuart got them married one way or another. Claire was born, and Kate continued to suffer. He was supposed to be taking her away to convalesce when their plane crashed—I've often thought it was a merciful release for the poor guy. Life with Kate would be unbearable. She never cared about anything but getting her own way."

Susanna surveyed her amiably selfish father and chuckled. "So that's why Stuart was so steamed up about Claire. I thought it was out of character."

"Is Claire consorting with jailbirds?" Simon said, faintly interested.

"No. A dashing banker, deadly respectable. Stuart's hysterical."

Simon grinned. "Bad for his image," he agreed. "Which banker? All the ones I know are overweight and preoccupied, not in the least amusing."

"Well," Susanna was cautious, "I should think this one would be amusing, if nothing else. At least to Claire. His name is Giovanni di Montefiorino, I think."

"Good God!" Simon's eyebrows reached his hair.

"The big league. You must get out as soon as possible. He'll not be blackmailed as poor old Hamilton was."

She hesitated and then said slowly, "Blackmail. It's not a nice thought. He more or less said the same thing himself."

"Did he? He's no fool. What did Claire say to that?"

Her brow creased. "I don't know if he's said it to Claire as well."

"You've met him? Interesting. What did you think of him?"

She opened her mouth to give him a succinct account of the abominable man, caught his expression and stopped herself. Simon, if he knew Giovanni, as he appeared to, would no doubt be on the friendliest terms with him.

"Is he a friend of yours?" she demanded suspiciously.

Simon smiled to himself. "We've met."

"Have you seen him with Claire?"

He looked affronted. "Do I spend my free time with my niece? Of course not with Claire. I thought the wretched wench was in Italy until you came up to London."

"She was."

"There you are, then. I wouldn't have seen them, would I? Johnny's been in London, oh—about two years now. God knows where Claire got her claws into him. Actually," he pondered, "I'm surprised she did. Bit youthful, I'd have thought."

Thinking of Simon's own tastes, Susanna preserved a discreet silence. He, however, was not deceived.

"And don't laugh at me, you hussy," he said without rancor. "Johnny isn't as old as I am. He doesn't need the same sort of reassurance."

"Johnny?"

"I've called him that since he was a kid."

"You've known him a long time, then?"

"Oh, yes." Again that secret amusement. "Stuart used to sponge on the di Montefiorino family shamelessly when we were younger. We used to spend all our school holidays there at one time, Kate and I. I remember young Johnny being born. He used to tag after me all the time when he was a kid. He was only a couple of years younger than Kate."

"Really?" Susanna was startled at the confusion of generations. "How old *is* he?"

Simon bent his mind on mathematical calculation. "Well, he's ten years younger than I am, and I'm forty-six. Aren't I?"

"Thirty-six?" she gasped. "Why, he's old enough to be Claire's father!"

"Don't be indelicate," he reproved her, and spoiled it all by grinning. "It's the purest chance that he isn't. He used to be crazy about Kate."

"How messy! Do you suppose that's why he's pursuing Claire?"

A waiter appeared on the horizon with their food. Simon looked at her pityingly. "My poor child, you need spectacles. Johnny doesn't pursue any woman—he doesn't have to. The one doing the chasing is Claire."

CHAPTER THREE

IT WAS LATE in the afternoon before Susanna finally left her father. He had stoutly refused to discuss Claire's problems throughout the meal and bent most of his attention on entertaining his daughter. Since he could, when he chose, be a very amusing companion, Susanna left him feeling a good deal more cheerful.

Nevertheless she was very reluctant to return to the apartment. Giovanni had promised—or rather, threatened—to return to collect his pulverized machine, and she did not want to be there when he did so. She hesitated between bolting into a movie for the rest of the afternoon and dashing back to the apartment to collect her sketchbook and taking herself off to St. Daniel's. There would surely be a small corner in the art school into which she could tuck herself until her evening class.

In the end she compromised and went shopping.

Before they parted Simon had pressed a check into her hand.

"How are you managing for money?" he had said casually. "You haven't got some dreary student job washing up or anything, have you?"

She had laughed. "I'm afraid not, daddy. I've got plenty of money. I could live off the remains of my salary for a year or so, particularly as we pay practically nothing for the apartment. Anyway, Stuart said he'd give me an allowance."

"Humph. When he gets around to it," Simon said

disparagingly, conveniently forgetting his own shortcomings in this respect. "You'd better have something to be going on with."

And he had ducked into a taxi before she had time to thank him or even to say goodbye. Remembering one of Simon's own maxims that the easiest way to waste time was by spending a good deal of money, she made her way to Knightsbridge with the intention of doing just that. Simon, she felt sure, would approve.

Mischievously she determined to return home a new and elegant Susanna. If she could not emerge as thoroughly from her chrysalis as Claire had done, she resolved to give her cousin a little sporting competition.

In the haste with which she had packed to accompany Claire she had brought hardly any clothes with her. Some disreputable trousers, a couple of sweaters and a shirt or two was the extent of her London wardrobe. Anything else—like the dress she had worn to lunch with Simon—she had to borrow from Claire. Not, she reflected ruefully, that the clothes she had left behind were any more flattering. Neat and serviceable was all that could be said for them.

She had often said that her interest in fashion was strictly as a spectator sport. But that was before she had spent six weeks watching Claire match her moods to an infinite variety of beautiful garments. Envy, she knew, was a distasteful emotion. And she did not precisely envy Claire. On the other hand, she had definitely decided that fashion was a game she, too, would like to play. And armed with her father's extravagant check, she set out to do so.

To begin with the shops were discouraging. The large ones were full of good clothes in dreary colors, and the small ones had badly cut eccentricities that almost made her despair. It was nearly six o'clock when she finally uncovered a clutch of shops in a quiet Victorian arcade. She was on the brink of abandoning her quest and returning to the apartment. After all, Claire would be home by now and if the unspeakable Giovanni had not yet left the apartment he could safely be left in Claire's willing hands.

However, the Dickensian window display caught her eye and she paused. There were only two models in the window: one was an evening dress, almost a crinoline adorned with lace and ribbons. It had obviously been lovingly put together from a Victorian original by an enthusiast and, almost against her will, Susanna was intrigued. The other, slightly behind it, was an elegant suit, high collared and severely cut in a stormy gray color.

She peered at it, her nose pressed against the windowpane. Her own face, distorted, was reflected back to her as if under water, her bright hair a wafting blond, gray eyes colorless. No, she acknowledged, not only did she not have Claire's elegance she would never acquire her cousin's cool beauty. Claire, she thought wearily, had all the natural advantages. She stuck her tongue out at her image. Well, she would console herself with the gray suit, shockingly expensive though she could see it was.

At first she thought the shop was empty. It was lighted by some unpleasant imitation carriage lamps with low-watt bulbs inside and full of models sporting cloaks and bonnets. Then, as her eyes grew accustomed to the contrived murkiness, she made out a diminutive figure among the garments that moved. Approached, the figure proved willing to get the suit from the window and to show Susanna to an ornate dressing room that resembled nothing so much as a box at Covent Garden with a huge mirror in it.

Scrambling into the suit unceremoniously, Susanna felt a little foolish. She was tired and grubby with her hair in tangles, and the suit demanded something different. However, she allowed, it fitted very nicely. She twirled in front of the mirror. The material was something stiff with a sheen to it that was not apparent until it moved. In the muted light it was a strange combination of darkest purples shot with jade and viridian. Her eyes widened. There was a witchery to it. It did not turn her instantly into a beautiful lady or even erase the sticky tiredness from her face, but it was a kind of talisman, something lovely of her own that she did not have to borrow from Claire. Recklessly she bought it, then wandered about the shop gleefully adding to her purchases.

By the time she left the shop it was nearly seven and dark. Even the shops that stayed open late were beginning to close their doors. The street lights glimmered in the half-light and the air was warm and moist. The odd sickly smell of tar and gasoline that she always associated with London assailed her nostrils and she plunged reluctantly into the stifling tunnel of the subway.

Claire was not in evidence when she reached the apartment, and she barely had time to seize her drawing board and charcoal before she dashed out again to class. She did notice that the living room carpet was once more free of junk but did not think to look to see whether the instrument itself had gone.

It was quite dark by the time she reached St. Daniel's and the school was quiet. Everybody was in class, and she was late. She made her way down the brilliantly lighted corridor, her heels echoing weirdly on the old marble floor. St. Daniel's had been built during the 1880s. Its original board of governors had included Lord Leighton and John Ruskin and the edifice, thanks to these gentlemen, resembled nothing so much as a Gothic railway station. Every room echoed. The corridors were tiled and reminded Susanna irresistibly of a Victorian public convenience.

She crept into her class as quietly as she was able on marble floors and creaking woodwork. There was the silence of concentration as she guiltily set up her board. Her instructor glanced across the room at her and raised a friendly hand.

Behind a barrage of electric lights a nude model wilted. The class must have been in session some time. Susanna looked at the clock at the end of the lofty studio. Nearly twenty minutes late! She had not realized the journey could take so long. Ordinarily she was ready, already doodling, by the time most of her fellow students arrived.

Soon enough—too soon, for Susanna—the model was allowed a rest and at once a cheerful hum pervaded the austere hall. Relaxing, Susanna savored the atmosphere. She belonged here. Here she was at peace, untroubled by her father's obscure amusement or Giovanni's disturbing arrogance, to say nothing of the miserable Claire. She worked hard all evening and gradually sloughed the distresses of the day like an unwanted skin.

At the end of the class she looked up to find her instructor at her elbow.

"Did you miss the bus?" he said sympathetically, his eyes on her drawing.

"Not really," she confessed. "I just had a busy day and time got rather out of hand."

"Uh—huh," he murmured, not really interested. "You know, this is coming along. I think we might find a corner for you in the end-of-term exhibition."

"Me? Or Susanna Shaw?"

He looked exasperated. "You. Your respected grandfather may have great pull with the plasterers, but not with me. Call yourself something else if it makes you any happier. You could do well—you ought to know that. Have you had the courage to plunge into oils yet?"

She laughed and shook her head. "No. I'm not good with color. It's a big step for such as me."

"You mustn't mark time," he said seriously. "I think you ought to try, at least. Soon. After all, you use pastels freely enough."

"But not with inspiration."

He snorted. "Inspiration! Now there's a word I hate. You buy yourself a bottle of turps, prime one of those canvases of yours and get going. Let me see, when do I next see you?"

"Next Tuesday," she said meekly.

"Right. By then I want that upper-class apartment of yours to be reeking with linseed oil and turps. You've got plenty of ideas. All you need is a little more enterprise."

"That," she said standing up, "is the story of my life."

He unclipped her sketch and sprayed it with fixative, glancing at his watch. "I'm not interested in your life, just your painting. I'll miss my train at this rate. See you on Tuesday, Sue. And remember, courage!"

COURAGE, SHE THOUGHT bitterly, letting herself into the darkened apartment. It seemed as if everyone wanted her to do things that she did not want to do and when she protested accused her, as Stuart had done, of cowardice. She wondered if her father also thought her a coward because she had not taken

Stuart's offer to study art all those years ago when she was Claire's age. But all she had wanted was to stay in the countryside that she loved. For that her secretarial training had seemed more than adequate. Now—how much had she missed? Was she already too late, her talent damaged beyond repair by her own willful neglect?

Her throat was dry at the thought. In a panic, she thought, *what am I going to do with my life?* Her classes were a temporary thing. She would stay in London only as long as Claire was prepared to endure her presence. When Claire left—or decided that Susanna must go—the classes would end for her. And then what? She swallowed. Back to Sussex to look after Stuart for the rest of her life? He undoubtedly expected it. Even if she married Roger, Stuart had plans to build a house adjacent to his own so that she could continue to supervise his household.

Susanna's mouth twisted. He had thought it a great compliment, too. Mrs. Rose was an excellent daily help, he had assured her, but she could not replace herself. He could not do without his Susanna. She would simply have to continue the job from a distance—a distance that Stuart intended to see was as narrow as possible.

She jumped as a key sounded in the lock. The front door opened and a light was snapped on.

"Sue!" exclaimed Claire, as her cousin blinked at her. "What on earth are you doing standing in the dark?"

"Meditating," Susanna said ruefully. "I've only just got back from school. I thought you'd be in bed by now."

Claire flushed. "I would have been, but Stuart phoned. He wanted to ask you how I was, so I told him."

Susanna regarded her with a good deal of amusement and some sympathy. "And worked yourself into a great temper doing it."

"Yes." Claire came inside and closed the door, glancing behind her down the corridor as she did so. "I went for a walk to cool my temper." She sat down, running her fingers nervously along the thin strap of her shoulder bag. "I, er, met Giovanni. He brought me back."

"Really?" Recalling the morning's interview, Susanna looked around her with new eyes. "I see he's collected his stereo."

"Yes." Claire was short. "It was gone when I got back this evening. He just marched in and took it when neither of us was here."

"He probably thought it would be the simplest thing," murmured Susanna diplomatically.

"Well, I think it was rude!" Claire sounded so much like a sulky child that even she seemed to realize it, for after a moment she gave a little laugh. "He's avoiding me, Sue," she said wretchedly.

Resisting the temptation to say, "Just as well," Susanna preserved an encouraging silence.

Claire fumbled for cigarettes and lighted one with fingers that trembled slightly. "His secretary has taken over where his mother left off," she said bitterly. "I hardly ever see him. Not at the office, anyway."

"Well, you see him at other times," Susanna pointed out. "Like this evening."

"This evening!" Claire was tapping cigarette ash nervously into a china dish. "This evening. He let me in, gave me one drink and brought me home."

"Late."

Claire shrugged. "I didn't exactly get there early. And then there was a phone call. I don't think he actually talked to me for more than ten minutes." She flung herself back in the chair. "He likes me. He's happy to take me around. But it's got to be where he wants to go, when he chooses. And no strings. He wants everything on his terms."

Susanna heard this with misgiving. "In that case, isn't it a little unwise to, er, be quite so available?" she hazarded.

Claire snorted. "Don't be so polite! Chase him is what you mean. Say it. And you don't know what you're talking about. If I weren't 'available,' as you call it, he would forget me altogether."

"In that case," said her cousin, suddenly impatient, "I don't see why you bother at all. I wouldn't."

"Don't you ever get tired of being perfect, Sue?" Claire shrugged her shoulders. "Oh, I'm sorry. I didn't mean that. I spoke without thinking. I'm not at my best tonight after shouting at Stuart over the phone and being turned out by Giovanni." She hesitated. "What did you think of him, by the way?"

"Stuart?"

"Giovanni," snapped Claire. "God, you can be annoying!"

Susanna thought about their encounter. "We didn't meet in the most auspicious circumstances," she said carefully. "I'm afraid I didn't really take much notice." Claire eyed her ironically, and she finished with a distinct note of defiance in her voice. "He's quite personable, I suppose."

"I'm glad you think so," Claire said mockingly. "Is that what you'll report to Stuart?"

"I don't intend to report anything to Stuart," Susanna said patiently.

"Oh, that's a pity." Claire stood up, facing her cousin with undisguised enmity. "Then I must give you something special to tell him!"

She swept out. Irritated and a little hurt, Susanna stared after her. She took a step forward and fell over Claire's carelessly discarded purse.

"Oh, damn," she exploded. "Damn, damn, damn!"

THE FOLLOWING WEEK brought no relaxation in Claire's hostility and an unprecedented amount of mail directed to the Marchese di Montefiorino. The latter Susanna duly parcelled up and forwarded to Giovanni's office. The former she ignored.

Her attempts at painting in oils alternately reduced her to impotent fury and to despair. Her tutor was encouraging when he saw her efforts, but she thought she detected disappointment behind his kind comments. This engendered a sense of failure.

The resultant comprehensive depression was not alleviated by a letter from Roger Thornfield. The weather was excellent. The end-of-season rugger-club dance had been well attended and Susanna much missed. Roger had made a point of visiting her grandfather. Mr. Shaw had been working in his studio but had been happy to show him his new work. He had not stayed long in case he disturbed the artist's concentration, but he thought his visit had been appreciated. He was her loving Roger.

As Stuart had already telephoned her with the request that she keep that idiot Thornfield out of his hair while she was away, Susanna knew exactly how much it had been appreciated. She laughed, but guiltily. Roger disliked Stuart almost as much as her grandfather disliked him, but was too kindhearted by far to admit it. Charitably, he ascribed Stuart's determined rudeness to him to the uncertainties of the artistic temperament. He would not, she reflected, be happy to learn that his future wife was also an artist. A mercurial bride would not suit Mr. Thornfield at all.

Stuart did not write to her at all. He would occasionally break off work and telephone, demanding, as Claire said, instant progress reports—uselessly for the most part, as Claire and Susanna seldom met except for the occasional encounter in the kitchen at breakfast time. Stuart was annoyed and reproachful, but seemed on the whole to accept Susanna's explanation that if anything were really wrong in Claire's life, Claire would tell her without her cousin having to snoop. Until one evening when he telephoned just as she was leaving for class.

"Oh, so you're in, are you?" he said unpleasantly, when she answered. "For a change."

"Yes, but not for long," she said. "I'm on my way out now. What do you want?"

He snorted. "Out every evening now, aren't you?"

"You know all my classes are in the evening," she sighed. "What is it? Hurry up, or I shall be late."

"You mean you're going out this evening as well?"

"Still life," she replied succinctly, edging her sleeve away from her watch. "Would you prefer me to stay at home and watch television with Claire?"

There was an unbelieving silence at the other end and then her grandfather said slowly, "You do know she's having a party tonight, don't you?"

"A party?" Stunned, Susanna sat down heavily on the floor. The telephone wavered at the edge of the table and she grabbed it and set it down on the carpet beside her. "Here? Tonight?"

"She phoned up specially to tell me," Stuart was grim. "She said she'd been out so much since she went to London that it was time she returned some of the—hospitality."

"I see."

"Well, I don't. Has she been out all that much? What on earth have you been doing, Sue? You're supposed to keep an eye on her, and now I find she's organized some orgy and you don't even know anything about it." He sounded petulant.

She chuckled. "I'll know all about it tomorrow if it is an orgy! I understand they're messy things."

"Don't laugh!" he roared, provoked.

"I can't help it. You sound like a character out of a French farce. Look, I can't stop, I'm late as it is. I'll phone you tomorrow."

"And the party?"

"I expect it will still be here when I get back this evening. If Claire doesn't throw me out as an enemy spy I might even catch the last of the crackers and cheese."

"I hope you enjoy yourself," he said sourly.

"Thank you." She made to put the phone down, but he interrupted.

"Have you met this man of hers yet? The Montefiorino boy?"

"The villain of the piece?" she teased him. "Yes. She's much keener on him than he is on her. I don't think you need to worry."

Doubtful noises emerged from the telephone, and she sought for further reassurance.

"Daddy likes him," she produced. "They seem to be old friends."

"That," said her grandfather with emphasis, "is no recommendation. And if you'd known your father as long as I have, you'd know it."

With which obscure valediction he ended the conversation. Perturbed but too late to ponder why, Susanna flew off to her class.

When she returned it was to unmistakable party

sounds issuing from the apartment. It was in a solid old building, but the music Claire was playing defeated even the Edwardian thickness of the walls and filtered into the corridor. The party sounded very cheerful.

After her initial hesitation, Susanna hitched her portfolio more securely under her arm and went forward. She was feeling for her keys in the back pocket of her jeans when she saw that the door was open. To facilitate entry or departure, she wondered cynically. She pushed it open and went in.

The noise was deafening. At first it seemed that the room was in total darkness and filled from wall to wall with people in an advanced state of hysterics. She stopped, blinking.

As her eyes became accustomed to the lack of light she saw in fact the room was by no means full. It was large and there could be no more than eighteen or twenty people in it. Most of them were dancing to the throbbing beat that issued from a machine that looked suspiciously familiar. Susanna glared at it. The first thing that Stuart would ask when he telephoned, inevitably, tomorrow, would be whether Claire's man had been at the party. Resolving not to speak to Stuart until she had had a long conversation with her cousin, Susanna made for the kitchen.

Candles stood around on various strategically placed tables. She concentrated on not upsetting one with her portfolio. So great was her absorption in this task that she did not look where she was going and walked into Claire, who was carrying a tray of food.

"Careful," she said, pardonably annoyed, and then, identifying her cousin, "Oh, hello, Sue." She sounded airy and obscurely pleased with herself. "Just got back? Have a sandwich."

Over the top of her portfolio Susanna said, "No, thank you."

Claire laughed merrily. "A drink, then. Come on, Sue, you mustn't be stuffy. Dump your stuff and join the party."

A particularly raucous bellow from a new record made Susanna wince. "Yes, I'll do that," she said mendaciously. Perhaps if she pulled the pillow over her ears she might not be able to hear the noise. Her room, after all, was at the far end of the apartment from the living room. With a small, embarrassed smile she escaped.

The kitchen at least was light. It was also full of Claire's guests. One young man in the process of raiding the refrigerator offered her some cheese in a charitable spirit.

She stood in the doorway, her mouth open in surprise, her portfolio clutched to her like a child's teddybear.

"Do have some," the young man urged her. "Rather superior mousetrap. Cheese is good for keeping you awake and this," waving a hand at the living room, "will go on for hours."

"W—will it?" said the startled Susanna.

"They always do," he explained, pouring red wine into a glass and offering it to her. "Let me take the shield," he said, relieving her of the portfolio.

"Th—thank you." She took the glass in nerveless fingers, looking around the kitchen. Another couple leaning against the counter were quite engrossed in each other. A girl perched on the table gave her a friendly smile. The man who was holding her hand ran uninterested eyes over Susanna and raised one eyebrow in acknowledgment of her presence. Her lips began to twitch.

"You're very kind," she said, sipping the wine.

"I'm George," he corrected. "And you look like someone who has had a party thrust upon her unawares."

She looked down at her stained jeans and shirt. Her fingertips were black with charcoal and she was quite convinced that some of the dust at least had transferred itself to her face.

"I'm afraid so. My name is Susanna and I live here."

"My condolences," said George. "That would be why we haven't met before. I wondered. I know everyone else here."

"Do you?" She was interested. "They all look very, er, sophisticated." She chuckled and corrected herself, "What I mean is that they all look very well dressed, not to say clean, compared with me. Who are they?"

"Do you want a breakdown by age, sex and marital status? Or will a collective description do?"

Susanna choked on her wine. "Oh, a collective description will be fine."

"Don't encourage him to be bitchy," said the girl sitting on the table. "He's a sour statistician who doesn't believe in people." She pulled at her companion's hand. "Come on, I want to dance."

"Statistician?" Susanna was interested.

"Me and my computer run the Banco Montefiorino," George assured her. "Which is where the rest of this menagerie come from."

"Oh, you *work* with Claire," she said, enlightened.

"It might be more accurate to say I work in spite of Claire," he returned dryly. "She's a distracting lady, your roommate."

"Does she distract you or your computer?" Susanna asked, amused.

"Neither," he said, a little too sharply. "The management wouldn't like it. Claire is strictly reserved for Montefiorino."

Susanna looked at her wine. "That wasn't the way I heard it," she murmured.

"I daresay not." George got off his perch and held out a hand. "Dance?" And as she went with him he added, "He's got the poor kid on a string, but that doesn't mean he'd let her go."

"Quite the dog in a manger," Susanna said lightly.

"Hmm. Have you seen their crest? It's on all the bank notepaper."

She shook her head.

"It's from some medieval medallion that belongs to the family. I think it was made for them. The family used to be huntsmen to a Tuscan prince and got fat on the pickings. The symbol is a man with two dogs on a lead. The dogs pull in one direction and he's looking in another. And that's our Giovanni. He never looks straight at what he wants, but he gets it all right. And keeps it."

Susanna shivered. "Poor Claire!"

The music took over at that point and conversation became impossible. George's style of dancing reminded her forcibly of a clockwork octopus and dodging his flailing arms made her distinctly breathless. As soon as she decently could she left him with a grateful smile. Nobody tried to stop her. She looked around her as well as she could in the half dark. Although she could make out the figure of her cousin in the far corner there was no evidence of Giovanni.

Her mouth twisted. Poor Claire indeed! She knit her brows. George, who had seemed to know, was convinced that Claire was the man's property. Yet Claire could not be more unsure of him.

She dodged an energetic couple and flattened herself against the front door as they passed. Simultaneously, the door was pushed, none too gently, from the other side and Susanna was almost flung to the floor.

"Steady," said a familiar voice.

A firm hand took hold of her elbow and steered her clear of the dancers. Curiously breathless, she found herself brought face to face with Giovanni. She shook off his hand.

"Susanna Shaw," he said, peering at her face. "How very unexpected."

She was offended. "I do live here."

"Yes, you do, don't you?" He was laughing at her. "So you more or less have to participate?"

"What do you mean?" she demanded, suspecting an insult.

"You don't really like parties, do you? It's only your duty to keep an eye on Claire."

"Nonsense," she snapped. "I'm enjoying myself."

"Splendid. Then you can help me enjoy myself."

"Oh?"

She could sense that he was smiling. "For a start you can take me somewhere where we can't hear that appalling noise. My stereo was never intended for that. Claire has no restraint."

Convinced that he was talking about more than the music, Susanna drew an indignant breath. "Then you should speak to Claire about it." She backed away from him. "It's nothing to do with me." She waved a hand at Claire's corner. "She's over there. Tell her. I'm sure," she said sweetly, "she'll listen to you."

She turned away from him and stalked into the kitchen only to find that it was deserted by now. He followed her.

"No doubt she would if she could hear me," he allowed. "She's an obliging child—don't you agree? How do you like the apartment?"

She remembered that it was his; he had lived here. It was a disconcerting thought.

"Fine," she said uncommunicatively.

It seemed he was interested in her life-style. "And living with Claire? Do you like that, too?"

There was no doubt about it, he was teasing her. Susanna raised her chin and looked him straight in the eye.

"I find it convenient," she said flatly.

He threw back his head and laughed. She glared at him. He threw up his hands. "Don't look so—icy. You're very entertaining."

"Because I find it convenient to live with Claire?"

"I doubt if Claire could say the same thing," he pointed out, still spluttering.

He won an unwilling smile from her. "No, probably not. But she would find it even more inconvenient to antagonize my grandfather. Stuart has a way of getting his own way."

Giovanni looked at her thoughtfully. "A family characteristic," he commented, and then, abruptly changing the subject, "You're Simon Shaw's daughter, aren't you?"

Remembering her grandfather's comment on the friendship, Susanna hid a grin. "Yes. He told me he knew you."

He made a face. "I'll bet! With illustrations. I should have realized when you said your name was Shaw, but it simply didn't occur to me. Frankly I find it difficult to imagine a daughter of Simon's in your position."

"Which is?" she prompted.

"Watchdog," he replied with perfect sangfroid.

"You aren't here to enjoy yourself, are you, Susanna? You're here to protect Claire from herself."

There was a pregnant pause.

"From you, surely?" she retorted gently.

He was about to reply but was interrupted by the appearance of Claire.

"Giovanni!" She tumbled artlessly into his arms. "I thought you were never coming."

He held her away from him, laughing. "If I'd known your taste in music, my child, I wouldn't." He brushed his lips lightly along her silken fringe. His eyes openly mocked Susanna's disapproving expression.

Claire gave a happy little laugh. She looked excited, like a child at her first party. "Well, tell me what you think I ought to play," she said, looking up at him.

"I told you she was an obliging child," Giovanni teased. "Come along, Claire, let's see if you have some more tolerable sounds out there."

The look she gave him was openly adoring. It sickened Susanna. He tucked Claire's hand into his own large one and took her back to the living room. She had not spared so much as a word or a glance for her cousin. Susanna shivered.

Suddenly all desire to sleep left her. She did not want to stay at the party but found it impossible to turn her back on it, so she drifted out into the living room and watched.

It was amazing how quickly Giovanni changed the atmosphere. To suit his own tastes, Susanna thought sourly. It was as if he were the only adult in the room indulging a lot of children. He might have been a favorite uncle. Everyone competed for his attention.

With the tempo and volume of the music reduced, he danced twice with a beautiful dark girl in a red dress. Then he sat down, talking to George and another couple. Claire hovered about him all the time—as if she were his slave, thought Susanna indignantly.

She moved restlessly. She was hot and uncomfortable with the beginnings of a headache behind her eyes. Claire was plying Giovanni with food and drink. Susanna's teeth came together with a snap.

"He's beautiful, isn't he?"

She turned to find the bright-eyed girl who had been in the kitchen earlier. Susanna stiffened, but the friendliness in the other's face was obvious.

"My cousin seems to think so," she admitted.

"We all think so," the other girl remarked. "He's nice, too. I've worked for him for three years. He's really kind." She sighed comically. "A girl doesn't have a chance."

"Against the other girls, I suppose," Susanna said dryly. She was tired of Giovanni's excellencies, she found.

"There are plenty of them," the girl agreed. She looked across at his dark head fondly. "Regular heartbreaker, our Giovanni."

"He's an arrogant pig," retorted Susanna angrily, on no evidence at all other than Claire's slavish devotion. In her indignation she spoke rather more loudly than she intended, and she thought for a moment that the object of her remark looked across the room at her. But the blood was no sooner rising in her cheeks than he looked away again and went on with his conversation, apparently uncaring.

She drew a shaky breath. "I don't see his attraction," she said more quietly.

Her companion looked a little offended. "You will," she prophesied.

Susanna was outraged. "Not me," she protested, her voice rising again.

This time there was no doubt he heard her. His eyebrows flew up and he was laughing at her. She blushed.

"I mean, he's nothing to do with me," she elaborated, hurriedly. "As far as I'm concerned he's strictly Claire's property."

"Giovanni?" was the unbelieving answer. "You really don't know him, do you?"

"And don't want to."

"That must make you unique," the girl said tolerantly.

Exasperated, Susanna left her and went, muttering, to her own room. It was only then that she remembered her portfolio of drawings still in the kitchen where George had put them. She stamped back down the corridor to rescue them. Left where they were, she thought grimly, they would be dowsed in wine and ice cubes before the party ended.

The kitchen was empty and in darkness. She had kicked off her shoes in her room and now she padded silently across the tiled floor. The portfolio was easily found. She retrieved it and made to escape. Her shin connected smartly with one of the stools pushed out of place by a past occupant, and she gave a yelp.

Almost at once the door from the living room opened.

"Claire?" said Giovanni, puzzled, looking in.

Simple horror kept her silent. She had been unpardonably rude to his face and behind his back. Stealthily she began to edge toward the other door of the kitchen that led to the central corridor of the apartment. But, of course, he knew where it was and heard her.

He shut his own door behind him, banishing the lights and sounds of the party. Like a hunter, he was breathing very quietly in the darkness. It was a game to him, Susanna thought wildly. He thought she was Claire and was teasing her. It was her own guilty conscience that filled her with this extraordinary fear.

She skirted the corner of the table and made a final dash for the door.

He was there first and stopped her easily, twirling her around so that she had her back against the door, laughing. With one hand on the door behind her, he was awesomely tall, and she shivered. He raised her chin with the other hand.

"Not Claire...." His voice drifted into a murmur against her mouth.

For the second time that night the portfolio slid from her fingers. His kiss was mischievous and strangely moving. Dazedly, she thought, *I don't believe it.* She put trembling hands against his chest. The warmth of his body was sufficient evidence of reality. Yet she felt as if she were caught in a nightmare. The dark, the silence, the obscure sense of powerlessness as if all her muscles had atrophied, froze any resistance she might have made.

Her thoughts were in chaos. *Claire... Stuart..... What am I doing?* And at last, as her hands crept helplessly around his neck, *why?*

For a moment only he held her so, strained against him, and his mouth grew fierce. Then, almost reluctantly, he unclasped the clinging arms. His fingers found the light switch at her back and turned it on. The metallic strips in the ceiling flickered whitely.

Susanna looked bewildered as if she had been suddenly and rudely awakened. Her eyes were dark with shock. She swallowed painfully, aware of a parched and aching throat. She blinked her eyes against the unkind light.

Giovanni looked unexpectedly grim. He looked, she thought agitatedly, like an uncle who had decided that the time has come to stop indulging the children. She felt a strange, muddled emotion: part guilt, part embarrassment and part an ignoble triumph that she had wiped the smile off his face. That face was a little pale and had a long charcoal smudge from her caressing thumb along his jaw.

"You'll have to have a wash," she said practically, in a high false voice. She spread her hands for him to inspect. "If I'd known, I would have washed my hands. I'm sorry."

For a moment he stared at her as if he could not make out her words, as if she were speaking a foreign language. Which, she realized with a shock, of course she was.

With an almost visible effort, he collected himself. "It was inevitable," he sighed. "Any other girl would plaster me with lipstick. But for you it has to be soot." He laughed, but for once it did not reach his eyes. They remained steady and quite unreadable.

Dismayed, she met his look. And then, with an inarticulate sound of distress compounded of indignation and a vague feeling that she for her own part owed him some sort of apology, she turned on her heel and fled.

CHAPTER FOUR

SUSANNA SPENT a sleepless night. It was unusual for her and was due, she assured herself fiercely, to the intrusiveness of the party. The noise came tantalizingly down the corridor. She could hear the murmur of voices without being able to make out what they said.

Eventually she gave up all attempts to sleep and tried to read. But it was useless. The print danced in front of her eyes, and she turned restlessly in her bed trying to find a comfortable position. But first her shoulder ached, then her elbow went to sleep and finally a cramp seized upon the muscles of her right arm. She sat up furiously. Angry tears coursed down her cheeks, and she flung the book away from her childishly.

She looked at her alarm clock. Still only half-past three. The sounds issuing from the living room were muted now. There was the faintest trickle of music and, as far as she could judge, no conversation at all. She wondered whether Giovanni di Montefiorino had left. A great desire to get out of bed and patter down the corridor just to glance into the living room took hold of her.

Susanna switched off her light and lay back against the pillows fighting the unworthy urge to spy on Claire. With the back of her hand, she wiped the tears off her cheeks. The hand was trembling. Upon consideration she found that her whole body was being shaken by spasmodic tremors. Shock, she thought, with wry self-mockery.

She sniffed. She felt feverish and bad tempered and thoroughly dissatisfied with herself.

It was unbelievable. It was unprecedented. It was unfair. She had never felt like this before. A perfectly casual kiss from a man she did not even like, and she behaved like a besotted schoolgirl. In fact, she thought absurdly, she had been a singularly levelheaded schoolgirl. How had she managed to avoid all the adolescent excesses to which she had seen her friends succumb, only to dissolve because Giovanni di Montefiorino mistook her for her cousin and kissed her in the dark?

"It wasn't even me that he was kissing," she reminded herself.

She began to nibble her thumbnail, a long-abandoned habit. It tasted, in spite of having been scrubbed, of charcoal dust. That reminded her of the smudge she had left on his face. She wondered if he had washed it away before he had gone back to the party. How would he have excused it to Claire? Would he have bothered to excuse it at all? Would he not rather think that what had happened was too amusing not to be shared? She felt hot at the thought. Perhaps he had told Claire all about his amusing mistake.

Except that he had not found it amusing. He had done his best to take it lightly, but he had looked—dismayed. Whoever he might enjoy kissing in darkened kitchens, clearly Claire's "dragon" was not one of them. There was an odd shame in that.

With resolution Susanna examined her feelings. It was, of course, humiliating to be cast into confusion by a kiss. It would have been more dignified to draw herself out of his arms without fuss—a polite, regretful refusal that put him at a proper distance and kept him there. She dwelt on the vision wistfully. Or alternatively she could have slapped his face. Traditional, perhaps, but it would have relieved her feelings, and she was never likely to have the opportunity again. It had been a great mistake to do what she had done—to melt into his arms without so much as a token protest as if she had never been kissed before.

But even that unpalatable memory, she thought, she could bear. She could take it as a salutary demonstration that nobody ever knew as much about himself as he thought he did and write it off to experience. If it were not for the picture of his face when he had looked at her. She could not banish that memory however she might discipline the rest of her recollections. He had not looked surprised. In fact, if anything, he looked as if an unwelcome suspicion had been confirmed. And when Susanna at last focused her dazzled gaze on him, he had looked angry.

And that, acknowledged the sleepless Susanna, hurt unreasonably.

The days that followed had an air of unreality. Susanna worked harder than she could ever remember doing before. Most of her days she spent at St. Daniel's. Toward the end of term more and more students left for one reason or another and space became obtainable. The evening classes fell off, too, until there was only her and a quiet middle-aged man left. He drew uniform compositions in gray chalk that enraged his teachers and seemed to fill him with quiet satisfaction. More than one of the teachers hinted that it might be appropriate to close the classes, but Susanna and her companion obstinately carried on.

When she was not at St. Daniel's she took her sketchbook to the zoo or one of the parks. To her instructor's annoyance she abandoned her oil painting with the vague excuse that she did not feel ready for it. He was suspicious and would have probed deeper, but the Easter holidays approached, and he was fully occupied with plans for transporting his family to the sea. And Susanna did not want to confide in him.

Susanna in fact confided in no one. Her strongest feeling was of a wish to be alone. As much as possible she kept away from the apartment, returning only to sleep. Her unfinished canvas hardened in the thin March sunshine. Claire, suddenly domesticated, began to paint walls and hang posters. Susanna ignored both. She did not so much as cook a meal or dust any of the Venetian glass that Giovanni had considerately left behind.

Claire would have been fully justified in complaining at her cousin's lack of conscience. Susanna avoided the housework blatantly, which was in itself sufficiently surprising, for it was Susanna who had run the Sussex house almost from the first day she entered it. But Claire did not notice her sudden loss of enthusiasm for domesticity and cheerfully did Susanna's share of the chores.

The Easter holiday came and went, and Susanna refused to hang any of her work in the end-of-term exhibition. Her instructor, accustoming himself to regard her as quite his most difficult pupil, was philosophical. Her grandfather was furious. Susanna was alternately reproached and reviled, and for a whole week he telephoned every evening to pursue the argument without once mentioning Claire's name. And every evening Susanna was out, and he found himself leaving messages with an unknown man who seemed to find it amusing that she was never there when her grandfather wanted to speak to her.

All of this Stuart Shaw complained of at length in what must have been the first letter he had ever written his granddaughter in his life. Susanna was appropriately repentant. She assured him that she would put some of her work into the end-of-the-year exhibition. She explained that she was not often at home because she was working so hard. She did not explain that she was working so hard to avoid Giovanni di Montefiorino.

The party seemed to mark a turning point in Giovanni's relationship with Claire. From being elusive to the point of invisibility, he became touchingly attentive to Claire's unexpressed astonishment. He was available to escort her anywhere whenever she asked. In his turn he took the delighted Claire to dinners and theaters with every appearance, as she assured her unreceptive cousin, of serious intent. He rode and skated and played tennis with her. But most of all he seemed to like dropping in unexpectedly at the apartment and staying for whatever meal was in preparation.

It was this proceeding that eventually drove Susanna out. Although he usually rang the doorbell she never forgot that he had not surrendered his key, and to her, his constant presence took on the quality of an invasion. She could not be comfortable in the apartment never knowing when he might walk in. It colored her movements about the rooms, her conversation, even her dress. After all, the first time they met she had been wearing a towel. She could not settle to work with the threat of his arrival constantly over her head. It was more peaceful, she reasoned, simply to remove herself from the danger zone.

She found it quite impossible to explain this to Stuart and, although for different reasons, to Claire.

It often occurred to her that Giovanni himself was well aware that she avoided him and was amused by it.

Not that she was altogether successful. Many evenings she returned to find him comfortably ensconced on the couch, one long arm flung across its cushioned back. She would stand in the doorway, her heart plummeting at the sight of him. Claire was usually perched on the arm or cross-legged at his feet. She would spring up, unaffectedly welcoming. And Giovanni would turn his head, ignore Susanna's expression and behave as if she and not he were the guest. His graciousness often made her grit her teeth, but she never allowed herself to respond sarcastically. For one thing it would have distressed Claire. For another, she admitted to herself, for she was a truthful girl, she did not quite dare.

And Claire was happy, of that there could be no doubt. Her old serenity seemed to have come back to her. The hours she was not with Giovanni were spent cheerfully, often in the company of other young men. Having secured his attention, she was content.

Susanna wondered at her. Susanna herself was always on edge in Giovanni's company. He had a critical wit that made her inspect her every word before she said anything to him. In certain moods a conversation with him, she told Claire tartly after one particularly unsuccessful evening, resembled a persecution.

Claire had laughed. "You let him get under your skin. You shouldn't. He was just feeling awkward tonight. He's tired. He's been on the phone to Rome most of the day."

"Is that any reason why he should come and ruin most of our evening?" demanded the carping Susanna.

"He's been on edge," Claire excused.

"You're very forbearing." Susanna tried not to sound disapproving.

"It's easy when you're in love." Claire's eyes softened, and she gave her cousin a pitying smile. "I wish you knew, Sue."

Exasperated, but unwillingly amused, Susanna laughed and left the subject.

However, there did not seem to be an hour of the day without danger of Giovanni, and she soon ceased to be amused. Even the mornings were not safe.

Drooping over her orange juice at seven o'clock Susanna was at first disbelieving and then outraged to discover Claire was intending to entertain him to breakfast. Emerging from her room in breeches and a sweater, with her long hair in an unbecoming net, Claire was about to go riding.

"You're up," Susanna said unneccessarily. She took a revivifying swig of orange juice. When her cousin did not disappear she accepted that this was no morning mirage and demanded, "Why?"

"I'm riding with Giovanni," was the airy reply. "He'll be here any moment."

In the act of sipping, Susanna caught her breath and snorted quite involuntarily. Claire regarded her with concern.

"You don't mind, do you?" she asked anxiously. "I thought he might come back for breakfast."

"Oh, no, I don't mind," said Susanna bitterly. "Why doesn't he come and live here?"

"Sue!" Claire shook her head. "This is heresy. Think of Stuart!" She paused. "Seriously—you don't really mind, do you? Not now you've met him? I know Stuart had some antiquated ideas and sent you here as a sort of duenna." She giggled.

"But now you know Giovanni you can see there's no need, can't you?"

"Can I?" she said ironically.

"Sue, don't be mean!"

"What you do is your own business, Claire. As far as I'm concerned it always has been."

Claire hugged her briefly. "I know that really. I always did underneath. I just felt a bit sore and lovelorn and didn't want an audience."

"And now you've recovered."

"Been cured," Claire corrected her. "Giovanni's being a lamb. He has the craziest ideas. Like this riding. He's seeing somebody at ten and has to be at his desk in his city suit by then, but he wants to ride in the park on a May morning. And you should see him—cream breeches, tailored hacking jacket, the lot. More English than the English."

The bell rang. She jumped up.

"Oh, that will be him now. I mustn't keep him waiting—we've only got the horses for an hour. We'll see you when we get back."

Susanna agreed with a sickly smile. She debated dressing and leaving the apartment before they returned but decided against it. She had no great fancy for sitting on the steps of St. Daniel's until the doors opened. It would be awkward, too, to explain to Claire that she was reluctant to meet Giovanni without giving her a sound reason.

And, she admitted, she did not even have sound reasons to give herself. He annoyed her, but that was not it. It was as if, in some mysterious way, he alarmed her, not by anything he said or did—her first fear that he would give Claire a comic account of her own foolish behavior at the party had long since disappeared—but by what he was. She tried to laugh at herself, but the sense of disquiet persisted.

In spite of Claire's confidence, Susanna mistrusted Giovanni. He was too indulgent with her, as if, whenever he chose, he could leave Claire and go back to other companions and a quite different life.

So she remained—with an effort—polite, which Giovanni received with barely concealed amusement. And, between them, Claire was entirely content.

The summer term went quickly—too quickly for Susanna, who did not foresee a comfortable summer unless she could persuade her grandfather that Claire was safe to be left alone in London. Stuart was engaged with a new piece of sculpture. He told her as much, implying that the empty house was to his taste.

"I haven't worked so well in years," was what he actually said. Interpreting, Susanna came to the conclusion that Stuart would not welcome her return. The impression was reinforced by Roger Thornfield's accounts.

Dutifully, he went to see Stuart Shaw every week, and dutifully, he wrote to Susanna about it. She gathered that her grandfather was keeping extraordinary hours and living on a diet of tinned soup and chocolate biscuits. Roger thought he was sinking into senility. Susanna, who knew that the regime described approached her grandfather's highest ideas of bliss, had no such fear, but she did realize that he was thoroughly enjoying his solitude and she sighed.

Perhaps she would be able to find herself a small cottage somewhere where she could retire to paint for the duration of the holiday. It seemed, she acknowledged pessimistically, unlikely. Cottages were not readily available in the summer, particularly not to impecunious artists. Susanna had discovered with some dismay how quickly her money had spent itself in London. She had recklessly spent her father's check on clothes—still for the most part unworn—and, as he had prophesied, her grandfather had not as yet remembered that he intended to give her an allowance. She was not destitute, but she was sufficiently short of money for the immediate future to provide some problems.

She decided to consult her father and duly telephoned him. After a fruitless week of calling his home, and with the end of term only a week away, she contacted his office. The secretary who answered seemed suspicious of her identity and refused to divulge his whereabouts. She did eventually concede that Mr. Shaw was out of London and volunteered the information that he was working on a newly acquired house for a valued customer. It needed almost total redecoration, even restoration in parts, and he expected to be out of town for the summer. Her tone said that she expected it, too, but totally disbelieved the official version. To some extent Susanna sympathized. Abandoning the attempt to convince the faithful secretary that she was not a discarded embarrassment from Simon's past, she offered an honorable compromise. Could a message be passed to her father?

The secretary said, without enthusiasm, that it might be possible and Susanna said, "Would you just ask him to phone me, please? He," with a certain satisfaction, "knows the number."

She placed little reliance on his response, however. If the message reached him at all it would obviously take a leisurely route. And even then he was unlikely to leap to the nearest telephone. Simon Shaw was unused to calls for help. If anyone suggested that he might be to some extent responsible for the well-being of his daughter, he would have replied indignantly that she was free, British and on dry land and more than capable of taking care of herself. In fact, the slightest hint of impending dependence on her part and he would not telephone her at all.

He had never quite accustomed himself to the way that his wife expected him to direct operations. When she died he had found with relief that Susanna seemed of an independent turn of mind, but women, as he knew, were changeable creatures. So he had left her with her grandfather before she began to show any signs of clinging to him. Their present excellent relationship was based on his bland confidence that she never would cling to him. The very fact that Susanna had never appealed to him before would make him wary.

Susanna abandoned hope of advice from that quarter and began seriously to consider taking a temporary job. After all, she was a fully qualified secretary. It ought not to be too difficult. But it was a depressing prospect.

To comfort herself she allowed George Mole to persuade her out for an evening. Ever since she had met him at Claire's party he had pursued the friendship. He was casual and lighthearted, and he knew London. He found her Gothic follies and Victorian passageways to draw in all the remote corners of the city. His hobby was making fantastic miniature robots capable of the most irrelevant tasks. Susanna would sit and watch fascinated as he tinkered with the intricate clockwork mannikins. They never talked about Claire or the Banco Montefiorino, although she had heard the whole case history of George's computer. It was very relaxing.

She returned from one of these peaceful evenings with George to find—inevitably—Giovanni stretched out comfortably on the couch reading an old color supplement and Claire talking agitatedly into the telephone.

"Ah, here she is," she heard as she closed the door behind her. Susanna greeted the intruder resignedly and found Claire waving the telephone in her face.

"It's your father," she hissed. "He's been calling every half hour and he's furious!"

"Oh." Susanna was surprised. She had almost forgotten the message she sent him and assumed that he had ignored it. Obviously she had misjudged him. "Hello, daddy," she said calmly. "I'm sorry I was out."

Simon Shaw breathed hard. "I thought," he said with great distinctness, "that you wanted to talk to me urgently. At least that was what my secretary told me. I thought you were ill."

"Did you?" She was intrigued. "But that was last week. What did you think I had? Sleeping sickness?"

"Don't be cynical," he said sharply. He sounded as if he had really been worried. "I've been abroad and only got back to London tonight."

"I see." Susanna was penitent. "I'm sorry, daddy, I didn't realize you were abroad. Your secretary only said that you were out of London."

"I've been moving around," he retorted irritably. "Don't change the subject. What's wrong?"

She transferred the receiver to her other ear and perched on the back of a convenient chair. Claire and Giovanni, she noted, were unashamedly listening.

"On the run?" she queried lightly. "From creditors or former secretaries?"

"Neither. I'm working." He sounded calmer.

"I've been going around the sales. What's it got to do with you, anyway? Are you trying to bully me as well as Claire? I'm sure father didn't tell you to look after both of us. Even he would realize that would be impossible. Now, do you want something or can I go and have something to eat and stop worrying?"

"Well, actually, I wanted your advice . . . " she began uncomfortably.

"Short of money?" Simon was good at grasping essentials.

"Yes," she said gratefully.

"That's easily remedied," he said with a sigh of relief. "Come and see me in the morning. Is that all?" he said as an afterthought.

She looked at Claire. "Er, no."

"Well, what else—oh, is Claire there?" said her quickwitted father.

"Yes."

"Hmm. We'd better meet later than. I'm seeing my, er, client tomorrow morning. Can you make teatime tomorrow?"

"Not really. It's the art school exhibition. I ought to be there. At least when it opens, even if I sneak out later."

"Good God, is it? The end-of-the-year thing that Stuart made so much fuss about? Are you in it?"

"Yes," she said to all three questions.

"Then I must come and inspect your work, mustn't I?"

"Oh, no, daddy," she said, embarrassed.

But he was firm. "But of course I must. Stuart will expect a full report. Besides," he added practically, "we need a new trainee. I might find someone possible."

"Thank you," she said dryly.

"Don't be silly, Susanna. You know we'd gladly

have you if you want to do it. But you say you don't, so we'll have to find someone else, won't we? It's only practical."

There was a variety of replies she could think of, most of them pointing out that it was not clear whether he intended to view the exhibition in his parental capacity or as a talent scout. Mindful of the ears on the couch, however, she contented herself with, "Quite."

"If it's the end of term, you'll be at a bit of a loose end, won't you?"

"Precisely," she said, pleased with his understanding.

"Bit tedious, chaperoning Claire, eh?" He roared with laughter. "Well, it's your own fault, you should've minded your own business no matter what Stuart said. What are you going to do now? Stay in London playing chaperon?"

"I hate you," she said with feeling. "That's what I wanted to ask your advice about."

"Oh?" There was a pause. "Do you want me to find you a job?"

"Well, not exactly. I was thinking more of helpful suggestions."

"And nothing would be so helpful as a cast-iron offer of a job." He sounded amused. "I think I may be able to help. I know somebody who's going to want a temporary secretary. How's your shorthand?"

"Short," she said crisply, certain he was laughing at her.

"Splendid. Well, I'll get in touch with this chap and see what he says."

"Is he a friend of yours?" she said suspiciously. She recalled Stuart's strictures on her father's friends.

"More of a business acquaintance," he replied, and added evasively, "at the moment."

He was still laughing when he hung up.

Claire and Giovanni were ostentatiously engrossed in each other. Susanna hovered.

"That was my father," she said unnecessarily.

"So I deduced," said Giovanni. Claire tucked herself further down on the couch and let her head droop onto his shoulder. He gave Susanna a bland smile. "It's a long time since I've seen Simon. How is he?"

Claire looked mildly astonished. "But I thought you said—" she began, wriggling around to look up at his face.

He interrupted smoothly, "That I must get in touch with him. I did. But I have not yet done so. When you see your father, Susanna," he told her, sounding like an aged pedant, "you must give him my best wishes."

"I will," she assured him sweetly, promising herself to deliver the unlikely message verbatim, "when I see him tomorrow."

She left them.

It was rather later than teatime when Simon joined her in the exhibition hall the next day. He was looking pleased with himself as he shouldered his way through the crowd of dignitaries and well-wishers.

"How are you, Sue?" he said, kissing her absently. "Sorry I'm late. Traffic's abominable. And I didn't leave, er, my client until forty minutes ago."

"Just one client?" Susanna looked her surprise. "All this time? Is it profitable to spend so much time on just one man?"

He patted her cheek. "You're a shrewd little

soul," he said indulgently. "Normally, no. This time, fortunately for me, he can afford it. And it's a big job. I've hardly started."

"Nice house?" Susanna steered him toward a display of fabric designs.

"It will be," he assured her confidently. "When I've finished. Now *that*—" he motioned at a length of bright green material "—is interesting."

Susanna left him happily browsing, fully expecting to be forgotten. From a distance she saw him pin down one of the brighter design students. He was waving his hands eloquently. She could imagine that he was sketching a brilliant future for the bewildered young man. In just such a way had he persuaded her mother to follow him to ever rosier horizons. He would find Talbot Carroll more difficult to convince, she thought grimly, amazed at the resentment that still remained. In ten years she had not lost the desperate indignation she had felt on her mother's behalf. It was pointless, and she tried to put it out of her mind, but the flavor of it always remained, souring her relationship with her father.

Unaware of her reflections, Simon returned to her side.

"Intelligent fellow, that," he remarked.

"You mean you've got him," interpreted Susanna.

He gave her a schoolboy grin. "Not quite," he allowed. "But he's interested. Good material there. Now let's have a look at your stuff."

This was so much an afterthought that Susanna laughed aloud.

Simon looked ashamed. "Forgot," he excused himself. "Hopeless parent. I never turned up for open-house days at school, either, did I? Do you feel I've got a lot to make up to you?"

She took his arm, suddenly affectionate. "No, of course not. Not to me. Come and admire dutifully, and then we can go home."

Her drawings were all together in a group opposite a huge sash window. Some were pastels, some pen and ink, but most were in charcoal. He stood in front of them in silence for some moments.

Then he said, very thoughtfully, "Are all these yours?"

"A hundred percent," she returned flippantly.

"Interesting." He continued to stare.

Susanna began to feel uneasy. "What's wrong?"

"Very little, I would say, from the look of these." He moved away from her to study a pen-and-ink sketch.

She followed him. "Southwark Bridge with attendant building site," she said.

He did not answer at once and then he said slowly, "I begin to see what Stuart means about your talent. What are you going to do about it, Sue?"

"Do?"

"Yes, do." He snorted. "You must know you have an extraordinary skill, to put it no higher. And you would have done nothing about it if Stuart hadn't flung you out to look after Claire. So now what? Come back here next year? Or new pastures?"

She shrugged. "I don't know. I don't want to make any plans at the moment. They'd have me back here if I wanted. But I don't really want to stay in London."

He looked down at her. "Because of Claire and this thing she's got for Johnny?"

"Among other things."

"That will be over by the time next term starts," he said cheerfully. "Of if it isn't you won't be able to do anything about it, anyway. But if it's getting you down, move out."

Susanna laughed. "It's not as easy as that."

He clicked his fingers. "Ah yes—money. I'd forgotten. I have a check made out to you, but I left it in the car. We'll pick it up on the way out. But I've had an idea. I'm going down to visit my own small work of art tonight. Come with me for the weekend."

Her eyebrows shot up. "Where is it, for heaven's sake?"

"Kent," he said in mild surprise. "Why?"

"You said you'd been abroad," she explained patiently. "It sounded as if you were redecorating an imperial palace. I thought darkest Africa at the very least."

"I was abroad on a buying trip. The house is very much an English residence."

"An English residence full of unplaced furniture and the smell of paint."

"Well, to some extent," he allowed. "But the kitchen and a couple of bedrooms are finished, and who needs more than that?"

"A bathroom?" she hazarded.

He dismissed the mundane consideration with a wave of his hand. "The bathroom is still in the state in which the last owner left it. Covered in tiles and fish prints—horrible! But the plumbing, to which I take it you refer, works."

She put her head on one side. "I'm tempted."

"It's in the middle of the Downs," he said casually. "The back garden goes down Wycliffe Hill."

Susanna drew him away from her drawings and began to parade him along the rest of the exhibits. Simon cast half an eye over them with supreme indifference.

"There's a swimming pool," he wheedled.

She capitulated. "I don't know why you want me to come, but I suppose I will."

"To cook of course," he said blandly. "There aren't any staff. Good grief!" as he stopped in front of a twelve-foot-high expanse of emulsion paint and plasticene. "What's that?"

"Another product of your prospective junior partner," she replied serenely.

"I don't believe it." He looked across at Talbot, improbably organizing refreshments.

"He's a man of many talents."

"Obviously." Simon was half fascinated, half appalled. "Heaven knows what the customers will say." He looked back at the canvas. "What is it?"

"Vegetable depression," said Susanna fluently. She had seen the conception of the great work. "You'll have to hang it in your office."

Simon, who worked in an elegant Regency building, closed his eyes. "You have a distorted imagination," he said. "Distinctly unhealthy. You need some country air. It will help you regain a sense of proportion. Let's leave this hall of horrors, and you can go and pack."

Susanna hesitated. "But what about the owner?" She knit her brows, struck by the sudden thought. "I mean, it's not very professional of you to start entertaining all and sundry in his new home, is it?"

"You can be my assistant."

"Oh, be serious, daddy. Won't this man mind you taking your daughter down there without so much as asking him?"

Simon patted her cheek for the second time that afternoon. It was an unaccustomed gesture, and she looked at him suspiciously.

"I've asked him," he assured her soothingly. "When I saw him this morning I just, er, mentioned it." His eyes widened innocently at her disbelieving expression. "Really I did, Sue. He won't mind." Simon was enjoying a private joke. He chuckled. "He won't mind at all."

CHAPTER FIVE

THEY HAD A PLEASANT DRIVE down to Kent.

"Summer has come," remarked Simon with great satisfaction. He had thrown back the top of his car and was sniffing the air appreciatively as they proceeded down a country lane. "The garden of England," he expanded lyrically. "It smells good."

"It won't smell as good to anyone behind us," pointed out his prosaic daughter. "They'll be breathing our exhaust fumes."

But Simon was not to be deflated. "Nobody ever comes down this lane," he said firmly. "It only goes to the house or the farm on the other side of the hill. By the time the next person comes along our exhaust will have dispersed."

"Over the fields of ripening corn," Susanna objected.

"Don't be sour," retorted her father with unimpaired calm. "I brought you down here for a little relaxation and peace. And that means my peace as well as yours. If you moan I shall throw you out."

"And if your client turns up he'll probably throw us both out," murmured Susanna provocatively.

Simon shook his head. "I don't know how you manage to look so like your mother and sound so like my father. You're a captious woman, Sue, and bossy with it."

She laughed. He did not sound disturbed. Susanna stretched her hands high above her head. She had taken off the silk scarf she had knotted around her neck at the start of the journey, and now she watched it ripple in the wind.

"You'll lose that," Simon remarked.

She felt it tugging at her hands. "I have others," she returned haughtily.

He gave her a quick sideways glance. "Oh, it is yours, then? I rather gathered that you held your clothes on an extended lease from Claire."

"Did you?" She was surprised. It was true enough, but she did not remember telling him, and even if she had, she would not have expected him to remember it. "It's so no longer. I spent all the money you gave me before Easter on clothes." There was a touch of defiance in her tone.

He negotiated a double bend neatly, and the car slowed as they began to climb a steep slope.

"I'm glad to hear it," he said calmly. "I suppose that accounts for your present lack of means."

She admitted it ruefully.

"Good. I hope you've got something pretty. I've grown tired of having a dowdy daughter. It's very depressing at my age."

"I'm not dowdy," she said, stung. "It simply isn't practical to wear anything but slacks most of the time. Stuart's house is lovely, but you never know when you're going to have to wade down the lane because it's waterlogged."

"That's reasonable," he allowed. "The driveway at this place is going to be resurfaced next week. I insisted, remembering the state that lane gets into. But even so, there's no need for you to dress like Calamity Jane all the time."

"I don't," protested Susanna. "Do I have to remind you that five days a week I used to work for Roger Thornfield? Solicitors don't like their secretaries to wear spurs in the office," she added sarcastically.

"I dare say not. But the things you did wear were hardly decorative."

She was torn between annoyance and curiosity. "I never realized you noticed or cared what I wore, daddy. I've never been very interested in clothes. I thought I looked reasonable."

"You looked neat and clean, like a Victorian parlormaid," he corrected. And as she choked with laughter added severely, "It's no laughing matter. It used to worry me. But I'm glad you've reformed. I hope you've brought a long dress with you this weekend."

Susanna was instantly suspicious. "Do you? Why? What have you got up your sleeve, daddy?"

"Me? Nothing. I just thought that if you're going to cook my breakfast and lunch I might take you out to dinner on Saturday night. In which case I would prefer you not to look as if you've just robbed a stagecoach."

She looked at him shrewdly. "Is that the truth?"

He laughed and dodged the question. "*Have* you got a long dress with you?"

"Yes, I have, as a matter of fact." She bit her lip. "But I don't know whether you'll approve. It's really only a summer dress. It's printed muslin with a big frill on the bottom. You won't find it very elegant, I'm afraid."

The lane narrowed, and the trees met above their heads. They plunged out of the pleasant twilight into blackness. Simon found the headlights and switched them on. There was a sudden blinding cone of light ahead of them, carving temporary clarity out of the trunks and bushes at the roadside.

Simon said abruptly, "Don't you want to be elegant, Sue? You're not unattractive when you want to be—why this resistance to fashion? Your mother was a fashionable woman."

For a moment, in her indignation, she was strongly tempted to say what she felt. "My mother was anything you wanted her to be. She dressed to please you, just as she played and worked and even thought to please you."

But she swallowed it and managed mildly, "I dress to please myself."

"And do you? Please yourself, I mean?"

She was rueful. "Less than I used to do since I've been living with Claire. Claire is stunning."

He considered this. "Claire is clever with clothes," he pronounced professionally, at last. "She puts a lot of thought into it. Now you . . . ."

"Are a hopeless case," Susanna supplied. "Never mind, daddy. You're quite elegant enough for both of us."

"You're just lazy," he accused. "You can't be bothered. . . ." He broke off, frowning. "And it's none of my business, I know. It's just that I hate to think of you living in Claire's shadow as you have been doing. She's a nice kid in her way. But you hardly have a great deal in common. And as for Stuart sending you off with her to mastermind her love life, he must be crazy."

"He didn't drive me out with whip and thong," Susanna objected. "I came of my own free will."

"Then you must have been crazy," her father said irritably.

"Yes, I think I was." Her tone was reflective. "At the time I thought Stuart was right—that Claire needed someone with her. She was so strange; nervous, even hostile, almost as if she were frightened and yet determined to go on. . . ."

"Hysteria." Simon braked at a sharp right-hand turn, and she shot forward, startled. "You should have worn your seat belt," he commented, unrepentant. Then, returning to the subject, "Claire is very like her mother. Kate always got hysterical over things she couldn't have. And she was so damned self-willed she'd go to any lengths to prove her point. I suppose Stuart was afraid Claire would try suicide."

"What?" Susanna was shocked as much by his indifferent tone as what he said. "Surely not?"

He shrugged. "Kate did—purely as a gesture. I wasn't impressed. Stuart was. So was Hamilton, poor fellow. Though I suspect he was a bit flattered, too. Hence the marriage."

"But surely—" Susanna thought of Claire as she had last seen her, bright-eyed and cheerful "—surely Claire is too sensible?"

He was turning into a pair of wrought-iron gates, overgrown with bramble. "I'll have to get someone to cut that down," he said in a preoccupied voice. "Claire? Oh, she's sensible enough. She's Hamilton's daughter as well as Kate's. I don't think she'd ever try to kill herself. But I do think she might go a little mad if she didn't get what she wanted. She'd get over it, of course, but in the meantime she wouldn't be very nice to live with. True?"

Susanna considered it. "Yes, I think so," she concluded slowly. "I don't know, because Giovanni—your Johnny—is being rather nice at the moment."

"To you," he said, amused, "or to her?"

"Her, naturally. I hardly ever see him. But at the beginning, when she was still suffering from, er, unrequited love, she was unbearable. I tried not to interfere. But it seems all right now."

He snorted, pulling up in front of a charming Queen Anne house. "Until Johnny goes marching home. Then the deluge." He got out of the car.

"Oh, well, let's forget that silly girl. This is supposed to be a holiday. Come and view my handiwork."

She did and was unexpectedly impressed. They went through a flagstone scullery to the kitchen. The remains of an ancient fireplace were visible. Simon had stripped the kitchen of most of its eighteenth-century features, however, and replaced them with large working surfaces and plenty of light.

"You should have seen it when I first came in," he said, pardonably proud. "Every time I stood up I hit my head on a beam. Riddled with worms, of course. They were just crumbling away. There was one little window above the sink and that was all."

Susanna looked at the huge window, which virtually covered one wall. "So you tore that wall out?"

He followed her eyes. "Oh, no. We knocked it about a bit, but the foundations and the central support remain as they were."

"Doesn't it—well—unsettle the place to be pulled around like that?" she demanded, fascinated.

"Undermine the fabric, you mean?" He shook his head. "Not if it's done properly. Oh, some old cottages might be shaky, I suppose. But this is a good stout little house. It was built by a prosperous gentleman farmer in the eighteenth century when prosperity bought something pretty permanent in terms of bricks and mortar."

"It looks it," she said dryly, looking at the window. "What did you do with the bricks and mortar out of there?"

Simon grinned. "Ah, I was rather clever. At least I think so, but I can see you aren't going to approve. The swimming pool that the previous owners built looked rather naked, so I, er, landscaped it."

"Land...?"

"Built a bit of a fringe around it," he said airily.

"In good crumbling eighteenth-century stone. It looks like a Versailles grotto—at least that's what I tell myself. Come and see."

"Daddy, you're outrageous!"

But she followed him. The pool was not a large one and was hidden from the garden to a great extent by a mass of tangled rosebushes.

"They want pruning," said Simon as they passed.

Where the rosebushes ended Simon had deposited his shattered masonry with a good deal of earth interspersed in which had been planted numerous rock plants.

"There you are," he said triumphantly. "Next spring a fairy pool."

"Chlorinated water and all," she agreed.

It looked inviting in the early evening shadows.

"I suppose—" she began.

"Yes, you can have a swim," her father said. "In spite of your insults. I'll take the cover off, and you can go and get changed."

Susanna looked at her watch. "But what about dinner?" she said, conscience-stricken. "After all, that's what I'm here for, aren't I? To cook."

He waved aside the objection. "You can cook to your heart's content tomorrow. There's always the pub tonight. Have your swim."

She took him at his word. Her bikini had been a last-minute addition to her suitcase and was easily extracted. She left the case by the car and went back to the pool. He had gone, and the swimming pool cover had been thrown carelessly under some birch trees at the edge of the garden. She changed quickly.

It was as well her father was not there, she thought. He would certainly not approve of her swimsuit, which was old and plain and infinitely more flattering to tanned skin. She stood still for a moment at the edge of the pool, savoring the twilight stillness and the smell of roses in the warm air. Then she plunged in.

The water was cool but not uncomfortably so, and she splashed about happily, turning somersaults. When she was exhausted, she turned on her back and floated, looking at the house. It looked very solid silhouetted against the evening sky. There were trees behind it, birch and oak, that might have been there since the house was built, she thought. There was an air of peace about the place. She had heard only one car pass by on the road while she was in the pool. For the rest, all she could hear were birds and the lazy hum of bees.

She got out regretfully. She was not cold, but she knew that she soon would be and cursed her stupidity in not providing herself with a towel. Perched on a tree root, with pieces of bark clinging to her wet skin, she turned the pile of clothes with her foot. Put them on? Or try to dry herself on a silk scarf? Susanna shook her head. No, the best thing would be to find her father and ask him to get the towel from her case. She stood up.

"Cold?" said a deep, amused voice that she knew instantly.

She froze, her thoughts whirling. What was he doing here? Had her father invited him? Was Claire with him? Had he been there all the time?

"N-not in the least," she denied untruthfully, and heard him laugh.

He strolled forward out of the shadows.

"Did you have a good swim?"

"Yes, thank you," Susanna said like a polite child. At a loss, she added, "What are you doing here?"

He bent over to pick up the plastic cover of the swimming pool.

"Here? I came out to see if you were ready to come and eat. You didn't seem to be—so I waited."

So he'd been lurking in the undergrowth, thought Susanna despairingly. And seen her romping like a puppy in the water. "I mean here at this house," she snapped, blushing unseen. "Did my father invite you?"

"Well, no, not really." He sounded apologetic, but she had the distinct impression that he was laughing at her. "Shall we cover the pool? Otherwise it gets full of twigs and rose petals. Which are quite poetic in their way, but the filter doesn't like them. Simon has had to have the filter unclogged twice so far, and he gets annoyed about it. Besides, it keeps the heat in."

As he directed, she took the other end of the plastic sheet almost in a dream. Between them they floated it on top of the water in silence.

"Thank you. Now it will be nice and warm for you to swim tomorrow morning if you want to," he said kindly.

An awful suspicion took hold of Susanna. He had sounded proprietorial.

"Daddy didn't ask you down here, did he?" she asked slowly.

"No." Giovanni gallantly gathered up her discarded clothes and motioned her to precede him into the house, "You could say I invited him."

Susanna began to shiver, more with temper than cold. So this was the identity of her father's client! He had taken good care to keep it a secret. He must have known she would never agree to spend the weekend in his house. She had been tricked. Irrationally, she found herself as angry with Giovanni di Montefiorino as with her father.

"And did you also," she said between her teeth, "invite me?"

He opened the heavy oak kitchen door for her to enter. "Of course," he said, surprised. "As soon as your father told me how worried he was about you. . . ."

"Worried about me!" She snorted. "All he was worried about was his stomach. He wanted a resident cook."

"Oh, you cook, do you?" Giovanni was pleased. He smiled down at her. "How fortunate. I thought Simon and I would spend all our time living out of tins and the village pub's meat pies. You are spending the whole weekend, aren't you?"

For a bewildering moment she stared up at him unbelievingly. Then, outraged, she grasped the truth. Simon had maneuvered her down here to cook for the pair of them while he worked and Giovanni no doubt lounged by the pool in the sunshine. She took a deep breath, preparatory to denouncing their deception, and found she was trembling.

"You *are* cold," he discovered. He urged her into the warmth of the kitchen, a solicitous arm around her shoulders. "Tonight there's no need for you to do anything," he explained generously. "Simon is heating some soup. You feel as if you need it."

Susanna sought in vain for words.

Her father was at the newly installed range, stirring something in a large pot. He looked up, a trifle anxiously she thought, as they came in. Giovanni exchanged looks with him, and Simon bent his head over the pot, stirring industriously.

"Ah, there you are," he said airily. "I was beginning to think Johnny had taken you into the woods to hear the nightingale. This stuff has lumps in it."

There was a pregnant pause. For a moment she

toyed pleasurably with the idea of sweeping out and leaving them to their own devices while she went back to London. But only for a moment. She was not dressed for dramatic exits, she thought wryly. The habits of a lifetime took over. The tension left her body and she laughed. Her host, reluctantly one might have thought, removed restraining hands from her shoulders. She went to her father and took the wooden spoon from him.

"You've overheated it," she said patiently, drawing the saucepan away from the hot burner.

She gave all her attention to the food. Her father, with a muttered excuse about garaging the car, disappeared. Giovanni watched her appreciatively.

"Have you been here long?" she said at last. His stare made her uncomfortable.

He stretched lazily. "No. I arrived after you. And found Simon here."

"Oh, yes, of course, I heard a car," she remembered. She sniffed the soup. "This would be better with some sherry or cream or something. I suppose it's too much to hope for?"

"I wouldn't know. I told the village grocer to send up a box of necessities."

"I don't think," she observed drily, "that sherry or cream would qualify."

He laughed softly and she turned an inquiring face to him.

For the second time that evening she blushed. Under his bright quizzical gaze her lashes fluttered down on her hot cheeks. She resumed her stirring with rapid uneven movements.

"Do you really intend to forgive us and stay here?"

She shrugged. "It's a free weekend in the country." She tried to sound indifferent. "With just the two of you to feed I needn't spend all my time cooking." A thought occurred to her. "I suppose it is just the two of you?"

Giovanni nodded solemnly. "Did you think your father would want you to cook for a house party?" he asked curiously.

"It wouldn't be out of character. He is—unpredictable." She discovered a French loaf on the windowsill and looked around for a bread knife.

"And would you have done it?" demanded Giovanni, still watching her.

She looked up at him suddenly, smiling. "Of course," she said serenely.

"You're very adaptable," he commented. His eyes lingered on her admiringly, and his mouth curled wickedly. "*Very* adaptable," he repeated.

Susanna was reminded of the bizarre figure she must make in her swimsuit at the kitchen range. Looking down at herself disparagingly, she chuckled.

"I ought to be wearing a white starched apron," she said with a rueful look at the oak beams. "And be head to foot in decent black."

He tilted his chair back and surveyed her under lowered lids. "Oh, I wouldn't say that," he drawled.

Flustered and determined not to show it, Susanna realized the only dignified course of action open to her was retreat. One hurried glance showed her that Giovanni was looking very pleased with himself. He rose. She fled.

In spite of its somewhat inauspicious beginning the weekend was delightful. Simon spent most of his time in an empty, first-floor room, which he grandly called his study, with numerous incomprehensible charts. Giovanni spent Saturday, as he complained to Susanna, collecting paint and carpets and meeting antiques off trains. On Sunday they disposed the antiques around the two rooms that were already decorated. Susanna cooked composedly meanwhile.

Giovanni had shown himself a little startled at the excellence of the food, but Simon was used to his daughter's skill and paid her no further tribute than to say that it would be a pity to go out for dinner on Saturday night when Sue could do all they needed very nicely at home. She had thanked him demurely for the compliment, but Giovanni had seemed uneasy at so much bland selfishness. Or perhaps, she had thought, it was not a guilty conscience so much as a fear of retribution. Probably he thought she would burn Sunday's lunch in revenge. But she was used to being taken for granted, she thought self-pitying. And anyway, it had meant she did not have to get dressed up. She was reluctant to expose the limitations of her wardrobe in Giovanni's worldly eyes. She thought of her gray Edwardian suit, long and graceful with its touch of magic, and regretted bitterly that she had left it in the apartment. It was paradoxically annoying that there would have been no opportunity to wear it even if she had brought it.

But that was the only annoyance in an otherwise perfect interlude. Sunday afternoon found Susanna snoozing among the roses, well content with her lot.

A shadow fell across her and she opened one eye. Giovanni, still dripping from his swim, was standing looking down at her.

"You look like the princess in the tower," he teased. "The one who went to sleep for a hundred years."

"Do I?" she was too drowsy to object as he settled himself down beside her. "The Sleeping Beauty?"

"That's the one. You have even," he leaned

across her and brushed something gently from her cheek, "got cobwebs on your nose."

"Haven't," she denied, without heat.

"Not cobwebs, perhaps. Leaves, though. And you've only been asleep since lunch. If you had been asleep a hundred years I would have had to dig very deep before I found you."

"And when you did," murmured Susanna, "I'd be covered in moldy rose leaves and fungus."

He shuddered. "Not nice to kiss at all." He leaned closer, and his breath fanned her cheek.

"And thorns," she added firmly, not opening her eyes.

"Horrible. It would be a brave man who kissed you awake."

"It's perhaps fortunate," said Susanna, tensing herself to resist further blandishments, "that I'm not asleep, and therefore not in need of waking."

There were movements beside her, but Giovanni was only stretching on the moss. He put his hands behind his head and looked dreamily up at the sky. She relaxed. A companionable silence ensued.

After a while she said idly, "Where's daddy? Still playing house?"

"Looking for a satinwood cupboard. He says I must have left it at the station. I don't remember it." Giovanni was dreamily indifferent. "If he can't find it, he's going down to the station."

"Oh."

There was another silence, longer this time, in which he appeared to go to sleep. Susanna moved a little away from him and sat up, resting her back against a gnarled tree trunk. She studied him thoughtfully.

Asleep he looked younger than she knew he must be. His dark hair was tumbled on his folded hands and had acquired its due complement of twigs and dust. The thick eyebrows which, when he was awake, so often frowned, in sleep gave him an oddly puckish air. He had a deep, even tan, which suggested that he had spent long hours sunning himself elsewhere than on a rose-scattered Kent hillside. She grinned to herself. Mediterranean sophisticate though he might be—Claire and Simon both insisted he was—at the moment he resembled nothing so much as a beguiling urchin. Awake he was formidable. Even when he was teasing her Susanna sensed a deep purpose in him that she did not understand but which warned her to tread warily. Asleep he was disarming.

With a little sigh of contentment she gave herself up to appreciation of her oblivious subject. He looked touchingly innocent. She knew an unworthy urge to smooth his hair and chided herself. Really, she was as foolish as Claire—and as encroaching. Giovanni did not want to be pursued by every woman he met. It was none of her business if a large, spiked rose twig attached itself to his hair. And yet he was so fast asleep . . . or was he? Very gently detaching the twig, Susanna saw indignantly that a faint disturbing smile was just touching the corners of the firm mouth.

"Well?" said Giovanni, not sounding sleepy at all. "Could you identify the body?"

She drew back, swallowing. He did not open his eyes. After a moment she said calmly, "Whoever pruned your roses left the remains on the ground. There was a nasty prickly bit in your hair. I removed it."

"How charitable!" He sounded ironic and even a little angry. "Is that why you were staring at me? Like a surgeon trying to decide where to slice."

"I didn't want to wake you," she retorted. "You seemed to be asleep. If you had been I wouldn't have disturbed you. Would I?"

He turned his head and looked at her. "No," he said after a moment's silent contemplation. "No, you wouldn't. You have a gentle touch. You're a very peaceful woman, Susanna."

She was amused. "That's more or less what my father said when he brought me down here. He didn't mean it as a compliment. Do you?"

"Of course," he said promptly. "Don't you think it's complimentary?"

"I do." Susanna looked at the vista of fields beyond the rose trees. They seemed to shimmer in the afternoon heat. She sighed. "I've spent half my life looking for peace. I value it."

"And have you found it?" His voice was grave. She gave him a quick suspicious look, but though he smiled at her there was none of that wicked teasing in his face. "Have you, Susanna?"

"I don't know," she said slowly. "One's ideas change, don't they? I thought I had found it. Before my grandfather routed me out of my stupor I thought I was happy in Sussex."

He took her hand and held it lightly. "You would be happy anywhere, Susanna. You have the art."

"No, I don't mean just the place. I was happy doing what I was doing. I was happy with the people I knew. I didn't keep asking myself all the time, 'Why do I do this?' 'Why am I not like that?' I didn't even worry whether what I was doing was worth doing. It was enough. And one day I would marry Roger and we would live near Stuart and...."

"Ah, yes, the rustic suitor." He spread out the fingers of her hand and inspected them closely. "No ring," he pronounced. "Therefore the lady is free.

Amazing, Holmes! On the other hand, no marks to suggest that there has been a ring and the ring has been returned. Therefore, my dear Watson, the lady has not made up her mind. She is, in fact, in limbo." His lids lifted in a sudden penetrating look. "Am I right?"

She tried to pull her hand away. He retained it easily, folding her fingers comfortably inside his own.

"Am I right?" he insisted.

"I suppose so," she said crossly. "I don't know who told you about Roger. I expect it was Claire, and I bet she wasn't—kind."

"It was not Claire," he said equably. "And is it unkind to say he's narrow and dull?"

"Was that what she told you?"

"Claire said nothing. I haven't discussed you with Claire. But that's what I was told, yes. Narrow and dull and death to your drawing. Is that unkind, or is it the truth."

She began to protest, paused and in her hesitation was lost.

"So you see," explained Giovanni, performing a complicated and expert contortion which brought her gently down on the moss with him leaning over her, "you are a sleeping beauty. And you do need waking up."

He proceeded to demonstrate.

After some considerable time during which Susanna had made only one intelligible remark—a weak and unconvincing, "Oh, no," to which Giovanni very sensibly paid no attention at all—she began to protest. He raised his head and eyed her reproachfully.

"What is it?"

Susanna closed her eyes briefly. Encouraged, he

bent over her again, only to be halted by a faint, deprecating cough. Displeased, he looked around.

"Don't let me interrupt," said Simon Shaw. He was grinning, thought his undutiful daughter, like a monkey. "I just thought I'd come and tell you I'm going to the station."

He paused hopefully.

"Good," said Giovanni.

"I can't find that cupboard. I know it was coming yesterday. Perhaps you missed it at the station. Do you remember how many boxes and crates you collected?"

"No," said Giovanni, not taking his eyes from Susanna's mouth which was still, to her chagrin, trembling.

"Oh." Simon's tones were wistful. "I thought you might come with me and show me where the other stuff was stored when you collected it."

Giovanni looked at him.

"No," he agreed. "No, I can see you won't. Well, I'll find it, don't worry."

"I won't."

"Er, no," agreed Simon, with a doubtful glance at Susanna. He began to back away. "Well, er, carry on." He raised a hand in farewell.

Susanna sat up briskly. In the distance Simon's car could be heard departing. Giovanni grinned.

"Enough," she stated quickly, "is enough."

One eyebrow rose, flagrantly teasing. She edged away.

"No," she said forcefully. "I daresay this is all very ordinary to you, but I usually spend my Sunday afternoons reading the color supplements."

He choked.

"Well, I do. I've never met anybody like you before." She recalled that Claire had said virtually the same thing about him. "You've been flirting with me," she accused.

He shook his head. "I know. It is shocking, isn't it? And now your natural protector has gone away and left you at my mercy." He leered at her.

"Giovanni!" She was on her feet and away down the hillside, half laughing, half alarmed. Behind her she could hear him roaring with laughter. She turned around and went back to him. Standing uneasily on the perimeter of the rose arbor, she watched his mirth in some dudgeon.

"You," she said resentfully, "are *not* very peaceful."

He raised his head from his hands. "Not like the absent Roger? Just as well. Too much peace is not good for you, Susanna."

"No?"

"No." He looked at her candidly. "Come, don't be angry with me. You sounded so . . . so prim. I couldn't resist teasing." Seeing she still frowned, he tilted his head up at her and said in a wheedling voice, "To make amends I will take us all out to dinner tonight."

"No more cooking?"

"Well," he said prudently, "there's always tomorrow morning."

She sighed. "Oh, very well. But I warn you," she said truculently, "I haven't anything grand to wear."

"Neither have I," he assured her mildly.

Her jaw dropped. "But daddy...."

"If Simon goes out to dinner in frilled shirt and a smoking jacket, he goes alone," Giovanni announced firmly. He stood up and hugged her briefly. "Susanna, you are a goose." He took her hand. "Come and paddle."

The rest of the afternoon passed pleasantly and

uneventfully. Simon returned with the missing furniture and was pleased to be told that Susanna was to be released from the kitchen.

"Although she likes cooking," he assured Giovanni, absently.

Susanna spent a good deal of time soaking in the despised bathroom before she emerged in her long muslin dress. Her hair, after its frequent dips in the swimming pool, was curling wildly, and she knotted it on top of her head in despair. She applied the Italian perfume that had been Claire's gift on her return, and then shook her head at her unsophisticated reflection in the mirror. When she went downstairs, one glance at Simon's face was enough to confirm her own estimate of her appearance.

"Neat and clean," he said resignedly, "as usual."

"I'm sorry, daddy, but if you wanted a daughter like Claire you should have worked at it."

"I know," he said gloomily.

"I think Susanna looks very charming," Giovanni interposed. "Like a shepherdess off a plate. Much too pretty to be crushed in the back of your old car, Simon. Or mine, for that matter. We shall have to take both cars."

"That's silly," Simon began to protest.

"Of course it is," agreed Susanna. "I can drive daddy's car and he can sit in the back. Then my dress won't get crushed."

"Why can't Johnny sit in the back?" he demanded.

"His legs are much too long, daddy." Susanna turned wide surprised eyes on him.

"We'll take both cars," he conceded hurriedly.

"Right." Giovanni was laughing. "Susanna can go with you and come back with me." Simon opened his mouth to protest. "That way I get to kiss the lady good-night," he explained.

The lady's father agreed to this disposal of her favors unhesitatingly and they set off.

"Have you enjoyed yourself, Sue?" he asked as they turned out of the gates. "I mean, you do like Johnny really, don't you?"

"He's amusing," she allowed.

"Yes." Simon sounded relieved. "Yes, I suppose he is. I've known him a long time, of course. I forget how he strikes strangers."

"He is not," she said with restraint, "precisely a stranger. He's been underfoot at the apartment for months."

"And you don't know what Claire sees in him," he supplied.

"Oh, no, I know what she sees in him all right." Susanna sighed. "I see all too clearly."

"Do you, Sue?" He sounded uneasy. He was concentrating fiercely on the road ahead, his brows knitted in a frown. "I've been feeling rather guilty about bringing you down here. I mean, I tricked you, didn't I? I didn't tell you Johnny would be here. When you said you didn't like him I thought it was all to do with Claire. It never occurred to me that you might be—well—personally involved."

"I'm not," she assured him. Unbelievably, it seemed that her casual father was trying to warn her against Giovanni di Montefiorino. A little late, she thought grimly. "I'm not."

He relaxed. "I'm glad. This afternoon when I interrupted you...."

"Him."

He gave a quick look sideways at her impassive face. "Interrupted him—I thought—that is, it occurred to me—"

"Yes?"

"Look, Sue, I don't want to interfere. Goodness

knows, it's none of my business. Johnny's a friend of mine. It's just that he's, er, very popular. Have a good time by all means, but don't get serious about him, like Claire did."

She was very cold in her pretty floral dress. "That way madness lies," she said lightly. "Don't worry, daddy, I'll keep a cool head."

He chortled, relieved, "Not too cool. You want to enjoy yourself," and closed the gap between his car and Giovanni's.

After that, of course, there was a certain restraint about the meal. Simon and Giovanni talked furniture for the most part while Susanna sat silently between them. Appealed to on the subject of pictures, she gave her opinion concisely and relapsed into silence again. Neither of her companions appeared to notice. And her anxious parent tucked her into Giovanni's car for the return journey with every appearance of serenity.

It was Giovanni who eventually broke the silence.

"My mamma would say that I ought to be making social conversation," he observed. "Am I boring you, Susanna?"

"No," she said, startled.

"Because you haven't said anything to me all evening. My mamma would say that I was either annoying you or offending you."

"Would she?" Susanna was fascinated. "Why?"

He looked at her, a quick gleaming look in the darkness. "Because my mamma is an expert on these things."

"What things?"

"The nuances of female temperament. She is an invaluable guide. Without her I would have married a bad-tempered harridan when I was twenty."

"Really?" Susanna was depressed. It was an effort to respond to his banter. "But your mother fought her off?"

"Yes. Every Italian mother regards it as her mission in life to protect her sons from designing women."

"How convenient!" Susanna could not prevent herself from sounding waspish.

"But it isn't. My mamma is in Italy. I am in England. Without a champion."

Was he, too, warning her off? She bit her lip. Shame surged through her, mixed with a kind of hurt anger. She drew further into her seat.

"Poor victim!"

"No," he said fairly. "It's not without its advantages. But it's very unnerving. I may find myself in love at any minute. It makes me jumpy."

"Rubbish," she snapped. She heard the viciousness in her tone and stopped. "I mean," she went on more moderately, "you don't just go splat and there you are—in love! It's a gradual process. You go through various stages. And you can draw back at any time."

"Can you?" His voice was quiet, but it demanded an answer. "Can you, Susanna?"

"Of course," she said sturdily.

He sighed. "How very English! Now Italian girls don't feel like that. Italian girls...."

But Susanna found she didn't want to hear about Italian girls.

"Haven't you missed the turning?" she said, not knowing or caring whether he had.

"No." Giovanni spoke evenly. "No, I don't think so. The gates are just around the corner."

They were. And as they pulled into the driveway she could see that Simon's car was already garaged. Giovanni drew to a halt outside the front door.

He did not move. Susanna found that the palms of her hands were wet with gripping them together. It seemed he was still interested in the philosophy of his countrymen.

"Italians," he ruminated, "look on love as a kind of divine madness. Inevitable, of course, but still madness."

She swallowed, but no words came. He drew her unresisting against his shoulder. His fingers were playing with her curls.

"Susanna," he whispered. "Lovely, lovely Susanna."

He kissed her for a long time, and this time he was not laughing. He was even a little cruel. When at last he let her go she could feel the anger in him. What was it Simon had said about Claire? That Johnny was out of her league. Simon would know. He and Giovanni were more than friends, they were two of a kind.

She drew away, her mouth stiff with the effort to control its trembling. Tears burned in her throat.

"Madness," she began. Her voice broke. She tried again. "Madness, I'm told, comes and goes with the moon."

She got out of the car. He made no move to stop her but sat very still watching her. She looked at the brilliant sky. A thin sliver of moon was all that it offered.

"And the moon's in its last quarter," she observed wryly. "New moon next week, Giovanni. Goodbye."

She walked away from the car. Once, she thought she heard him call her name, but she did not falter.

Madness, he had called it, and he did not lie. She must have been mad. And was still, she thought, looking blindly around the lighted kitchen.

She did not see her father, emerging quietly from the pantry, but he caught the despairing look on her face, and his heart sank.

"Sue?" he said diffidently, wanting to help, to take the expression of pain out of her eyes, not knowing how.

She found him. "Daddy, you were right. I should have listened to you. I overestimated my cool head."

He would have put his arms around her, but she shook her head.

"I'll be all right, daddy. Let me go to bed. But—I'd rather not see him in the morning. Could you—could you wake me when he's gone?"

Simon was dismayed. "But, Sue! You can't be serious. You—you're overwrought. Too much champagne."

"Too much of your precious Johnny," she lashed out. She pressed her fingers to throbbing temples. "Daddy, please!"

"No, no. This is melodrama."

She had once said much the same thing about Claire's agonies, she thought. Nemesis indeed! "All right, melodrama. I still don't want to see him again."

Simon was dismayed. "But—but—"

Help came from an unexpected quarter. "But you're going to work for me," said Giovanni from the doorway.

She whirled to face him, the muslin dress billowing.

"It's all arranged," he said expressionlessly. "Simon arranged it. My secretary—whom I believe you have met—is going home to stay with her fiancé's parents. Therefore I instantly need a secretary until head office sends a replacement. Preferably one who understands Italian. Simon offered you." A bleak smile. The anger he held in check was almost tangible. "I accepted. You're coming to work for me. Just," he added softly and very cruelly, "like Claire."

CHAPTER SIX

IT WAS A NIGHTMARE. Looking from Giovanni's impassive face to her father's anxious one, Susanna did not even try to conceal her dismay.

"Oh, no!" she cried.

Simon rushed in. "Don't be silly, Sue. It's not like you. Think how convenient it would be. It's very lucky that it should happen at just this time."

"Convenient for whom?" she demanded bitterly.

"You and Johnny both, of course." Simon was surprised. He saw the ironic smile playing about his friend's mouth and added hastily, "You said you needed money."

"Not that badly," said Susanna despairingly. "Oh, daddy, why didn't you ask me?"

He cast another quick glance at Giovanni. Susanna turned her back on them and stared blindly out into the darkened garden oblivious of this byplay. Giovanni ignored it. He was studying the back of her head with its revealingly disheveled curls.

Lacking help from that quarter, Simon said in an injured tone, "I wanted to surprise you."

She gave an unamused laugh. "You certainly did that!"

Again he looked appealingly at Giovanni, and this time it seemed that help was coming.

"You're not very flattering," he interposed, waving Simon out of the room. "Your father thought, as I did, that you would be pleased to have a ready-made job offered you—temporary, well paid and not boring."

"Yes, Sue. It wouldn't be dull," agreed Simon eagerly, at the door. And as she did not turn her head, he added, "I don't understand you, I don't really. Perhaps you can make her see sense, Johnny."

He shut the door smartly behind him. The sound brought Susanna spinning around. Indignantly she confronted Giovanni, now leaning negligently against the wall, his arms folded across his chest. He held her eyes calmly.

"Well?" she demanded.

He shrugged. "Your father is overly optimistic. No one could make you see sense at the moment. Nor even the demands of common politeness."

"Politeness?" she gasped.

His deep lids veiled his eyes. He appeared to be playing with some spent matches scattered on the table. "You've embarrassed your father," he pointed out. He made a careful square with the matches. "And you have left me in a considerable difficulty."

"I'm sorry about that," Susanna replied with awful sarcasm.

"You should be. It will be impossible to find an adequate secretary at a moment's notice. I could have found somebody last week if I'd known you would let me down. As it is—" He shrugged.

Susanna drew a long breath. "Are you trying to blackmail me?"

His eyes lifted at that. Their expression disconcerted her. He had seemed indifferent enough, a little displeased perhaps, but not overly concerned. But his eyes belied his cool voice. They were black with temper. She retreated instinctively. Swiftly his eyes were veiled again. He began to construct a triangle from the matches.

"Blackmail wouldn't do me any good. You're not in a mood to see reason."

Susanna's hands clenched on the sink behind her. "Reason! Are you out of your mind? I'm not the one who's being unreasonable. Do you really expect me to come and work for you, without a murmur of protest? What about Claire? What about—" She broke off, furious.

The fingers pushing the sticks around the table stilled. Not looking at her, he prompted gently, "About...?"

She flushed. "You—I mean, tonight," she muttered.

His eyebrows flew up, and he looked at her in honest puzzlement. "Tonight? What crime have I committed tonight—oh," as enlightenment dawned, "do you mean because I kissed you?"

She nodded silently.

He sighed. "Susanna, how old are you?"

"Twenty-four," she told him reluctantly. "What has that got to do with it?"

"In twenty-four years," he said patiently, "you must have been kissed before."

There was an outraged pause and then Susanna said viciously, "Not by prospective employers."

Unexpectedly he laughed. "Do you mean that honest Roger kept his hands off you?"

"Certainly. In the office," she said haughtily.

There was another silence while he measured her with his eyes.

Then, "So will I," he offered, more than a suggestion of laughter in his voice.

She glared at him.

"In the office," he added mischievously—and before she could find words to vent her feelings, added, "Look, Susanna, it's only for a couple of weeks. A month at the outside. And then you can go off to Paris or wherever artists go nowadays for the rest of the summer. I really would be grateful if you'd help me out. To be honest, I'm desperate."

She had the oddest feeling he was sincere and hesitated. It was not in her nature to be disobliging. If her father had offered her services to anybody else she would have gone uncomplainingly, and she was well aware of it. Nor was she entirely sure just why she recoiled so violently from working for Giovanni. It was an instinctive recoil that had nothing to do with Claire or her own disapproval of the man. It was almost as if she were frightened of him—which was ridiculous. And yet the suspicion remained, dark and unconfirmed, that she was somehow the victim of a conspiracy between her father and Giovanni, whose purpose she could not guess and yet was convinced was to force her along a path she would not have trod willingly. She put up her chin.

Giovanni saw the gesture and interpreted it in his own way. "Frightened?" he murmured provocatively. "Even if I promise not to assault you in working hours?"

Susanna drew herself up. "I'm not frightened of you or anyone else," she said untruthfully.

"Then come and work for me."

"On my terms?"

Suddenly he was impatient. "On any terms, so long as we can get it settled."

She sighed. It seemed inevitable. There could surely be no harm in it. And yet it was against her better judgment that she at last said reluctantly, "Very well. For a month, no more."

She looked sharply at him, but his face only registered tiredness. There was no unchivalrous signs of triumph.

"I'm overwhelmed," he said ironically. Standing upright, he stretched. "Lord, I'm tired! We'll work out the details in the morning. The best thing will be if I take you back to London and fill you in on the job on the way. You won't find it too difficult. Normally one of the juniors could take over quite well for the time being, but we're particularly busy at the moment, and I'm assured no one can be spared." He yawned again largely. "Oh—and Susanna, I'm sorry about—tonight." He imitated her phrase teasingly. "I didn't mean to upset you."

He lounged away from the table and came to her, taking her chin between finger and thumb. Susanna stared up at him mutely. She had the feeling that he was not nearly as sleepy as he said he was. He stared down at her thoughtfully.

"Are you a changeling, Susanna? You're a very strange person to find in your family. But having found you—" he pinched her chin indulgently "—I shall behave accordingly." He released her with an unexpected suddenness. Susanna gasped. Giovanni gave her a gentle smile. "Sleep well," he said.

When the door had closed behind him Susanna found herself staring at it stupidly with uncontrollable tears drying on her cheeks.

In the next week she found that Giovanni was as good as his word. The job was not unduly difficult, although she was very busy. The departing secretary proved to be the bright-eyed girl to whom she had spoken at Claire's party. Having worked for Giovanni for three years she had everything at her fingertips and initiated Susanna into the mysteries of banking routine with the minimum of fuss. To her relief, Susanna found that most of the business was conducted in English, and she only had to use her Italian on the telephone or occasionally in conversation with other members of the bank.

Giovanni, when he spoke to her, was impeccably polite in English. His secretary, who was used to an altogether friendlier approach, had looked a little startled at the formality with which he addressed Susanna. Not knowing that Susanna was grateful for it, she tried to excuse the lapse.

"He is worried at the moment," she explained. "His father is very ill. He feels he should go home more often, I know, but—" she hesitated and then said in a rush, "well, you'll find out soon enough, and I'm hardly breaching professional confidence to tell you—we're about to float a Eurodollar loan."

Susanna looked puzzled. "But don't you do that all the time?"

The other girl laughed. "Of course. But not big ones. This is enormous. It's the largest thing the Banco Montefiorino nas ever been involved in. It takes a good deal of work—and it has to be kept secret. And timed properly. Giovanni has to keep his thumb on the pulse of the market all the time. When he decides the moment has come—pouf—we, or rather you, will all work like mad for forty-eight hours and then collapse."

"It sounds exciting," Susanna observed, surprised.

"It is. But it also means that Giovanni hasn't been back to Italy since the pressure came on. And he won't go back until it's off and the loan has been floated. So he worries."

Rather unkindly Susanna remarked that she had not noticed signs of undue worry.

"Haven't you?" She found herself being studied with some amazement, "Ah, but then you haven't known him very long. He's very quiet and sober at the moment."

"He certainly seems to be working very hard,"

admitted Susanna. She had been surprised to find how seriously Giovanni took his career. He was often at his desk long after his staff left, she knew. Frequently he looked pinched and tired in the morning, too, but she was more inclined to ascribe that to the toll his amusements took. She could not imagine him working over his papers late into the night however severely he might drive himself in his office.

Fortunately he worked so hard that there was little time for him to exchange more than the usual courtesies with Susanna. She had resolved to set and maintain a great distance between Giovanni and herself and had found, a little ruefully, that this was hardly necessary. He was polite. He was not unamiable. And he was totally preoccupied. Instructions came for him almost daily from Italy in the heavy white envelopes with the Montefiorino crest embossed on the back. Susanna quickly learned not to open these, but to lay them on his desk as soon as they arrived. Nor did she open the airmail letters that came by express post from Florence. She had been told that these were from his mother. They became increasingly frequent until, at the end of her month with him, they were arriving every day. After reading them he would often emerge from his office looking bleak and plunge into a fury of dictation.

At these times her kind heart nearly got the better of her, and she was often tempted to break her resolve not to get involved with the devastating director of the Banco Montefiorino. Only the reflection that he would hardly welcome expressions of sympathy from her restrained her. On one such occasion he interrupted her conscientious typing abruptly.

"Susanna, would you see if you can book some rooms in a London hotel for some friends of mine?"

She took up her pencil and note pad. "Of course. How many rooms? When will they be arriving."

He ran his hands through his hair. "Next week, damn it."

"Next week?" She gaped at him. "But there won't be anything—not in London. Not at a moment's notice."

"I know, I know." He looked at her almost beseechingly. "I could have told them—but look, Susanna, they're friends of my father's. In fact, they're his guests really. I shall have to do something, even if it means putting them up myself. Phone around and see what you can find. A suite, a penthouse, anything."

"I'll try," Susanna said doubtfully. "Who is it for?"

He smiled at her gratefully. "A Signora and Signorina Gabrielli, a mother and daughter. I'm sure they wouldn't mind sharing a bathroom or a sitting room."

"How fortunate," said Susanna waspishly, envisaging an afternoon calling hotels.

He leaned on her desk, over the typewriter. "Don't," he advised, "try my patience, Susanna. I've had a good deal to put up with this last few weeks. Not the least from you. If you make me angry I might say something we shall both regret afterward."

Indignant at this unprovoked attack, Susanna defended herself. "I don't see what I've done to upset you. I do my work as well as I'm able. You knew when you bullied me into it that I would be ignorant."

He made a helpless gesture. "You do your work admirably—as you know. But when I walk into the office in the morning the temperature is arctic. I cower behind that door—" he waved a dramatic hand at his office "—and feel your disapproval through heaven knows how many thicknesses of wood. What's the matter with you, Susanna? Would it hurt you to unbend a little?"

Oddly, he made her feel ashamed of herself and her petty resolve to keep him at a distance. "No, of course it wouldn't," she answered him honestly. "I didn't know you wanted me to. I'm sorry."

Interrupted in the middle of a diatribe, he seemed to find himself without anything to say. His hand fell and he stared at her disconcertedly. Then, "Truce?" he demanded suspiciously.

She smiled at him. Susanna's smile was one of her greatest charms, warm and unaffected, and he had been offered a glimpse of it on too few occasions. Giovanni blinked.

"Truce," she agreed solemnly.

"And you'll find these rooms for me?"

"I'll do my best," she temporized. "But you know...."

"Yes, I know." He straightened, sighing. "Anyone but my father and I'd write and tell him how impossible it is to wave a wand and produce London hotel rooms out of midair. But I can't do that to my father."

Susanna looked at the names on her pad. "I know," she said in a low voice. "I wanted to tell you. I'm sorry."

He looked a little startled. "Er, thank you." He moved away. "Let me know if you find anything. Oh, and tell them to send the bill to us here."

"I take it the cost is unimportant?"

"Of course," said Giovanni serenely, a look of secret amusement on his face. "Of course."

The search proved an extended one as Susanna had prophesied and she was not in a very good mood when she reached the apartment that evening.

Claire was already there, the windows flung open to the dusty evening air and a large jug of ice-cold lemonade sitting temptingly on the windowsill. She looked up as Susanna came in.

"You look hot, Sue," she remarked. "Bad day?"

"Horrible," her cousin agreed, flopping onto the couch.

"I thought there must be some crisis on hand when you didn't turn up for lunch," said Claire tranquilly. "Want to talk about it?"

Susanna had at first been afraid that Claire would resent her working at the Banco Montefiorino. It had the look of deliberate spying and Susanna would not have blamed her. However, Claire had received her advent almost with relief. It occurred to her cousin that she was finding the discipline of working for someone else a little harsh. Claire, after all, was still a schoolgirl in age, she reminded herself. And she was beginning to look drawn and discontented. They saw very little of each other during the day but usually contrived to meet for lunch, and on these occasions Claire seemed subdued. She continued to spend most of her evenings out of the apartment but, Susanna suspected, fewer and fewer of them were spent in Giovanni's company. At any rate Claire had become less wary and ready to take offense at her cousin's mildest remarks.

Now she poured lemonade into a frosted glass and brought it to Susanna.

"Thank you." Susanna took a refreshing drink. "I didn't even get any lunch today. I've been gasping."

Claire nodded sympathetically. "It's hell at the moment. I've been locked in my cubbyhole translating a report on closed-circuit television systems, of all things. I suppose it's to do with this X International loan everyone's talking about. Giovanni seems to be working on it eighteen hours a day. I haven't seen him for weeks."

"He's very busy," agreed Susanna. "He seems to spend so much time in the city with other bankers that all his paperwork has to be done after everyone else has gone home. Fortunately he hasn't asked me to stay late yet."

"Would you?" demanded Claire curiously.

Susanna grimaced. "Claire, look at me, I'm exhausted! The phone doesn't stop ringing all day. Of course I wouldn't, if I could get out of it." She stretched. "I'm all sticky," she complained. "And bad tempered. He wanted me to book hotel rooms today—for next week, if you please. I must have phoned every hotel in London."

"So it's true," said Claire. Her shoulders dropped.

"True?" Susanna was lost.

"That the neglected fiancée has pursued him to London. I'm not altogether surprised. Though I bet it wasn't Paola's idea."

Susanna closed her eyes. "Claire, I've had a long, hard, hot day and my brain is not at its clearest. If you have a point, make it. If not, stop twittering."

"It's not a point that will interest you," said Claire stiffly. "Merely—Paola Gabrielli is about to heave into view. Isn't she the girl you had to get rooms for?"

Susanna's brow creased. "I don't remember the name. I wrote it down, but . . . . It's a mother and daughter," she added helpfully.

Claire's brows rose. "Signora Gabrielli? Good lord! I thought the old *marchesa* would come to do her own dirty work. But I suppose with her husband ill she thinks she ought to stay at home."

"Do I understand that there's a formal engagement?" Susanna was intrigued. In her experience

Giovanni did not behave as if he had any commitments to any woman in the world.

"There will be," Claire said grimly. "His mamma has been working on it." She bit her lip. "It's an understood thing. The Gabriellis are partners in most Montefiorino projects. In one way, I suppose it was inevitable. But the *marchesa* didn't really start pressing it until last year, when he started taking me around. If she's despatched Paola to London, without coming herself to oversee proceedings, she must think things are pretty desperate. Poor old Giovanni! And poor me."

Susanna was amused. "Is she really so terrible?"

"Paola? Paola's a spiteful little bitch," said Claire with feeling.

"I remember Giovanni telling me that his mother regarded it as her sacred duty to protect him from designing women."

"You can laugh," said Claire resentfully. "You haven't been on the receiving end of the old hag's protective instincts. And Giovanni thinks she's perfect." She lighted a cigarette and drew a long breath of smoke into her lungs. Her mouth twisted at the taste. "Oh, well, it had to come."

"What had to?" Susanna tried to infuse her tone with sympathy but only succeeded in sounding weary. Claire did not appear to notice.

"This. It's the end of Giovanni and me. He'll be married by the autumn—you wait and see."

But Susanna was too busy to speculate on his marital intentions. The next week was desperately full, and she never managed to snatch more than a cup of coffee at her desk at lunchtime. She saw little of Claire, who, perhaps sensibly, played tennis every evening until the light failed. She saw even less of Giovanni, who communicated with her by dictaphone and scribbled notes that she found on her desk in the morning. Her month was up, but no replacement secretary had arrived from Italy and she had not the heart to leave.

He was out on the day that the Gabriellis were due to arrive, and in the absence of specific instructions, Susanna sent a car to meet them and take them to their hotel. She then dismissed them from her mind and settled down to typing the numerous letters that Giovanni had already dictated.

She was, therefore, totally unprepared for Paola Gabrielli's descent upon her office in the afternoon. She had just finished a particularly complicated telephone message to an absent colleague of Giovanni's and had prevailed upon the messenger boy to bring her an ice-cream cone when he returned from dispatching the lunchtime post. So she had pushed her chair away from her desk, kicked off her shoes and tucked her legs under her and was licking luxuriously when the door of her office was thrown open and in stalked an infuriated beauty.

Susanna's first thought was that her visitor looked like the malevolent witch-queen from her childhood fairy-tale book. So amazed was she by the apparition that she sat staring, her mouth open foolishly and the ice-cream cone poised like the Olympic torch.

"What," demanded the visitor, "is this?"

Susanna got to her feet, running the back of her hand across her mouth, which was generously smeared with ice cream. A little helplessly she looked around for somewhere to place the cone and ended by balancing it precariously in a thick, glass ashtray. She rubbed her sticky hands down her creased poplin slacks.

"Can I help you?" she said weakly.

The beauty surveyed her. "Where is the *marchese*?" she snapped.

"The—the—which *marchese*?"

"Are you stupid? The Marchese di Montefiorino, of course. Where is he? Why did he not meet me at the airport?"

Susanna swallowed. "Are you—I mean, forgive me, but surely you must be the Signorina Gabrielli?"

The lady's eyes were not friendly. "Of course," she said disdainfully. "Please answer my question."

"The *marchese*?" Susanna shook her head, bewildered. "But I thought he was ill and still in Italy. I'm afraid I haven't his address...."

The Italian girl clicked her tongue impatiently. "Don't be insolent! You know perfectly well who I mean."

Susanna knit her brows. "Giovanni?" she hazarded tentatively. Now she came to think of it, that was how his letters had been addressed, but as he always signed his own correspondence with a boldly legible flourish he never required her to type in his name and title and so she had dismissed it from her memory.

Paola Gabrielli looked affronted. "Certainly I call him Giovanni," she said with emphasis. "But surely it is a great impertinence for you to do so?"

As this had not previously occurred to Susanna she was disconcerted. "I suppose it is," she admitted after a moment. "I'm sorry, Miss Gabrielli, but he's out at the moment."

"Where?"

Susanna began to feel hunted. She could hazard a guess as to Giovanni's whereabouts, but was also fairly sure that he would not welcome the interruption of even so decorative a lady as Paola Gabrielli into delicate and confidential negotiations.

"I'm not altogether certain," she temporized. "But he usually telephones during the afternoon if he's not going to be back before I leave. If you care to go back to your hotel I'll tell him you've arrived and want to see him...."

She broke off at the undisguised fury in the other girl's face.

"You will not tell me what to do—" she began in a venomous tone, but Susanna's attention was distracted by the imminent dissolution of her ice cream.

She scooped it up, looked around wildly for blotting paper and finding none licked the drips comprehensively from the side of the cone. To Paola it was a calculated insult. She began to rage in Italian. Listening, shocked, to the display of temper Susanna reminded herself that Miss Gabrielli did not know she spoke Italian and so could understand every uncomplimentary word.

Even in a tantrum, she thought dispassionately, Paola was a very pretty girl. Not tall herself, she was a giant beside the dainty Italian. Dark expressive eyes were set under delicately etched brows in a heart-shaped face full of character. Noting the petulant mouth and the whole suggestion of evil temper in that face, Susanna was sure that such unattractive features were only permitted to reveal themselves to subordinates whose opinions did not matter. She took another quick necessary lick at her ice cream and Giovanni walked in.

Instantly Paola stopped ranting. She gave a little gasp, rearranged her expression to one of melting grief and cast herself upon the new arrival. He greeted her enthusiastically. Susanna finished her ice cream unobstrusively.

Eventually Giovanni held the girl away from him.

"Paola, my dear, you look lovely. I meant to meet the plane, but I got held up."

"I was sure something must have happened," she said, with a triumphant little glance at Susanna, now hunting for her shoes under her desk. "So I let mother take your car to the hotel and came straight here by taxi."

Giovanni looked startled. "My car?"

Susanna held his eyes compellingly. "I sent the chauffeur to collect Signora Gabrielli at the airport, as you told me." His surprise turned to amusement as she added with belated conscientiousness, "Sir."

"Of course," he said smoothly. "I forgot. I was at a conference, Paola, and I've only just emerged. In fact I've got to go back at once to collect some papers they're having made up for me."

She pouted charmingly and protested.

"No, really! I only dashed away to, er, see if Miss Shaw knew whether you had arrived."

Which, thought Susanna cynically, was probably true.

"I'm sorry—" he said apologetically but firmly.

"But you can't leave me so soon. I've got lots of messages from your mother."

"Yes, I'm sure," he said patiently. "But I can't wait. Those things have to be collected."

"Send someone else," she offered caressingly. "Send Miss er, then you can take me to lunch."

"Paola—" he began, but she interrupted by winding her arms around his neck and kissing him.

Susanna curbed a desire to detach the clinging creature and averted her eyes tactfully. She heard Giovanni laugh.

"Oh, very well. Susanna?"

She looked at him.

"Would you mind?" he asked winningly. "You

could take my car as Signora Gabrielli has the bank's chariot. Or better still take Claire, and she can drive you. Then you won't have to park it. She can drive around until you emerge."

Susanna, thinking of Claire's new license and Giovanni's new car, shuddered. "I'll take George," she said firmly. "From the statistics section," she explained as he knitted his brows.

He looked as if he would argue, but Paola was tired of the subject, and he had little alternative but to acquiesce

"Very well," he said as he was being urged out of the door. "But tell him to be careful. If he gets caught for speeding I won't pay his fine."

"I'll tell him," Susanna promised, and telephoned the statistics department.

George was delighted to leave his computer for the sunshine. He had already settled himself in Giovanni's car and was awaiting her with a pleased expression when she came out of the elevator.

She climbed in beside him as he said, "You know, it's a shame to run a beautiful machine like this in the city."

"Well, don't run it too fast," she said, passing on Giovanni's message and adding, "I think he meant it."

George shrugged, swinging the car up the ramp and out of the underground parking area. "He's had his knife into me for weeks. Forget it. Where are we going?"

She told him and he groaned. "Cheapside at this hour! I'll be lucky if his precious car doesn't get scratched to ribbons. Oh, well, it's an hour off, I suppose. Could we squeeze in a drink, do you think?"

Susanna laughed. "Definitely not. It's too hot.

I'm too busy and the whole object of your coming with me is that I don't go mad trying to find somewhere to park."

"It would be worth it," he said gloomily.

"I'll pick you up a popsicle," she promised, and told him about her encounter with Paola Gabrielli and the ice cream.

When he finished laughing he said soberly, "Be careful, Sue. She's a nasty enemy, and she's a lady with a lot of power around here."

"So Claire said." Susanna shrugged. "That's all right. I'm only temporary."

"Huh," said George disbelievingly, snaking to a stop outside a concrete-and-glass building. "Off with you. I'll drive around the block and see you back here."

He was as good as his word and in ten minutes they were speeding back. The traffic was dense and the sun glinted blindingly on the metaled roads and gleaming car hoods. More than once she saw George wincing as if he were dazzled or in pain. Waiting at traffic lights to turn left, he ran a finger around the inside of his collar. His forehead was beaded with sweat.

"I should have brought my sunglasses," he said, starting off with a jerk and turning the corner too sharply.

The Banco Montefiorino was on the right. A steady stream of cars came toward them and George braked hard in the middle of the road. Susanna rocked with the machine as it lurched forward and found that she felt a little sick. She would be glad to be back in her cool office.

George saw an opening in the traffic and darted into the gap. His hands were wet on the wheel and it slipped in his fingers. Panicking, he braked, skidded, braked again as, with a screaming of torn metal, another car ripped into the side of them.

Susanna, faintly surprised, was aware of a pain that surged through her body like a thunderbolt as she was flung forward, and for a moment, she knew no more.

When she stirred she found she was no longer among the hot leather of the car seats but, blessedly cool, was being carried down a subdued corridor. It was not an unpleasant sensation, and she stirred comfortably like a cat stretching.

"Be still," said a voice that she ought to know.

Obediently she subsided. Her brain felt light and helpless. She could not remember where she was or what she was doing or meant to be doing. All that was obvious to her was the feel of cool silk under her cheek and a warmth behind it against which she rested contentedly like a child.

Eventually she was set down, and she murmured complainingly. She tried to cling to unreality, but all too soon she began to recover.

"No," she whimpered, creasing her eyelids against the light. "No!"

Whoever it was who had held her so gently drew away. Her hands fluttered after him and fell. Tears began to surge in a painful silent tide down her face. She had a confused impression of activity. Doors opened and shut and somewhere in the distance, she could hear George's voice, loud and defensive, and smoother professional tones in her ears.

At a sudden stab of pain, she opened her eyes. A harassed-looking man was running his hands around the base of her skull. He smiled down at her abstractedly.

"How do you feel? Is there any pain?"

Her eyes closed briefly. "N-no."

"No headache? Do you feel hot? Sick? Dizzy?"

She bit her lip. "Yes. No. All of those. Mostly sick, I think."

There was a sharp movement behind the doctor. Her eyes flew open and found Giovanni standing with Paola by the window. The doctor must have heard it, too. He straightened and turned to him.

"She's in shock," he said briefly. "No other damage that I can find. We'll take some X rays just to make sure. But I'm pretty certain she'll be all right." He smiled down at Susanna reassuringly. "It won't take long. You'll be home in a couple of hours. I'll call an ambulance."

The door closed behind him. Giovanni was staring at her with a very strange expression on his face. Paola took his arm. Susanna stared at the bloodred nails against the silk of his shirt until they danced, enormous, in front of her eyes. With a little moan of pain she turned her head away from them.

"She *is* hurt," she heard him say.

"Nonsense," said Paola briskly. "The doctor told you. With the heat and probably no food except that disgusting ice cream she just fainted from shock. Leave her alone. She's weak, not injured."

But she was, thought Susanna, as the door closed behind them. Mortally injured. She had committed the final appalling folly of falling in love.

CHAPTER SEVEN

THE JOURNEY in the ambulance was hot and uncomfortable, and Susanna found the pain in her head redoubled. No one came with her and for what seemed ages she lay uncomplainingly on a stretcher in the radiology unit. When the X rays had been duly taken she asked, childishly, for permission to leave, at which the young radiologist looked faintly shocked. Eventually she was taken to an empty room at the end of the corridor where, at least, she fell asleep.

Sometime later she sat up wearily, pushing her fingers through her hair. The electric clock above the foot of her bed said nearly six. She must have slept a long time—although it had hardly felt like sleep, she thought wryly. The half-subdued images of her unpleasant dreams clung about her like cobwebs. She shook her head impatiently. She was feeling the pressure of a hard week's work and the insufferable city heat, she assured herself. No more than that. When she got home to Sussex and had time to put things into perspective, she would realize how impossible it was that she should really be in love with Giovanni di Montefiorino. She was no child and no innocent. She knew his reputation, and she had experienced enough of his charm to be sure it was deserved. He was not the sort of man she could imagine herself being in love with for long.

But the pain lingered like a toothache.

She looked around, wondering vaguely how to announce to the world that she was awake when the door suddenly swept open. A nurse appeared with, mysteriously, Giovanni at her shoulder.

"How are you now, then?" she demanded cheerfully.

"Oh—fine," said Susanna, confused.

"There," said the nurse, beaming at Giovanni. "I told you. They don't need any more X rays, and you can take the lady home as soon as she feels well enough. I looked in earlier," she told Susanna, "but you were fast asleep. I'll just get your purse and you can be going. You'll be glad to get home."

She bustled out past the frowning Giovanni. He came into the room looking very grim.

"Are you better now?"

"Y-yes, thank you." Susanna found her voice faltered and was angry. "I'm sorry to be so silly."

"You're not silly," he said curtly. "You're exhausted. I've been overworking you. You should have told me. Now you'll be ill."

He did not look very healthy himself, she thought. Under the even tan the skin of his face was taut and there were greenish shadows under his eyes.

"I'm all right," she said deprecatingly. "It's just the heat. We both felt it, George and I. How is George?"

"Worried." His tone was vicious.

"Worried? Why?"

"He nearly had you killed, and he quite wrecked my car."

She remembered the thud as the two vehicles collided and winced. He saw it.

"Don't think about it," he said roughly. "I shouldn't have reminded you."

"I don't remember much. It must have been

worse for George. After all, he was driving. He isn't hurt, is he?"

There was a little silence before Giovanni said expressionlessly, "No. The other car hit you broadside, right across the passenger seat. Fortunately he wasn't going very fast."

"Poor George," she said compassionately.

He gave a mirthless laugh. "And poor me! Paola and I were just coming back. We saw it happen."

Susanna stared at him. Rigid, he was standing with his back to her looking out at the street. She had the impression that he was not seeing the scene in front of him at all. His voice was clipped. She had the feeling that he had been very badly frightened.

"I'm sorry," she said helplessly.

"You're sorry!" He swung around on her fiercely. "Susanna, I—"

But the door opened again and the friendly nurse came in.

"There you are," she said. "Your purse is in a bit of a state, I'm afraid. Still, it could have been you. Look on the bright side, that's what I always say. I've told the porter you're leaving. If you'd just sign on your way out."

Torn between the ruins of her purse and Giovanni's appalled face Susanna found herself giggling hysterically. It had certainly come off badly in the impact. It had been ripped apart. Somebody had bundled all her possessions onto it as if it were a piece of newspaper. His brows twitched together. He bundled it up unceremoniously under his arm.

"I'll get you another," he snapped. "Get up if you're going to. I'm driving you home."

"No!" She recoiled sharply.

"Not in the Maserati—your boyfriend effectively disposed of the inside door. I've got the bank's Austin here. You can sit in the back if you like."

Susanna trembled. Now that she knew the state of her treacherous heart she did not want to be alone with him. What if she were to give herself away? What if he already guessed and that was why he was being so considerate?

"I would rather not—" she began, but he stopped her.

"You have no choice," he said firmly. "The only say you have in the matter is whether you feel strong enough to walk to the lift or whether I borrow a wheelchair."

"I can walk," she murmured.

He looked down at her, a faint smile breaking through the unfamiliar sternness. "Then walk," he said, offering his arm.

They did not talk on the way back to the apartment. Susanna was still shaken at finding herself again among London traffic, although the afternoon temperature had subsided and a cooling breeze came through the open windows. Giovanni seemed preoccupied, even remote. Although he was faultlessly kind, Susanna felt his mind was on other things. From the look of his face, rather disquieting things. And it seemed to her that it was with relief that he eventually handed her over to Claire.

Claire was nearly hysterical. Sent home with instructions to prepare to receive an injured Susanna, she had been told neither the extent of the damage nor when to expect her. Consequently she had waited, in a fever of apprehension, for nearly four hours. All possible comforters from barbiturates to a hot toddy had been prepared. Susanna must go to bed at once. Susanna must see a doctor. Susanna must not think of going to work tomorrow.

Susanna set herself to calm her.

But Claire had been badly frightened. "Why

didn't Giovanni take you straight to the hospital?" she raged. "Why didn't someone call me? George said you were as white as a sheet."

"George?"

"He's been phoning every ten minutes or so to find out how you are. He wanted to stay with you, but Giovanni threw him out. He's been out of his mind."

"Oh, dear," said Susanna guiltily. "What a fuss about nothing! If he phones again I'll tell him to stop worrying."

"No, you won't." Claire was autocratic. "You won't tell him anything because you're not speaking to him. I will tell him you're resting. And you will be," she insisted as Susanna opened her mouth to object. "We're both having an early night. You've had a shock, though you may not want to admit it. And so," she added dryly, "have I. Bed, Susanna, before you collapse."

Eventually her well-wishers did not allow Susanna to return to the bank until after an extended weekend. She was grateful for their kindness but would infinitely have preferred to be at work. It would have distracted her from her new-found problem.

As it was she occupied her time by sketching Giovanni from memory. She had never had a flair for portraiture, and she found it extraordinarily difficult to achieve a likeness. Superstitiously she felt that if she could paint him it would in some way exorcise his image. Once trapped on canvas she could banish him to a dark cupboard—or even paint over him. And he would cease to trouble her dreams.

While Claire was out Susanna would pin her experimental sketches around her studio and try to paint. She felt embarrassed and even a little ashamed of what she was trying to do and never allowed Claire to guess at it. For her part Claire, knowing that Susanna had hesitated a long time before beginning to use paint, tactfully made no inquiries.

Nevertheless Susanna was glad to return to work. She was painting well, she knew, but it was disturbing to spend her days coaxing Giovanni's features out of the shadows she had bestowed on her canvas. She had an uncomfortable feeling that she was creating him in her own image, resembling her, pleasing to her, and it seemed to diminish his stature. She was glad to put it away although it was only half-finished.

Although there was a great deal to do when she finally sat down at her desk, she saw little of Giovanni during the next weeks. He seemed to have forgotten altogether that she was supposed to be temporary and gave no sign that another secretary would ever arrive from Italy. She would almost have thought, if it had not been nonsense, that he was avoiding her.

However little she saw of him, Paola Gabrielli spent a good deal of her time sitting around in Susanna's office waiting for Giovanni to telephone. Susanna found it rather trying as she liked the Italian girl no better on further acquaintance and, in any event, had enough to do without running the errands that Miss Gabrielli felt she was entitled to impose on her. She managed to remain civil, but could never be as servile as Miss Gabrielli seemed to expect.

In particular, she resented her attitude toward George. Susanna had always had a great deal to do with the statistics department in the course of her work, and since the accident, George had constituted himself her guardian. Therefore, he often dropped into her office and usually stayed for coffee when he did so. Susanna was so busy that he mostly made it himself, but he did not seem to mind. He did not even mind making coffee for Paola Gabrielli when, as all too often happened, she was present. So that her rudeness to him was all the more unforgivable.

"Does Giovanni know how much time you waste with Miss Shaw?" she demanded nastily one day.

George chuckled. "I expect so."

But Susanna had been angry. Taking a sheaf of papers from him, she had said evenly, "Collating the computer printouts is part of my job, Miss Gabrielli. Without George's assistance I couldn't do it."

The other girl had laughed dulcetly. "Then the sooner he finds someone more competent, the better."

Susanna bit her lip. It was hurtful to be told the truth in such a way. But it was not in her to deny that it was the truth. "Of course," she agreed quietly. "But while I'm here I'll do my best. So I'm sure you'll forgive me if I ask you to go so that I can concentrate."

"Are you dismissing me?" Paola Gabrielli demanded disbelievingly. The large eyes stared at Susanna, who returned the gaze steadily.

"If you'll excuse me...."

With a squeak of pure rage the other girl swung on her heel and swept out.

"Game, set and match," said George, amused. He plugged in the electric kettle. "At least we can have our morning refreshment in peace."

Susanna found she was trembling with suppressed fury. "Yes," she agreed unsteadily. "But I think you're wrong, George. That was only round one, and I would say the honors were even."

"Ah, but the onlooker sees more of the game." He brought her coffee. "If you ask me, the lady's jealous."

"Jealous?" She took a quick sip of the scalding liquid. "Jealous? Of me?"

"Yup. Giovanni likes you. He trusts you. He leaves you alone to get on with your work without popping in every half hour like a slave driver. In fact, he treats you as an adult. Can you ever see anybody treating that young lady like that?"

"He doesn't have to treat her like that," she objected justly. "She doesn't work for him."

George laughed. "She wouldn't be given the chance. She's strictly for amusement only. But because you're not—and because he was so worried about you after the accident—she thinks you have something special for him. You and I know it's nonsense, but that's the way her mind works. She was there when he got you out of the car, and she heard the things he said to me." He made a face. "He has an evil temper, and he was very fluent. And I'd just ruined his brand-new Maserati. Obviously it was nothing to do with you, really."

"Obviously," agreed Susanna, depressed.

"But you can't expect Paola to see it like that. After all, she has a lot to lose. She hasn't come all this way, and with mamma's blessing, to let him get away now."

Susanna rocked back in her chair thoughtfully. "You really do think he'll marry her?"

He perched on the edge of her desk. "Certain to, I'd say. He's walking very warily. He has even—" a bitter note crept into his voice "—stopped seeing Claire."

"I know," she said. "But I thought—well, I don't know what I thought. Except that I wouldn't have expected him to do what his family told him to do quite so meekly. Claire said he would marry Paola, but it seems so cold-blooded. Not like him."

George considered it interestedly. "I don't suppose it is like him," he said at last. "Or at least as he would like to be. But it's the way he's been brought up. The divine right of money. You can't understand it, Sue, anymore than Paola Gabrielli can understand you. You just have to accept that it exists and forget it if you can. After all, you're going back to college in the fall. Then you can forget all this."

She agreed without noticeable enthusiasm, and he left her.

Meanwhile Paola and her mother remained ensconced in their hotel running up bills that made Susanna, who paid them, raise her eyebrows. Giovanni, however, seemed unconcerned and even warned her that there would be a new spate of them when the Gabriellis gave a cocktail party at the end of the month.

"I told Paola to go to a caterer's and charge everything to me," he told Susanna lightly. "Don't query the account, just pay it." As she nodded mutely he added, as an afterthought, "You'll be coming, of course."

Susanna raised her head, and her eyes flashed. In spite of being in love with him she was by no means blind to his faults and his tendency toward the dictatorial was, in her estimation, one of the worst. "Is that an order?" she said coldly.

He laughed at that, a flicker of the old mischief on his face, before he corrected himself soberly, "I hope Miss Gabrielli will have the pleasure of Miss Shaw's company at her cocktail party."

"It depends," said Susanna blandly, resolving to spend the time in Sussex, "what I'm doing on that date."

But in the end her resolve not to go had to be abandoned. For one thing, the projected loan on which Giovanni had been working seemed to have come to a crisis, and she was warned that she would probably have to stay late at the office to prepare last-minute additions to the prospectus. For another, Claire, who was looking thin and pale and spending sleepless nights drinking coffee, was quite determined to go. Stuart Shaw was in the middle of organizing an exhibition of his new work and had long since lost interest in Claire's affairs. But Susanna, sensing a recklessness and deep unhappiness in her cousin, felt that perhaps Claire needed more support than she had given her so far. It would be very unkind to abandon Claire to Paola without reinforcements, she thought.

As it happened the evening of the party was one on which she had to work late. She took her gray suit to the office and changed there. George, who had offered to drive her to the party, tore himself away from his computer to collect her at seven o'clock. She had not seen Giovanni all day and devoutly hoped she could avoid him similarly during the evening.

She was adding a final nervous powdering to her nose when George walked in. He stopped instantly, a look of great surprise on his face.

She gave him a mock curtsy, the gray skirt rustling and swirling as she did so. He did not return her smile.

"Well?" she said, disappointed at his reaction. She had so loved the garment herself. "How do I look?" she prompted.

He hesitated. "Lovely. You look—lovely and strange. Not like my Sue."

She swirled away, pleased. "Ah, but I'm not your Sue. Not tonight anyway."

"No you're not, are you?" His tone was unwontedly sober and she stopped, apprehensive. He came close to her and put his hands on her shoulders. "Look, Sue, I know this isn't the time," he glanced around the dusty, paper-filled office, "or the place, heaven help me. But I want to say something. I've wanted to for a long time."

Susanna stared up at him. Her ephemeral satisfaction with her appearance died as if it had never been. His eyes were serious.

"No," she pleaded. Distressed hands were pressed against his shirt. "Please don't, George."

But of course he ignored it. "I love you, Sue. I think you already know that. I want you to be my wife." He put a gentle finger against her lips. "No, don't say no. Don't say anything now. I know there's someone else. Claire told me you'd left some chap behind you. But if you're honest, you'll admit you've forgotten him a long time ago. Haven't you, Sue?"

She swallowed a lump in her throat. Looking into his kind, honest eyes she knew she had to admit to him what she had not so far dared to admit even to herself. Gently she drew away.

"I won't ever forget," she said quietly. "If I told you anything else I'd be deceiving both of us."

At the pain on her face, his hands went out to her, but there was a sound from the doorway.

"Forgive me," said Giovanni, looking irritated. "I hadn't realized Susanna had finished. I was going to offer her a lift, but it seems I'm unnecessary." He nodded to them bleakly. "No doubt you can find your own way there. If I don't see you again, I hope you enjoy yourselves."

Enjoy themselves! Susanna's thoughts were bitter. How could he be so unknowing, so uncaring?

And yet, paradoxically, it was a consolation to know that he had not guessed that she hung on his every word, blanched at his frown and preened in his favor like any of the rest of his obsequious girlfriends. It was a consolation that nobody knew. Even George thought that her unrequited love was for poor forgotten Roger.

Congratulating herself on her powers of deception, she did her best to enjoy the party.

It was very noisy and crowded. Susanna's ideas of cocktail parties had hitherto been based on the polite gatherings in the vicarage or the not so polite but infinitely more amusing evenings that Stuart occasionally held, where conversation was usually lively rather than loud. She disliked being elbowed out of the way of hurrying waiters. Even more, she disliked having to exchange polite nothings with bored strangers. There must, she thought, scanning the room for Claire without success, be a couple of hundred people present.

She did not see Giovanni, but Paola had greeted her with deceptive sweetness. Paola was beautiful in an Oriental-style gown that had a design of jade and emerald peacocks worked on golden silk. She had not Claire's elegance, thought Susanna, but she had an eccentric style of her own. Certainly Giovanni would never have bothered with her if she had not been a rare creature. She wondered idly what his own mother could be like.

Nothing, she was sure, like Paola's. Signora Gabrielli was as tiny as her daughter but without her presence or her vivid features. She was neatly and obviously very expensively dressed, but she looked out of place at Paola's side. Susanna thought there was a distinctly depressed expression on the *signora*'s face. About halfway through the evening, to her very great surprise, Signora Gabrielli accosted her.

"You are Miss Shaw," she said in a soft, charming voice. "I have heard of you. I was so sorry to hear that you were hurt. Are you now recovered?"

"Fully," Susanna assured her, touched.

"I am glad. But it will make you all the happier to leave, no?"

"No," she said fairly. "It could have happened anywhere at any time. It was nobody's fault. I shall be glad to leave the bank to get back to college."

The *signora* looked at her shrewdly. "Ah, yes, you are an artist." She sighed and the short jeweled fingers turned the stem of her glass around and around. She had not drunk from it, and Susanna wondered if she liked champagne, which was all that had so far been offered her. "You are lucky to have a talent," Signora Gabrielli said, after a pause. "I would have liked—It is a great boon to a woman if she can earn her own living."

Susanna was amused. "Well, I could do that anyway, talent or no talent. In fact, I don't think I'll ever make any money as an artist."

"You do it for the satisfaction only?"

Susanna nodded, her eyes dancing at the other's puzzled expression.

"And that, too, is a great boon," the *signora* murmured. "In my day our only ambition was to find a husband and have a family." She almost managed not to look at her daughter, chatting vivaciously in another group. "Perhaps that is very Italian. My own children feel like that and certainly my mother-in-law does. But I do not know that it is enough. I do not know that it was ever enough."

They both looked at Paola. She had caught sight of Giovanni who was standing by a heavily curtained window. He was looking straight at her. Imperceptibly one eyebrow rose. Like a dealer, thought Susanna indignantly, bidding at an auction. At once Paola turned away from the people she was with and began to make for the window. He disappeared behind the curtain.

Signora Gabrielli was speaking. With an effort Susanna brought her attention back to her.

"Of course," she was saying thoughtfully, "it all depends on the husband."

"Of course." Susanna heard the weariness in her own voice and blushed as Signora Gabrielli stiffened.

But there was great kindness in the woman's expression. "You are very young, Miss Shaw," she said obscurely. "And very lucky, you will realize one day. At your age I had two houses to run and a baby and a husband who was at work all day. Believe me, you've nothing to regret."

"I never regret anything, anyway," said Susanna haughtily.

The *signora* laughed. "Bravo, Miss Shaw! That also I envy you. And now, if you will excuse me, I must see to my daughter's guests as she does not appear to be doing so herself. Goodbye, Miss Shaw. It has been so nice to have met you. I trust it will not be long before we see you again."

They shook hands formally and the *signora* drifted away, her glass still untouched in her hand. Susanna, who felt she needed fortification, acquired a handful of tiny pastries from a passing tray and looked around for a drink. She spied George and was about to ask him for help in the search when she discovered that a flushed and tearful Claire was leaning on him. Alarmed, she went to them.

"Claire, my dear, aren't you well?"

George cast her a furious glare. "Not here, for God's sake," he hissed. "Take her outside. I'll get some brandy."

Obediently Susanna took Claire's elbow and steered her, unresisting, to an open window. On the terrace Claire turned away and blew her nose.

"Have you a handkerchief?" she muttered. "I've used George's."

Silently, Susanna produced the required scrap of lace and linen, which looked hopelessly inadequate beside the fistful of used tissues and sopping man's handkerchief that she received in exchange. Her lips twitched, but she preserved a tactful silence.

Claire blew her nose again, harder.

"Thank you," she said. She swallowed. "I'm sorry to cause a scene," she added, sounding woefully young. "I didn't think. Can we go home?"

"Of course." Susanna was calm. "But as George has gone to fetch you a brandy it would be polite to wait until he comes back with it. Besides," she said practically, "he can drive us, which will be much more convenient than hopping about waiting for taxis."

In the darkness Claire gave a tearful smile. "What if George doesn't want to leave yet? You're a bully, Sue!"

"Nonsense. He might just as well make himself useful. I'll feed him a reward. I expect that's what's wrong with you, too. They must have stocked up with people so that you don't notice there's nothing to eat. I'm starving!"

The banter had the desired effect. Claire giggled. "Fodder is a bit sparse, isn't it?"

"Well, the caterer's bill suggested there would be mountains of it, so it must all be secreted somewhere. Do you want to hold out looking hungry until they produce some for very shame?"

"No." Claire sounded happier. "No. I want to go home. I've made rather a fool of myself, Sue."

"Oh?"

She nodded. "It's my own fault. I—wanted to speak to Giovanni."

Susanna controlled her rising anger. "Was he unpleasant or merely elusive?" she demanded in a light tone.

"Neither." Claire sniffed and began to pleat the handkerchief between her fingers. "He was quite kind really. He said—he said—oh, he said I was very young, and I had a life of my own to lead in London, and I wasn't to bother about him any more. Bother!" She choked. "He did everything except say he was bored with me."

"Oh, yes?" said Susanna mildly. Her fingers were curled into the palms of her hands.

Claire noticed nothing. "I told him it wasn't a question of bothering. I told him I was in love with him. And—he laughed!"

At her tragic tone Susanna, too, had difficulty in not laughing.

"And he said—he said—it had been amusing and now it was over. We had entertained each other, no more. And I said I didn't believe him. And he said that he didn't care if I believed him or not, but he was going to get married and his wife wouldn't be very pleased if I still expected to—" She broke off. "Oh, what does it matter, Sue? He doesn't love me—I've known it all along, really. He didn't even love me in Florence. I just hoped and hoped that—"

Susanna was very still. "Going to be married?" she said in a strange tone.

"Yes." Claire was too taken up with her grief to observe that her cousin put a hand on the back of the wrought-iron chair as if she could not stand unsupported. "I—ran away. I couldn't bear it. And then Paola came."

"You mean you spoke to her?"

Claire shook her head vigorously. "No, she came out on the terrace. She didn't know I was there. I was hidden behind a pillar. But he knew. He must have known. It was horrible—like a sort of display. He—kissed her. I mean, not like he kisses me but—he went on and on. As if," there was a horrified disgust in her tone, "he were eating her." She pressed her hands to her cheeks. "I'm sure it was deliberate. To show me."

Remembering him calling Paola across the room to him, Susanna had no hesitation in believing her. Somewhere under the numbness she was aware of a sense of outrage that he should treat Claire in such a way.

"Forget it," she advised curtly. "Forget him. He's not worth anything else."

Claire looked at her with drowned eyes. "You don't believe that! You know he's worth everything...." She began to sob again.

Fortunately George reappeared with a tray of drinks. With presence of mind he whipped the napkin from the tray and offered it to Claire to dry her tears. Then, after an invigorating drink of champagne, he turned his attention to Sue.

"What on earth's got her into this state?" he said under his breath.

She drew him away from Claire into the lee of the window. They were almost in the room and the sound of voices and glasses clinking drowned her words so that Claire could not hear them.

"Our lord and master," she said succinctly.

"Di Montefiorino?" George looked aghast. "What's he done to her?"

"Nothing spectacular," said Susanna, smiling unpleasantly. "Merely detached her. He thought she might prove a premarital embarrassment."

George looked relieved. "Well, you can't blame him there," he said. "Young Claire can be a bit, er, pressing."

"And so," she pointed out, "can he. What he needs is a taste of his own medicine."

"I daresay," George retorted. "But who's going to give it to him? I don't see the fair Paola playing fast and loose with him." An idea occurred to him and he chuckled. "Unless you take over, my love. Do you fancy a spot of torpedo work on the lethal Giovanni?"

"I might," raged Susanna. She could see Claire huddled on one of the spindly chairs, the picture of mournfulness. "My goodness, I might!"

There was a sudden movement behind her, and she turned to find herself looking straight into Paola Gabrielli's face. It was full of spite and a curious triumph. Susanna recoiled and the expression died, to be replaced by the irreproachable mask of the hostess.

"I hope you are enjoying yourselves?"

George assured her incoherently and untruthfully that they were.

"I am so glad. But I'm afraid I have bad news for you both. The *marchese* has asked me to tell you that it will be necessary for you both to go back to the bank. He said the time has come. It sounds very dramatic!" She gave a tinkling laugh.

George looked at Susanna dismayed. "That must mean the loan is on the air tomorrow. I foresee an all-night session. What are we going to do?"

"I shall have to go home and change," said Susanna, with a meaning look at the terrace. Perhaps you could drop me off?"

"Of course." George was relieved. "With pleasure. And I'll wait and take you on to the bank. It will probably be quicker in the long run."

"Thank you." Susanna nodded dismissingly at Paola who, however, refused to be dismissed. What on earth was she to do, she wondered desperately. She could not expect Claire to walk through the party looking as she did. Inspiration came. George could take Claire down the fire escape that led to the street. She said to Paola, "We can leave through this exit, can't we?" The other nodded and showed every sign of escorting them to George's car. Hurriedly Susanna improvised, "I'm afraid I've forgotten where the cloakroom is. Perhaps you'd show me?"

Paola was not going to triumph over the distraught Claire if she could prevent it. It seemed that she could. Paola acquiesced and led her back through the crowd while George made good his escape via the terrace.

Paola escorted her to the steps of the hotel.

"Good night, Miss Shaw. It has been a great pleasure. I am sure the *marchese* will miss your help when you leave. It is to be soon, I understand?" She smiled meaningly. "A great pity. I do not think we will meet again."

CHAPTER EIGHT

BOTH SUSANNA AND GEORGE were part of the team that worked all night. In the deserted building just the one small area was filled with light and activity. It was almost, she reflected in a brief moment's respite, like a newspaper office. The staff wore an exotic array of unlikely garments. George was still in formal clothes although he had discarded his tie and dinner jacket. She herself had changed into the first clothes that came to hand, which had proved to be a pair of paint-smudged jeans and one of Claire's freshly laundered tennis shirts that had found its way into her room. Giovanni himself was in flannels and a cool poplin shirt while the janitor, routed from his bed to act as messenger between the three rooms, was still wearing his pajamas under a khaki overall.

It was insufferably hot. George swore over the computer. The girl who typed his instructions into it on a large keyboard that resembled Susanna's electric typewriter was nearly in tears on several occasions. Giovanni telephoned Zurich twice and Florence once. And Susanna did her best to keep the proliferating paper in order and record proceedings suitably.

With daylight the atmosphere became more tense, and by the time Claire and the rest of the staff arrived at the bank, the director and his staff were in a state of acute nervous tension. Susanna had expected it to subside when the details of the loan were published, but although the frenzied activity to some extent regulated itself, the anxiety remained at fever pitch.

For the next two days she worked ten hours a day, falling into bed when she got home without so much as a cup of coffee. As far as she could see Claire had recovered. She was a little subdued but cheerful enough in the office. George, a little shamefaced, said he had arranged to drive Claire down to Sussex to spend the weekend with her grandfather. Susanna, surprised, agreed that it was a good idea and looked forward to a whole weekend in bed undisturbed.

When George finally left the office on Friday night it was nine o'clock. Resting her forehead momentarily in her hands, Susanna wondered how Stuart would take this new addition to Claire's life and decided he would approve. Of course, in spite of his proposal to herself, she had long suspected that George's heart really lay with Claire. Whether Claire knew of it or whether he knew himself, she could not conjecture. But she thought that a few days under Stuart's eye would probably decide it for both of them.

She sighed and raised her head wearily to find Giovanni looking at her.

"Oh!" She was disconcerted. "I'm sorry I didn't see you. Did you want something?"

"Something more?" He smiled briefly. "Poor Susanna! You've pounded that infernal machine valiantly. No, there's nothing more to do. You will be glad."

"Yes," she agreed. "I did secretarial work for nearly six years until I went to college, and I wouldn't go back to it for anything."

He leaned against the desk, his hands folded

across his chest, watching her lazily. "So I can't tempt you to stay?"

She shuddered. "Not for any money."

"I'm sorry. Although in a way it's just as well, because my new secretary is arriving on Monday. I forgot to tell you. I won't be here myself; I'm taking a week's break from all this. You can come back and meet her and show her the ropes if you like. Or better still you can pack up now and leave her to find her own way around."

She felt hollow. So he was getting rid of her!

"I'll go now," she said brightly. "I'd like a holiday too."

"Good!" He straightened decisively. "Then you'll come down to Kent with me."

"What?"

"To Kent. To my house. If you remember, you said it was very peaceful or something equally flattering. It could have been designed by Simon with you in mind. I'm going. So come."

"What now? Tonight?"

"Now, tonight," he averred. He looked at her amusedly. "Come along, Susanna. You're a country girl. You must be as sick of the city as I am myself."

"Well, yes," she admitted. "But I could go to my grandfather. . . ." Her voice trailed away as she thought of sharing the house with Stuart's inspection of Claire's new boyfriend. That at least would not be very peaceful.

He watched her. "I don't think I'm flattered, to be compared with your grandfather and found wanting!"

"In this case," she said slowly, "you're not wanting. Stuart can be very disturbing at times."

"And I can't?" He was mock hurt. "Susanna, if you continue to insult me like this I will withdraw the invitation, and then I shall have to drive down on my own."

"Which would, of course, be disastrous," she retorted.

He wrinkled his nose at her. "Well, boring. Come on, Susanna. Don't you ever do anything on the spur of the moment?"

"Of course I do," she said, affronted.

"Well, then. . . ."

"All right." Suddenly she was breathless and laughing. A little something, she told herself, to remember him by. She would clearly never see him again. Paola Gabrielli had told her as much. "All right. Let me get a change of clothes."

"We'll stop and pick them up," he promised. "And bring something to swim in. It's going to be a beautiful weekend."

IT WAS. They arrived after midnight to find the house in darkness. Susanna was in the same room as before, and she fell on the bed without even undressing or brushing her teeth. Stuart would have been horrified at such slovenly habits, but she doubted whether her father would mind when she eventually appeared for breakfast next day. He was definitely, she thought inconsequentially as she drifted into sleep, not a toothpaste-conscious parent.

She was awoken by the sun shining through the open curtains on her eyelids. A glance at the bedside clock, which had stopped, was unhelpful. Her watch, with what degree of veracity she was not sure, said it was eight o'clock. Cursing her ingrained habit of early waking, she lay for some moments drinking in the sunshine.

The room was one of Simon's more extravagant

efforts, carpeted and furnished in a deep apricot material that was almost identical in color with the wooden doors and sills. It was a room to trap sunlight. Even the pillow, she thought amusedly, turning her head on to it, was the same shade of rosy yellow. It would be very warming in the winter. Now it had a quality of fantasy about it as if she were cradled in a sunbeam.

She stretched, yawned, stretched again and tried to compose herself for more sleep. It was impossible. At last she gave up the struggle, showered and pulled on a bikini. She was much too lazy to swim, but she could sunbathe on the lawn. That, she reflected, was the second best thing to sleeping. She had no doubt that her father would not leave his bed for hours and suspected that Giovanni was of the same kind.

She pattered quietly downstairs and let herself out of the kitchen door.

Susanna had been basking for some three hours when Giovanni eventually joined her. He had brought a good thick towel draped over his arm, which announced his intention of swimming eventually, but for the moment he seemed content to settle beside her and resume his interrupted slumbers.

After a moment she said idly, "Is Simon not up yet?"

"Simon?" He neither turned his head nor opened his eyes, but she felt him tense.

"My honorable father," she explained.

"Your honorable father, as far as I know, is going about his business in London."

"What!" She sat up as if she had been shot. "Do you mean he's not here?"

He opened one eye and looked at her. "Darling, he's my interior decorator, not my servant."

"But he was here last time," she said helplessly.

"Last time," he closed his eyes again, but his voice, though casual, was very precise. "He brought you. This time I did."

"Q.E.D." she said with something of a snap. A week's holiday in Kent in a peaceful family atmosphere was one thing, a week of sunshine and roses and the unpredictable Giovanni was something very different. Particularly as her heart was fairly unpredictable, too, at the moment.

"Did you think your father lived here?" Giovanni was annoyed.

"N-no. I suppose I just didn't think. I was so tired last night. And Kent sounded heavenly."

"So it is." He relaxed again enjoyably. "So enjoy it and stop worrying."

"But I don't think I should. I mean, we don't really know one another very well and—well, it's not as if we're old friends or anything. What will people say?"

He opened the other eye and looked at her ironically.

"Susanna, you can't be that innocent! You know perfectly well what people will say. And you don't care a fig, and neither do I."

She clasped her hands worriedly. "But Claire—"

"Has gone to Sussex with her new boyfriend," he said fluently.

"How did you know that?" she gasped.

"I told him to take her," he said with complete sangfroid. "I find it's no good leaving these things to chance."

She surveyed him unflatteringly. "You're immoral," she told him.

"Immoral? Me? When I've played the fairy godmother and sent them both off to a weekend of bliss?"

"Not," she said with restraint, "with my grandfather. Purgatory would be more like it. He has strong views on granddaughters' suitors and will probably make poor George endure hell—just to see if he can stand it."

One raffish eyebrow quirked. "Oh, well, I expect he'll be able to," said Giovanni unrepentantly. "Love is a great strengthener of the sinews, I'm told."

"And the eardrums, I hope." Susanna was gloomy. "He'll have to listen to Stuart holding forth about modern art and the Philistine society."

"Very interesting," he commented.

"Oh, damn you!" Susanna was finding it impossible to be amused. "Why didn't you leave us alone?"

His mouth took an ugly twist. "Work it out, darling. I'm going to swim. By the way, there's something for you on the kitchen table. I forgot to give it to you before."

He left. She stared after him, her blood churning in anger and something like fear. She remembered George had once told her about the Montefiorino crest. They look in a completely different direction from what they are after, he had said, but they always get what they want in the end. Giovanni, it seemed, had arranged this situation with diabolical cunning, not hesitating to make use of other people to do so. But what could he possibly hope to gain from it? And with his marriage imminent how did he dare risk Paola's fury if, as she surely must, she found out?

Deeply disturbed, Susanna made her way into the kitchen. On the table was an enormous handbag, big enough to fit her sketchbook and a fine selection of chalks into it if she so wished.

She looked at it, stunned. Then, not for the first

time that week, she sank down onto a convenient chair and sobbed her heart out.

Then, because she was a sensible girl, she dried her tears, splashed water on her face and went out to confront the enemy.

Once again he gave the appearance of being fast asleep. Susanna marched up to him.

"What," she said, waving the bag under his nose, "do you mean by this?"

He looked surprised. "I told you I'd buy you a new one. The other, if you remember, died an unnatural death in my car."

"Oh." The wind taken out of her sails, she collapsed beside him.

"What did you think it was for? Services rendered?"

"The thought did just cross my mind."

"What a lurid mind," he said peacefully.

"Well," she defended herself, "you have rather a lurid reputation to maintain. I thought I might be the instrument of it."

"Don't be silly, Susanna. What are reputations? Words and wind. I'm no foul ravisher and you know it. In fact," he pondered, "it's difficult to imagine quite what a foul ravisher would do. But I'm sure he wouldn't arm the lady for the fray."

"Arm—?"

"I'm sure you wield a deadly handbag," he observed. He reached out a lazy hand and plucked her down on the grass. "Relax. Forget the world, the flesh and the devil. And all your unworthy suspicions as well."

She smiled unwillingly. "You're too persuasive. I don't trust you."

Unexpectedly he exploded. His eyes were dark with anger as he glared at her.

"Damn it, woman, what do I have to do?" He bit it off. "I don't know if you're deliberately spiteful or just simple-minded, Susanna Shaw, but you're pernicious. And you get right under my skin. Go and swim before I forget my party manners and wallop you!"

She retreated. He was left, brooding, his knees hunched under his chin and his brows knitted fiercely above his nose. She flung herself into the cool water, trying to still the alarm that ran like quicksilver through her veins. Of course he wouldn't really hurt her. He had no reason to. But temper was not reasonable, and she had seen black temper on his face.

She kept a safe distance from him throughout the day.

With manifest indifference he swam, and ate and drank and lounged in the sun while she hovered, never out of earshot, never within touching distance. At last he lost patience and brought her a goblet of cool, dry wine.

Susanna took it from him carefully, not touching his fingers. "Th-thank you."

"Tradition of the house." He studied her face. "What is it with you, Susanna? You're never the same two hours running. First you're sweet as pie and then—"

She sipped her wine. "Then—"

He grimaced. "Wormwood! What have I done to upset you now?"

"Nothing," she denied. "And I'm not upset."

"No? Then what are you?"

She moved away from him. "Unsettled. I don't understand it myself. I can see I'm not the ideal houseguest. I'd better leave. If you'll just run me to the station...."

He said, very softly, "Chickening out?"

She flushed. "Of course not! It's just that...."

"You feel unsettled," he nodded. "Well, so do I. It's the weather. Among other things."

Susanna did not ask what other things. She was aware of them. Again that sense of danger took hold of her, keeping her immobile when she should have fled, speechless when she should have defended herself with the armor of polite conversation. She looked at him helplessly.

Giovanni strolled over to her. He took the goblet from her hand and put it carefully down on the grass. Like a trapped rabbit she watched him. She was in his arms, hardly aware of it, as he held her looking down into her dazed eyes.

"This," he murmured, "should have happened a long time ago."

She had no reserves left, no defense. Her eyelids fluttering, she said no, as she had said once before.

But he took no notice. The sky was darkening suddenly and great drops of rain splashed down on them. He seemed not to notice that either, flexing his hand against her taut throat until she felt she would choke with feeling.

Then abruptly he let her go. She swayed.

"Thunder in the air," he said lightly, cheerfully. The lines of strain had gone from around his eyes. He was himself again, wicked, laughing and wholly in command of the situation. "You'd better go and get dry."

"Yes," she said thickly.

It was raining quite hard and there were distant flashes of lightning beyond the hill. As yet they heard no thunder. He gave her a little push.

"Well, go on."

She could not bear to leave him. Like Claire, she had no pride left.

"You—" she said appealingly, her hands reaching to him.

"I have to cover the pool, you know. Go indoors, for heaven's sake!"

And, as she supposed they all did, she went. Went with dragging feet and furious rebellion in her heart. But went.

To her surprise she found the kitchen full of appetizing smells. She halted in the doorway, sniffing appreciatively. By what spells she wondered, her mood lightened, had Giovanni conjured this magician's feast into being? It smelled, as all the best meals do, of garlic and lemon. She closed her eyes, savoring it.

"Good evening, miss."

Her eyes flew open. She found herself being regarded by a small woman in an enormous apron.

"Oh, er, good evening," said Susanna, at a loss. "I'm sorry I didn't see you. I was enjoying the smell. I hadn't realized how hungry I was."

A gleam of approval appeared in the other's eyes.

"You'll be ready for your dinner, I dare say. Not touching a mouthful of my good cold lunch that I left out, set and ready. I suppose," with barely veiled disgust, "the master forgot it."

"Well, er," Susanna dissembled unconvincingly. "It was hot. We, er, we've spent all day in the garden. We weren't really hungry."

"The master must have forgotten it," the little woman nodded, undeceived. "Men!" she added with comprehensive bitterness. "Can't keep a thing in their heads unless you write it down for them."

To Susanna's astonishment she began to dart about the kitchen, taking pots and plates from various cupboards and assembling them all on the scrubbed wooden table, talking, half to herself, all the time.

"I told him I'd laid it out in the dining room. All he had to do was take the covers off." She stopped momentarily and surveyed Susanna with puzzling sympathy. "All them foreign servants. Never done a hand's turn in his life, I dare say. He'll be a trial to the poor girl that marries him. He should have known better than to bring a young lady down here on my day off if he can't take care of her properly. I don't know what his mother would say!"

Susanna blushed. "I didn't know it was your day off," she murmured, not admitting that she hadn't known of the lady's existence at all. "I hope you haven't come back early just to cook dinner for me, Mrs.—"

"Miss," she snapped. "Miss Bird. I'm always back for supper on Saturday, miss. I meet my sister in Canterbury and the last bus leaves at four. I needn't have gone really. I'd as soon have stayed. Then you'd have got your lunch. But master wouldn't have it." She brooded. "He wouldn't let me bring you in a tray this morning, either. Said you'd be tired and to leave you to sleep, he did. And if he remembered your breakfast it's more than I bargain for."

There was a telltale pause. Susanna felt guilty without knowing quite why. She felt, vaguely, that it was her duty as Giovanni's guest to defend him to his staff. On the other hand, she could not say truthfully that he had offered her anything more substantial than fruit or wine all day.

Miss Bird's eyes sparkled. "You must be fair famished," she concluded triumphantly.

"I really haven't been very hungry," Susanna offered weakly, and encountered a fierce look. "But I am now," she added. "Something smells delicious."

"Coq au vin," said Miss Bird with satisfaction.

She glanced at the clock. "Dinner will be in half an hour. I told," ominously, "the master."

"Oh, er, yes, of course. I'll go and change," said Susanna, correctly interpreting Miss Bird's severe look. She fled to seek out of her sketchy wardrobe something worthy of coq au vin.

Of course, she found nothing and had to content herself with a shower and some brave makeup to compensate for her ordinary working-day clothes. She hoped Miss Bird would not be offended and came downstairs with a wary eye on the kitchen door.

Giovanni, who was emerging from the dining room, raised his eyebrows.

"You look very guilty," he remarked. "Come and have a drink. She's given me five minutes before we have to sit down to eat. I take it you've met Miss Bird."

"Yes," she agreed, following him. "She doesn't approve of me."

"Nonsense," he said bracingly. "She's on your side. Do you want gin or is wine all right?" He poured it out as she nodded and handed it to her. "It's me she doesn't approve of. You're the victim. I forgot to feed you. She'll probably write and complain to my mother."

Susanna spluttered, "They've met?"

"Oh, no. But in default of a wife, Miss Bird thinks my mother ought to take responsibility for me. She doesn't hold with men. You may have noticed."

"Yes," she agreed. "Why doesn't she leave you?"

"Love," he said darkly.

"What?"

"Love," he repeated. "For the kitchen. Your father has apparently built every irresistible gadget known to chefs into that kitchen. She can't bear to leave it. So she has to tolerate me. But not," he said with a quick glance at his watch, "my unpunctuality. If you don't want tea at six o'clock tomorrow morning we'd better go and eat. Her revenges are not subtle."

Miss Bird appeared to have forgiven him the omissions of the day however. She plied them both with enormous quantities of delicious food and even offered, smilingly, to wait up to brew them more coffee if they should want it.

Giovanni stretched. "No, no, Miss Bird. We're quite capable of making coffee ourselves. I'm positive Miss Shaw is dying to play with the gadgets her father installed. You may safely leave me in her hands." And he smiled blandly across at her.

Miss Bird looked pleased. "I'll leave everything ready," she said to Susanna conspiratorially. "Good night, sir. Good night, miss."

"And what," demanded Susanna irately, as the door closed behind her, "do you think I am?"

"A nicely brought up girl who never makes a scene in public," he said, walking around the table and kissing her lightly. He chuckled. "You should have seen your face! Though why, considering you type and file and answer the telephone for me to admiration, you should balk at making my coffee, I fail to understand."

"It's not the same thing," she began indignantly when, apparently struck by a sudden thought, he held her away from him.

"Can't you make coffee?"

"Yes, of course I can, but that's not the point. I ought not to have to in somebody else's house. I'm your guest! You ought to make coffee."

"I never make coffee if there's a woman to do it for me," he said calmly.

"No?" She took hold of her temper. "And I suppose there usually is?" she said sweetly.

He shook his head, laughing down at her. "By no means."

"You amaze me. You mean you sometimes have to do things for yourself?" She was obscurely angry. "I would have thought you'd arrange things better than that. You always seem to have everything under control."

He pulled her against him then.

"I don't have a damned thing under control," he said roughly. "And you know it." He brushed his chin over her soft hair. "Oh, Susanna, Susanna."

The disputed coffee cooled, and the shadows lengthened. At last he drew away.

"I think," he said gently, unevenly, "that it's time you went to bed, Susanna."

"Or Miss Bird will complain to your mother?" she murmured mischievously.

"Very probably." He raised her chin with one finger and kissed her briefly. "And very rightly. As you have pointed out, I'm your host." He detached her clinging arms. "We can continue tomorrow," he added kindly.

At which piece of blatant and entirely justified vanity Susanna flounced off to her own room without the civility of bidding him good-night.

She slept well and came down the next morning rather late and more than ready to put the odious Giovanni in his place. Giovanni was nowhere to be seen but an early visitor had already brought her car screeching to a halt outside the front door and was stalking into the house. Susanna felt hollow. She went forward to greet the infuriated woman with the calm of despair.

"Good morning, Miss Gabrielli," she said brightly.

"You!" spat Paola. She looked hot. She added a good deal of Italian that Susanna found difficult to follow precisely. The general meaning, however, was unmistakable.

She flushed slightly. "You'll want to see Giovanni," she said cravenly.

Paola was still in the middle of explaining that she never wanted to see him again when he appeared.

"Giovanni!" She ran to him. "Why do you do this to me? Why do you fall into the arms of this—this creature? Why do you make such a fool of yourself? It is only revenge to her!"

"Revenge?" He passed his hand over his face, sounding more amused than anything else. "Paola, my child, I've only just woken up. What nonsense is this?"

Susanna had an awful premonition and made a sudden movement of protest, which Paola saw with triumph.

"Ask her," she hissed. "It was all a plot." She looked at him scornfully. "They planned it—that stupid George Mole and that Claire and—her!"

"No, it wasn't like that!" Susanna cried, and looked up, for interminable minutes, to find his eyes on her, suddenly cold and distasteful.

"It's true?" he said at last.

She halted. "In a way—"

He shook off Paola indifferently. "Go home," he said indistinctly, not looking at her. His eyes slid over Susanna as if she disgusted him. Paola fell back looking shocked and almost frightened.

"I never meant to hurt you," Susanna began clumsily.

"Really?" One cynical eyebrow rose. He ignored the cowering Paola.

She looked at him, handsome, indifferent, masterly in his disposal of unwanted females. *One day it will be me*, she thought. He struck her sharply across the cheek.

"Get out," he said.

She did.

CHAPTER NINE

It was a miserable journey. Having left all her money at the house Susanna had to rely on helpful motorists for transport. Those she met were kind enough, but hardly anybody was out on a warm Sunday on the quiet roads on which she was traveling. It took her nearly four hours to cross the county boundary into Sussex, and then the weather broke and it began to rain.

By the time she reached Stuart's house her heels had blistered where shoes not meant for extensive hikes had rubbed the flesh. She had had to walk the last seven miles of her journey and was wet and exhausted. Claire, letting her into the house with undisguised astonishment, exclaimed over her.

"Sue! You're soaked to the skin. What on earth happened?"

Susanna pushed her sopping hair out of her face. Her cotton skirt clung to her, turned almost to black by the water it had absorbed. "The long walk home," she said through chattering teeth.

"What?" Claire was blank, torn between amusement and outrage. "Look, you'd better come into the kitchen where it's warm. We haven't lighted any of the fires. The rain came on so suddenly. And it's not really cold, is it?"

Susanna shook her head wearily and allowed herself to be swept along on the tide of Claire's chatter. There was no evidence of her grandfather or George, and for that she was grateful. Unprotesting, she stripped off her sodden garments and shrugged herself into the stout, flannel dressing gown that Claire brought down from her wardrobe.

"I've switched on the electric blanket in your room," Claire announced.

Susanna was huddling over the range. Above it, her clothes steamed, filling the kitchen with the smell of laundry. She nodded dully. Claire began to heat milk.

"A hot drink and then bed for you, Sue." Busy with the saucepan, she avoided looking at her cousin. "What really happened? Did you have a brainstorm or something?"

Susanna gave a harsh little croak of laughter that brought on a fit of coughing. "No, I told you," she said, when she could get her breath. "I walked home."

Claire swung around. "From London?" she said disbelievingly.

At first she thought Susanna would not answer, but, after an extended silence, her cousin said reluctantly, "Not exactly."

The milk began to come steaming up the sides of the saucepan. Claire swept it clear of the heat, poured it smoothly into a mug and handed it to Susanna, who took it silently. She looked utterly dejected, huddled in her dressing gown, warming her hands around the mug of boiling liquid.

Claire began, "Sue—" but she was interrupted.

"Look, I'm sorry, but I don't want to talk about it."

"About what?"

Susanna gave a twisted smile. "About the gigantic fool I've just made of myself. I'm not going to tell you all the gruesome details, so you can stop looking hopeful. But take my word for it, I couldn't have been much more stupid."

"You?" Claire's tone said more clearly than any words that she did not believe her older cousin capable of folly.

"Me," she agreed tiredly. She sneezed convulsively. "And now it looks as if I've got pneumonia on top of it."

Claire eyed her uneasily. This was a Susanna she did not know.

"Don't you think, perhaps," she offered tentatively, "that you should stay in bed for a few days? Not come back to work, I mean. I can explain to them at the bank...."

"There's no need. I left on Friday."

At her abrupt tone, Claire's eyebrows flew up. She looked thoughtfully at the bedraggled figure. "Oh," she murmured noncommittally.

"The permanent secretary is in transit," Susanna said with an oddly defensive note in her voice. "I wasn't needed any longer. There's only four weeks to the start of term. I thought I'd have a holiday."

"Well, you've certainly started it in style," Claire observed.

Susanna's eyes looked past her as if at some scene in her mind's eye that offended her. Her mouth turned down sharply. "Oh, I have," she agreed with bitter self-mockery. "I truly have."

There were noises in the garden that made them both look up.

"Stuart and George," Claire explained. "They went for a walk. I expect they got caught in the rain like you."

Susanna rose in a flurry. "I don't want to see them," she said breathlessly. "I'm going to bed. Tell Stuart I'm home and full of cold." She retreated, clutching the hot milk to her like a talisman.

She did not emerge again until Claire and George

had left for London. Her grandfather had paid her a dutiful visit, his tall head bent painfully in order to accommodate the sloping ceiling of her bedroom. He had looked uneasy and bad-tempered as he had always done whenever one of them was ill and Susanna apologized for being a nuisance. She could feel his annoyance at having his comfortable life disrupted. What she did not detect was his very real anxiety for her.

Stuart Shaw was not a particularly observant or considerate man, and when he had dispatched Susanna to London to look after her cousin it had been as much with the object of clearing his house of distractions, while he worked on his new commission, as with any clear idea of what she was to do there. He had not seen her since. Now her appearance shocked him. She had lost weight, and her eyes seemed to have sunk into her head. But it was the expression in those eyes that disturbed him most. It was bitter, as if she hated all the world and herself in particular. It was not a feeling with which he was unacquainted, but he had never expected it to infect his gentle Susanna, and he was furiously resentful that it should have done so.

During the next weeks he waited patiently for her to confide in him, but she did not. Superficially at least she regained her composure. As soon as her cold left her, she resumed her ordinary pursuits, walking, riding, keeping his house for him with unobtrusive efficiency. She might never have been away. Except for the wardrobe of fanciful elegancies that Claire sent down to her from London and a certain withdrawn look about her sometimes.

She met the faithful Roger Thornfield with composure rather than enthusiasm and Stuart gathered from the half annoyed, half relieved expression on the latter's face that she refused his eventual proposal of marriage. Susanna herself never mentioned the subject.

Their days passed serenely enough. Claire wrote to say that she was leaving her job and returning to Italy. By chance, George Mole had been posted to Venice, and they were traveling together. They were leaving almost immediately, and Claire had no time for more than an excited telephone call to her grandfather. She was sure Susanna would not mind clearing out the apartment and handing it over to the next tenant, Giovanni's new secretary.

When Claire's instructions were made known to her, Stuart thought she turned a little pale. But she said quietly that of course she would do as Claire asked. She would have to go to London, anyway, to look for somewhere to live during the coming term.

"Perhaps you could share with this Italian girl?" suggested Stuart, inspired. "After all, it was big enough for you and Claire. She might be glad of the company."

Susanna's hands clenched slowly until she found her nails were digging painfully into her palms. But she said, calmly enough, "It's not very convenient for the art school. I don't want to be too far away this time. Some of my classes could start at nine, now I'm a full-time student."

Stuart seemed convinced of her reasoning and, to her immense relief, abandoned the subject.

The only other threat to her composure during these precarious weeks had been when her grandfather said casually when she had just risen from her bed, "By the way, a Signor di Montefiorino telephoned while you were ill."

She had felt as if the fever were back. Her pulse quickened erratically, and she had to grasp at the banister rail for support.

"Who?"

"Signor di Montefiorino," Stuart repeated cheerfully. "I think that's what he said. He wanted you, but I told him you were ill in bed, and he said he'd call back." He reflected. "Seemed quite bothered," he added informatively.

Susanna swallowed. "The name," she said carefully, "would have been Montefiorino."

"What? Johnny Montefiorino? The one little Claire's been breaking her heart over?"

A little wryly, Susanna agreed to his identity. Stuart was amazed.

"But he sounded perfectly reasonable," he said, bewildered.

"He would," she agreed. "But if he phones again will you tell him I've gone away, please, Stuart?" He looked at her sharply, and she continued with admirable indifference. "He'll keep pestering me about where I left files and whether I sent letters, if you don't. It's all perfectly clear. His secretary will just have to find her own way around. But I have left, and I don't want him to think he can still treat me as an extension of his office."

"Of course," Stuart acknowledged, satisfied. "I'll ward him off."

Which he did with such success that Susanna heard no more from the troublesome Giovanni.

To fulfill Claire's request, Susanna begged a lift from Roger Thornfield who happened to be going to London to meet a client. He took her uncomplainingly, and she knew a moment's compunction at using him for her own convenience. He had taken her rejection of his proposal without resentment and she felt uneasily, from the calm way in which he continued to do what she asked him, that he might feel that it had not been final. She knew she had to make it quite clear to him that she would never marry him, but short of telling him that she was irrevocably in love with Giovanni, she did not quite see how to do it. And anyway, it hardly seemed an appropriate moment when he was driving her to London and had engaged himself to drive her back that evening.

He left her at the art school, having carefully written down the address of the apartment and traced the route to it on the A to Z map. A little impatiently, Susanna bade him farewell and ran up the steps of the school.

The accommodation office gave her a list of addresses, and she tramped determinedly from one eccentric landlady to another until eventually she found herself in possession of an attic studio in Islington and a list proclaiming the house rules. It was a depressing prospect, but it was—provided that she did not indulge herself with such luxuries as baths or electric fires or record players—cheap. Cheap enough, she hoped, for her to survive on the allowance that Stuart would eventually get around to giving her.

She went back to the old apartment to collect her belongings.

After the dingy prison for which she had just negotiated, it seemed a haven of light and comfort. Even with dust sheets flung carelessly over the furniture, it had a welcoming, lived-in appearance. Claire had obviously done her best to tidy it in her unpractised way so that the result was an oddly haphazard disarray. She had covered the television meticulously, for instance, but completely forgot to remove the old magazines and newspapers from under it. Here and there was mute evidence to her hurried departure. She had left behind the paraphernalia of living: a pen, some stamps, a couple of unwashed teacups, a box of matches.

Susanna lighted a cigarette and strolled through the apartment. Claire had obviously done her best in the time she had. Even Susanna's studio had been attacked with vigor, although it bore signs of having been hurriedly abandoned. The portrait that she had started of Giovanni had been pulled out from its place among the other canvases and stood against a collapsed easel in front of the window.

She surveyed it dispassionately. It was not at all bad, she decided. Even half-finished it had something of the restless quality of the man. In fact, it was probably best half-finished. It showed all the important things in his face. If she had to go back and conscientiously draw in ears and hairline she would probably kill it. She put it away from her.

Lighting another cigarette, she began to work systematically to clear the apartment of the debris of their occupation. Soon enough she had dusted and vacuumed until it was restored to immaculate vacancy and had amassed a pile of rubbish to be thrown away. She put it all in a cardboard box and set it in the middle of the living-room floor.

She stood back and surveyed it. It was in almost exactly the spot where she had first seen Giovanni when she had thought him an electrician come to repair his own record player. She grimaced. She had set off with such prejudices, and they had all melted under the influence of his charm. It was humiliating. Tears began to prick her eyelids, and she felt very tired. She sank into the embrace of the sheeted couch, kicking off her shoes as she did so. Her watch said it was still only half-past four. It would be a good hour before Roger came to collect her even if he did not lose his way. She giggled at the thought. She might just as well rest.

But sleep would not come. She felt strangely desolate in the quiet room. An ashtray caught her eye, one she might have used herself since she had been in the apartment, which she had forgotten to empty. She pulled an envelope out of the rubbish box to empty the ashes into it and stopped. It was addressed to Claire from the Montefiorino bank. Obviously it had held a salary check or some such thing. And there on the back was the emblem she would never now forget.

Susanna looked at it: the huntsman in his medieval dress, the heels of his boots dug into the grass as his twin hounds pulled at their leashes. And all the while his head was turned; he was leaning backward in his attempts to hold them, but looking behind him all the time.

"Poor dogs," said Susanna foolishly. She traced the embossed design with a fingertip. "Poor dogs," The envelope fell through her fingers and she began, at last, to cry.

She fell eventually into an uneasy sleep, her legs cramped under her, her head pillowed on her hands.

So she did not hear a key turn softly in the lock and the front door swing open. A chime from the doorbell might have woken her, but Giovanni's soft-footed entrance did not disturb her at all.

He did not see her on the couch, and after one amused glance at the pile of rubbish in its box, he went through the kitchen to the rest of the apartment. When he returned, his face was puzzled as if he had expected to find something that was not there. And then he caught sight of her.

He stopped so suddenly that he dislodged a small table lamp that fell to the floor with a soft thud. Susanna stirred, murmuring.

Her hair, tumbling over a submerged cushion in a patch of evening sunlight, seemed to catch and hold all the colors of the sun. Watching her, Giovanni drew a little breath of pure pleasure.

Susanna was dreaming. It was not a pleasant dream, and it was one she had had before. She knew it was only a dream and she had only to wake up to escape, but somehow she could not. She was in an icy cave and outside she could hear wolves baying. They knew she was there, and they were going to pursue her into her sanctuary and rend her to pieces. She was alone. Nobody knew she was there and nobody would come to her aid.

She cried out, seeing the great teeth of the first beast—and found herself caught and soothed and lifted out of her dream into sunlight.

"Hush, my darling, hush," Giovanni was murmuring, brushing the hair away from her face lovingly.

Her lashes fluttered. "G-Giovanni?" she whispered.

He was sitting beside her on the couch, cradling her against his body. "Of course," he said calmly. "I knew you would have to come and collect your paintings. So I have come here every day."

Susanna struggled away from that seductive arm. "Why?" she demanded abruptly. She sat up, wincing from the pain in her stiffened joints, and glared at him. His eyes she found, disconcerted, were dancing with laughter and very close.

"You are a very silly girl," he informed her. "And you deserve not to be told...."

And he did not tell her in words. But there again, she reminded herself, returning his kisses in despairing idolatry, he could not tell her anything she did not know already: that she was his creature to do with as he willed. Fighting for sanity, she wrenched herself out of his arms and away from the couch.

She closed her eyes against the hurt expression on his face.

He stood up, watching her. "You are not," he said with fierce quietness, "going to walk out on me again. I spend my time kissing you and standing back like a fool while you run away. Not this time, Susanna."

She retreated, afraid and oddly ashamed, when the doorbell pealed loudly.

"That will be Roger. He's taking me back to Sussex," she said thankfully. Her heart was thumping painfully.

"Oh, is he?"

Giovanni strode to the door and flung it open as if he were throwing down a challenge before a rival in more violent days. Roger looked astonished and rather apprehensive to find himself being scrutinized by arrogant dark eyes.

"Is, er, Miss Shaw ready to come home?" he said hesitantly.

"No."

"Oh." Roger was nonplussed. He peered around the tall figure in the doorway, looking for Susanna. "Will she be long?"

"Yes," said Giovanni uncompromisingly. "She will be as long as I can keep her. I shouldn't bother to wait if I were you."

"I would prefer," said Roger, with touching loyalty, "to hear that from Miss Shaw."

Giovanni regarded him smolderingly, and he shuffled under the animosity but held his ground. At last, grudgingly, Giovanni said, "Very well. Susanna, come here."

She came, very pale and bright-eyed. Her usual composure had deserted her, to Roger's astonishment. For a horrified moment he wondered if the bad-mannered barbarian had actually laid violent hands on her. But although she was unduly tremulous, she did not seem afraid, and his alarm died as quickly as it had been born.

Giovanni looked down at her as if he were a puppet master and she a doll under his control. She seemed not to notice, and in one of Susanna's independent spirit this was sufficiently amazing for Roger to be rendered speechless.

"I think you'd better go on ahead, Roger," she faltered. "I'll get the train. I don't know how long I'll be. But I still have—things to do here."

"If I have to," said Giovanni arrogantly, "I'll chauffeur her home myself. Goodbye."

And the door was closed in Roger's astonished face.

Behind the stout oak door Susanna was glaring at Giovanni, who had leaned his back against it and was rocking with slightly hysterical laughter.

"How dare you?" she hissed.

"I didn't dare not to," he told her, choking. "He had everything set to lead you straight out of here, bar the red carpet."

"You're mad," Susanna stated flatly. "Just because Roger has gone it doesn't mean you've got me trapped here. I can walk out whenever I like."

"Sure. As long as it's when I like."

"You are the vainest, most insufferable man I've ever met!" she gasped. "I'm going. Now. Like it or not, you can't stop me short of force."

"Precisely," he said with great satisfaction.

Her temper died. "You wouldn't," she said slowly. At the look in his face, "You couldn't."

"Couldn't? Couldn't what? Keep you here by force? Of course I could." He laughed softly. "But I won't. If you want to go, go."

He was between her and the door. She looked at him mistrustfully.

"If you've got something to say, say it," she said brusquely.

"I haven't."

"Then I'll go."

Her voice was ridiculously uncertain. She put her chin in the air and marched to the door. It was walking straight into his arms. She jerked her head away.

"Let me go!"

"You don't mean that," he said with superb assurance.

"I do. I do!" She was frantic. Every atom of her body responded to him. "You're just like daddy," she lashed out at him. "You don't care who you hurt as long as you get what you want!"

Abruptly his hands loosened their hold, but she was too worked up to see his expression.

"You and he—you're like a disease. I watched my mother die of it. In the end she just didn't care anymore what happened to her. When daddy had finished with her there wasn't even a person left. He was cruel and callous and heaven knows how many other women there had been—but she could not live without him. When he left that last time, she just had nothing left. So she died." Her voice shook with a pain she had thought she had come to terms with long ago.

Giovanni said coldly, "What has that to do with you and me?"

"Everything." She shook her head dazedly. "Nobody is ever going to do that to me."

"Agreed." He sounded grimly amused. "I wouldn't give much for the chances of anyone who tried. For God's sake," and the anger ripped out at her, "stop being so melodramatic! Look at the truth. I love you. You love me."

"No, no, I don't," she protested.

"Then why," he said, very softly, "that gallery of horrors in there?"

He jerked his head toward the rest of the apartment beyond the kitchen. Bewildered, Susanna knitted her brows in suspicion. Slowly it dawned on her that he must have found her portrait of him and all the preliminary sketches. She turned crimson.

"Well?"

Furious with him, she snapped, "Why don't you leave me alone?"

He sighed elaborately. "Why don't you listen to me, Susanna? I love you."

"And what does that mean?" she said nastily.

His eyes gleamed. "It means that at the moment I'm curbing an almost irresistible urge to beat some sense into you."

"I see. Is that something special, or did you do as much for Claire and Paola?"

"Claire and Paola," he retorted, "have never made me as mad as you do."

"I'm sorry," she said politely. "I'll leave you to regain your temper."

He glared at her. "I warn you, if you leave me now I'm not chasing after you again."

"Again?" Susanna raised her eyebrows. "I haven't noticed much chasing so far."

He shook her. "You ran away," he said. "I chased up here after you. You didn't come. So I went back to the house in case you'd gone back there. You hadn't and you didn't. I phoned Simon. He didn't know where you were. I phoned your grandfather. He said you'd gone away—I didn't know where. I thought you might have gone to the friends in Florence that Claire stayed with, so I went over there. I combed the city for you. I came back here and tried again. I even pumped Claire, but she wasn't telling." He let her go suddenly and ran his shaking hands through his hair. "In God's name, Susanna, where have you been?"

She swallowed. "In Sussex," she said in a small voice.

"But your grandfather said—"

She hung her head. "I know. I didn't want to talk to you. It wasn't his fault, I made him."

"But why? Oh, I know I behaved badly, but wouldn't you have been hurt if somebody admitted to your face that they had only pretended to be in love with you to revenge some imaginary slight to a hysterical teenager?"

She flushed. "Put like that it doesn't sound very nice. And I never really meant it."

"Then why say you did?"

"I didn't. All I said was that I'd said it. And I had," she insisted with dogged logic. "I was in a temper and Claire was wretched, and I said you needed a dose of your own medicine and if necessary I'd give it to you. But—I wouldn't have really. I wouldn't have known how. Anyway, I was afraid of you. I wouldn't have tangled with you for any money, Claire or no Claire."

He was honestly astounded. "Afraid of me?"

"You teased me all the time. I never knew where I was with you. Sometimes I thought—" She bit her lip and turned away from him, reddening.

There was a little silence. Then he said in an odd voice, "You didn't know where you were. Nor did I. You were a chameleon. I didn't know what to think. Claire told me you were her 'dragon,' but that was obviously untrue...."

"Why obviously?"

He looked at her mockingly. "The first time I saw you, you were wearing a very insecure bath towel."

She blushed again and pressed her hands to her too revealing cheeks.

Giovanni said very gently. "Dragons don't blush. So you weren't a dragon. But you were—hostile. I never knew what I'd done to offend you. So I went from bad to worse, didn't I? I never thought that I might have had a bad advance press from Claire. To me Claire was a lonely kid in Florence with no talent, abandoned in the middle of a pack of crazy artists. She was lonely and a little frightened." He shrugged. "That was all. I knew she thought she had a crush on me, but I didn't think anyone else would take her seriously, let alone her own family."

Susanna did not turn to him. She said, "It seemed so real."

"Claire has as big a talent as you have for self-dramatization," he observed drily.

"But you went on seeing her," she said, unheeding. "What was I to think?"

He sighed. "Susanna, you don't understand. I saw, as you put it, Claire and probably three or four others. It was very ordinary. The only special one that happened was you—" He hesitated. "I don't suppose you remember—but that party Claire gave—I kissed you because I thought you were prim and needed shaking up." His eyes dwelled on her untidy hair. "I was the one that took the shaking up. I'd never known anyone like you. You took me right off balance."

"Why?" It was almost inaudible.

"You're—I don't think I can explain it." He came to her and clasped her face between his hands. "I think the word is innocent. Claire isn't innocent. Simon isn't. Not one of your damnably intrusive family is innocent. But you are." He traced the outline of her mouth lightly. "The original fairy princess." He grinned wryly. "I wasn't prepared for it, so I made every mistake in the book."

"I seem to have made a few myself," she offered. "Always running away."

He hugged her. "It was good for me. I'd planned everything like a campaign. I didn't think anything could go wrong. I got Simon to bring you down to the country—I reasoned that if I could get you away from Claire onto neutral territory—but it didn't work, did it?"

"Probably because daddy wasn't neutral."

"Simon? But he's a friend of mine."

"He's my father," she reminded him gently. "He didn't want to see me unhappy."

"God, what a family!" he muttered. He kissed her almost savagely and then held her away, looking at her glowing eyes with satisfaction. "Listen, Susanna, I don't care if I have to take on an army of cousins and uncles as well, I am going to marry you. Is that clear?"

She nodded. "But what about your mamma?" she said mischievously.

"I have already seen my mamma. She had a full report about you from Signora Gabrielli, and she fully approves. In fact," he added bitterly, "she thinks it's a huge joke that you've led me such a dance."

Susanna looked up at him. "But Paola?"

"But Paola," he mimicked. "What about Paola?"

"Doesn't your mamma want you to marry her?"

He shuddered. "She'd shoot me if I did! Paola's her goddaughter and she knows her very well indeed."

Susanna bent her head. "I was very jealous of Paola," she admitted.

"Oh, were you? And did you think that I wasn't jealous?"

"You? But there was no one."

He snorted. "How was I to know that? You thought I was in love with Paola, didn't you? How did I know what sort of man you might imagine yourself in love with?" He raised her head with a gentle hand under her chin. "I wasn't worried about George Mole," he said reflectively. "I could always have sent him to the Sahara if you lost your head. But I confess Roger Thornfield bothered me. You were so determined you wanted peace, as you call it, and it seemed to me that he could give it to you." His eyes were serious. "And I can't, my darling. You know it. You said I was like your father...."

Suddenly he looked hurt and very young.

Susanna said humbly, "I was in a panic, and I'd been told a lot of rubbish. Forgive me?"

"I've known Simon a long time," he said bleakly. "I know what he is as well as you do. Except that when I was younger I never thought about your mother. I simply admired him tremendously. He had style."

"He still has," she pointed out. "But not the kind of style that is conducive to a good marriage."

Looking down at her, he said slowly, "Yes, I know. It never occurred to me before. I suppose I wasn't thinking about marriage before." He squared his shoulders. "So you'll have to make up your mind, Susanna. Will you risk it?"

She looked at him suspiciously, but he was perfectly serious, even a little anxious. There were little flames in his eyes, but he was scrupulously not touching her. Susanna put her arms around his neck very slowly, holding his gaze.

"If you'll have me," she whispered.

She felt him tremble, and he caught her against him fiercely. He kissed her as he had never kissed her before with a kind of famished exultation that showed her how afraid he had really been that he would lose her. She clung to him gladly, swept along like a leaf in a strong current, without will of her own, conscious only of his strength and the wild beating of his heart. When he raised his head she was shaking, helpless against him.

For a moment she stared up at him almost blindly, still new to the delirious storm that had shaken her. Then eyelashes fluttered as realization came and she smiled at him shyly but very openly.

He was watching her face with passionate attention. But his voice, when he answered her, was full of laughter.

"Oh, I'll have you," said Giovanni.